D0648455

THE ENDLESS VESSEL

ALSO BY CHARLES SOULE

The Oracle Year
Anyone

THE ENDLESS VESSEL

A NOVEL

CHARLES SOULE

HARPER PERENNIAL

NEW YORK • LONDON • TORONTO • SYDNEY • NEW DELHI • AUCKLAND

HARPER PERENNIAL

HarperCollins books may be purchased for educational, business, or sales promotional use. For information, please email the Special Markets Department at SPsales@harpercollins.com.

FIRST EDITION

Designed by Jamie Lynn Kerner

Fire emoji on page 327 © Lidiia Koval/stock.adobe.com

Library of Congress Cataloging-in-Publication Data has been applied for.

ISBN 978-0-06-304304-6 (pbk.)

23 24 25 26 27 LBC 5 4 3 2 1

For Amy.

BOOK I

THE JOURNEY

I. ONE

PARIS.

48°51′36.9″ N, 2°20′07.2″ ‘“E

FRANÇOIS LEDUC WAS SO HAPPY.

He was an old man, and soaking wet. His joints ached as he ran, especially his bad hip. His wingtips squelched with every step. His drenched suitcoat slapped at his sides, heavy like raw meat. But as he sprinted through the Louvre, he felt nothing but joy. He had a job to do, a purpose.

All around him were masterworks. This was the ground floor of the museum's Denon Wing, home to many works of Renaissance genius. Just then, François was rushing through Salle 403, the Michelangelo Gallery. He ran between two famous, superb marbles by the gallery's namesake, his *Rebellious Slave* and *Dying Slave*, each originally intended for the tomb of Pope Julius II. But the room was not only a shrine to Michelangelo. It was packed with sculptures by other great masters, all nearly as exquisite—Giambologna's lovely bronze *Flying Mercury*, a number of Bernini marbles. Monsieur LeDuc had spent his career amid these pieces, ensuring the world could view and enjoy them.

Now water streamed over the sculptures, showering down from high above like they were caught in a summer storm. François could do nothing about that. The museum's sprinkler systems were automated, activating whenever the temperature rose to a sufficiently high level. Rivulets washed across ancient, priceless carvings, dripping off the stone and metal into puddles on the floor. A surreal sight, but water was no threat to these works, or even the hundreds of paintings being similarly saturated in other galleries. The museum's restoration department could handle the damage. In the centuries since these pieces were created, most had survived worse than a soaking.

Fire, though . . . fire was another story. Flame would be the end of even these long-enduring works. It would swallow the paintings whole, blacken and shatter the marbles, melt the bronzes into puddles. The Louvre was burning, and if the blaze was not suppressed, François LeDuc would be one of the last people alive to set eyes on its treasures.

The inferno had surged up from the museum's lower levels, appearing everywhere all at once. François suspected the blaze began in one of the basement workshops, where craftsmen worked with volatile substances used to preserve and restore great works of art. Resin and liniments and a long list of chemicals and compounds, inflammable one and all.

Whatever the fire's cause, it ate through the museum's galleries like a starving beast, racing from one to the next, gleefully gulping down the genius contained within.

One small blessing: it was Tuesday, and on Tuesdays by long tradition the museum closed its doors. On any other day LeDuc would be fighting his way through a crush of fleeing patrons. But this evening he had the halls to himself, as far as he could tell.

François raced through Daru Gallery, Salle 406, his feet loud against the stone floor even against the roar of the approaching flames. At the end of the gallery lay a broad set of marble stairs, now become a series of ten-centimeter-high waterfalls. The old man hauled himself up, passing the lady from Samothrace in all her glory at the first landing. The iconic sculpture—*Winged Victory*, most called it—was wreathed in smoke, firelight flickering on its polished surface.

It almost improves it, he thought. *Gives the piece an apocalyptic air that's really quite—*

François LeDuc slipped, flailing wildly, certain he was about to fall backward and break his neck with his task unfulfilled.

His palm found the brass banister and he grasped it tightly, wrenching his wrist but finding his balance. François took a moment, his heart pounding. It would not do to avoid a fall only to succumb to a cardiac episode.

His equilibrium returning, Monsieur LeDuc looked back down the steps at the sculpture gallery. Flames and smoke obscured the worst of what was happening . . . but his imagination supplied the details. Centuries-old stonework heating beyond tolerance, the clean white marble turning black, cracks obliterating the delicate carvings.

A disaster. And somehow, not even a single member of the museum's fire brigade was in evidence. The Louvre kept forty-eight firefighters on permanent staff. None of those were to be seen, nor any from the city itself. Perhaps the firemen of Paris were busy elsewhere. These days, after all, there were so many fires.

Then again, LeDuc thought, surveying the ongoing immolation of his beloved museum, *perhaps it is not that there are so many fires, but that there are so few firemen.*

The Louvre was dying, but the gigantic old palace was strong. François thought it would survive long enough for him to do what he needed to do. He continued up the stairs, choosing his steps carefully.

LeDuc emerged into the upper level, the section he considered his own personal kingdom. He was the *directeur des peintures* of the Louvre Museum. He had personally selected many of the paintings on display in these halls, anointing works he believed should be moved from the limbo of the storage vaults into the light and air and attention of the galleries. François LeDuc knew every painting here as well as he knew his own face, from the famous to the obscure— Ingres's *La Grande Odalisque* to Raphael's *Balthazar Castiglione* (a personal favorite).

Smoke thickened the air. François took short, quick breaths, tasting a horrible chemical residue on his tongue—burned paint. He swallowed, feeling pain in his raw throat, wishing he had thought to wet a scarf to breathe through. The curator crouched as much as his elderly back would allow, trying to get underneath the choking haze, and kept moving. Not far now.

The second floor boasted enormous floor-to-ceiling windows more than four meters tall. François glanced through one as he hurried past, then froze. He had a good view of the Louvre's northern half, the Richelieu Wing, utterly engulfed in flames. The huge structure wasn't just ablaze; it was gone, transformed into a seething, twisting block of fire.

LeDuc's curatorial mind began cataloguing everything being consumed within that inferno, but he yanked himself back to the moment. He could not dwell. Perhaps later.

Movement in the corner of his eye shifted his gaze to the left, to the large lawns of the Jardin des Tuileries, a massive stretch of parkland running from the Louvre west along the Seine, thirty hectares in all.

Arrayed in the park was a massive crowd, watching, standing vigil—but not all bore witness in stoic silence. A not-insignificant portion seemed consumed by a bacchanal. They danced around smaller fires of their own; drummers pounded out rhythms as they swirled and spun, waving brightly colored flags. The dancers were tiny from this distance, but their energy, their motion—the very *insistence* of their celebration—hotter than the flames devouring the Richelieu.

LeDuc knew who they were. The beautiful fanatics of Team Joy Joy, L'Équipe de Joie, dancing to the beat of their own extinction. He wondered if they'd started the fire. Seemed like the sort of thing they would do.

François LeDuc moved on from the window. He was the *directeur des peintures*. He had responsibilities.

He passed through a final archway into room 711, Salle des États, stumbling through the intensifying smoke and heat.

François slowed. He'd made it, and just in time. There she was.

He looked at the great lady, his mind flooding with facts about the work despite the smoke and the stench of melting paint and the sprinklers still raining down water from above. Painted by Leonardo da Vinci around 1513. A jewel in the collection of many French sovereigns from Louis XIV to Napoleon. And once French sovereigns were no longer *en vogue* due to the Revolution, it ended up in the Louvre. It had remained here ever since, barring a brief sojourn in 1911 to Florence after the painting was stolen by an Italian ne'er-do-well named Vincenzo Peruggia, and a United States tour in the 1960s due to the particular request of a president's wife.

Of all the many works in the Louvre, François thought this one might survive the fire. Attempts to destroy this particular piece were not uncommon; someone had even once attacked her with acid. She attracted venom from lunatics, anarchists, even self-appointed critics who felt her importance to the cultural landscape was overstated. But despite their efforts, she remained, growing more precious with time. More than ten million people visited the Louvre each year, and many bought their tickets solely to see this one piece.

The lady was strongly protected, befitting her status as the museum's greatest treasure. A clear enclosure of reinforced glass surrounded the painting, bulletproof and climate-controlled. Its systems maintained a constant internal humidity and temperature and were specifically designed to survive a fire. François knew it was strong enough that firemen should be able to sift through the Louvre's ashes, wipe the soot from the still-intact enclosure, and see that famous smile, preserved for future generations.

"Ha," François said.

Future generations, he thought.

The smile.

Everyone was so focused on the damn smirk, and yet he'd always thought it was the least interesting thing about the piece. Why didn't people talk about the sfumato technique Da Vinci had invented when he created it, an utterly unique method of layering paint to bring in light and depth? Or the perspective tricks employed to depict the landscape behind the figure, the unusual chemical blends in the paints, and more besides? The work was a cavalcade of technical advances for its era, all of which (in Monsieur LeDuc's opinion, a weighty opinion indeed) vastly outweighed a single woman's smile. An *ugly* woman's smile. La Gioconda was no great beauty.

François pulled a key ring from his pocket, selecting one, then flipped up a recessed panel in the wall next to the case, revealing a keyhole and numerical keypad. He inserted the key, turned it, tapped in a nine-digit code, and the sealed box opened with a soft whoosh of perfectly temperate air.

He looked back the way he had come and saw that the fire had already swallowed the corridor he had just passed through. He was running out of time.

François lifted the painting off the wall. For all its momentous reputation, it was light. Easily carried.

He brought the work to the next gallery, number 701, the Salle Denon. This was on the building's exterior and so included more of the tall windows overlooking the central courtyard, bordered by tall, heavy curtains of red velvet. François set the painting on the floor next to one of these. Another quick fumble through his key ring and he unlocked the window. François could have smashed it, but he found himself reluctant to damage the museum. Perverse, considering the circumstances.

The curtains blew inward with a huge sucking rush of air once he threw open the window, the flames sneaking up behind him and greedily gulping at their new source of oxygen. It wouldn't be long now.

With some effort, François shoved the long curtains out into the night, letting them ripple up to either side. He thought they might serve as flags, drawing attention to his location, and sure enough, when he looked at the park, he saw faces turning to look. He wanted the attention of the revelers, with their drums and symbols and chants, and they complied, staring at him expectantly, all those Joy Boys and Joy Girls.

François LeDuc stepped up into the window and held the painting above his head. A cheer arose from the dancers as they recognized what he was holding. Of course they did. It was the most famous painting in the world. Not the *greatest* painting—he would give that title to Friedrich's *Wanderer Above the Sea of Fog*, though the old curator was willing to accept that taste was subjective, and ultimately Friedrich didn't sell tickets like Da Vinci.

Everyone had to see the *Mona Lisa* before they died.

François could feel the flames at his back. He didn't look. He didn't want to lose his nerve.

The heat built, leaping quickly from uncomfortable to the edge of pain to something nearing agony. He wondered if he was already aflame.

François did not lower the painting. He held it high, displaying it to the sea of faces. He would hold it up as long as he could. He wondered if Aunt Jane was out there somewhere, if she was watching what he was doing. He thought she probably was. She led Team Joy Joy; she was its guiding light and inspiration. This was not an event she would miss. He wondered if she was proud of him. He hoped so.

François felt searing pain in his fingers. He glanced up, and saw the *Mona Lisa* was burning. A spark must have landed on it, instantly setting the ancient frame and the even older paints and varnishes ablaze.

He smiled, a true, unambiguous ear-to-ear grin.

Good, he thought. *No miraculous escape for* La Joconde *this time.*

She had survived acid and war and time itself, but François LeDuc had ensured her reign was done. One less distraction for humanity, one less thing to prevent people from accepting the truth of the end to come. For this *was* the end, the last generation. It was, and he knew it, and everyone outside and across the world needed to know it. That was why he was doing this. He was making his final moments matter. There was joy in that, if you just allowed yourself to see it.

The joy. The joy. The joy.

The fire kissed François LeDuc and he lifted the painting up, the great masterpiece, letting it burn before the eyes of the world.

He smiled.

I. TWO

HONG KONG.
LAN KWAI FONG DISTRICT.

22°16′51.9″N, 114°09′12.4″E

"Pity Party's raging tonight, eh?" Reed said, surveying the bar.

"Give us a minute, will you?" Lily said, staring at her tiles. "Trying to survive here."

Reed had just thrown FAVOURITE at her, using the V off HAVEN and the T off DAFT, crossing a double word score on the R. Thirty points just off the letters, plus the fifty-point bingo for using all seven tiles in one play, which put him ahead by forty-three points.

"Shitfire," Lily said, glancing at the score sheet, then back at the smiling summer sausage of a man sitting across the booth from her.

Reed was at Pity Party almost every time Lily went. They played Scrabble most of those nights. The man was an English teacher at the international secondary school over in Tai Tam. He knew his words, and often pulled intense, game-changing plays like FAVOURITE out of nowhere.

"The game's not over yet," Reed said, in an accent that summoned up lagers and sunburns and not being too bothered about all that much. "That Z in the southwest could hook into that triple word with the right tiles. If the stars align, you'll leave me in the dust."

"Eh," Lily said, staring at the pathetic array of tiles on her tray.

Reed offered up a sympathetic nod. He drained the last of his beer.

"You'll get me next time," he said, scooching his way out of the booth. "I'm going to get another beer. You like something? On me. I am gracious in victory."

"Sure," she said. "Get me one of whatever you're having. Why buy yourself a drink when you can buy someone *else* a drink, right?"

Without looking, Lily pointed to her left, toward a sign taped to the wall espousing that sentiment along with the other rules for Pity Parties:

Good Vibes Only

Don't Step on Other People's Joy

No Smartphones. Wordys Only

Reed headed for the bar, and Lily took a last swallow of what was left of her existing drink: soda water with a few dashes of orange bitters, an in-between concoction that was basically plain old H_2O but worked as a decent role-play of an actual cocktail. She was drinking it for two reasons.

First, it was cheap. Hong Kong was a crushingly expensive city; she'd lived there for five years and was still stunned by the total every single time the clerk rang up her groceries at the ParknShop near her apartment.

Second, alcohol was a depressant, and seeking out depressants in the Grey world seemed foolish. That wasn't a hard-and-fast rule. Lily drank from time to time—and if Reed was buying, why not?—but she didn't booze very often.

Not a universal policy, Lily thought, glancing up from her Scrabble tiles to take in the bar and its many increasingly soused customers. Reed was right. Pity Party *was* raging that night.

The bar, D'Aguilar's, was a tiny rattrap dive on the edge of Hong Kong's Lan Kwai Fong nightclub district. A few dozen people could cram it from wall to wall—and they had. This particular Party chapter was all expats, hailing from various Commonwealth nations and former bastions of Empire around the world. Australians like Reed, New Zealanders, a South African, an older Canadian couple. The rest, like her, were Brits.

People were chatting, dancing to a pretty good DJ (currently spinning Prince's "Gett Off"), drinking, watching the subtitled movie being projected on the wall (*Happy Madison,* a weird choice that only made sense in the context of the Pity Party's stated goal toward uplifting entertainment), playing games, or just sitting, soaking in a thickly manufactured stew of positivity.

Pity Parties had started in America . . . in a city named Pittsburgh, which was funny but also wasn't. They'd spread all over the world in no time. No surprise there. You had to do *something.*

Lily sighed, slouching deeper into the booth, feeling the seat of her jeans snag on the ancient cracked leather. She pushed her hands into her hair, knowing it made her look like a circus clown with red curls flying out every which way, not caring. She stared at her rack of tiles, then back to the Scrabble board, then back to the tiles. Her letters were terrible, a mix of vowels and a few high-scoring consonants she'd saved for a perfect opportunity that had failed to arise. But . . . there was something there. Lily's mind below her mind saw something; she just needed to figure it out.

Lily's eyes on her tiles. Back to the board. The tiles. The board was nearly full, with everything from ARENA to ZAXES. (That last had almost garnered a challenge from Lily, but she knew better. If Reed played it, it was a word.) There were no obvious spots for a high-letter-count play (not that she had the tiles for that anyway).

But that shouldn't matter. Scrabble wasn't about words, about vocabulary. You won by treating it like a puzzle, a maths problem with many solutions. It was about the potential of the board, running the numbers, pulling points from all those double-letter and triple-word squares, making a lot out of a little. Reed's last play had altered that potential, both creating and destroying opportunities. The trick was to *see*.

Her mind snapped into a deeper place, and she finally understood what she'd been trying to tell herself for the last five minutes. Lily picked up five tiles and placed them on the board, crossing the U in FAVOURITE.

"Shitfire," Reed said from behind her.

"Don't fret," Lily said, marking up the score sheet. "There's always that Z in the southwest."

Reed set one of the two fresh pints of San Miguel he was holding in front of Lily, then deposited himself back on his side of the booth with a healthy grunt.

"QUACKY, Lily?" he said. "*QUACKY*? I hate it . . . and I'm in awe of it. What's the damage?"

"Triple letter on the Q and the K, and an additional eight points for making YEAST with the Y . . . That's sixty-two total. Puts me up by nineteen."

Reed stared at his tiles for a few moments. He had three left and Lily had two.

"Bah," he said, spinning his rack around to show her an R and two I's. "I could try to eke this out, but there's not enough firepower here to catch up, and we both know it. Well done, Ms. Barnes. Really thought I had you this time."

"I'll clean up," Lily said. "I am gracious in victory."

She picked up the Scrabble board and folded it so all the tiles slid to the middle, then took the tile bag in her free hand and let the little squares cascade into it with a pleasing rattle of wood on wood.

Reed's eyes roved across the packed bar.

"No surprise it's crowded tonight, considering," he said, taking a pull of his beer.

Lily raised an eyebrow.

"You didn't hear?" Reed asked.

Lily went very still. Her ears tingled, her stomach hollowed out—feelings she had come to recognize as her body's attempt to inoculate itself against incoming bad news. These days—and for some time now—the news came in any flavor you wanted, as long as you wanted awful. There were no good surprises anymore.

"What happened?"

Reed sighed. He reached into his pocket and pulled out his phone. He pulled up something on its screen, then offered it to her.

"It's a Wordy," he said.

"It's fine," Lily answered.

She trusted Reed.

He handed her phone, and she saw the homepage of Hong Kong's most prominent English newspaper, the *South China Morning Post,* rendered entirely without images. The phone was indeed a Wordy, as Reed had said, set for text only, no images or video or audio. She relaxed a little. You couldn't be too careful.

The headline, in enormous type: THE LOUVRE BURNS, with a subtitle beneath it in smaller text: THE WORLD MOURNS.

Does it, though? Lily wondered.

Lily felt sick to her stomach, but not, she was unsurprised to realize, *that* sick. Things were just different now. She remembered when Notre Dame Cathedral in Paris went up in flames, back in 2019. That one she'd felt in her gut. She was already in Hong Kong by then; she'd come over straight from finishing her engineering degree at the Imperial College London. The cathedral caught fire around 6:00 p.m. in France, midnight on Lily's side of the world. She was out that night clubbing with David, so she was still awake and saw the coverage beginning on her phone. They'd both stayed up all night watching it as if they had no choice, like standing vigil over the slow death of a loved one.

But now, reading a newspaper account of the loss of one of the world's greatest cultural treasures, Lily's strongest feeling was resignation. Of course the Louvre would burn. It made perfect sense.

She read on. The museum was still ablaze. Efforts to extinguish the fire had largely been abandoned; most of its treasures were lost forever. The only small blessing was that the Louvre had an expanse of parkland bordering it on one side and the Seine on another, natural barriers that helped the firefighters prevent the fire from spreading beyond the museum.

A paragraph caught her eye:

> *While Leonardo DaVinci's* Mona Lisa *was kept in a protective enclosure that could, potentially, have survived the disaster, those hopes were dashed when François LeDuc, head of the Louvre's Département des Peintures, was seen in an upper-floor window of the museum with the masterpiece. He held it above his head as if presenting it to the assembled onlookers, remaining in that position until both he and the painting burned. Mr. LeDuc was one of only three individuals with the necessary key and passcode to the* Mona Lisa's *enclosure. We spoke to Dr. Elaine Ng, staff psychiatrist at Hong Kong Adventist Hospital, who stated, "This isn't an official diagnosis, but Mr. LeDuc's actions are consistent with the behavior of a Grey-afflicted individual affiliated with the Joy movement. It felt like he wanted that painting to burn, and he wanted the world to see it happen. It's hard to think of any other explanation for a man who spent his career protecting great works of art."*

She handed Reed's phone back to him.

"Sorry to be the bearer of bad tidings," he said.

"Don't be," Lily said. "I get the paper. I'd have found out in the morning anyway. And with full-color photos to boot."

"That's one nice thing about all of this, eh?" Reed said. "The newspaper's back. I missed it."

"I did, too, which is funny," Lily said. "I should be too young to care. Print media's been on life support for most of my life. I suppose I have some nostalgia for it because my parents had papers around when I was small. My mum liked the gossip and scandals in the *Daily Mail*, and my dad read the *Telegraph*. Any-time I touch newsprint, it brings me right back to those days."

"What are you, thirty?" Reed asked.

A blunt question, but because Reed had erred in the right direction, Lily found it easy to forgive. Plus, he was an Aussie. Such things were to be expected.

"Thirty-two," she said.

"I got a few decades on you," Reed said. "Had a paper round when I was a kid. Those are back too, I hear. Gainful employment for the youth of today. All the printing presses are firing back up, now that no one wants to use these anymore." He held up his phone. "You can't hack the front page, after all. Can't make someone see or hear anything they don't want to. Simpler's better, sometimes."

Lily nodded.

"I like that you can *finish* the newspaper too," she said. "It's . . . finite. You can read it and be done. Better than just scrolling constantly, seeing the next bit of nonsense to come across all your feeds."

This is a very Pity Party conversation, Lily thought. *Two people convincing themselves things are fine. Just fine.*

"You ever go?" Reed asked. "To the Louvre, I mean."

"Once," Lily answered. "My dad went to Paris for business—

some neurology conference. We took the Eurostar train over together, under the Channel and back up again. He gave me some money and sent me to the Louvre to kill a day. I tried to appreciate the art, tried to be a lady of culture, but I was thirteen. It was too much. I ended up just wandering around, looking for any paintings I halfway recognized. Spent the last few hours sitting in the cafeteria. But it was a nice day."

"I'm sure. I never went myself. But let's shift away, yeah? How's the new job? Don't know that I've seen you since you started. What is it again?"

"You remember the Lego, right?"

Reed nodded.

Lily tended to describe her job to laypeople in as simple a fashion as possible—"what I do is like building a Lego set." The comparison wasn't too far off. She was a materials engineer. The idea was to combine substances in configurations or combinations that didn't already exist in nature, to create materials with purpose-built properties that were particularly useful in some specific way.

It was a weird, unique job that Lily greatly enjoyed. It really was like playing with a building set—but instead of molded plastic, the blocks were atoms and molecules. Her field brought the world all kinds of interesting things. Flexible glass, inflatable aerogel spacecraft, nano-lens invisibility cloaks. Lily used the Lego analogy when explaining her career to a stranger, but in her heart, she saw it more like being a wizard. A potions master at a school of sorcery, mixing bits of this and that to make some magical new thing.

"Right," Lily continued. "So I was working for that electronics company in Sha Tin, helping them design lighter, stronger alloys for their phone cases. It was interesting enough. Let me keep my work visa so I could live here. But what was I doing, really? Phones? Who did that help? Everyone already has a phone, and making a better, more expensive version . . . it was just spinning the wheel, right?"

"Sure," Reed said, his tone neutral.

"So I looked for something that would . . . you know. Let me feel like I was *doing* something. I found a place in Sham Shui Po, this company CarbonGo, and they—"

"What's the fucking point, Lily?" Reed said, his voice not cold, exactly.

Disgusted, maybe.

"What?" Lily said.

"What are we doing?" he said, his voice quiet, barely audible over the DJ, now playing something by the Happy Mondays.

Disgust was shifting to another emotion Lily knew well, one she and everyone else alive at that moment was very finely attuned to—despair.

"I started learning the piano," Reed said. "I feed a stray cat that comes by my window. I teach my students. I come here every week, and I play board games and get drunk and watch Andy Samberg movies."

"Adam Sandler," Lily said, unable to stop herself.

Reed gave her a long, considering look.

"They played *Hot Rod* last week," he said. "Anyway. You quit your well-paying job to do something else, and I'd wager the new one's some humanitarian thing, something you think will *change things*."

He lifted his beer and drained it in four long swallows, then reached for Lily's and slid it over in front of him.

"Nothing's gonna change, Lily Barnes. The Grey's coming for all of us, and that's *right*. It's what humanity deserves. I can sit here and cheerfully lose to you at Scrabble and do it again next week, but when I lie in bed awake tonight in the small hours I'll feel the Grey rising in my head and heart, and maybe I'll push it back and maybe I won't, and I can feel it right *now*, Lily. I can feel it, and I just want to jump in and let it all be *over* . . . stop *struggling*—"

She reached out and took Reed's hand. The contact shocked him into silence, like he'd been dunked in ice water. Lily wondered when someone had last touched him at all. He was divorced, she knew.

"It's not a struggle, Reed," she said. "It's a fight."

She held his hand tighter.

"It's a choice," she said.

He looked at her. His eyes were wet.

"Isn't it?" Lily said.

Reed took in a deep, shuddering breath.

"Yes," he said. "It is."

He squeezed her hand once, then let go.

"Thank you," Reed said. "I'll be all right. Just a low moment. Don't worry about me."

Lily nodded. There was only so much you could do.

"You'll be fine, Reed. I know you will. I need you here. Who else in all of Hong Kong gives me a run for my money at Scrabble?"

He chuckled.

"Next time let's put some *actual* money on it," he said. "Might be just the motivation I need. One more?"

Reed pointed at his empty glass.

"Sure," Lily said, despite not really wanting to keep drinking. You did what you could.

Lily Barnes had another beer with her friend and listened to the DJ, who was really quite good. In time, she left the Pity Party and caught a taxi she could mostly afford, let herself into her apartment in Hong Kong's Mid-Levels district, undressed and got into bed.

And there the Grey waited for her, the same rising tide of nothing Reed was so afraid and certain of, a cold silver sea.

Lily remembered walking into the Louvre, having found her own way there on the Metro from Gare du Nord after telling her father she was old enough to handle it. She remembered how good it felt to be walking through that gigantic museum on her own, exploring, going wherever she wanted. No thirteen-year-old kid would ever have a day like that again.

Now, Lily cried.

She fought and struggled and almost went under. Because, ultimately, why not?

Why not? she thought. *Because you are better than that. Because you are making a difference. Because there is a reason you are alive, and because you are needed, and because you have a purpose.*

She told herself these things over and over.

Eventually, exhausted, she slept.

I. THREE

HONG KONG.
MID-LEVELS.
22°16′48.0″N, 114°09′01.2″E

6:20 A.M. TEN MINUTES BEFORE HER ALARM WAS SET TO GO OFF, Lily lay awake listening to Hong Kong's morning song. Traffic, construction—it all started early in the city . . . or never really stopped, even these days. Wisps of industrious noise drifted up toward her windows, thirty-five stories above the sidewalk.

Hong Kong was a vertical city. There wasn't much usable land, especially along the coast and on the little speck of an island just offshore that contained many of its most famous, wealthy, and historical neighborhoods. You literally couldn't build out, so buildings built up. One of the most conspicuous symbols of wealth in this place was a two- or three-story home that lavishly ignored all the valuable airspace above its roof that could be occupied by apartments. Homes like that, actual "houses," could mostly be found at the top of the mountain range that divided Hong Kong Island neatly in two, largely occupied by tycoons and movie stars.

Lily Barnes was neither, and so she lived in a compact one-bedroom apartment in a neighborhood called the Mid-Levels. Her building was a skinny, apartment-filled spike levering high up above Robinson Road, in a complex of identical constructions collectively known as Palm Court, a small part of the irregular pincushion that was Hong Kong Island, one of the most densely populated places on the planet in terms of people per square kilometer.

"Get up," she said out loud. "Get out of bed."

She didn't. She'd been awake since three.

Her alarm went off, and she slowly wormed a hand out from beneath the covers to tap her phone to silence it.

Lily lay still. The enormity and effort of just . . . *being alive* during this meat grinder era of history was all around her, waiting to welcome her back to all its strain and stress and fear. She considered staying in bed, refusing to engage with existence, doing nothing that would require reckoning with the state of the world.

A ray of sunlight slashed its way into her bedroom, created by the imperfect seal of her window shades against the frames. She still wasn't used to Hong Kong sunshine, even after five years there. It was a cliché that it rained all the time in England—there were plenty of sunny days—but the light in London was gauzy, veiled. Polite and proper. Hong Kong's sun was a thug kicking in your door.

"Get up," the sunlight said. *"Get out of bed. If you don't, I will burn this planet to a cinder."*

Not if I have anything to say about it, Lily thought.

She sat up. The woes of the world reasserted themselves. She got out of bed, put water in the kettle, and set it to heat for tea. She wasn't hungry—and what did it mean to wake up after a full night's sleep and not be hungry?—but popped a piece of toast in the toaster.

On the mat just outside her apartment door lay the *South*

China Morning Post. It boasted the same headline as the article she'd read on Reed's phone the night before (THE LOUVRE BURNS; THE WORLD MOURNS) but now accompanied by a huge color photo of the burning museum. The paper went into the recycling bin, unread.

Lily had her toast and tea. She spent a few minutes adding pieces to her latest self-designed Lego model, a particularly complex protein molecule with a pleasingly asymmetrical structure. Once it was complete, she'd add it to the shelf with the others, where delicate structures of brightly colored blocks rested atop tall stacks of boxes containing brutally challenging jigsaw puzzles. The molecule was nearly done, but Lily set it aside after only a few minutes. She didn't want to be working on puzzles for fun just then. She wanted to work on puzzles for work.

Lily showered and dressed in slacks of light cotton and a linen blouse, the only fabrics that made sense in Hong Kong's heat and humidity. She wrestled her hair into a messy ponytail, a bundle of wiry orange springs. She threw on sunglasses, grabbed her satchel, stepped into the sensible flats she kept on a mat just outside her door, and joined the crowds making their way down the endless terraces of the gigantic escalator the city had installed to aid with the daily commute down from the Mid-Levels.

In many parts of the world the Grey had greatly reduced the number of people going to work each day as many of the afflicted just stopped leaving their homes. That was not the way in Hong Kong; the huge escalator was as crammed as ever. Industriousness was coded into the city's stones and bones. Hong Kong's people were, in many ways, the work they performed.

It was quiet, though. None of the normal loud chatter in Cantonese and Mandarin. People were keeping to themselves. That was another side effect of the Grey, and one Lily didn't mind. Westerners weren't uncommon in Hong Kong . . . but few with Lily's particular combination of characteristics. She was a tall, pale, skinny, curly-haired redhead. Open stares, even the occasional old lady touching her hair on public transit——before the Grey it was constant. Now, though, people didn't much look at anyone. That suited Lily well enough.

Once off the escalator, it was a quick walk through Central to the MTR and then under the harbor and back up again into Kowloon, just seven stops to Sham Shui Po. Her employer, CarbonGo, Ltd., had its offices on the top floor of an ancient high-rise, its exterior speckled with the musty dark growth endemic to any building steeped in Hong Kong's steamy tropical miasma. It was an ugly pile and no mistake, but the company needed access to an urban rooftop to test its products, and this was what her boss could afford.

A little bakery sat just down the block from Lily's building, one of her favorite places in the city. She cut through the pavement traffic, angling toward the shop and slipping inside. She still wasn't hungry, but knew better than to embark upon a day in her lab without more fuel than a bit of toast and jam. The establishment was tiny, about two meters wide, basically a closet. It housed a waist-high glass case that did double duty as a counter and display for various pastries, rolls, and other delectables.

Standing behind the case was the bakery's proprietor, a tiny woman in her early twenties sporting a name tag reading *Charmaine* in careful, hand-lettered cursive. She'd made a go of creating something special here. The shop wasn't just your standard croissant-and-coffee stand. Everything was cute, everything was unique—a donut stall with patisserie dreams. The cupcakes were architecturally frosted, the Danish had unusual fillings like lychee or pomelo, the bread was so freshly baked, it steamed when you pulled it apart. Each day Charmaine filled the glass case with delights, and then a steady stream of customers ensured it ended up empty, waiting to be restocked the next morning with whatever she dreamed up during her predawn baking hours.

Today, just before 8:00 a.m., those shelves were already nearly bare, and the goods on display looked wilted, old. Grey. Charmaine was behind the counter as always. She looked grey too. Her hair hung lank; she looked as if she had slept in her little baker's uniform. Her name tag was tilted a bit, askew, and that told Lily more than anything else. The effort required to set it right—so minimal, and yet it remained unfixed, unadjusted.

Usually, everything in this shop spoke of effort and care. A reflection of the mind of its proprietor. Today, Lily thought it was still a reflection, but of a deeply altered mind. Her heart broke. What she might have felt for the Louvre, she was instead feeling here for a little sidewalk bakery on Hai Tan Street. The Louvre, she supposed, was a genocide. This was a murder.

"Good morning," Lily said.

Charmaine looked up at her, but she wasn't seeing Lily. Her eyes were looking at something else very far away.

"Hello," she said, her voice like a splotch of wet cement.

"Can I get . . . ," Lily began.

None of the pastries looked particularly appetizing, but she couldn't just walk away.

"How about that sweet bun? And a tea?"

Without responding, Charmaine reached into the case with her bare hand, Lily noticed; normally she would, without exception, use tongs. She put the bun on the glass countertop, which was smeared with icing or oil and scattered with crumbs. A paper cup of tea arrived a moment later, conspicuously not steaming.

"And that's . . . ," Lily prompted. "Forty, right?"

Charmaine considered for a slow moment, then nodded.

"Yes," she said.

Lily pulled out two blue Hong Kong dollar twenties and put them down on the countertop. Charmaine looked at them. Didn't pick them up.

"I hope this doesn't seem rude," Lily said, "but maybe you

should go to the clinic? Or call your family or talk to some friends? I'm happy to sit with you for a while. Honestly, it would be my pleasure."

Charmaine gave Lily a long stare.

"I'm fine," she said.

Lily opened her mouth to push but stopped herself. This was one of the worst things about the Grey. *There was nothing you could do.* She had learned that in the hardest possible way.

Twenty-seven percent of the world's population was afflicted by the disease. The Grey wasn't garden-variety clinical depression. It wasn't an imbalance in brain chemistry, and it didn't respond to SSRIs and the other common medications. Therapy, exercise, sleep . . . all the standard treatment methods didn't make a dent. The Grey was a creeping, relentless malaise, a dark growth on the soul, and once it took you, you were lost.

Humanity had been formally aware of the problem for a little over two years, but it was assumed it had just gone unnoticed for some time before that; humanity, as a species, was always somewhat down in the dumps. It wasn't until it started affecting individuals with absolutely no reason to be depressed—stable, successful people, or children—that the reality of what was happening became clear. And then a darker realization: it wasn't just that the Grey could hit anyone at any time . . . it was *transmissible.* Sometimes it spread within families, or a whole office might come down with it all at once.

Scientists were torn on whether it was a disease at all in the standard sense. They had not been able to find a transmission vector—not a virus, not a bacteria, not a prion, not a fungus—but it was spreading somehow. And without a sense of *what* was spreading, the world's doctors could only watch and despair.

One common theory: everyone already had the Grey. It was a species-wide affliction connected to the very nature of being a human being. Some people were just better at fighting it off. Deeply negative events in a person's life could trigger the onset of the condition, as if a person's spiritual bulwarks had been breached. This was the reason for things like the Pity Parties. You did what you could to build up your defenses, and when something terrible happened in the world, you told yourself everything was fine. Just fine.

But a blast of bad news wasn't the only way people succumbed to the Grey. There were other ways you could get it.

Charmaine's phone sat on the counter near the cashbox. Lily wondered if the woman had maybe clicked on a link she shouldn't have, watched a video clip she thought would be fine, and gotten the Despair Manifesto instead.

Lily pulled her mind away. Even thinking about the Manifesto felt dangerous.

She thought instead about the flavors of Grey and which might have afflicted Charmaine. There were three. Sometimes people who got it soldiered on, just . . . reduced. This seemed to be Charmaine's path. She had shown up to her bakery and was going through the motions. Other times people went dark, unable to leave their homes or their beds, barely able to take care of themselves. Many of those ended in suicide. At the opposite end was the third way the Grey could appear, the rarest path—a twisted joy, misery manifesting as mania. Those people were dangerous. They wanted to share the good news.

The minds of just over a quarter of the planet were stuck in one of those traps, and no doctor had figured out a reliable treatment, much less a cure. Once you got the Grey, that was that. Twenty-seven percent. About two billion people.

The world was still running, but the gears were starting to stick, the engine winding down. The obvious conclusion: if enough humans stopped caring about keeping society going . . . it wouldn't keep going.

The only real defense against the Grey seemed to be *purpose*.

People with a firm sense of themselves and their reason for existing had a lower infection rate and were less deeply affected if they did catch the disease.

Lily would have thought Charmaine had that purpose, running her cute little bakery and inventing her special little cakes. Apparently, lychee Danishes weren't enough.

Charmaine's gaze had withdrawn again.

"Have a nice day," Lily said, taking her bun and her tea and leaving the bakery.

She was sad about poor Charmaine, but if there was one thing Lily Barnes had learned in the Grey world, it was this: do not dwell. Out on the street, she dropped the bun and tea in a trash can and headed up the block to her building at 52 Hai Tan Street. She could feel her mind limbering up, resetting itself to tackle the problems to come. She felt anticipation, resolve.

Purpose.

Lily walked past the elderly security guard dozing at his desk and took the tiny elevator to the top floor. She let herself into the empty office—she was early; she was almost always early—and headed to her workspace, plopping her satchel on her desk. She loved this job. CarbonGo wasn't a particularly impressive organization, and she wasn't paid all that well compared to what she might have earned at an aircraft manufacturer or SpaceX or even back at the electronics job she'd left a few months earlier. But CarbonGo had something the other gigs didn't—a morally defensible line of business.

By working here, Lily could, without any sense of hyperbole, tell herself she was saving the world.

CarbonGo was in the climate change mitigation business: trying to cool things down on a planetary scale. More specifically, they were concerned with finding a technological solution to removing carbon dioxide from the atmosphere.

That task was not particularly difficult. Any halfway decent secondary school science teacher could pull carbon dioxide from the air. The trick was to do it on a massive scale. For millennia, every tree that was ever burned, every bit of coal, every barrel of oil, had put carbon into the air. Now all of that had to be sucked back out and stored somewhere. CarbonGo thought that unbelievably gigantic task might be accomplished by developing small devices—"scrubbers," in industry parlance—that could be placed all over the world in high-exhaust urban environments and chug away vacuuming carbon out of the air.

A good trick—actually, two tricks, from an engineering perspective. Carbon scrubbers weren't complex. They consisted of a chemical sponge called a sorbent, which soaked up carbon dioxide from the air while leaving all the other gases behind. Finding the right material to act as a sorbent was trick one. Trick two was figuring out way to squeeze the sorbent "sponge" to release the CO_2 into a storage medium—tanks, or perhaps limestone or concrete—anything that would either lock it away out of the atmosphere or let it be reused.

Both of these processes were well understood, and many methods existed to do both. The problem was the *cost*, usually described in terms of dollars per metric ton of extracted CO_2. The best tech out there could do it on an industrial scale at about US$58 per ton. The goal was US$30 but, honestly, the lower the better. The cheaper it was, the more people would use it.

Lily's work for CarbonGo involved trying different combinations of atoms to build a perfect sorbent that would both efficiently vacuum up CO_2 like a magnet to iron filings while also releasing it upon as low an application of energy as possible.

Lily powered up her computers; most of her work was done using advanced modeling software. Much cheaper than producing actual prototypes. She leaned forward as the screens lit up, preparing to lose herself in ratios of potassium oxalate monohydrate and ethylene diamine for the next eight to twelve hours, solving the puzzle that would save the world.

"Ms. Barnes," a voice said, behind her.

She turned to see the company's owner, Danny Chang, walking across the lab. He had thinning hair and a bit of a middle-aged paunch, and favored tailored suits that did their best to hide the second attribute (as not much could be done about the first). Lily liked him, liked his focus and general lack of frivolity. What Danny Chang lacked in sentimentality he made up for with efficiency, not something you always found in the nonscientific mind.

Danny held something in his hand: a cylinder about twenty centimeters long, maybe eight centimeters in diameter. It was a rich shade of blue, a sapphire color with shadowy accents. Lily had never seen a color exactly like it. That was interesting because colors came from the way stuff reflected light, and an unfamiliar color meant the *stuff* was unfamiliar too. Not a common experience for someone who worked in materials science. But even more interesting than the cylinder was the fact that Danny Chang was smiling. A huge no-joke grin was plastered across his face.

Lily tensed. Smiles could be very dangerous these days. People with the third form of the Grey, the Joy variant, tended to smile a lot.

The eyes, everyone said. You had to look at the eyes.

But Lily didn't sense anything off as her boss approached. He just seemed legitimately excited. She barely recognized the emotion.

Danny held up the cylinder, showing it off.

"You see this?" he said.

"What is it?" Lily asked.

"Salvation!" her boss said.

Lily's gaze shifted to the cylinder. Now that she could get a better look, the thing's essential oddness was amplified. It wasn't just that blue color. The finish was like nothing she'd ever seen. It was reflective, but in a way that almost seemed to take in the light, change it, and send it back out warmer. It made her want to touch it, hold it, put it in her bed on a cold winter's night. Not that Hong Kong had those.

The device had openings at either end. One looked like an intake. The other, a hatch.

"Let's go upstairs," Danny said. "I need you to test this, make sure it's real."

They went into the hall outside the office, then climbed a set of fire stairs and exited through a rusty steel door to the building's roof, where various generations of the company's CO_2 scrubbing technology worked away, resembling rooftop HVAC units of various sizes. Some of the earliest, power-hungry models were deactivated to save on the electric bill, but the others hummed along, sucking carbon dioxide out of Hong Kong's atmosphere a molecule at a time.

The city stretched away in the distance, all skyscrapers and mountains and sea. At ground level, Hong Kong was an anthill. But from high up the city was beautiful, a metropolis built into a stunning natural environment with an eye toward integration, not conquest.

Danny handed Lily the blue cylinder; lighter than she expected. He gestured toward a locked, rust-speckled steel cabinet set next to a workbench at the far end of the roof. It contained a power system and diagnostic tools used to test new prototypes.

"Hook it up," he said. "Give it a try."

Lily frowned.

"It's a scrubber? Where did you get it?"

"Doesn't matter," Danny said. "Just connect it, run a pass, tell me the results. Little panel on the side opens, and it only has a few controls. Very easy to use, I think."

Lily was intrigued. She took the cylinder to the workbench, unlocked and opened the cabinet next to it, and attached the device to power. She opened up the strange gadget's control panel to see that it was indeed simple.

The activation button for the thing was obvious; she pressed it. A small, pleasant hum commenced. Inside the steel cabinet was a small glass tank, airtight, with sensors attached that measured the mix of atmospheric gases within. Lily placed the blue cylinder inside, sealed the tank, and stepped back.

Out of the corner of her eye, Lily could see that Danny could barely contain himself—he was shifting his weight from foot to foot, almost dancing.

They watched the device in silence until it abruptly seemed to complete its cycle. The small hatch on the end of the cylinder opened smoothly, revealing a solid, milky-white cube a few centimeters on a side. The testing tank had a built-in diagnostic system that could determine how much CO_2 had been removed from the internal atmosphere and how much power was used to do it. Lily looked at the readout.

"Holy shit," she said.

"I take it the results are good," Danny said.

"Remarkable," Lily answered. "Hard to believe, actually. Is there a mechanism for releasing the carbon dioxide from the sorbent, though? Doesn't matter how easily it takes the stuff in if it's too pricey to get it back out."

"Watch this," her boss said.

He stepped past her, then opened the testing tank. He grabbed the little white cube and stood back, looking around the roof.

"Ah," he said, striding over to a clay pot pushed up against one edge of the roof's retaining wall, a rainwater-filled remnant of some prior tenant's attempt at a rooftop garden, now a mosquito nursery. Danny tossed the cube into the murky water, and a massive surge of bubbles exploded from its surface, bubbling up over the sides of the pot and spilling onto the roof tiles.

"What? No," Lily said, amazed.

The bubbles seethed up from the pot for another thirty seconds before slowing, a fizzing, frothing sea of carbon dioxide released back into the atmosphere.

"No energy required at all to pull the carbon dioxide out of the sorbent," Danny said, grinning at her. "You can put it in water and then collect the gas. Or you can just dispose of the sorbent cube however you like."

"But that's . . . that's . . ." Lily ran the numbers in her head. "At that power intake level for the gas collection, that's maybe . . . a dollar per ton?"

"Lower, maybe, depending on where it's deployed and how we develop markets for the offset."

"But . . ." Lily was having trouble processing this. "Where did you get it? Climeworks? Carbon Engineering?"

Those were the two primary competitors to CarbonGo—the market leaders in the field.

"Pff," Danny scoffed. "They wish. This will put them both out of business. No competition for CarbonGo, Ms. Barnes, not anymore. We're about to corner the market."

Lily turned to look at the blue cylinder again, sitting innocuously inside the diagnostic tank. A magical, impossible thing. A few thousand of these devices could rebalance carbon dioxide levels across the planet. Fit them into factory smokestacks and car exhaust systems and jet engines, and that'd be it. An actual, realistic path forward to ending global warming. Lily detached the device from the cables inside the test tank and tested its weight in her hand. It was light. So light, for everything it could do and mean.

"I need to make another one of those cubes, study its properties. A room-temperature stable, water-soluble suspended matrix of CO_2? I mean, dear god, Danny. Maybe it could be used as a building material, or an insulator, or . . . ," she said.

"Ms. Barnes," Danny said, his tone changed, now almost apologetic.

Lily looked back at her boss. He had the most awkward expression on his face. He held out his hand for the cylinder. She passed it over. Danny turned, heading back toward the door leading back inside. He talked as he walked, clearly expecting her to follow. She did. He was, after all, her employer.

"Lily, you've been an excellent employee, but you must understand that I no longer need a materials engineer. The company no longer requires a development arm. I have the finished product we were working toward, and it exceeds our wildest projections. I will need every resource I have for marketing and manufacturing. You understand, don't you?"

Lily understood. Danny Chang was low on sentimentality, high on efficiency.

"You're letting me go," she said, hearing an echo in her voice of the tone Charmaine the baker had used to say "I'm fine."

Danny nodded.

"I will make sure you get an excellent severance package. You've been a true asset to my business."

He held the door for her when they returned to the main office, to her lab, to the place she'd been as happy as it was possible to be these days. Danny walked over to a safe set on a countertop, tapped out its combination, and opened it. He placed the cylinder inside, closed and locked the safe, then turned to smile at her.

"Ms. Barnes, be happy. We both wanted the same thing. To give humanity a chance against climate change. Just because you didn't do it doesn't mean it wasn't done."

He extended his hand to her.

"Does it matter who saves the world, as long as it is saved?"

They said the best way to push back the Grey was to have something in your life you really believed in, something central to your identity. A purpose.

And just like that, Lily Barnes no longer had one.

I. FOUR

HONG KONG.
SHAM SHUI PO.

22°19′51.9″N, 114°09′27.4″E

LILY WAS RELEASED FROM EMPLOYMENT—LET GO, SACKED, fired, kicked out on her arse—around 10:00 a.m. It took another few hours to work out the details of her disentanglement from CarbonGo, Ltd. Danny Chang wanted her to sign an intimidating nondisclosure agreement in exchange for a generous severance offer of six months' pay and benefits—buying her silence about his mysterious device, in other words.

Once the paperwork was finally finished, Lily tossed the few personal items she kept at work in her satchel, and out the door she went, with no particular destination in mind. She no longer had anywhere to be.

The district where CarbonGo kept its office, Sham Shui Po, was well-known for its gigantic consumer electronics markets. Lily wandered through endless narrow stalls featuring gaming consoles and smartphones and cameras and audio components and computer parts in versions both knockoff and (possibly) official, with garish, hand-lettered signs in English and Chinese advertising the lowest prices on the planet. She didn't see any of it.

She got noodles at a stall she knew, found a park, and sat down on bench in the shade to eat. She was surrounded by the sounds of Hong Kong's endless traffic, shouted Cantonese, vivid scents both horrid and sublime. None of that, not even the taste of the noodles, made it to her conscious brain.

Lily set aside the empty carton. She dug through her satchel until she found a puzzle, just a child's novelty toy. A small, flat square of plastic inset with smaller tiles in a grid, each with part of a larger image on them, mixed and scrambled. One square of the grid was empty, and the tiles could be moved in and out of that empty space, shifted until the image was reassembled. This one had originally had a picture of a clown, but you could barely see it now. The image was all but worn away from hours and hours of insistent, repeated solving.

Lily solved it again now, and felt a little better.

She found a convenience store, where she bought a notebook and a bottle of water. Then she returned to the park and tried to execute her normal response whenever life threw her a crisis—figure out her next steps in minute, bullet-pointed detail. For most of an hour the pages stayed blank as Lily stared out into the distance, thinking, remembering.

Then half-formed ideas began to appear in the notebook, sketches, little bits of chemical formulae and theories. Lily considered the endlessly deep, rich blue she'd seen on the scrubber's cylindrical casing. She listed out elements and compounds that might generate such a shade. Synthetic sapphire, cobalt chloride, copper sulfate pentahydrate . . . she had no bloody idea. But, by god, she *wanted to know.*

Lily should have been shaking with anger or fear. Maybe catatonic with shock. Those were all hovering around the edges, but mainly she felt . . . hope. It washed through her, bright and unfamiliar, underscoring how deeply her worldview had become dominated by a creeping, low-level despair. How bad it had really gotten.

The thing was, materials science—her field and career—was about *building things*. And for that field even to exist, you needed a forward-looking world, with humanity trying to improve itself through technology. Materials science was about finding the next new thing that could do the next new thing. It made the impossible possible. But after the hammerblows to humanity's psyche brought by pandemics, the creeping dread of climate change, political upheaval across the globe, and now, of course, the Grey, believing the world had much to look forward to was starting to feel like an act of extreme naïveté.

So, to see something truly new, something that suggested someone out there was still making things, was still committed to progress, on a scale so significant that they had produced technology Lily couldn't begin to understand . . . yes, hope. She felt quite a bit of hope, no matter what that bizarre carbon scrubber might mean for her own professional prospects.

Where did it come from? Lily thought, sitting in the park, smelling roasting chestnuts from a street vendor, staring at a sketch she'd made of the cylinder in blue ballpoint pen.

Lily knew every player in her professional field. The two most likely suspects to have created something like the device—ClimateWorks out of Switzerland and Carbon Engineering in the southern US—hadn't ever produced anything near it. It would be like the Wright brothers inventing their little fabric-and-sticks airplane for Kitty Hawk and then, the next summer, rolling out a fighter jet.

The technology she'd seen was decades away. Some of what the super-scrubber could do had to incorporate technological advances the carbon capture industry predicted *would* happen but hadn't yet. It was like evidence of time travel—which, actually, was one of Lily's working theories. A miracle, in a world that sorely needed some.

Who made the damn thing, and how did Danny Chang get his hands on it? Why wouldn't he tell her what it was? What was with the secrecy?

The most incredible thing I've ever seen, and I got to play with it for all of five minutes before Chang sacked me, she thought.

An idea appeared in Lily's head, so fully formed that it had clearly been building for a while, gathering strength until it was ready to formally present itself to her consciousness.

Lily frowned.

Don't, she thought. *Don't even think about it. Things are bad enough.*

She turned to a fresh page in her notebook and wrote the word "PROSPECTS" across the top.

The six months' severance from CarbonGo would see her through for a bit and let her remain in Hong Kong on her current work visa. (She made a note to confirm that. She didn't want to add deportation to her list of woes.) She wondered if her prior employer, the cell phone manufacturer, would take her back—but she was sure they'd already replaced her. She considered the idea of looking for work back in the UK, and frowned at the thought. No, thank you.

There were definitely engineering gigs in China, but the process to get a work permit in the mainland was brutally difficult at the best of times, and—

Lily scratched it all out, big blue ragged sweeping cross-outs all across the page.

That idea she'd had wasn't going away. It was dancing, wiggling right in her face, not letting her think about anything else until she gave the persistent bastard its due.

Lily knew she should go home. Figure things out. Plan her

next steps. She closed her notebook and tossed it and her water bottle in her satchel, stood, and walked to the park's exit.

The sensible thing was to turn left, toward the MTR stop that would take her back under the harbor and then up again to the Pedder Street exit from the Central stop, just steps from the Mid-Level Escalators, their downward flow now reversed for the evening to take commuters back up to their flats. The smart thing to do was to go home.

Instead, Lily did something deeply foolish. She turned right.

She walked back to Hai Tan Street and found herself a spot in the Pacific Coffee down the block from her (former) employer, at a table with a good view of the building entrance. She checked her watch—analog, a Swatch she'd bought at the big mall in the Admiralty District over on the island. Another thing about a world in which the Despair Manifesto might pop up on any screen at any time—watches were back. It was only about 4. Plenty of time.

Plenty of time to reconsider, Lily, she thought, but she also knew she was kidding herself.

There would be no reconsideration. What she was about to do was her plan all along. If not, then she'd have gone home straightaway after being fired instead of bumbling around in the gadget markets for hours and then parking herself in a blazing-hot city park within walking distance of the CarbonGo offices.

Lily waited and watched, an untouched latte on the table in front of her. Most of her former coworkers left around 5. She'd made a list in her new notebook and checked them off one by one. The last, Danny Chang himself, exited around 6. She hunched her shoulders when she saw him leave, wishing for a hood or a hat to cover up her hugely conspicuous redheadedness, but he didn't even glance in her direction. Preoccupied with the billions of dollars he was about to make, probably.

One more hour for safety, which conveniently let darkness fall over the city. Lily left the coffee place—whose owners were undoubtedly pleased to see her loitering backside finally depart their premises—and crossed the street.

The lobby guard was a wizened man whom she believed lived at the security desk. She'd never been there at any time of day when he wasn't sitting there behind his little bank of camera monitors. Nine out of ten times, though, he was asleep, gently dozing with his head tilted back—and this was very much one of those times.

The lobby had a security camera, but the corresponding monitor was blank. The camera had broken six months earlier and stayed that way. Lots of things were breaking these days, and few were getting fixed.

The elevator had a camera, too, though, and that one was working. Lily could see the monitor on the guard's desk showing the empty little cube of the car. She had no interest in leaving a record of her presence that evening, which meant the stairs. Fifteen or twenty flights later Lily reached the top floor, breathing hard, her heart pounding. Some of that was exertion and some was nerves, and she decided not to speculate too much as to the allocation.

At the door to CarbonGo's offices, Lily produced her key. Danny Chang hadn't asked for it when he fired her; too excited or distracted, she supposed. Either way, a stroke of luck. There was a slim possibility he'd changed the locks that afternoon, but she didn't think it likely. The office door used an actual key in an actual lock to turn actual tumblers. Cylinder locks required a locksmith to replace, and in the Greying world, getting a locksmith (or any tradesman) out on short notice was becoming an increasingly difficult chore.

Lily put her key in the lock turned it, and the door opened. She went in, the motion-sensor-activated lights coming on automatically. That was encouraging. If the lights were off, the office had to be empty.

I've officially broken and entered, she thought, a shameful, zesty buzz running up her spine. *Or at least entered.*

Lily went to the lab, past her former workstation, to the safe sitting on its counter against the wall—an imposing dull black metal box about half a meter on a side. She hesitated. It was entirely possible this was all for nothing. Danny Chang might have taken the safe's contents with him when he left the office. Or he might have changed the code—though she doubted Danny even knew she had it. She'd seen it on a piece of paper once and unconsciously memorized it because it was a chunk of the hexagonal number sequence: 6152845.

After donning a pair of latex gloves from a box at her workstation to avoid leaving prints (Lily felt rather clever to have thought of that), she entered the code, not sure if she actually wanted it to work, part of her hoping something would prevent her from continuing her little crime spree. The safe opened with a small, satisfying click.

There sat the super-scrubber, just where Danny Chang had left it, gleaming that strange warm gleam under the lab fluorescents, the rich, shadowy sapphire shine. It rested atop a small stack of paperwork. Lily brought it all to her workspace, device and documents alike. She quickly checked her equipment, pleased to see that her mass spectrometers and gas chromatographs and scanning electron microscope remained present and accounted for. She'd need them.

Lily looked at the papers first. They appeared to be a contract, dense with unparsable legalese. She snapped images of the pages with her phone's camera but didn't spend much time on them. She could review them later. The real prize was the device, just waiting to yield its secrets to the powerful tools at her disposal.

She selected a thin-bladed probe from her toolkit and dug in. The scrubber didn't want to open—it was well-made, with no obvious fasteners or screws. Finding a way to access its inner workings was a challenge. But Lily was meticulous, and it was just another puzzle. Eventually she found a path, and the shell opened, revealing . . . beauty.

The cylinder packed an enormous amount of functionality into a very small space. There was just a lot of . . . *stuff* inside it, components Lily didn't recognize. It reminder her of a cross section of a nautilus, or some other complicated sea creature. The device wasn't alive; it was definitely a machine, but not laid out like any technology she was familiar with. Shaking her head at the very audacity of this thing's existence, she decided to start by examining the shell.

Every material, from the simplest hydrogen atom to the most complex engineered structures, had a set of properties inherent to it. Density, mass, elasticity, conductivity, magneticism, radioactivity, and many more. Many ran in families; for example, metals, generally speaking, were more conductive than organics. When confronted with an unknown material—which didn't happen to Lily very often—the trick was to run analyses to determine the values of the various properties so as to classify it into one family or another.

Whatever the scrubber's shell was made of, it had no family. It was an orphan. An alien orphan from space.

Under Lily's microscope, the shell had an extremely complex composition. It was crystalline, but the shapes were impossibly regular, maintaining precise edges and angles down to the highest magnification her equipment could manage. She thought perhaps the shell could also serve as a storage system for carbon dioxide pulled out of the air before it was dumped into whatever that little milky cube was made of. It reflected blue—maybe there was some cobalt in there—but from certain angles it was refractive . . . and it refracted *red,* all the way at the other end of the spectrum. The thing was insane, impossible.

And that was just the casing. The innards were just as confounding, just as impressive.

Lily used her probe to delicately sift through loops of spongy, organic coils she thought were the gadget's analogue to wiring.

It was awe-inspiring merely to be in the cylinder's presence, to commune with the revolutionary mind that had designed it. Lily was an expert at how things fit together. She knew how things worked. But before this divine device she was like a dog at the cinema.

The craziest ideas from the list she made in her notebook, aliens and time travel and the like, were seeming saner by the second. This thing was not from the world she knew. That much was clear.

Lily pushed aside another coil of wire, digging deeper into the scrubber's workings. This revealed a structure buried beneath: complex, with more of the spongy conduits looping in and out of a chip or processor of some kind. The way the wires were arranged looked almost like laces on a boot, if the wearer was trying a little too hard to be unique with the lacing pattern, trying to signal their specialness even down to their footwear.

Lily froze. Her heart stopped. Her heart broke.

"No," she said.

Her hand jerked involuntarily, yanking the probe out of the device. The violence of the motion pulled the thing off the edge of her worktable, and in her shock Lily reached to catch it.

Too late. The cylinder fell to the stone floor of the lab. It landed. Hard.

A sound somewhere between crunch and crack.

Lily held her breath.

She didn't want to look . . . but how could she not?

On the floor, bits of the device were scattered in a small arc around the shell. Components she could barely identify made of things she didn't understand.

A machine that could have reversed climate change. Literally saved the world.

Wrecked.

Her fault.

Lily stared at the ruin, trying to decide if she should make an attempt at fixing it, knowing there was just no way.

Maybe Danny can just . . . get another one, she thought.

Call up whoever he'd got it from and ask for a replacement. After all, the idea couldn't be to just have *one* scrubber. That wouldn't achieve anything. Thousands if not millions would need to be manufactured to make a dent in atmospheric carbon levels.

Then again, maybe he couldn't get another. Maybe there was in fact only one. Maybe Lily Barnes had ruined something irreplaceable.

All Lily knew for certain was she'd broken the scrubber and could not fix it. She had, possibly, destroyed a potential cure to one of the diseases afflicting this dark world. This dying world, if she didn't put too fine a point on it.

Lily turned and left the lab. (Left? No. She ran.) She headed for the elevator, then skidded to a stop as she remembered it contained a working camera.

So, the stairs. Lily plunged down two at a time. Between the third and fourth floors, the sole of her left shoe slipped on the bare, polished concrete, and her foot shot forward and down. Her Achilles tendon rasped along the step's sharp, ragged edge, and the jolt of her foot landing twenty centimeters lower than expected reverberated all the way up to her hip.

"Fuck," she shouted, mostly from shock, though pain roared up in her ankle almost immediately.

Lily slowed down, took a breath.

"Stop it," she told herself. "Get your shit together."

She limped the rest of the way, hesitating at the fire door that led to the lobby. Surely the security guard was awake after that yell. She closed her eyes for a moment, rehearsing what she'd say when he questioned her.

Just popped up to grab something I left in the office, she thought. *Took the stairs to get a little exercise. That was silly of me: I slipped. No, I don't need any help. Thank you.*

She wasn't sure how much English the fellow had; it had never seemed like much. Then again, you didn't need to speak English to remember to tell the cops that the tall ginger Western lady was hanging around the office after hours, acting weird.

What are my other options here? Am I going to sleep in the goddamn stairwell?

No . . . no, she was not. Lily pulled the door open, moving with confidence, as if she belonged there, as if everything were good and right in the world. *Just popped up to grab something I—*

The lobby guard was still asleep, earning his pay as effectively as ever.

Lily slipped out, wandering-limping south, heading toward the harbor. She stopped at a twenty-four-hour Wellcome pharmacy to buy some antiseptic wipes, some ibuprofen, and a plaster for her ankle. It wasn't great—every step hurt—but it wasn't agonizing. She could walk.

And walk she did, until she found herself outside the huge McDonald's in Tsim Sha Tsui, right by the water's edge and the ferry terminals. It had a sign bolted to the wall next to its entrance proclaiming it as one of the world's busiest, and it seemed it. Even at 3:00 a.m. the place was half-full.

Fast food was something Lily tried to avoid. Another way to bolster the old mental health, like not going too heavy on the alcohol. A sense that you were taking care of yourself, making good decisions . . . It made for one less source of anxiety, one fewer pathway through which the Grey might make an inroad. When things were going well, Lily ate as though she owned stock in a health food store. Smoothies and tofu and the like.

Lily got a Big Mac and a coffee and a large fries, consumed it all in ten minutes, and felt sick immediately. Then she got herself an apple pie and ate that too.

The rest of that night she spent lurking at a table on the restaurant's third floor, staring moodily out the window at the harbor, sucking down coffee and breathing grease. She tried every mental contortion she could devise to convince herself to return to the lab, to use her tools to fix the scrubber. To do something to make this right. Anything. Anything she could.

She was still trying to convince herself when the sun rose. Too late. Danny Chang might already be back at the office. There was no going back to fix anything. It was done.

I. FIVE

THE OUTER HEBRIDES. LOCH RODEL.

57°44′13.9″N, 6°58′12.9″W

LILY BARNES WAS TEN, OUT ON THE SEA WITH HER FATHER, IN A little rented skiff built for zipping around the waters off the Scottish coast. They were enjoying the day. It was cold but sunny, and her father was an excellent sailor. Lily was sitting in the bow, her eyes closed, smelling the earth-stone-fire scent of her father's pipe tobacco and feeling the whoomph as the boat smacked against each wave, the cold salt spray against her face bracing and delightful.

Then a gust of wind; she remembered that too, clearly. It came crosswise to her and pushed her sideways, and she clutched at the boat to regain her balance. And then a huge impact, a *KNOCK* out of nowhere, some hard part of the ship's mechanism swinging around to crack her in the side of the head, and then she was in the water.

She wore a life jacket, but it was adult-sized and loose fitting. Even worse, she hadn't latched the strap that went between her legs—she hadn't closed the circuit, as her father always told her to do.

Hitting the water yanked her arms up above her head, and the life jacket was too big, and out she went, stripped clear of the item that was supposed to save her life, like a banana squeezed out of it its skin. The shock of it so strong that Lily opened her mouth to scream and breathed in seawater, icy-cold brine. The life preserver stayed on the surface. Lily sank.

She was deep before she knew it, too terrified to swim. It was *cold*, and she had gone from a nice crisp autumn day with the sun shining to dying in the East Atlantic in no time at all. Panic wasn't even the word for what she felt. It was being alone, with no way, no way at all, to prevent what was happening to her.

Pain in her lungs, her throat, her stomach, her heart, in her head, and the one thing she knew was not to breathe because there was nothing to breathe, but she was going to anyway—she had no choice—and then a new pain, on her scalp. This pain she knew. A schoolyard pain, from the rare squabbles she got into with classmates when things turned a bit mean.

Someone was pulling Lily's hair, yanking on it, and she felt outraged despite her imminent death. She reached up, found a hand tangled in her hair, followed it up to a bony wrist and a strong, hairy forearm, velveteen and fine and slippery from the sea.

Then up and into the light again, and Lily was gasping, choking, unsure whether she was breathing in air or shoving water up and out of her gullet. Both, really.

The hand in her hair released and moved to encircle her, a firm ring around her chest and under her armpits, and she was moving, being pulled as she spluttered and wheezed, her eyes stinging from the salt, everything in revolt.

Back aboard the little sailboat she and her father had rented for a nice day off the coast, just a two-person, single-mast vessel, barely more than a dinghy. Her father thumped her back, hard enough to hurt, and she remembered being angry at him—fathers shouldn't hit their daughters—and she coughed and choked and eventually drew in huge, painful gasps of air. She was freezing, too, and there were no blankets, no way to get out of the wind in that tiny little shell. The best her father could find was a bit of extra sailcloth stuffed up under the bow, and he took that and wrapped her in it. It stank and was a little damp, but it cut the wind.

"You're all right," he said. "Just a little dunking, nothing to worry about."

But she heard the tremor in his voice, so unusual and unexpected and unlike him, and even more than the fact that he had dived into the freezing waters off the Scottish coast to save her life, that was how she knew he loved her.

Twenty-two years later, just after dawn, Lily crossed Victoria Harbor aboard a green-and-white ferry named the *Morning Star*, returning to Hong Kong Island after her night in Kowloon. She stood at the rail on its upper deck, hiding behind her sunglasses, her satchel resting on the ground between her feet like some strange pet.

All around the ferry, boats skimmed the low waves of this notoriously busy patch of ocean, from massive container ships to teakwood pleasure junks to tiny, precarious vessels that seemed unfit even to serve as pool toys. Cargo skiffs piled high with net-wrapped bundles and fishing boats and unlicensed water taxis and makeshift craft lashed together from spare tires and Styrofoam, wreathed in grimy smoke pouring from their ancient engines.

Lily ran her hand along the wooden rail, smooth and shiny from the touch of millions of hands over the decades this particular workhorse of the Star Line had been in service. There were faster ways across the harbor, but the Star Ferry was always crowded, always popular. Part of that had to be the price—the ferry was cheap, less than a cup of tea. But Lily thought it was also because the big old tubs did in fact take their time, ambling ponderously between Tsim Sha Tsui and the Central Piers, refusing to be rushed. A Star Ferry ride offered ten minutes of serenity in a city defined by its relentless pace, a chance to soak in one of the world's great cityscapes.

I. M. Pei's Bank of China Tower was the obvious showpiece on the island side, but bordering it and extending far to east and west were dozens of other architecturally unique spires. At night gigantic signs on the buildings lit up, neon scrimshaw Chinese characters for happiness and luck and longevity, reflections flickering in the harbor chop. They boasted video screens as well, huge *Blade Runner*–esque slabs that once displayed advertisements and film trailers, but those had been dark for months now. Another little gift from Team Joy Joy and their efforts to spread the Despair Manifesto.

The mainland view was good, too, if you could ignore a break in the skyline yawning like an empty tooth socket. This was the former location of the Hong Kong Cultural Centre, destroyed by bombs planted by the Joy Boys. Now the once-beautiful building was a barely cleared tangle of wreckage, awaiting a rebuild Lily was pretty sure would never come.

The *Morning Star* chugged slowly across the oil-streaked waves, and Lily used the time to try to figure out what the hell she would do once it docked. Part of her was still, limply, trying to convince herself to return to CarbonGo and face the consequences. But . . . no. She'd committed crimes. Theft, destruction of property, who knew what else? Hong Kong residents had come to understand one thing very clearly since the brutal suppression of 2019's democracy protests and the subsequent imposition of sweeping new security laws: the HKPD did not fuck around.

Lily liked her life. She didn't want to throw it away over what was really just an accident. Not her fault. She wasn't in her right mind when she broke the scrubber—not after what she'd seen when she opened it up.

So, no. Lily wouldn't go back to the office. But she couldn't go home, either. Danny Chang might have gotten to the office early, already called the cops. He liked her, Lily knew, but he wouldn't hesitate, not with business on the line.

Lily set that problem aside, letting her mind shift to a different conundrum—the impossible device that had caused all the trouble in the first place. She took out her phone and opened its photo app, pulling up the shots she had taken of the paperwork she found in Danny's safe with the device.

On this second, more focused analysis of the documents she was struck by their essential weirdness. The paper was some strange stuff that looked like parchment but was probably some alien material the people who devised the cylinder were able to access. Lily zoomed in as much as she could, finding no grain, no evidence of the fibers you'd normally see in plant-based paper. It was uniform, perfect, and at higher magnification it looked as if the text was not printed but typed.

She zoomed back out, focusing now on the words themselves—dense, mind-numbing paragraphs, riddled with "but for" this and "in the circumstance of" that. All had titles, but Lily was not a lawyer. "INTELLECTUAL PROPERTY TRANSFER AGREEMENT" and "WAIVER OF RIGHTS" and "CERTIFICATE OF AUTHORITY" didn't mean much to her.

Confoundingly, most of the documents seemed to be one-sided, requiring agreement only from CarbonGo, which meant only Danny Chang had signed them. It wasn't until the last page of the transfer agreement that Lily found a sort of signature in bright blue ink. Not a name. More like an icon or rune, intricate, a sculpted tangle of shapes like figure eights or infinity symbols. But above that, these words:

FOR CALDER & CALDER, INC.

Lily thought about that. Calder & Calder.

She closed her photos and pulled up an internet browser on her mobile, something she hadn't done in a very long time. Her phone, like most these days, used the Wordy operating system—text based, supposedly secured against incursions from Team Joy Joy. She typed "Calder & Calder Inc" into the search box, and her thumb hovered over the button that would bring up results. She hesitated, frowning.

Too risky. You heard stories. People logging into their banks' websites to pay a few bills and finding the Despair Manifesto waiting. Children left alone, watching a cartoon on a tablet, their parents returning to see their son or daughter staring blank and cold, thinking things no child should have to think, swallowed by the Grey. Something like that had happened to the vice president in America, she'd heard—and if it could happen to him, with all the security and technology the United States could presumably bring to bear, it could certainly happen to Lily Barnes.

She closed the browser. She couldn't take the chance. But she knew someone who could.

I. SIX

HONG KONG.
REPULSE BAY.
22°14'21.8"N, 114°11'34.6"E

THE NUMBER SIX BUS WAS A DOUBLE-DECKER, AND LILY ALWAYS liked to take a seat on the upper level. It let her glide along above the fray as the bus made its way through evocatively named districts like Admiralty and Happy Valley, cresting the mountains and descending to the south side. There, Hong Kong revealed its pretty face.

There was no denying that Hong Kong was a capital-*C* City, one of the world's densest in both population and sheer number of structures, filled with traffic and exhaust and pedestrians and cacophony of all types. But it was also, if you knew where to look, a tropical paradise. Hong Kong's natural beauty was hard to imagine from the depths of Central or Kowloon, but once you hit the south, every curve of the mountain roads revealed emerald peaks and island-dappled bright blue sea stretching to the horizon.

It was still early, and the morning light cast the sea as a sparkling sheet of turquoise, its brightness hard to look at. Lily felt her heart lift, even through the exhaustion. She had been up for twenty-four hours, in near-constant motion, with repeated spikes of anxiety and adrenaline. McCafé lattes could do only so much.

Lily watched the sea for the entirety of the forty-minute ride to Repulse Bay. Far on the horizon, a coil of deep, black smoke. She wondered what it was. Lots of fires these days.

In her hand, she held the little plastic tile puzzle. She wasn't trying to solve it, just shifting the tiles around with her thumb, keeping them in constant motion.

The bus stopped below her destination, a huge complex consisting of two broad residential towers in pastel colors. The buildings were built in curves against the mountainside like a series of vertical waves, a slow, lovely ripple. In one of the two towers was a massive square opening cut right through the middle. Legend had it that the building was designed this way for the purposes of feng shui, to allow the dragons that lived atop the mountain access to the sea below. It had to be something along those lines, because these buildings rested on some of the most valuable real estate in the world, and the gigantic square hole represented tens of millions of dollars of potential apartments.

The fact that a choice against commercialism and profit had been made in Hong Kong, the most commercial, profit-driven place Lily had ever known, was pleasing. One of those nice little contradictions about the city.

She entered the building's lobby and headed to the eighteenth floor in the western tower. Originally a series of apartments, this floor and the two above it had been converted into something else.

A reception desk awaited outside the elevators, beneath a large sign in warm pastels reading THE ASCENDANCE INSTITUTE, where a young woman in a concierge-like uniform waited. Lily didn't recognize her, even though she had visited this place many times. (Not recently, though, Lily could admit. It had become too hard.)

"Hello," the receptionist said, "how can I help?"

"I'm here to see a guest," Lily said. "David Johanssen."

"Of course," the receptionist said. "Is he expecting you?"

"No. I should have called ahead. But we know each other. I've been here often. You can check. I'm sure he'll want to see me."

Lily was not, in fact, sure, but she had to think David would at least be curious. The two of them hadn't ended poorly, they had just . . . ended. Like many things in the Grey world.

"I'll just call the back, then," the receptionist said, lifting a phone handset from her desk. "You can have a seat."

Lily did, noting new magazines on the lobby's coffee tables since her last visit. Magazines were back, too, just like newspapers.

She sat, considering many things, but mostly that impossible, undeniable pattern of wires she'd seen inside the carbon scrubber. Before she wrecked it.

"You can go on back," the receptionist said after about ten minutes. "Mr. Johanssen is in the solarium. You know the way?"

"Absolutely," Lily answered. "Thank you."

The receptionist nodded and buzzed Lily through the security door into the facility.

She hadn't lied to the receptionist. Lily did know this place, and even liked it. All light and windows, everywhere you looked it was sea or mountains or tasteful, inspirational design choices. The carpet in the hall was a lovely blue-and-green pattern, the walls a pale yellow. It smelled clean and fresh, without any institutional aroma.

Of course, that was all a bit of a mask. The Ascendance Institute was indeed an institution, just a very expensive one with a very select clientele. Clients like David Johanssen, who looked up as Lily entered the solarium, a faint smile on his face. A false, forced smile. She hadn't seen him offer a true smile in . . . so long, she couldn't remember the context. She could remember what that last smile had looked like, his face and eyes alive with mirth and life, but couldn't remember what had engendered the reaction. Maybe her. She chose to think so.

"Hello, Lily," David said. "It's been a little while."

"I know," she answered. "I'm sorry I haven't been along to visit sooner."

"That's all right. I'm fine," he replied.

David was sitting in an armchair beautifully upholstered in maroon and orange like a tropical flower, before a massive floor-to-ceiling window commanding an incredible view of the South China Sea. He looked good—clean-shaven, his dirty-blond hair cut and combed, in slacks and a T-shirt with a thin cardigan over it. Thin but not emaciated. But Lily knew that, left to his own devices, without the constant attention provided by the Ascendance Institute, David would be as ragged as a scarecrow.

The sun poured in, soaking everything in radiance. Lily understood the intention; it was impossible not to be inspired by a view like this, uplifted . . . unless you had the Grey. Which David did.

But he was important to his employer, a multinational management consulting firm, one of those entities hired to solve the problems of other massive corporations. David was, or had been, a forensic accountant. He followed money along incredibly convoluted paper trails, the financial equivalent of a twenty-year set of dreadlocks. He found treasure intentionally hidden in far-flung corporate jurisdictions, ferreted out ultimate owners and beneficial shareholders and silent partners. He knew the world beneath the world—at least, the world that revolved around banking and corporations and finance law. Nothing could be hidden from David Johanssen.

So, when the Grey took him, David's employer paid for him to be installed here, a place where the disease could, in theory, be treated. Lily had seen nothing to suggest any improvement in the eight months David had been at Ascendance, but even the fact that he *was* still here, still alive, could be seen as a good thing. Beating the odds.

"How are you, David?" Lily asked, smiling at him.

"Fine, as I said," he answered. "I mean, just look at that."

He waved vaguely at the view.

She could tell he didn't want to talk, that speaking even this much cost him an unfathomable amount of effort. He was utterly closed off, a wall—the same emotional zeroing out you got from anyone inflicted with the Grey. Lily was not a therapist, but she thought such an obvious lie—"I'm fine"—how could it help anything? Charmaine the baker had said those words too.

Admit you need help. Admit you're drowning, otherwise no one will know to reach for you.

"I was wondering if you might be able to do something for me," Lily said.

David cocked his head, puzzled. Her request was odd, not in their current dynamic. They didn't ask anything from each other anymore.

"What?" he asked.

Lily didn't answer right away. Her eyes flickered to an end-table next to David's chair, holding a laptop and a small stack of file folders. He usually had something like that nearby when she came to see him—projects his employer left in case he felt the urge to work at any point. She suspected that did not happen very often, and wondered how long it would be before the company decided the exorbitant cost of Ascendance was throwing good money after bad and left David to fend for himself. Lily thought about what she would do if that happened—no, *when*, because he wasn't getting any better. No one was.

David was the first good relationship decision Lily had made in a long time. Ever, maybe. Her past in that arena was marked by failure after romantic failure. Her general pattern was to abandon situations that threatened to deepen before the other person left her first. Or she chose people she knew would hurt her so she would have an excuse to leave herself. Or she picked people she was certain wouldn't interest her for long.

Then she met David, decided to stop being afraid, and it was good. He was American, from a place called Kalamazoo in a state called Michigan, which delighted her. Kalamazoo. It sounded like the catchphrase for a children's show wizard. Kalamazoo! David told her there was very little magic in Kalamazoo, other than perhaps a good brewery or two, at least compared to Hong Kong. They agreed to disagree, and Lily resolved never to visit David's hometown. She preferred the whimsical version in her head.

Fortunately, David seemed as uninterested in returning home as she did. They had both, for different reasons, chosen to get as far away from their birthplaces as their credentials could get them. They met in early 2019 and spent a year traveling as much as their jobs permitted—Bangkok and Tokyo and Saigon and Sydney—and then when the pandemic hit they decided to move in together rather than be alone. The next few years were spent realizing how well they actually *worked*. If they could still enjoy each other's company after quarantine with nothing *but* each other's company, then, really, they could handle anything life might throw at them.

Hiking had become a godsend for them during the Covid lockdowns. The city had hundreds of kilometers of staggeringly gorgeous mountain trails both on the island and the mainland, and it was one of the few activities you could do with everything shuttered. They loved it so much, they kept it up once the pandemic eased. She remembered sitting with David on a huge flat stone atop the highest part of a trail called the Dragon's Back, the whole world spread out below them, like they were on a throne, and then—

Lily pulled her mind away.

And then David got the Grey, and Lily was faced with the question of figuring out what to do with and for this wonderful man who loved her and vice versa but who was, by all indications, irrevocably changed, that wonderful man never to return. She was still wrestling with it when, thank god, David's company decided to pay for his treatment.

Lily pointed at David's laptop.

"I was hoping you could do some research for me. Look up a company name I came across. I would do it myself, but . . . you know."

His brow furrowed. He glanced at his computer. David *did* know, as well as anyone. Googling in the Grey world was a minefield. It was safer with Wordy browsers, sure, but opening yourself up to the Internet in any way was a scary prospect with the Despair Manifesto prowling out there like a shark beneath the waves. The exception, of course, was if you already had the Grey. In that case, you had nothing to worry about. The damage was done.

David shrugged, picked up the computer, and flipped it open.

"What's the name?"

"Calder & Calder, Inc."

"What do they do? Any idea where they're based?"

"I don't know. I'm sorry. Just the name."

David shrugged again and looked at his screen. He typed for a moment.

"David," Lily said, reaching out, putting her hand near but not on his arm, "the sound is off, right?"

The Despair Manifesto was strongest if you watched it, but there were accounts of people getting the Grey just from listening to it too.

David snorted, something that under different circumstances might have been a laugh.

"Always. One of the house rules. We can't use screens in view of other people without their permission, either. Good sense, I suppose."

Lily leaned back in her chair, listening to him type, listening as he murmured to himself, guiding himself through whatever labyrinth of forms and filings he had discovered. She looked out at the beach below and the sea and islands beyond.

The coil of black smoke still drifted up toward the sky, far off toward the horizon. She still wondered what it was. But really, when was a fire large enough to be seen from miles away ever a good thing?

"Well," David said, and Lily looked back at the man she'd actually allowed herself to love. "This is interesting," he finished. "Very."

David's eyes were bright. She recognized him, actually saw him, the person she knew and adored and missed with all her heart, for the first time in almost a year.

"Tell me," Lily said.

"I searched the global databases, went deep. Only one business entity comes up in the records under that name. Calder & Calder."

"Is that odd?"

"Maybe a little, but Calder isn't really that common a name. I checked. It's mostly an American surname, and it pops up in about one in every fifty thousand people these days. Here, also, you'd need two of them, like a father-and-son business, something like that. Odd or not, only one company seems to have used the name."

"What is it?"

David took on a bit of a lecturer's pose in his chair, old mannerisms resurfacing. Lily's heart lifted.

"Calder & Calder, Inc., was formed in the States, in Massachusetts, in 1777, as a for-profit stock corporation. It looks like it was a textile manufacturer with a shipping arm to take its products around the world. That lasted until the early 1800s, when things went pretty quiet. That makes sense, though. A lot of wars around then—the American Revolution, the Napoleonic Wars. They took a toll on international trade.

"The company pops up from time to time during the nineteenth century, but not in a substantial way. Banking records here and there—funds transfers and so on. It has the feeling of a family business that makes its fortune and then supports the kids for the next generation or two until the money runs out."

"Is that it, then?" Lily said, disappointed. "Nothing else?"

"Calder & Calder all but disappears in the early twentieth century, but when I broaden the parameters beyond just corporate and banking records, I get a few hits. The most recent was in 1942. Bills of lading, manifests for cargo being transported from eastern Europe to Britain and the US."

"What does that mean?"

"Lily, who knows? You have to understand, I've got some powerful tools here, but I spent about ten minutes on this. I found the scraps floating on the surface. I'd have to dive deep to see what else might be out there."

"Of course, David," Lily said. "I realize that, and I appreciate you helping me at all. Does the company still exist?"

"As far as I can tell. I don't see anything about a dissolution. Again, though, the records aren't great. This company is two hundred and fifty years old and did most of its work in the early nineteenth century."

David paused for a moment, reading something off his screen.

"It had an office here, though."

"Really?" Lily asked.

"Mm. It makes sense. Hong Kong is one of the world's great ports. Has been for centuries. Calder & Calder had offices in Boston, London, Batavia, all over the world. The office here was in Shek O. The building's still there—or at least there's something at the address. It's not leased by them anymore, though. It's something called Coriander & Associates, Ltd."

David typed for a few seconds.

"Huh," he said.

"What?"

"All the other Calder & Calder offices—most, anyway; some aren't around anymore—Coriander leases or owns them too."

Lily thought about this.

"Can you give me the address of the one here?"

He glanced at the screen again.

"14 Big Wave Bay Road."

"That's not too far. I'm going to check it out. Do you want to come? I can tell you what this is all about on the way. You won't believe it."

She stood up, smiling, excited, slinging her bag over her shoulder.

"You can still sign yourself out, right? They don't keep you here or anything?"

"I can go if I want," David said. "I can."

"Then let's go," she said, talking fast, trying to capture the moment while it lasted. "There's a lot to this. It's important, might even be world-changing. There's this device. I've never seen anything like it before. I don't know who built it, but it could be a chance to do something special. It's like . . . a *mystery*, David. You're so good at things like this, and I know you enjoy puzzling things out. If we went together, I know you could help. Maybe it could help you, too. We could just—"

His face closed. She could see it happen, like a thick blanket being dropped over a fire. His eyes shifted, looking out the window, away from her.

Lily stood there for a moment, waiting for David to look back. He didn't. She reached into her satchel and pulled out the tile puzzle. She held it out him.

"Do you remember when you gave me this?" she said.

His gaze moved from the window to the little plastic square in her hand.

"You said you thought I'd like it because it can only be solved because of the hole in it. It's the empty bit that makes the whole thing work. It was the most beautiful thing anyone's ever given me."

David looked back at the sea.

"You go on ahead, Lily," David said. "I think I'll just stay here. It'll be lunch soon."

"All right, David," Lily said. "Whatever you think."

She left.

I. SEVEN

HONG KONG.
BIG WAVE BAY.
22°14'27.5"N, 114°14'47.4"E

FISH AND BARBECUE AND SEAWEED ON THE BREEZE. THE SCENTS OF Shek O, a small oceanside village at the far southeast tip of Hong Kong Island; a strip of weekend beach bounded by little clusters of easy restaurants and sunscreen shops. Swimmers bobbing in the waves and, farther out, windsurfers whipping along. A good place, was Lily's assessment; nice to think good places still existed.

14 Big Wave Bay Road was a three-story building, once white with black shutters, now grey with shutters a slightly darker shade of grey. Window box aircon units protruded wartily from several windows, shuddering and dripping. Cracks spidered the concrete walls, and vines speckled with orange-red blossoms crawled up one side of the building before curtaining off the roof.

The building was obviously pre-handover, a remnant of Hong Kong's century and a half as a British colony, an era ended in 1997. Lily was shocked to see something so ancient still standing. Hong

Kong constantly, obsessively remade itself. If a building wasn't historically significant or otherwise notable, it was just a matter of time before it was demolished in favor of a condo tower. It was one of the city's unwritten laws. But somehow, Number Fourteen remained, standing moderately tall, this anomaly, this anachronism.

A sign to one side of the front door on a tarnished brass plaque: CORIANDER & ASSOCIATES, LTD. Below it, the same symbol Lily had seen on the contract at CarbonGo, an intermeshed tangle of infinity symbols.

Progress, she thought, feeling a little thrill.

The door was unlocked. Lily pushed it open and stepped inside, the sweat chilling on her skin at the transition into air-conditioning. She pulled a thin sweater from her satchel and slipped it on; she always brought layers with her for exactly this purpose. Hong Kong could change from oven to igloo with a single step indoors. She looked around, her eyes adjusting to the interior light.

Most of the ground floor was an open space, and Lily's first impression was *Museum*. Her second: *Art gallery*; third: *Charity shop*. Finally: *This is some truly weird shit*. The odors were dust and leather and very old floorboards. Framed items covered the walls, and display tables and glass-domed pedestals stood here and there, their contents confounding, impossible.

The display nearest the door contained what Lily thought at first had to be a flower, inside something like a dusty terrarium. The thing had the correct shape and structure—tiny purple blossoms on green stems clustered together into little balls like dandelion fluff. But if it was a flower, she'd never seen anything like it. It was bizarre. As she stepped closer, the purple flowers shimmered to red, then bright yellow. Lily considered whether it was an LED, electronics, but on closer examination . . . no. It was definitely a plant, definitely alive. Tiny insects—probably insects; she really had no idea—flitted around the blossoms like gossamer pinprick angels. And all of it under glass.

Lily was no botanist, but she knew plants respired, and it didn't seem like that would be possible in a sealed terrarium . . . though "terrarium" suggested earth, and this thing was growing out of soil that looked like a pile of metal shavings. No earth she knew.

The next display was a glass-topped table, its treasures hidden inside—all no less odd. A crystal ball. A strip of thick white cloth with a ragged, rust-tinged hole in it. A long metal rod, cracked along its middle, with a trigger assembly on one end and a strange, deflated sac just below it. Lily could not help but think of testicles—but she had absolutely no idea what the device might do.

On a podium past the table rested what looked like an old pulp magazine. The cover was ragged and torn, the date on the cover November 1947. The title was mostly missing; it read *Chronicles of the Laz* and then it cut off. The cover image, what remained of it, depicted a rocky red shore and storm-tossed waves and part of what looked like a person in a space suit, but . . . scaled like chain mail? That was all she could glean from the cover, and she didn't want to risk opening an eighty-year-old publication lest it crumble in her hands.

Lily moved on to the framed pieces on the wall. She stopped before a photograph of an insubstantial shape shrouded in fog. It was impossible to tell the size of the thing—there was nothing for scale—but it felt both man-made and huge. If ever a thing deserved the term "looming," it was this angular, irregular object.

Another photo, this time a black-and-white image of a small group having tea around a table set up in a jungle meadow, servants in the background. It felt like a safari outing from the Victorian era: pith helmets, puttees and so on. Not really so unusual. Any British citizen would be familiar with similar images from museums and history books, remnants of the vanished Empire. But Lily had never encountered such an image where one of the subjects looked to be made of solid metal. It was hard to tell due to the monochrome nature of the shot, but Lily Barnes, material sciences engineer, knew her metals, and she would have bet the figure's weight in gold that it actually *was* gold.

Mysteries and oddities in all directions. A circus sideshow mysteriously assembled inside a beachfront villa in Shek O.

The next framed item was not a photograph, but a legal document. Very old, the paper browned and mottled, brittle and weathered. Lily bent for a closer look. The document bore a date from about two and a half centuries back. It was numbered 0045 and covered in ornate handwritten script in what seemed like far too many fonts, like the person who had inscribed the thing desperately wanted everyone who saw it to step back and murmur to themselves, *Goodness. That there is calligraphy.*

It read:

> THESE ARE TO CERTIFY THAT EUGENIA GREAVES IS ENTITLED TO ONE SHARE IN THE CAPITAL, OR JOINT STOCK, OF CALDER & CALDER, INCORPORATED, TRANSFERABLE AT THEIR OFFICE ONLY, PERSONALLY, OR BY ATTORNEY.

Then a seal stamped into the parchment, two ornate versions of the letter *C*, one reversed so it faced the other, embossed into a raised circle of bright blue wax, and more words: WITNESS THE SEAL OF THE COMPANY, THE NINTH DAY OF JULY, 1790.

It was signed by the company's secretary, someone she thought was named Milton Tenenbaum, if she read the signature correctly.

"May I help you?" someone said from behind her.

Lily turned, caught, irrationally certain she was about to be arrested for her many crimes against CarbonGo. But the person who had spoken was not a black-clad member of the HKPD. It was a tall man, dark-skinned and middle-aged, in an orange suit with a yellow shirt and a bright blue tie. Most would have looked like a clown in such a getup, but this man possessed and occupied it utterly.

"Oh," Lily said, whipping up a smile. "I'm sorry, I didn't mean to intrude. The door was open."

"Yes, it was," the man said. "But in order to walk through it, you had to choose it out of all the doors in the entire world. And then you chose again—to enter without knocking. Which suggests two important questions to me. Two very important questions."

He inclined his head politely.

"Who are you and what the hell are you doing here?"

Lily liked this man.

"I'm Lily Barnes," she said, holding out her hand.

"I'm Mr. Coriander," the man said. He shook her hand with a dry grip, a brief clasp and release. "I am in the midst of a busy day, and this is a private place of business. If you don't mind . . ."

"Of course," Lily said. "But wait. I've answered your first question. Don't you want to know the answer to the second?"

Mr. Coriander considered.

"I suppose I do," he said. "To be honest, my life is full of unanswered questions. Built around them, in a way. It would be nice to have one go in the other direction for once."

Lily thought this was an entirely bizarre thing to say, but very much in keeping with everything she'd encountered since she stepped through the door of 14 Big Wave Bay.

She was still standing in front of the framed ancient stock certificate and gestured to it.

"I'm curious about this company, actually. Calder & Calder. Can you tell me anything about it?"

Mr. Coriander stepped up next to her, peering at the document as if he'd never seen it before.

"I'm sorry, no," he said. "As far as I'm concerned, it's just decoration. Came with the building."

"I see," Lily said. "This used to be their office a long time ago. They were a shipping company active in the 1800s."

"Fascinating," Mr. Coriander said, not sounding particularly fascinated.

"You work for Coriander & Associates, Ltd.?" Lily asked, realizing the stupidity of her question as soon as she asked it.

Coriander looked at her. His face betrayed nothing, but his eyes . . . they had taken on a certain gleam.

"I should think it would be obvious that I do," he answered. "All my life, in fact."

"Well, you might be interested to know that Calder & Calder had offices all over the world, in major ports. Every single one is now occupied by you guys. Coriander & Associates. And you really don't know anything about them?"

The shine in Coriander's eyes sharpened.

"May I ask you a question, my dear?" he said. Ordinarily the familiarity would bother Lily, but the "dear" fit this man the same way as the orange suit. He meant nothing by it.

"Sure," she said.

"Have you, by chance, encountered something amazing?" Coriander asked. "Did something happen to you that should not have happened, and now you can't let it go until you understand how and why it could have come to pass? And you found little hints or clues that ultimately led you here?"

Coriander was smiling. Lily did not know him. She was not in a position to trust him, and the stakes were high. And yet . . .

Her eyes flickered past the odd man toward the weird objects displayed in the room, this space pregnant with impossibility. She'd examined at most a tenth, each more bizarre than the last.

She slipped her satchel from her shoulder and set it gently down on the nearest glass-topped table. From within, she pulled out Danny Chang's miracle carbon scrubber, its case still open, its inner workings still smashed and unsalvageable. Of course she'd stolen it from the office. Of course she had. In for a penny, in for a pound.

Lily presented the device to Mr. Coriander, rotating it, showcasing all its alien glory.

"This device could solve the climate change crisis," she said. "I work in that field. I'm an engineer. The technology here is decades beyond where we currently are. Maybe a century. It's . . . broken now, but I've seen it work. It's real. I have no idea where it came from, and I need to find who built it."

Mr. Coriander raised an eyebrow. His body language shifted. He now seemed delicately tensed, focused, readying his faculties like someone about to perform brain surgery, or wrestle a crocodile into submission.

"May I?" he said, gesturing at the device.

"Be my guest," she said. "You can't bang it up any worse."

For at least a minute, Coriander gently examined the scrubber, moving its components aside with his fingertips, lifting out broken bits and holding them up close to his eye, squinting. He oohed and aahed over certain elements that seemed to mean a great deal to him.

He replaced a tiny coil of sponge wire back in the case, then looked at Lily and crooked a finger at her.

"Come with me, if you please."

Coriander led the way toward the back of the room across squeaking floorboards, then disappeared through an open door. Lily followed him into a small, immaculate office space furnished completely in antiques. Fountain pens and inkwells and leather-bound ledgers and a worn, brutally carpentered wooden desk that could have stopped a charging rhino. Coriander stood behind it, dialing a number on a rotary phone. It looked ancient, a vulval pink plastic confection Lily guessed was from the 1970s or '80s.

He held the handset to his ear, waited a moment, then spoke.

"It's me," he said. "I believe we may have another Intercession."

He paused.

"Yes," he said. "Just get here."

Mr. Coriander hung up the telephone, took a deep breath, then released it. He looked up at Lily, smiled, a broad, warm grin, and Lily realized how much she missed expressions of genuine happiness, how rarely she saw them in this world even among people who had thus far evaded the Grey.

He walked across his office, stopping right in front of her. He took both of her hands in his, clasping them with a warmth and intimacy that was not warranted but she could not deny.

"Ms. Barnes," Coriander said, "welcome to the Wonder Path."

I. EIGHT

LOS ANGELES.

34° 36′ 41.256″N, 118° 11′ 23.28″W

Aunt Jane danced. The music pounded every part of her, every inch from toes to tail, and what was better than that? Bass and bass drops and treble spins and melody when it made sense, but you really didn't need it, did you? All you needed was a fucking *beat.*

Well, a full dance floor might have been nice, even a partner or two . . . but that wasn't in the cards these days. The world was in a weird place, but she could fix it, bring it to where it needed to be, and then every club in every country in the world would be *full.*

Jane danced, and danced, and danced. Her eyes were closed most of the time, but every once in a while she looked up. The lights were good in here, blue and green and red spotlights swirling and clashing in time to the music. She liked this club, a West Hollywood place called the Cathedral, and came often. She hoped it stayed open for a long time. Right up until the end.

Swirl, sway, move, sex, twist, joy joy joy.

Aunt Jane danced. Closed her eyes and spun.

She was so happy. Happy at what she was doing at that moment, but also happy at the gifts she was giving to the world. Everyone deserved to be happy. She could never have guessed that she, little nothing Jane Morello from Staten Island, would end up being so important to the world. But there it was, and there she was, right in the middle of it.

She opened her eyes and saw one of her closest friends and allies, one of the very first Joy Boys. He was smiling at her.

"Lorenzo!" she shouted, pulling him in for a hug.

The embrace became an excuse to dance, all close-up and nice, and she made him do it. She felt his stubble against her cheek and his wiry little body beneath his clothes. He was stiff at first, but he got into it pretty quickly. She knew she was nice to dance with. She felt good. And dancing felt good. Wasn't that the point of being alive? Feeling good?

A minute or two of the bounce bump grind on the dance floor, and then Lorenzo leaned in and whispered in her ear.

"Can we talk for a minute? I have a few updates."

"Sure thing," Jane said, and held him closer. "Go."

Lorenzo seemed a little surprised she wanted to keep dancing. He shouldn't have been.

"We got the admiral," he said. "She was heavily protected, but we were able to get the Manifesto into a satellite video call she was making home to her family from the South Pacific. We weren't sure if it'd work—that's one focused lady—but we got her."

Jane's heart leapt. The admiral was one of the key components of building the Pyre. She was one of the biggest pieces of firewood, if you wanted to push the analogy. Jane wasn't sure if the Pyre would work at all if they didn't have her.

"Is she on the team?" she asked. "She's a Joy Girl?"

"Not quite yet," Lorenzo replied, "but the door's open. She'll go in for treatment at the Navy's facility in Bethesda, and we've got a Joy Boy in their psychiatric unit. He'll spread the good word to her."

"Oh my *god,*" Jane said, pulling Lorenzo into another embrace. "You're *amazing*!"

"I just believe in the cause," he said, smiling.

A little more dancing—this song was really good, and the Pyre was actually going to happen; she could *feel it*—and then she looked at her friend again.

"You said you had a few things to talk about. What was the other one?"

"Connie's here," he said. "He wanted to give you a report in person. I wasn't going to bother you, but then he told me what he did, and I thought you might want to hear it."

Jane gave Lorenzo a hopeful look.

"He do something good? Spread that joy?"

Lorenzo tilted his head in a noncommittal way.

"He should probably tell you. But you don't have to talk to him. It's not important, just felt like something you might want to get involved with."

Jane shot her lieutenant an exasperated smile.

"You are being *weird*, Lorenzo," she said. "But sure. I like Connie, and you've certainly got me curious."

They walked off the dance floor together. Jane blew the DJ a kiss as they went; a thank-you and a promise to return just as soon as she could.

Outside the club, a black van waited, parked just at the curb. More of Jane's people waited near it: Annette and Yuri. They smiled when they saw her. Team Joy Joy, being joyful.

Annette opened the rear doors of the van, and Jane stepped inside. There, waiting for her, was Conrad Ellis, a bearish man in his late forties. Normal in every way except for his smile, a big, broad, heartfelt grin that crinkled his face and sparked up his eyes, and, Jane knew, touched his heart.

People had mostly forgotten how to smile like that until she'd come along. If Aunt Jane could feel good about anything she'd done, it was reminding people of what happiness actually felt like. Conrad's smile wasn't something he put on like a mask to make other people feel comfortable or to convince himself he felt different than he actually did. Conrad Ellis was *lit up,* inside and out.

"Connie!" she said, reaching out to embrace him.

Conrad held her for a good seven or eight seconds, a firm, strong embrace. She let it go on as long as he liked; you didn't end a hug unless you had to, she believed. She had plenty to give. Let Connie have as much as he needed.

But eventually he let her go, settling back and looking at her with a pleased expression.

"Lorenzo tells me you did something cool you wanted to tell me about?" Jane asked.

"I did," Connie replied. "Did you hear about that implosion in Reno? That apartment complex that just fell in on itself?"

Jane nodded, a sinking feeling in her chest. She suspected she knew what Conrad was about to tell her.

All those people, she thought.

"That was me," he said, proud. "It wasn't easy. I had to rig the charges just right to get it to implode properly, and my Joy Boys out there didn't have the training I do—you remember I've been doing building demolition for fifteen years. Anyway, I had to triple-check their work, all while trying to keep out of the security guards' way. Pain in my ass, let me tell you."

"It happened at night, right?" Jane asked, her voice quiet.

"Yeah," Connie said. "Set the charges off at 3 a.m., when everyone was asleep. Maximum occupancy period. Got as many as I could."

"Over a thousand people," Jane said, remembering more details from the article she'd read about the story.

"I figure, like, twelve, thirteen hundred. I hope you aren't annoyed I wanted to tell you in person, but none of it would have happened without you, so I thought maybe, you know, you'd want to hear about it in person. What do you think? Good work, huh?"

Jane felt despair welling up inside her. How could things have gone so wrong? She was so meticulous about her message. She released podcasts and video clips and written materials to the team regularly, and thought they presented a consistent, clear worldview. How could Conrad Ellis—clearly not a stupid man—have so catastrophically misinterpreted the goals of Team Joy Joy? It was times like this she wondered how she would ever complete the mission. The Pyre suddenly seemed farther away than ever, despite the success Lorenzo had reported with the admiral.

"Will you record a broadcast with me, Connie?" she said. "I was going to do one tonight, if that's all right with you."

Conrad's face lit up.

"Of . . . of course, Aunt Jane. I'd be, uh . . . I'd be honored."

Jane glanced at Lorenzo, who had been listening to the conversation. He held up a waiting smartphone and started recording a video clip. The message would be sent out online, and people who wanted to see it could easily find it. Not everyone was avoiding screens. Not everyone was afraid of joy.

Aunt Jane pushed the bad feelings down, letting a smile spread across her face. She could feel it bubbling up from deep inside. She knew she wasn't beautiful, really. No one in her entire life had treated her like she was. But she knew she looked beautiful when she felt like this.

She looked at the lens of Lorenzo's phone and began to speak.

"Hello, ecstatic beings! It's your Aunt Jane, here with the latest dispatch from the Happiness War! I have a special guest with me tonight."

She gestured at Connie, who leaned forward, his expression eager.

"This is Conrad Ellis. Say hi, Connie."

The big man waved, suddenly shy.

"He just told me he was responsible for the destruction of that apartment complex in Reno last week. He did it for Team Joy Joy, believing it would move our goals forward in some way. Now, you know me—I am a very happy person. It takes a lot to bring me down. But I gotta tell you, I'm not feeling great right now."

She pointed a thumb at Conrad.

"Because Connie here fucked up real bad."

The man seemed puzzled now, not sure what was happening. Jane reached out and took his hand, turning to look at him.

"I want to try to explain this to you, my friend," she said to Connie, looking the big man right in the eye, "so you can learn, and everyone watching can learn, if they don't already know. Team Joy Joy is not about killing people. We're not about destruction for the sake of destruction. I don't want to burn everything down, leave people hurt and sad. I mean, you think I talk about joy and happiness all the time as a *joke*?"

"I . . . I don't . . . ," Conrad said.

"It's okay," Jane said. "We all make mistakes. But it's pretty simple. Do you remember when you were a kid, the way you felt on the first morning of summer vacation? You didn't have to think about any of the homework you did in that last year, or exams, or your teachers, or any of it. It was all *behind* you, and so you were free, and you were happy in a very particular way. You were *unburdened.*

"Imagine if you could feel that way all the time! That's Team Joy Joy's mission. We're trying to give humanity that summer feeling every day. And why? Why do we work so hard?"

She screwed her face up into a sad, cute little expression, an *Aww, dang it* kind of look, the face you make when you open the freezer and remember you finished the ice cream two days back.

"It ain't easy to get your head around, but the truth is humanity's over. The planet has gotten sick of us, there are too many people, not enough resources, madness is seeping in around the edges. We're done. Anyone with half a brain can see it. Even more . . . we *feel* it. That's where the Grey comes from, I think. Deep in our bones, in our hearts, in our very souls, we understand there's a wrongness to us. We can't fix it, we can't make it better, and it's getting worse!"

Jane rearranged her face into a thoughtful, resolute expression, the look of someone getting ready to give the pep talk to end all pep talks, *Jerry Maguire* and *Braveheart* and *Independence Day* and *The Pursuit of Happyness* all piled together.

"So now we have a choice. We can struggle against the inevitable, waste our last years fighting a fight we can't win . . . or we can *accept the truth*. We can *enjoy the time we have left*. My dad did that when the cancer came back the third time. He spent his last six months reading his favorite books and eating his favorite foods and watching his favorite movies and spending time with his favorite people until the moment he breathed his last breath—and he never regretted it."

Jane remembered her father lying in his bed, dying—but serene, even through the pain. Yes. That was the path.

"When the Grey comes to a person, we feel it in one of three ways. Everyone knows that. Either our soul is diminished, it is killed . . . or it is *set ablaze*. That's what happened to me. I have the Grey—that third, fiery version. Everyone in Team Joy Joy does. And we consider ourselves *blessed*. We have let go of our troubled pasts and unattainable goals. We are completely in the now and seek only happiness for ourselves. But my little contribution—my little idea—was that maybe I could help other people feel the way I do. That was the whole idea behind Team Joy Joy, the reason I started it.

"Trust me. There is no future. The quicker you accept that, the happier you'll be. We want that for you. Team Joy Joy is committed to taking away things that distract you, trick you into thinking about a tomorrow that will never come to pass.

"That is why we burned the Louvre and all those other museums. We don't want you guys wrapped up in thinking about the art humanity has created or might make down the road. It's why we hit the stock markets. What are you saving for, investing in? Come on. Paying attention to all that stuff is like doing homework over summer vacation. There's no homework. Not anymore. We just need to get out there and play. That's the *truth*. It's what we're trying to teach you. It's why we do all the things we do.

She held up a hand, palm out, and tapped her closed fist against it, emphasizing the words of Team Joy Joy's mantra.

"Yesterday is gone. Tomorrow is a fantasy. There is only now, now, now. And, if you want it . . . joy, joy, joy."

She looked back at Conrad Ellis, who had a confused, almost wounded look on his face.

"But I told you Connie here fucked up, and I can tell he's wondering what he did wrong. He's thinking, 'But Team Joy Joy burned the Louvre! How is what I did in Reno any different?' Isn't that right, my friend?"

"I mean . . . kind of," he said, speaking slowly, cautiously.

"Totally get it," Jane said. "Let me explain. We lit up the Louvre on a Tuesday night, Connie. The museum's closed on Tuesdays, and it was after hours, when almost no one was there. The point wasn't to kill people, it was to take away a distraction. All that art, all that effort spent preserving it for the future, all that time wasted going to see it . . . what if that was used for just . . . being happy? Focusing on the world as it is now, not on what it might be like in ten years, or twenty. There *is* no ten or twenty years. This is all we got, and we should act like it."

She took a deep breath, knowing she had to get this right. She couldn't have another Reno on her hands, someone doing something so awful in her name.

"When you killed all those people, Connie, you stole their chance to find that truth. You robbed them of their opportunity to *find joy*."

She held out her hand to Lorenzo without taking her eyes off Conrad Ellis. A weight slapped into her palm. A pistol, with the round cylinder attached to its barrel that meant it was silenced, a little quieter than the ordinary variety. The cops were still around and might respond to a gunshot. After the Pyre that wouldn't be a problem anymore, but that was still a ways off. Best to not take chances.

She lifted the gun and shot Connie in the head before he knew what was happening. He fell, now just a big old sack of nothing.

Jane turned back to Lorenzo's camera. She sighed.

"I didn't like doing that. Maybe I could have brought Connie around eventually. But here's the thing. We're running out of time, and I have to choose my teaching moments. So listen up."

Here she pointed the gun barrel right at the lens. Lorenzo held it steady, not flinching.

"If you do something in my name, or the name of Team Joy Joy, you better damn well do it for the right reasons. I hate pain, and suffering, and fear, and sadness, and despair. I am doing everything I can to eradicate them from the world. If you create them, you are my enemy."

Jane looked right into the camera, smiling, still feeling the power of that smile deep inside her soul, knowing it was the kind of smile that people believed in, the reason she could pull together the incredible, world-changing movement that was Team Joy Joy. The one that made her beautiful.

"This is your Aunt Jane signing off. Remember, friends, embrace joy. Joy's all we got."

Her grin widened.

"Because nothing's gonna change."

I. NINE

HONG KONG. BIG WAVE BAY.

22°14'27.5"N, 114°14'47.4"E

MR. CORIANDER LIFTED HIS TEA BOWL TO HIS LIPS AND TOOK A silent sip, watching Lily through wafts of rising steam.

Lily left her own tea untouched, letting it cool.

They were seated on a long bench built into a little circular nook tucked into a corner of the gallerylike open space of the Coriander & Associates office, at an antique mahogany table beneath a hanging lamp with a green shade. It felt like a seating arrangement one might find in the dining room of an old London social club.

Coriander's demeanor had reversed itself upon her reveal of the carbon scrubber. No more suspicion, no more acting put out that she had invaded his place of business. They had become, apparently, the very best of friends. He had insisted on preparing tea, and chattered on all the while about how pleased he was to meet Lily, how exceptionally clever she was to have found him, how the strange items on display in his office were just a taste of the marvels to come. Johnny Hospitality through and through . . . and yet his gaze kept wandering to Lily's satchel, currently resting between them on the red velvet banquette, with the scrubber safely secreted away inside.

"Please, try the tea," Mr. Coriander said. "It's a special blend from very far away. Very hard to obtain. Fit only for special occasions, which this certainly is."

Lily didn't need the reminder. Coriander's tea was as unusual as everything else in this place—bright turquoise, for one thing. She lifted her bowl, holding it gingerly by the rim. A tiny sip, and she tasted . . . an absence of taste. The taste of the scent of the air after a hard rain.

"Well, that's unique," Lily said.

"Of course," Coriander replied. "May I ask you a question, Ms. Barnes?"

"Be my guest. But I'll probably be more inclined to answer if you answer some of mine," Lily said. "Give-and-take, right?"

Coriander's mouth twitched.

"Nothing would give me greater pleasure," he said. "If all goes well, you will end this day knowing things you never thought possible—things very few people on earth know."

Lily was leery of hucksters, leery of grand proclamations, a lesson drilled into her by her mother. "Promises are like bananas. Very hard to keep," Adriana Barnes said, all the time, a short phrase suggesting a lifetime of being let down by people—mostly men—whose promises turned brown and mushy after far too short a time.

"Your answers will come in due time," Coriander said, "but if you'll permit me, I'd like you to tell me what the following things have in common."

He set down his tea and reached into the coat of his bright orange suit, withdrawing two round objects, one much smaller than the other. He placed the first object on the table and slid it toward

Lily. She looked. A small dial with a floating needle, wavering, rotating, then finally settling into stillness.

"A . . . compass?"

"A compass," Coriander repeated, then began counting items off on his fingers. "The eruption of Mount Krakatoa in 1883. The Fox sisters. And this."

He held up the second round object between thumb and index finger—a white circle about a centimeter across.

"A pill," Lily said, hearing frustration edge into her voice.

She was not fond of guessing games. *Just tell me,* she thought. *Why all the theater?*

Then again, she was speaking to a man wearing a tangerine suit who called himself Mr. Coriander. Expecting anything less than theatrics was probably foolish.

"An aspirin," the man said, clarifying more than correcting, which was nice. He set it down on the table, then looked at Lily expectantly.

Her eyes flicked between the compass and the little white lozenge. Her mind looked for some connection between the two, plus a volcanic eruption in . . . the 1800s? In Hawaii, maybe? Lily wasn't great with history or geography. In school, she'd been a science and maths kid through and through.

And the Fox sisters? Who the hell are they?

"I'm lost," Lily said. "The compass and the aspirin are both pieces of technology. Man-made. Beyond that, I have no idea."

"Ah, but you see, Ms. Barnes," Mr. Coriander said, leaning forward, "they are *all* man-made."

"One of the things you listed was a volcano," she said, dubious.

"So it was. The Krakatoa explosion, and the other things I mentioned, all came from the same source as that marvelous little device of yours."

Coriander gestured at Lily's bag, and she fought the urge to pull the satchel over to her lap to keep it safe and secure. Honestly, leaving outright was seeming more appealing by the moment. But where could she go? Home? Surely not. Danny Chang might have already called the police, and her flat was the first place they'd look.

"Can you please explain what you're talking about, sir?" Lily said. "I just want to fix the device I showed you and learn more about where it came from. I don't understand why you won't just be clear with me. Can you help me or not? This isn't a game to me."

"The Wonder Path is no game," Coriander replied.

"Okay, so what is it, and why is it relevant to what I'm asking you?"

"My, you are direct," he said, his warmth fading a bit.

"Yep," Lily said.

Mr. Coriander frowned and set down his tea. He looked out at his collection of oddities for a long moment, brazenly stared at Lily's satchel for another, then seemed to come to a decision.

"The answers, such as they are, are not mine to give," he said. "Not on my own. There are protocols to be observed. You've stumbled on a sort of organization, or a club, Ms. Barnes. Our traditions are firm and go back rather a long way."

He stood.

"I have a busy afternoon ahead," Coriander said, "preparing for guests. If you are interested and patient enough to remain here until the evening, I can promise you the explanations you seek, via an evening of excellent conversation and stimulating cocktails, and the best beef chow fun you have ever had."

He chuckled.

"Or perhaps that's stimulating conversation and excellent cocktails. I do hope you'll stay."

With those words, Mr. Coriander retreated, heading to the back office, presumably to focus on whatever additional members of his club might be on the way.

A weariness hit Lily. This was the first moment she had stopped moving since Danny Chang first showed her the device back in Kowloon. Only a day ago, and it felt like a week. Lily blinked once, hard, squeezing her eyes shut and opening them. She reached for her tea, then realized the bowl was empty. The liquid had completely evaporated in the few minutes since Coriander had served it to her.

I barely even got to taste it, she thought, feeling an inexplicably deep sense of loss.

Lily realized she had already decided to stay.

She checked her phone—2:00 p.m. Hours to kill before dinner. Lily considered, then tapped in a number.

"Thank you for calling the Ascendance Institute," a pleasant voice spoke into her ear. "Please enter the extension you would like to reach, or remain on the line and an attendant will be with you shortly."

Lily hit another four digits and waited as she heard a phone ring one, twice, three, and four times.

"I'm sorry, the resident you're trying to reach is unavailable," the receptionist said, breaking into the line, her voice familiar from that morning. "May I help you?"

"Hi—this is Lily Barnes. I was just there earlier today, seeing David Johanssen. Is he in a session, something like that? Or—"

"Obviously I can't discuss that, Ms. Barnes, but I can tell you that Mr. Johanssen has requested to be put on a no-contact protocol, in consultation with his doctors."

"Since . . . this morning?" Lily said, incredulous.

"Apparently so. You can leave a message if you like, but as you're probably aware, it will be screened by Institute personnel for content that could negatively affect the resident."

Lily processed this.

"Tell him . . . tell him the research he did for me took me to some really interesting places and I'd love to talk to him about it, if he's willing. And if not, that's fine too. I just want him to know I'm grateful for his help."

"Very good, Ms. Barnes. And he knows how to reach you?"

"We were together for years. *Yes,* he knows how to reach me," Lily snapped.

Silence for a moment.

"Will there be anything else?" the receptionist asked, her voice fifteen degrees cooler.

Lily didn't care. She was rejected, hurt, and angry at herself for allowing herself to hope.

"Not a thing," Lily said, and hung up.

She realized there was now a chance the woman might conveniently forget to pass along the message—why should she do Lily any favors? Then again, it probably didn't matter whether David knew she wanted to talk to him. He had already sent her his own message via his no-contact request, and it couldn't be more clear.

Lily pulled up a news browser on her phone, saw a headline about a live execution performed by Team Joy Joy, and felt her soul clench. She very deliberately buried the phone deep in her bag, though she left the ringer on in case David somehow decided to call her, hating herself a little for not just letting him go.

But then, hope—even misguided, foolish hope—meant the Grey didn't have her. Wanting David, even if David didn't, couldn't want her, was an inoculation against giving up completely. A . . . purpose.

Sure, Lily thought.

She stood, slinging her bag across her chest. She walked to the back office, where Mr. Coriander was speaking quietly into his pink landline telephone.

He looked up as she approached.

"Excuse me a moment," he said into the handset, then gave her an expectant look. "Leaving, Ms. Barnes?"

"Just to get some food," she said. "I haven't eaten since last night. But I'll be back soon, and then I'll stay for dinner."

He grinned, that shocking, open smile that felt like sunlight pouring directly at her. So rare these days.

"I am enormously pleased to hear that. Please feel free to browse any of the exhibits in the outer room . . . and you might enjoy this as well. Just don't take it out of the building, please."

He opened a drawer in his desk and withdrew a book, a slim, wide volume, the sort of thing you'd place on your coffee table to impress visitors. It was worn, the dust jacket yellowed and tattered.

Through the Doors: The Lost Paintings of Frances Agron, 1891–1894, Lily read, the words in a rounded, lush font she thought might be Art Deco, above an image that looked like a view through a doorway into somewhere . . . other. A landscape—probably—but depicted in a deeply abstract way, with odd, vivid color choices. The ground was deep red, and the vegetation (or people, or animals, or structures) was a mix of yellow, purple, and orange against a blue-green sky.

Lily could not identify what she was seeing, but she knew exactly what she was feeling. It was the sense of a road curving out of sight around a bend. A sealed envelope addressed to you in handwriting you immediately, regrettably recognize. A person telling a joke in a language you do not speak, their listeners convulsing with laughter. A smile from a beautiful stranger. A wrapped gift with your name on it. Frances Agron's painting communicated precisely and perfectly a single, focused emotion: curiosity.

"Who is this painter?" she said. "I've never heard of her."

"No one has," Coriander said. "But now . . . you have. Such is the Wonder Path."

"Yep," Lily said.

Coriander clearly wasn't going to explain a damn thing to her until he was good and ready. No point in trying to force it. She walked back to the main room, the one she was already thinking of as the museum, and left the volume of Frances Agron's work next to the equally unexplained compass and aspirin sitting on the table in the little corner booth.

Outside, she followed Big Wave Bay Road back to the beach, catching glimpses of surfers and ocean as she walked past the low, pastel-colored buildings bordering the sidewalk. Between the road's end and the sand beyond was a stretch of shacks selling good, cheap seaside food Lily smelled well before she saw it—noodles and fried fish and cuttlefish on sticks. Her stomach roared to life.

Chips, maybe, Lily thought, figuring she'd get herself something she could wolf down to blunt the sharpest edge of her hunger, and then take a moment to see what else looked good. Ice cream, maybe. There was always an ice cream place by the beach.

Her phone rang, singing "Barbie Girl" to her, an instrumental loop of the tune's chorus. Ringtones had survived the technological terrorism wrought by Team Joy Joy—Aunt Jane's people hadn't yet figured out how to transmit the Despair Manifesto that way, so they were still safe to use. Lily dug through her satchel, scrambling to pick up the call before the song got stuck in her head.

"Hello?" she said.

"Lily, it's David."

Her heart leapt.

"I'm so glad you called," Lily said. "I wasn't sure if the girl at the front desk would pass along my message. I got a little testy with her. Anyway, you won't believe what I found down in Shek O."

"I'm sure it's fascinating," David said, sounding not fascinated at all. "But that's not why I'm calling. The police were just here."

Lily stopped walking. Children raced past her, laughing, holding ice cream cones, with drips melting down their hands. Nothing frozen lasted long in Hong Kong's sun.

"They were asking about you," David went on. "I had to tell them you'd been here—they already knew, from the front desk. They wanted to know where you'd gone."

The pieces came together quickly in Lily's mind. Danny Chang must have reported the theft of his device and pointed the police at his former materials engineer. The cops then began interviewing her known associates, with her Grey-afflicted boyfriend (*ex-boyfriend*, she reminded herself) high on that list.

Her ears felt hot. Her pulse throbbed in her throat.

"Did you . . . tell them where I went?" she asked.

A little pause. Lily would have said maybe David was offended, but she didn't know if that happened to him anymore.

"No," he said.

Lily closed her eyes. She blew out a long, slow breath.

"Thank you, David," she said. "I . . . don't know what to say."

Of course she didn't. If there was a right and proper way to acknowledge that someone had lied to the cops to save you from a lengthy stint in a cell, or even a work camp if things got bad enough . . . she didn't know it.

"Lily, you and I aren't what we were, but that doesn't mean I want you in jail. Anyway. I just thought you should know. Be careful."

He hung up.

Lily no longer felt hungry. She turned and hurried back along the road to Coriander & Associates, sweat dripping down her back and panic rising in her gut, her eyes scanning the people at the food and souvenir stalls for any hint of HKPD black.

Mr. Coriander called out from his office as she entered.

"Back already, Ms. Barnes? I hope you found somewhere to eat."

"I'm fine," she said. "Just going to sit for a while. I'm exhausted."

Lily's heart pounded, an incessant throb that wouldn't let her think.

She slipped back into the booth in the corner, where the compass, the pill, and the book of paintings remained on the table.

Things with nothing in common that apparently had something in common.

Exhaustion rolled over her. She slipped her arm through a loop of her satchel, ensuring that if Mr. Coriander—or anyone else—tampered with it, she would know. Then Lily lay down on the padded bench, curling herself into its arc, her feet dangling off the edge, and closed her eyes.

LILY WAS BACK ON THE BOAT, IN THE HEBRIDES, WITH HER FATHER at the tiller. She wasn't doing anything in particular, just sitting near the bow, one hand dangling over the side, each wave giving her fingertips a little kiss.

She was happy for no special reason, despite the cold and the way the wind cut right through her. She was out with her dad on the sea, and he was talking about something she wasn't really paying attention to—some rock or funny bit of cloud he could use to find his way, probably. Her father loved that, loved knowing where to go just because he was smart enough to figure it out.

He was happy, so she was happy.

She lifted a hand from the gunwale to push her hair behind her ear, which meant she was no longer fully anchored in the boat. Then, because the sea's law said it would take you the moment you gave it even the tiniest opening, a gust of wind caught the sail and moved its boom about a meter—just enough to smack Lily and send her unbraced body into the freezing pit of the North Sea.

Lily sank, and sank, and the cold took her and got into her bones, and she was too shocked to try to swim or save herself, the wind knocked right out of her—but in the dream, she wasn't afraid. She knew what would happen. Soon her father would grab her by the hair and pull her up and—

He was below her. Fathoms down and falling, his skin bleached grey, his eyes empty sockets, his fingernails black, his mouth open, drowned, dead for a week, dead for a month, maybe preserved a bit by the cold water, but gone, and he wasn't going to—

LILY LIFTED HER HEAD, HER NECK CRAMPING, TRYING TO REMEMber where she was.

She grabbed the edge of the table and levered herself up, to see four people standing just outside the little circular nook where she had fallen asleep. She recognized two.

"I'm sorry to wake you, Ms. Barnes," Mr. Coriander said, "but everyone has arrived. Why don't you freshen up . . ."

He lifted an ice-filled tumbler adorned with a tangerine-colored umbrella that precisely matched his suit.

". . . and we can begin."

I. TEN

HONG KONG.
CORIANDER & ASSOCIATES, LTD.
22°14'27.5"N, 114°14'47.4"E

MR. CORIANDER HAD NOT LIED. DINNER WAS EXTRAORDINARY.

A Cantonese feast, spread over eight courses. It began with dim sum and moved on through various delicacies—roast goose with cranberry sauce and braised abalone and poached lobster in soup and the promised beef chow fun. A riot of spice and heat, with dishes appearing on a disk-shaped roundabout in the middle of a huge mahogany table in a dining room revealed at the end of yet another corridor in the Coriander & Associates offices.

Char siu pork dumplings, vegetables in pungent sauce, lamb with cumin . . . everything delicately deposited onto plates by the catering staff Mr. Coriander had hired in, with tea and wine and the white-lightning local liquor called baijiu and water and beer, an unending and constantly updated set of dishes rotating slowly back and forth, moved by hand and appetite and whim.

Lily had enjoyed astonishingly good Cantonese food in her time in Hong Kong—even the town's street meat was exceptional—but this took the art to a new extreme. The rice alone. Perfect white, steaming domes in small porcelain bowls, sticky with a precise, non-gluey tension allowing easily chopsticked mouthfuls, and tasting of a round, sweet blandness that complemented and enhanced anything with which it was paired. Lily could have eaten nothing but rice and been entirely satisfied—but she was ravenous and piled her plate with a bit of everything. She dug in, and as she ate she took the measure of the four people with whom she shared the magnificent spread.

Mr. Coriander had called these people a club and implied they had old roots. Beyond introductions, he had volunteered very little. The man might not have lied about the quality of his food, but he had so far not lived up to his promise to give Lily the answers she was looking for.

To Lily's left, Coriander was busy with the goose. To her right was a crass, elderly Filipina named Maria Santa Cruz, and beside her another woman, an Australian in her late forties, though possibly younger and simply sun-weathered in that leather-cured Aussie way. Her name was Elizabeth Porter. Lily knew essentially nothing about either woman. But to her right, and Coriander's left, completing the circle, taking a sip of tea, was someone about whom Lily knew many details, with a face she would have known anywhere.

Peter Match. The singer. From somewhere in America.

Lily tried to keep her eyes off him, tried not to stare as she shoveled dumpling and string beans into her mouth. Peter Match was famous, truly famous, worldwide. He gathered attention to himself the way a black hole sucked in light. It wasn't just the man's status as a minor cultural icon, either; it was the fascinating, jarring reality of seeing him outside his usual context. Lily knew Match from music videos and interviews and his films, where his bronze skin was unlined, his face perfected and enhanced. Looking at him across a table of Cantonese delicacies, with his features unsmoothed, his shoulder-length dark hair rumpled and lank, his famous tattoo of a lit match on the side of his neck poking up just above his collar—his presence here was impossible, and Lily couldn't look away.

Peter Match wasn't eating, just taking sips of tea, his eyes flickering around the table. He rarely joined the increasingly lively discussion, and even then offered just a grunt or a nod. He didn't seem grumpy or off-putting, though. The singer was cheerful, comfortable, usually smiling. Just a warm, easy, unworried presence.

Then again, he's famous, rich, and barely forty, I'd say—what does he have to worry about? Lily thought.

"Perseus? *Perseus*? You're a goddamned fool, Elizabeth," Maria Santa Cruz said, punctuating this with one of her chopsticks, held out like a dagger toward the Australian woman.

"You're going to stab me with that, Maria?" the Australian said. "Go ahead and try. I'll take that thing off you and shove it right in your ear, you obstinate old bitch."

The two women had been arguing for ten minutes, the tension between them rising with every exchange, about things Lily couldn't parse. It all felt familial, obsessive—old grievances being aired. The word "Intercession" came up a lot—the capitalization was obvious—and the two ladies were apparently willing to battle to the death about whether various historical events could be classified as one.

"You're too young to remember the seventies and eighties, Beth," Maria said, stabbing her chopstick into a pile of chicken and chilies on her plate as opposed to Elizabeth Porter's face. "The Cold War and the arms race had the world under a shadow for forty years. America and the Soviets did terrible things in the name of their ideologies, fighting all those proxy wars. You'll never convince me the Intercessionists had any part in creating that."

"Maybe the Cold War was the best option for the world," Elizabeth said, unwilling to be convinced. "Maybe the Intercessionists saved us all and we just don't know it."

Maria groaned.

Peter Match's tea cup clinked against its saucer. Lily looked at him. His eyebrow twitched upward—he smiled at her. She got the sense he found all of this funny.

"Ladies, please," said Mr. Coriander. "These are old, well-trodden roads that pose questions we cannot properly answer without new information. Speaking of which . . ."

He turned to smile at Lily.

"We have eaten, we have reconnected . . . Let us turn to the main event. Ms. Barnes, will you show us what you discovered?"

Lily froze, a dumpling halfway to her mouth.

Ah. Right, she thought. *I'm the reason these people are here.*

She completed the dumpling's journey and methodically chewed it, her eyes moving from face to face. They all had expectant looks, even Peter Match. Lily swallowed, took a sip of water, cleared her throat.

"I believe," she said, "you were going to tell me what the hell's going on?"

"I will," Coriander replied, his voice mild. "*We* will."

He gestured to the rest of the table.

"He's telling you the truth," Elizabeth said, her face sincere, her eyes shining. "We're all in this together. We all had to give before anything could be given to us. But we did, and it was worth it. You'll see."

Lily didn't want to give. She wanted to leave. But she glanced at Peter Match, who gave her the tiniest, subtlest nod.

She knew that liking this rock star's songs and liking this rock star's face didn't mean she could trust this rock star. And yet . . .

Lily removed the carbon scrubber from her satchel. She held

it out, and four sets of eyes drank the thing in. They all clearly thought the object answered a question Lily had not yet been asked.

"If you wouldn't mind," Coriander said, gesturing to the lazy Susan. "So we can all have a look."

Lily pushed aside a few plates denuded of everything but a few wisps of sauce. She set the carbon scrubber down, then forced herself to lift her hand from the device. Immediately, Maria Santa Cruz spun the roundabout to bring the scrubber to her. She picked it up, brought it close to her eyes.

"Have we ever seen anything like this?" she said, without looking at the others.

"Not exactly," Coriander answered. "But the material used for the exterior has the same patterning we saw in the Geneva fragment."

"The Geneva fragment is unverified," Maria said.

"Almost *everything* is unverified," Elizabeth said. "Now spin the thing around so I can have a chance. You're hogging it."

"You're a hog," Maria snapped, but she put the device down and let Elizabeth rotate it toward her.

Elizabeth picked up the scrubber and performed her own inspection. She looked across the table at Lily.

"Coriander was a little unclear about what this thing does. We got the story secondhand. Can you tell us?"

Lily sighed, but there didn't really seem to be much point in holding anything back.

"I'm a materials engineer," she said. "I work for a company trying to build an atmospheric scrubber to pull carbon dioxide out of the air, to help offset climate change. My boss handed me that device a few days ago and asked me to test it. That's the whole story."

"Did it work?" Elizabeth asked. "I bet it did. Better than anything you've ever seen."

"It's a miracle," Lily said simply. "It performs a thousand times better than the best scrubber I've ever heard of. It's basically a magical artifact. My best hypothesis is aliens."

That was actually not Lily's working hypothesis, or at least not all of it, but it would take more than a fancy dinner and a nod from a rock star to get her to give up the full story.

Elizabeth and Maria exchanged a knowing glance.

"Must be an Intercession," Elizabeth said. "The Eleventh, I wager."

Maria nodded and looked back at Lily.

"We're quite well hidden, you know. How did you know to come here?"

"I followed a trail of bread crumbs. Corporate records and such."

"The Wonder Path," Coriander announced, beaming.

Peter Match snorted, the first sound he'd made in a while.

"The rest of us don't call it that," Elizabeth said to Lily.

"What better name is there, Ms. Porter?" Coriander interrupted, indignant. "Something wonderful exists in the world, something hidden, something magical. Certain special souls find hints of it left scattered around the globe. As they investigate, their understanding grows, and they find others who have made similar connections. No matter how far along this road they travel, at every step, they encounter . . . wonder."

"Uh-huh," Elizabeth said. "Herbert, you know as well as we do that it ain't just wonder on the Wonder Path. Plenty of horror too. Now, if you don't mind, I have a few questions for Lily here about—"

"I actually do mind, Elizabeth. I don't want to be rude, but I came here because that machine is broken," Lily said, causing Peter Match to glance up from his own study of the device, "and I'd like to fix it. It could literally save the world, and I—"

She took a breath.

"What is this? Who are you people?" Lily said. "Please. This is driving me insane."

"We wouldn't want that," Elizabeth said. "Enough insanity in the world these days, eh? I'll start."

She lifted her beer to her mouth, drained what was left, and set the glass down. She looked at Lily.

"Out there," she said, gesturing vaguely, as if to encompass the greater world outside the building, "somewhere, is a group of people who can do incredible things. They have technology beyond anything the rest of us have, and other abilities besides."

"Like . . . superpowers?"

"No, not really," Maria interjected, earning her an annoyed glance from Elizabeth. "They're just very smart people with extraordinary resources. Sometimes they use those resources to . . . do things."

"They *intercede,*" said Mr. Coriander.

"To help? To make things better?"

"Mostly. Not always."

"So you think my scrubber is them trying to do that?"

"We do. We think it's the Eleventh Intercession."

"What were the other ten?"

"That is a subject of much debate among our members," Coriander said. "The group in question is extremely secretive."

"That's an understatement," Maria chimed in.

Not promising, Lily thought.

"Who are they?" she asked. "Where are they from?"

"We don't know for sure, though we have suspicions," Coriander said. "Initially, they were connected to a business called Calder & Calder."

I knew it, Lily thought. *Score one for the impeccable research skills of David Johanssen.*

And that made her sad, but she locked the thought away and refocused on Coriander.

"But whether they started Calder & Calder," he was saying, "or merely worked with it, we do not know. The short list of things about which we are certain begins in the early nineteenth century, when my own family entered the employ of the business. For about a century we were their agents, their go-betweens, conducting business on their behalf. Collecting money owed, buying things they needed, managing correspondence . . . all very discreet."

He paused to take a sip of his cocktail, recently refreshed by the caterers.

"My great, great, great, great great great great grandfather," Coriander said, orating, clearly enjoying himself, "ran the London office. For many decades, all seemed well. But around the start of the twentieth century, Calder & Calder stopped using their offices or communicating with their agents, including my family. They just . . . disappeared. We Corianders continued to maintain their operations, as we had never received any instructions to the contrary, but we never heard from them again."

Another languorous sip of the cocktail, and this time Lily was sure it was done for dramatic effect.

"Of course, we did our best to investigate. From time to time we saw evidence that our former employers still existed and occasionally influenced world affairs in ways large and small. Because of those actions, we came to call this unique group the Intercessionists, though I have no idea what they actually call themselves."

Lily looked at the group.

"So then"—she looked around the table—"are you all Mr. Coriander's . . . cousins or something?"

"God forbid," Elizabeth said, though she threw Coriander a wink. "We're just the people who believe, Lily."

"We are chroniclers, Ms. Barnes," Mr. Coriander said. "We consider it something of a calling to pull together whatever little pieces of information about the Intercessionists we can. And, of course . . ."

He gestured at the device, which had made its way back around the table to Lily.

". . . we are here for those who find their way to the Wonder Path. It happens from time to time. Perhaps a person's life is touched by an Intercession, or they come across an odd contradiction they can't explain, or meet an unusual person they cannot forget. Whatever the first step, people follow the Path until they find me or one of my relatives across the world. Just as you did, though I will admit you got to us much faster than most."

"I'm highly motivated," Lily said. "What do you think these, uh, Intercessionists are actually up to? What's their purpose?"

"A very good question," Maria said, holding up a finger. "Lately, they've been *up to* quite a lot. They've been more active in the last year than for the entire last century."

"It's the Grey, we think," Elizabeth agreed. "They're trying to push it back."

Peter looked up at this, giving a thoughtful nod. He pulled his phone from inside his coat—a blue leather jacket that felt extremely rock star, conveying luxury and filth in equal measure—and began tapping away with his thumbs.

Texting Damon Albarn or Bruce Springsteen no doubt, Lily thought.

"Okay, fine," Lily said. "But the Grey is new, and these people have been around for hundreds of years, right?"

"They have," Coriander said, with a genteel nod. "And so, my dear, they obviously have some other motivation or purpose beyond curing the Grey. But what that is, we do not know."

"People argue about this stuff," Elizabeth said. "It's one of the biggest things we fight about."

Lily considered.

"Can you put me in touch with them?"

"Absolutely not," Coriander said, his good humor replaced with flat, definitive certainty.

"They don't want to be found," Elizabeth said.

Lily frowned.

"What does that mean? Why not?"

Mr. Coriander took a breath, then forced his face back into a smile.

"That is a mystery the people gathered before you are content to leave unsolved."

"I don't get it," Lily said. "You spend all this time, gather all this stuff in your museum, make your little club, and you don't want to know the answer?"

"Of course we want to know," said Maria. "But let me agree with Elizabeth, for once. The Intercessionists *do not want to be found.*"

"That doesn't work for me," Lily said, pointing at the carbon scrubber. "I need to fix this thing. Can't you point me in the right direction?"

Coriander sat back, considering. Peter Match looked up, his mouth twisting into something like a frown, then went back to texting.

"Perhaps we can help each other," Coriander continued, smoothing his pumpkin-colored lapel with one hand as he gestured at the carbon scrubber with the other. "As we study your device, we might see things you would not on your own. In fact, there's a broadsheet from the 1830s you might find interesting. The original is in the office of our Buenos Aires chapter, but we have a copy here. We can review it together over brandy."

Lily saw a path stretching before her, a treasure hunt, poring through dusty archives, finding clues, traveling the globe. Meeting other searchers, making new connections, learning an entire secret history, piece by piece. The Wonder Path.

Fuck that, she thought.

"No," Lily said. "I'm sorry, but no. I don't have time for that. Thank you for dinner, but I need to go."

Mr. Coriander seemed taken aback.

"You'll find it's harder to walk away from all this than you might expect."

Was that a threat? Lily thought.

Coriander's eyes flickered back to the carbon scrubber, still on the lazy Susan in front of the still-texting Peter Match. Its path back to her would spin it past Coriander in one direction and Elizabeth and Maria in the other. Any of them could just reach out and grab it, and if they did, what was she supposed to do? Call the cops to help her get back the thing she'd stolen in the first place? Unlikely.

Lily could feel the situation spinning out of control. She felt herself sinking, down into the cold dark, felt her emotions beginning to flail and thrash.

"I'll walk wherever the fuck I want," she said, knowing she was escalating, turning a situation that might have gone bad into one that definitely would. "I'm leaving."

Lily placed her hand on the edge of the lazy Susan, deciding to spin it past the two women instead of Coriander. They hadn't shown his naked, obvious desire. A nice, easy, clockwise rotation, which would bring the device back to her without sending it caroming off the table.

A gentle push. The roundabout did not move. Lily's fingers skidded off the thing. It was as if it was locked in place.

She glanced away from Coriander. Peter Match had his hand on the roundabout, holding it, with the scrubber still directly in front of him.

Lily sank deeper, really struggling now, running out of air.

"Let go," Lily said. "I don't care who you are, asshole. It's mine. *Let go.*"

"Why?" the rock star said, his voice shockingly rough, like two pieces of lava rock scraped together.

Lily snapped out of her spiral, just a bit, too surprised to speak.

Peter Match's singing voice was legendary. Notably smooth and precise, like honey poured over ice. What Jimi Hendrix was to guitar, Peter Match was to singing. Fluid and virtuosic and constantly surprising.

So how is it, Lily wondered, *that his speaking voice sounds like his vocal cords are a couple of rusty bedsprings?*

Peter Match raised an eyebrow, his hand still on the lazy Susan.

"Why do you want to find the Intercessionists?" he rasped.

"Because I need to," Lily said.

They looked at each other for a long moment. He gave her an easy smile, nodded, and lifted his phone. A voice spilled from it. Computer-generated but far from unpleasant—not so different from what she'd expected Peter Match to sound like.

"I know everything they do," the voice said, and Lily realized Peter hadn't been texting at all but typing out this message. "I paid Coriander a million bucks to see everything in his archives. I'll tell you whatever you want to know."

Maria gasped.

"You traitor! You're one of us! You'll be excommunicated!"

Peter gave her an *Oh, wow, that* would *be terrible, wouldn't it?* look, and the phone kept talking.

"You know how Coriander told you that the Intercessionists stopped using those offices where his family worked? He neglected to mention that they never pulled their money out of their bank accounts, and his people stole every penny. Took them a while to blow it all, but over a hundred years, they got it done. Now, they're selling what they have left—the story. They find rich idiots and bring them in, taking donations to give them little glimpses at their secrets, but never give out enough information for someone to find the Intercessionists on their own. They're con men. Cowards, too, terrified to go look for the thing they're obsessed with. Or maybe they're afraid the people they stole from won't be too happy if they remember Coriander's family exists. The Wonder Path is real, and it's got miracles waiting at the end, but they're too chickenshit to follow it. It offends me, down to my bones. Not my style, and I don't think it's yours."

He picked up the carbon scrubber from the lazy Susan and held it out to Lily.

With his own voice, that steel-wool-on-cast-iron croak, he spoke.

"What do you say we take a walk?"

I. ELEVEN

HONG KONG.
SHEK O VILLAGE.
22°13′52.8″N, 114°15′00.8″E

"I NEED TO GET OFF THE STREET," LILY SAID.

Peter took this in stride.

He gestured, two fingers pointing straight up the block, then turned it into a thumbs-up.

"No problem," he rasped, and began walking in the direction he had indicated.

Lily was left to interpret this. She decided *Come with me and we'll get you sorted* was the most likely meaning. She followed Peter along the pavement, thinking, *God, the man must be baking.* He wore black jeans, tight, and motorcycle boots, and that blue leather jacket over a loose-fitting green shirt. An outfit for a thoroughly air-conditioned club, not a stroll through a seaside village.

She kept her head down, letting her hair hang in her face, hoping that would reduce the chances of her being spotted on one of the CCTV cameras installed everywhere in the city after the 2019 protests and the 2020 lockdowns. Hong Kong was always fairly well surveilled, but the Chinese government used the opportunity provided by the pandemic years to build out their network. Now cameras sat on every street pole and lamppost, in every alley, their feeds linked to facial recognition algorithms the authorities could access as needed.

The city's invisible eyes could already be searching for one Lily Florencia Barnes, born in Gloucester, England, a Hong Kong resident since 2016. It would take no more than a few keystrokes on some computer at HKPD HQ.

Not to mention that Lily was currently less than a meter from an extremely well-known rock star who, while perhaps not as immediately recognizable as he might have been in Los Angeles or New York, still had the vibe of a Someone. The nature of Someones was to generate curiosity about anyone the Someone was with. Who was that person? How did they rate the Someone's company? Were they, in fact, interesting in some way themselves? Perhaps, for instance, of great interest to the police?

Lily slipped a pair of sunglasses from her satchel and put them on, wishing for a hat, a huge, floppy, 1940s-starlet chapeau that would shroud her face in gloom.

Peter stopped.

"Get in," he said, the words scraped from his throat with a rusty spoon.

Lily looked up from her feet and saw a car, white, shining in the sun. The vehicle had no straight edges—it was all curves, ripples on a river. She recognized the logo on its hood—an Aston Martin. Her father had driven one for a bit. Her dad's car was a pretty standard sedan, though. This was . . . a swirl of cream stirred into a coffee and set upon four tires.

Peter didn't speak again; he just opened the driver's-side door and lowered himself into the . . . cockpit. That was the only appropriate word for the vehicle's interior.

Lily hesitated—strange car, strange man—but not for long.

She had to get off the street. She slipped around the vehicle's hood—the passenger's-side door was already levering itself open via Peter's activation of some slick, insectile mechanism—and got in.

"Beautiful car," she said as the door slid silently shut, sealing them inside a dark technological cocoon, tinted windows offering welcome protection from prying eyes and tropical sun alike.

Peter made a small noise of agreement and threw her a smile that made Lily's heart stutter. His voice might be shot, but his charm remained a nuclear weapon.

The car slipped away from the curb, silent, like a predator fish moving through a reef.

Lily felt cold. The car's climate-control system was as powerful as its engine, and its interior had rapidly become a refrigerator. She rubbed her arms, feeling goose pimples beneath her palms. She hated being cold.

Shek O rolled by out the window. Lily watched the sea. Took deep breaths. Got her sweater from her satchel, put it on. Worked the tile puzzle for a while.

The car came to a roundabout, three choices available—north, south, or back the way they'd come. Peter entered the circle and took a loop. He looked at her. The question was clear.

"The police are looking for me," she said.

Peter raised an eyebrow.

"Because I stole the carbon scrubber," Lily said, answering the obvious question, tapping her bag. "It belonged to my employer, but . . . I was poking around in it and broke it. I panicked and ran. I had this idea I could fix it, make everything right. I know, it was foolish. My boss called the cops. I'm sure they're keeping an eye on my apartment. I don't know where to go."

Hong Kong seemed so small suddenly. It was an island, for god's sake. Even if she could find a place to hide, she was utterly ill-prepared to be a fugitive. She had no safehouses, no caches of gear and passports and ready cash. She was just a very ordinary woman who had made a remarkably stupid mistake.

Lily's phone buzzed in her bag. A text: To Ms. Lily Barnes: Please report to the police station at 6 Lok Man Road in Chai Wan to assist HKPD with inquiries.

A chill in her guts, completely unrelated to the arctic levels of the car's AC. She showed the phone to Peter, who shrugged. He was maintaining shocking levels of equanimity at Lily's various revelations. On the other hand, she supposed he'd done nothing wrong, and rock stars probably had entire teams on retainer to get them out of all manner of trouble. He took another turn around the roundabout, literally spiraling.

Lily could relate.

This is getting out of control, Lily thought, feeling the waters rise up around her again. *I have to do something or I'll end up in prison.*

She lifted her phone and dialed. A familiar voice answered after two rings.

"Lily," said Danny Chang. "What are you doing? This is not like you."

"It's not what you think," she said. "I didn't steal it to . . . steal it. I just wanted to know more about it. You understand. I know you do."

"The device belongs to me and my company. It's not yours. You *did* steal it, whatever your reason."

"I know. I can't wait to give it back to you, I promise. I know what it can do. It needs to be out in the world, doing its thing. But . . . can you just tell me where you got it? It's very important. Can you contact the people it came from?"

"Bring me the device and we'll talk about it."

"Absolutely, Danny—but who gave it to you? This thing . . . it's like . . . magic. Please. I have to know."

"It doesn't matter now, Lily. That's all over. I was having discussions with their reps about how to manufacture the scrubber in bulk—they would have provided schematics and fabrication recipes, everything—but when I told them their prototype was missing they cut off all contact."

"But how did you find them?"

"They emailed me. I thought it was strange, of course, but saw no reason not to see what they had. Just . . . bring it back, Lily. You are not a bad person. I understand everything. We can set it right. Save the world like we always talked about. I won't press charges. Just bring it back."

"I can't, Danny. Not yet."

"Lily . . ."

A long silence.

Danny spoke again.

"I did not think you were this person, Lily. I'm sure you're afraid, not thinking rationally. Own up to your mistakes and return to the right path, or the consequences will be the result of your own choices."

Lily's lips tightened. She ended the call and stared down at her phone.

Peter cleared his throat. They were still in the roundabout, circling. He gave her phone a meaningful look.

"They have that," he said.

Lily realized what he meant. Her cell. She was holding a tracking device constantly broadcasting her location in what was literally a surveillance state.

Everything was collapsing. She had no idea what to do. She powered down her phone, with no idea if that would actually solve the problem.

"Why are you doing this?" Peter said, enunciating carefully, each word paid out like a poor man's coins. "You had an out there, with your boss. You didn't take it."

She chose her response just as carefully.

"I didn't just steal the scrubber. I broke it. I have to fix it."

Peter grunted, clearly unsatisfied.

"When I was a kid," Lily said, trying to find a way to explain this to him, "I almost drowned. I was on a boat, and I fell into the sea off the coast of Scotland. It was freezing, dark. I tried to swim, but my clothes and shoes were soaking wet and dragging me down. I panicked and ended up just thrashing around, making it worse. My dad saved me."

Lily sighed. This next part she was barely able to admit to herself.

"A lot of things have happened in my life that made me like to be . . . focused, I guess. In control. When I feel that way, I'm good. I feel like I can think; I make good decisions. But sometimes it's not like that for me. Sometimes it feels like I'm back under the sea and I just start . . . flailing. Trying to find my way back to the boat.

"Right now," she said, "I'm in the ocean. I need to find my way back."

She tapped her satchel to indicate the scrubber within.

"This thing is how I'll do it. The only way. It's why I lost my shit at Coriander's when I thought he was going to take it from me. Does any of this make sense?"

Peter nodded once, slowly. Lily knew she'd given him, at best, half an answer, but he didn't push it. He glanced at her and raised an eyebrow, clearly communicating the words *What now?*

"I know where I have to go," Lily said, "but I have no idea how to get there. It's impossible."

"Tell me."

"England. Might as well be Mars."

Peter nodded and said, "I can do that."

He accelerated, a grin ripping across his face, and the Aston Martin finally left the roundabout, slicing through traffic to take the exit headed north. Lily was shoved back into her seat, the engine thrumming with a low bass note she felt deep in her chest.

"Where are we going?" she asked.

Peter looked at her, still smiling. He pointed a single finger. Up.

I. TWELVE

HONG KONG. LANTAU ISLAND.

22°17′53.3″N, 113°54′49.7″E

PETER MATCH DROVE ALONG A CAUSEWAY HEADING WEST FROM the city. The road skimmed across the surface of the sea, eventually reaching an island called Lantau. Lily had been here before—she and David had hiked its trails and had made the obligatory tourist pilgrimage to the gigantic Buddha sitting atop one of its peaks.

Just off Lantau's northern shore was a second, much smaller island called Chek Lap Kok, 80 percent of which did not exist until the Hong Kong government dredged it up from the ocean in the 1990s and which Lily had not visited in quite some time. This was because Lily hadn't left Hong Kong in years, and Chek Lap Kok's primary feature was one of the world's busiest airports. Hundreds of flights per day traveled through the massive complex: passenger, cargo . . . and what a sign at the last exit off the ring road around the airport called "business aviation"—private jets, in other words.

The Aston Martin steered into this heavily secured section of the airport, access granted after Peter flashed an ID at the security gate. Lily was not given a second glance.

Peter navigated through the airport, eventually pulling up twenty meters from a sleek white bullet of a plane parked on the tarmac. A member of airport staff, sharp in a navy blue uniform and cap, was waiting.

"Fully fueled and ready to go, sir," the attendant said, stepping up as they got out of the Aston Martin. "Your flight plan has been filed, and we'll return your car to the garage for you. Customs and immigration will be along shortly."

Peter nodded, tossed the man his car keys, and climbed up a short set of steps leading into the plane's interior.

"Madam," the attendant said, gesturing for Lily to follow.

Lily climbed the steps and found herself in a slim tube she knew was made of a titanium-aluminum alloy, softened by white leather and polished wood. Peter waited in the aisle.

"I won't make it through immigration," she said. "I don't even have my passport with me. I don't have anything."

"Go back," he said, gesturing to the rear of the plane. "Wait. Toilet."

"Won't they search the plane? I'm"—Lily searched for the proper word—"wanted."

He made a sound, a skeptical little snort, and again, emphatically, indicated the back of the plane.

Lily shrugged and squeezed past him.

If nothing else, she thought, *I'll have a glamorous story for the other inmates about the time the police dragged me out of the loo on a rock star's private jet.*

A thin door at the rear of the plane slid open at the touch of a button to reveal a surprisingly spacious lavatory, not the cramped cabinet Lily was accustomed to from literally every other flight she had ever taken. A few bauhinia blossoms in a bud vase perfumed the air—another feature she had never seen in the standard model.

Lily wouldn't have minded using the facility, but she had no idea when the customs officers would be aboard and didn't want to alert them with an ill-timed flush. She sat on the toilet lid—more white leather, the item doubling as a seat for passengers who wanted to, say, freshen their makeup in the tastefully lit mirror above the sink. She pulled the tile puzzle from her purse and started sliding the squares, not even looking at the thing, not trying to solve it.

Voices from the cabin. Greetings offered in an official-sounding tone, but cordial, respectful. Nothing from Peter in response, but no surprise there.

This plan cannot work, Lily thought, her thoughts accelerating. *The customs people will check the toilet. They have to. It's their job. And once they find me, will they take me straight to jail? Is there . . . a warrant out for me? This is all so fucking—*

A noise from the cabin, a soft *ka-thunk,* and then . . . steps, walking toward the back of the plane, toward her hiding place. Lily braced herself. A knock on the door, gentle.

"Okay"—so quiet she could barely hear it, a whisper of sandpaper on stone.

Lily opened the door. Peter was already headed back toward the cockpit.

"They just . . . left?" she called.

Without turning back, Peter gave her yet another thumbs-up, then rolled his fingers into a *Follow me* gesture. The confidence of the move was breathtaking, his utter lack of surprise that things had worked out as he'd expected, the shield from consequence and scrutiny provided by his wealth and fame.

And . . . he wasn't wrong, she thought, following him forward.

The cockpit was small but, like everything else on the plane, beautifully designed. It used every centimeter of space without feeling cramped. Peter lowered himself into the pilot's seat on the left and buckled himself in, pointing at the copilot's seat for Lily. She followed suit, levering herself down, sliding her legs down into the well below the copilot's . . . steering wheel? She didn't think that was right.

On the console before her was a wild complexity of dials and buttons and switches, all within easy reach, and all of which she intended to firmly ignore.

"How did you get the immigration folks to let us go without searching the plane?" she asked, looking at him.

Peter briefly paused flipping switches and pulling levers to make the universal gesture for money—thumb and index finger rubbing together. Lily didn't know if he meant wealth or bribery, and as the plane began to taxi down the runway, she realized she didn't care.

She was leaving Hong Kong. Somehow, impossibly, she was escaping. She had a vague notion that her immigration status was about to become nebulous. The chain of title to her person in the records of the world would shortly be broken—but that was a problem for some other Lily Barnes down the road.

Then they were in the air.

For a while, that was enough. They sat in silence, climbing up above the green mountains and turquoise sea surrounding Hong Kong, breaking out into a bright world floored by clouds and roofed by sky. The cockpit's windshields dimmed automatically. The plane leveled out, and Lily watched Peter flip switches on the console, ending by pressing a single button labeled AFC.

He took his hands off the controls, and Lily must have reacted in some way that telegraphed her immediate surge of terror. He chuckled, a weird little granite sound, and pointed back at the button he had just hit.

"Autopilot," he said. "Food?"

She nodded. Despite the banquet at Coriander & Associates, she was starving again. The stress, perhaps.

Peter opened a locker between the seats, revealing wrapped sandwiches, snacks, bottles of water. He gestured at it, a clear invitation for Lily to take whatever she liked. For his part, he selected a plastic bottle containing a thick pink liquid. He opened it and took a long swig, then sighed in relief.

Lily selected a chicken sandwich and a bottle of water, then closed the locker. She unwrapped, took a bite, thought, watched as Peter drank again from his bottle.

"I want to ask you something," she said. "But you aren't much of a talker, and I don't want to make you if you don't want to."

He gave her a wry little smile and raised an eyebrow. An inquiring eyebrow. Lily took that as a signal to go on.

"Why are you helping me?" she said. "You just smuggled a fugitive out of Hong Kong. You're flying me to England on your private jet, and I can't imagine how much it costs. Jet fuel must be insanely expensive. Clearly you're beyond rich, but still. We just met.

"I'm no one, again, we *just met,* and you're Peter Match. You're famous. If you get in trouble, you have a lot to lose. I'm just some woman. Why are you doing this?"

He watched her, and Lily was sure he wasn't going to answer, or if he did, it would be one of the one-word, noncommittal responses he seemed so fond of.

"I don't talk much because it hurts," he said. "A lot."

He held up the bottle of pink liquid, now about two-thirds gone.

"I have throat cancer. Pretty far along. This helps."

His voice did sound a bit smoother—scraped from his throat with a finer grain of sandpaper, maybe. But now it was Lily who had gone silent. Peter Match, noted possessor of one of the loveliest voices in popular music, had throat cancer. She reeled at the precise, calculated injustice of it. Evidence of a lower power.

"I've tried everything," Peter went on, his eyes hooded. "Every treatment you can name. Nothing's kicked it back. It took my voice. Soon enough, it'll take the rest of me. So now I'm looking into the things you can't name. The Hail Marys. The miracles."

He pointed at her bag, resting on her lap.

"Things like that gadget you found, and the people it came from. If anyone has a cure for what I've got, it's them."

Lily looked down at her satchel, then back up at the singer.

"I don't understand," she said. "You were part of that club. Coriander's people. They know more about that group, or society—whatever it is—than anyone else. And you left to go with me?"

"Coriander and his crew don't really want to find the Intercessionists. They just want to *know* about them. Pretend it makes them special. They're terrified to actually look."

He grimaced and took another swig from the bottle.

"I don't have time to be terrified."

Lily thought this through. She was amazed—stunned, really—that Peter Match didn't have the Grey.

"I'm so sorry," she said.

Peter shrugged.

"Don't be. My life has been . . . you wouldn't believe me if I told you. For twenty years I've made my living doing the thing I love best. I'm so good at it that people get happy just hearing me do it. How can I complain? If I die, I die. I'm not going to turn into some grouchy asshole just because my number's probably up. I've had a thousand people's luck in one lifetime."

He swallowed, a shiver of pain rolling across his features. That little speech clearly cost him. Lily didn't want to make him talk again, but she couldn't just leave it there.

"But still . . . okay, your illness—I'm so sorry, truly," she stammered, the awkwardness of the situation overwhelming her. "But, uh, anyway, that explains some of what you're doing, but it doesn't cover why I'm here, sitting in your airplane, flying over . . ."

She gestured vaguely at the sky outside the cockpit.

"China," Peter said. "About a third of the route's over China. Then a bunch of time over Kazakhstan and Russia. Little bit over northern Europe at the end."

"Isn't that out of the way?" she said, running the geography in her head.

"It's a great circle route. You don't fly straight to a destination once it's over the horizon. You use the curve of the earth to get there in a shorter path."

"Are you dodging the question?" Lily said.

"No," the singer said. "I'm here because you want to find the Intercessionists too. But also . . . I think you know something no one else does. Connected to that thing you found. I saw it in your eyes when back in Shek O. You figured something out."

Again he gestured at her bag.

"Coriander and the others weren't going to save my life. But maybe whatever you've got will get me a little further down the road. Even if it doesn't, it's better than waiting to die. As far as the plane . . . you never have to twist my arm to spend time up here."

Peter looked out at the clouds.

"I picked up flying when the Grey came, and no one trusted pilots anymore, because you never knew if they had it and would crash the plane, or, later, when Team Joy Joy showed up, if the Despair Manifesto might come over the radio and do the same thing. I could afford a plane, and figured I could do the rest myself. Signed up for lessons, and here we are. Great blue yonder."

They both watched the sky for a few minutes.

"What do you think it is?" Peter said.

Lily didn't know what he meant.

"The Despair Manifesto?" she asked.

"No. The Grey," he responded, looking straight ahead.

"Huh, okay," Lily said, a little surprised at the non sequitur. "Sure. Well, you remember I said I'm a materials engineer? I study . . . *stuff* for a living. The materials of matter. Why aluminum is different than steel, and why they're both different from cellulose. Everything—*everything*—has a fixed set of properties that fit together to create what the thing is. Mercury has a really high density, and if it wasn't precisely that dense, it wouldn't be mercury. I like that. It's exact, measurable."

Peter looked at her, raised an eyebrow. She lifted a hand.

"I'm getting there. So. One of those properties is called the yield point. It's connected to elasticity, which is another property everything has. Rubber is more elastic than stone. But the thing about elasticity is that it has a limit. Everything you stretch reaches a point where its flexibility runs out, and it won't return to its original form anymore. It's still itself . . . but it's in a new configuration. You can do it with a rubber band—or anything, really.

"I think that's what the Grey is. Humanity reached its yield point. Everything bad and quick and enormous happening in the world all at once stretched us too far, so we can't get back to what we used to be. We're something different now."

Peter stared at her.

"That's interesting," he said. "I wouldn't have said it exactly that way, but—"

He stopped, reached up, rubbed at his throat. His voice had gone rough again.

"I should stop talking. Starting to feel like I'm blowing a chain saw. I've got painkillers, serious ones. But I won't take them while we're up here," he said.

He finished the last of the pink drink.

"This is all I get until we land in England."

He looked at her, suddenly very intent, a shadow in his eyes.

"I got one last question, Ms. Barnes. Were my instincts right? Do you know something no one else does? Can you help me find these secretive fuckers?"

Lily felt pinned, a butterfly on a mounting board, but she understood. If her throat was eating itself, her remaining days measured in double digits, she'd snatch at any lifeline on offer. Peter Match had helped her, at real risk to himself. He deserved a little hope.

"I think I can," she said.

Lily opened her bag and brought out the largest fragment of the shattered carbon scrubber. She showed it to Peter, pointing at the intricately woven nest of wires at its heart. He leaned forward, trying to see what she was indicating.

"The wires here," she said. "You see how they're arranged in a pattern? It's like a personal statement. A signature that no one would ever recognize but me."

"Whose?" Peter said.

"My father," Lily said.

The singer's eyes widened.

"He died when I was fifteen," she said. "A car accident."

His funeral. Everyone just sort of stunned at the service and the reception—her mother, the relatives, her father's friends and uniformly weird colleagues, and of course Lily. This wasn't one of those situations where someone died after a lingering illness and people had time to make peace with the loss. Dr. Frederick Barnes had given a lecture at Oxford, called to say he would be home in time for dinner, and wasn't.

Her father's little sedan had collided with a truck carrying liquid propane, and . . . well, one could imagine. The lorry driver had made it out with just minor burns and scrapes. Her father had a different experience. The casket, resting on a stand at the front of the viewing room, was firmly and emphatically closed.

But the closed casket was an opportunity too. Because Lily didn't have to look her father's corpse in the face, her mind could give her a gift. It built for her a nice, cushiony reality in which the funeral was nothing more than just another boring church service her mother had dragged her to. It wasn't so unusual for Lily and

Adriana to do things, just the two of them. Her father was often away for work, traveling to London or other parts of the country for meetings and conferences, even the occasional overseas trip.

In fact, Lily and Adriana had gone to the shops together not long before the funeral service, to find a black dress for Lily. Just the two of them.

Just another shopping trip. Just another hour spent in church. Just another day with mom.

Lily and her mother kept the magical thinking going for years. Their lifestyle didn't change much, thanks in part to a hefty insurance payout upon her father's death, and Adriana's whip-smart management of those funds and the family's other assets. They didn't move to a new home. Lily's mother didn't date, at least not as far as Lily was aware. Lily stayed in school, worked hard, got good grades, as she had always done.

The death of Frederick Barnes was a Schrödinger's cat, not real until it was observed, and observation was a choice they both refused to make.

This status quo remained in place—at least for Lily—for several years, until a chemistry class during her first year at university. She was reviewing a table listing the temperature at which various fuels burned. Her attention was focused on the number for liquid propane burning in open air: 1,980 degrees Celsius. Another temperature ran through her mind, a fact remembered from a morbid phase in her tweens, focused on Tim Burton films and entire buckets of eye shadow, which was this: crematoriums operated at 1,000 degrees Celsius.

Lily stared at the chart, her hand trembling.

The math was simple enough. The temperature inside her father's little Vauxhall sedan as it burned was nearly twice that required to reduce the human body to ash. Frederick Barnes was gone, gone from this earth, vaporized and atomized in an inferno of liquid propane.

She exploded into tears right there in the classroom, became a sobbing mess in the space of a heartbeat. She had to be escorted from the class by her close friend Evie, who was shocked to learn that Lily was upset at the death of her father and then amazed, even a little resentful, to learn it had happened just before they'd started university. Lily had never said a word.

Lily also didn't share this story now, fifteen years later, as she and Peter Match traveled thousands of miles above the surface of the earth, crossing over Kazakhstan or Lithuania or wherever they currently were. She told herself that giving him these details would be a kind of imposition. Just . . . common. Nothing a famous person would be interested to hear or should be expected to indulge.

Peter was still looking at her. His mouth twisted a little at the corner, an expression of awkward sympathy Lily knew well from other times she had revealed her little family tragedy to friends.

Lily thought Peter might leave it there. But she didn't know. There was an off chance the world-renowned composer of gorgeous lyrics and melodies might drop some beautiful, unforgettable sentiment just for her.

Peter gave a single, curt nod and looked back at the device in her hands.

So much for sentiment, she thought.

"Right, sorry, I was explaining the wires," Lily said. "My father—his name was Frederick Barnes—was a psychologist with a sideline in neuroscience. He studied the mind and consciousness. He wanted to know where our selves come from. Our personalities. How much was a reaction to external stimuli and how much, if anything, was baked in from birth."

"Nature versus nurture," Peter said as he made a few adjustments to the plane's instruments.

"Sure. He was a bit of a hippie. Got very into the metaphysical, even did a lot of experiments with altered states of consciousness. He was . . . away a lot. Literally and figuratively."

"Acid?" Peter asked.

"Oh, yes. And peyote, and mescaline, and all sorts of things. He wanted to see what happened to the brain when it was pushed to new places. He was an interesting person."

"Good dad?" Peter said.

"When he was around," she answered. "Anyway, he invented a bunch of gadgets to help him analyze what was going on in the brain. Like EEGs, but customized. When he died, he was trying to build a device that would map a person's consciousness, like a visualization of their soul."

"Trippy."

"Yep. Anyway, he had a particular way of wiring things up in his inventions . . . wove them together in a kind of pattern. Very distinctive. He said it conveyed a certain metaphysical power to the devices and increased their overall efficiency by, like, ten percent. Nonsense . . . but he used it a lot. I saw it often when I was a child. And when I opened this thing up back in my lab in Hong Kong"—Lily pointed at the carbon scrubber—"there it was again. The Mechanical Mandala, big as life."

Peter learned forward, took another peek inside the device, then looked back up at Lily. He raised an eyebrow.

"No, I don't know what it means, Peter," she said. "Maybe my dad licensed or sold a design to your Intercessionists before he died, and some version of his little wiring trick made it into this device. Maybe it *does* do something important and helps make this thing work. I have no idea.

"But it's . . . his, somehow. A piece of him that found its way to me. No . . . that's not right. This was sent to me. This was purposeful. There's a story here, a message."

A puzzle, Lily thought.

"A Wonder Path," Peter said, his voice hushed.

Lily touched the mandala wires inside the broken cylinder, gently moving her fingertip along the loops and crossings.

"I hope so," she said. "I'm going to follow this thing back to where it came from. Maybe it'll end up helping us both."

Peter nodded, then flipped open a storage compartment in the instrument console between them, revealing a thick, square wallet of black canvas with a zipper along its edges.

"Movie?" he said. "Long flight yet. Discs. Not online."

"Sure," Lily said.

And so they settled in and watched the tenth and supposedly final film by Quentin Tarantino. Once it was over, Lily fell asleep, awakened later by a very full bladder. She attended to that requirement, then returned to the cockpit. Peter Match was staring out at the night sky, alert. She wondered if the pain kept him awake.

They didn't talk much for the rest of the flight. They landed some hours later at Heathrow Airport, just outside London. Lily hid in the lavatory again while the immigration authorities cleared Peter Match to enter the United Kingdom. This occurred with no more fuss than he'd encountered when they left Hong Kong.

Another sports car waited on the tarmac, once again an Aston Martin. Peter had a type, apparently. This was an older model, that classic low-slung look Lily associated with spy movies. They drove nearly due west for just over two hours to a low stone home not far from Gloucester, with outbuildings scattered around the grassy meadows surrounding it.

Lily got out of the car, walked to the front door, rang the bell. She no longer had a key. Hadn't for a long time.

The door opened. A tall woman stood there, late middle age, slender. She had olive skin and dark eyes, hair cropped short in a style younger than her years would ordinarily support if not for her strikingly beautiful face. A shifting scrum of emotions fought a mighty battle for control over the woman's expression—shock, joy, and perhaps even a touch of anger.

"Hi, Mum," Lily said.

I. THIRTEEN

GLOUCESTER. PINETUM DRIVE.

51°52′07.2″N, 2°18′53.5″W

Adriana Barnes ushered her daughter inside—few words were offered, and just a short, awkward embrace—then vanished into the kitchen to prepare tea. Adriana had been born in Spain, but the rules of British hospitality were deeply imprinted upon her after decades in the north.

Lily took a seat in the living room, in an armchair with a white-on-blue fleur-de-lis pattern. The room looked as it had on her last visit five years before, and for the decade before that. The decor still worked, though—a nice mix of what Lily's limited expertise classified as "modern" and "classic" that registered as timelessly eclectic.

That wasn't a bad descriptor for Adriana herself. She looked as beautiful in her late fifties as at any point in Lily's youth. This was a surprise visit. Lily hadn't called ahead, and her mother hadn't had time to put on makeup or do her hair or select an outfit. She was in jeans and a T-shirt with a long cardigan over it, her hair pulled back in a bun, secured by a few chopsticks. After returning to the living room with the tea, Adriana had curled up on her sofa with her legs tucked beneath her.

She was gorgeous. Regal.

Like national heritage or athleticism or an obvious disability for others, Adriana Barnes's beauty was deeply central to her entire life, the way she navigated the world. Her looks gathered attention from men and women alike, with sexual interest beside the point. People paid attention to Adriana in the same way they paid attention to a particularly vibrant rainbow, or a gorgeous antique Rolls-Royce on the roadway, or a whale leaping from the sea. A *Well, you don't see* that *every day* sort of focus.

Lily's mother didn't seem bothered by that attention, or even pay much notice to the many privileges it offered her. She didn't bemoan *or* celebrate the fact that what she was, most people were not.

That "not" category included Lily. They were both tall and slim, but that was as far as the resemblance went. Lily's skin was an intermediate shade between her mother's olive and her father's solid British paleness. She had that red hair, utterly unlike her mother's silky dark waves, probably derived from some relative farther up the chain on Frederick's side. It all combined to create a woman who could not be called ugly, but who wasn't the showstopper that her mother was. Lily Barnes thought she possessed the appeal of a well-designed ad on the wall at a tube station or a pleasant song on the radio. Interesting, quite nice, well done . . . but you didn't spend much time thinking about it later.

That hadn't mattered when Lily was young, but as she grew, it became increasingly clear that the two women moved through different worlds. Adriana was one of the world's most historically valuable things—a staggeringly gorgeous woman. Lily was something that, traditionally, generated a more complex response—a very intelligent woman not particularly interested in whether other people enjoyed her company.

Lily was fairly certain she and her mother loved each other. She was also certain that the moment her father died, they could no longer understand each other. Frederick was the bridge between them, the translator, the person they loved in common, the thing that made them even partially the same. With him gone . . . their lives diverged almost immediately, even while Lily was still living in this house. They could no longer see each other in each other.

While her mother poured the tea, Lily did a more focused scan of the living room, confirming that very little had changed in the past five years. A few pillows, perhaps. A fancy TV—that was new. But the couch was the same; the chairs were the same. Most telling, so were the photos on the wall. Images from Lily's youth, pictures of her and her father, pictures of the three of them, pictures of Adriana and Frederick—every combination, but nothing more recent than seventeen years back.

No evidence of anyone else in her mother's life. Adriana could have had a thousand lovers since her father's death—and possibly had; it was probably effortless for her—but it seemed like the long-term-partner-seeking impulse in her mother's life had ended the day Lily's father died. Adriana had never replaced Frederick Barnes with anyone else, though she seemed to restrict her life in no other ways. She had a vibrant social life, loved to dance, and had traveled often in the pre-Grey world. She sent Lily photos from exotic locations posing in bikinis and gowns that begged the question of who was taking the pictures.

Lily's impression was that Adriana had filled her life quota of exactly one marriage, to the man she chose, had the child she would have with that man, and there was no point in trying for something else that would never possibly measure up.

Was that right? Or good? Lily didn't know. It was a choice, and certainly not hers to make. The choice she *had* made was to leave Gloucester as soon as she possibly could, to begin her own life, first at university and then on the other side of the world.

"So you're finally back from Hong Kong, darling," Adriana said in her mild (and of course impossibly lovely and elegant) accent. "I almost wish you'd stayed over there. Planes are such a risk these days. Will you not have a biscuit? I have those ones you like."

The lovely little serving Adriana had set out on the coffee table did in fact include bourbon creams, Lily's longtime favorite sort of biscuit. She hadn't tasted one in ages. In the best of times they were challenging to find in Hong Kong, requiring a trip to one of the specialty shops that sold foodstuffs imported from Britain for the expat community. But these were not the best of times, and most of those shops had closed after the Grey exponentially increased the difficulty of international shipping, already complicated by the 2020 pandemic.

Lily took one of the biscuits and bit off half, savoring the dark chocolate filling. Stale but good—though she'd have taken an actual glass of bourbon just about then. Perhaps after dinner she and Peter could swing down to the Chester in town and see about finding the real thing. She hadn't been to that pub in ages, and she—Lily caught herself, amazed at how casually she assumed she and Peter Match would be doing anything at all together.

"Good?" Adriana asked.

"Mm-hm," Lily said, swallowing. "I didn't take a plane to get here. Well, I did, but not the usual way. It was safe."

Her mother raised an eyebrow.

"What's the unusual way to take a plane? Did you ride on the wing? Doesn't sound very— Wait. Lily. Did you get a pilot's license? Did you buy your own plane? This is wonderful news. Give me ten minutes to pack a bag. I haven't been to Goa in ages. Or, better yet, let's go to the States. Did you hear what Team Joy Joy did to the Statue of Liberty? I'd like to see that in person."

"I came in my friend's plane, Mother."

Her mother glanced out the window at Peter Match, leaning against the Aston Martin's hood and smoking a cigarette. Lily supposed that when you had late-stage throat cancer, one or two puffs wouldn't make much of a difference.

"He's got a plane *and* that fancy ride? Well done, dear."

"It's not like that. We're just friends."

"No man flies his 'just friend' halfway around the world in his private plane. I'm glad you found someone new after David, Lily. I worry about you, all alone on the other side of the world."

"You . . . worry about me? About me being alone?" Lily said. "Since when?"

A look of surprise crossed Adriana's face.

"Why, always, dear. I'm your mother."

Lily wanted to let it go. She knew she should. But it was impossible to be in this house without thinking about her father, and the time after her father, and so—

"You stopped being my mother as soon as we got home from the funeral," Lily said.

The surprise on Adriana's face turned to shock.

"*What?*" she said. "What are you talking about?"

"Do you know how badly I needed you? I was only fifteen years old, and you *left* me, Mother."

"I didn't leave you! I was here the whole time," Adriana said.

"Not here," Lily said, waving an arm in a wide circle that encompassed the house, then pointing at her heart. "Here."

"You left *me,* Lily," Adriana said, her face reddening. "The first moment you could, first to university and then to Hong Kong. *The other side of the world.* How dare you turn this around on me!"

Her lip curled.

"You didn't need me, Lily. You made that very clear. And just look how well you've done, with your vibrant life full of laughter and airplanes and love."

"Mother, you know what?" Lily said. "Fuck you."

Oh god, Lily thought. *I didn't mean that. I love you. I just miss you. I'm in trouble, and I wish I could ask you for the kind of help I really need, but I'm so afraid you'd say no, and so I'm taking all that fear and just—*

Adriana had gone very still. She turned to look out the window, where Peter was still working on his cigarette, his head tilted up toward the sky.

"Your friend out there won't even be that if you leave him sitting out in the drive. I've taught you better than this, Lily. Invite him in."

"He's not much of a talker."

"Then he can sit and drink his tea. I'll do all the talking."

Adriana stood, walking purposefully to the kitchen, presumably to grab a third cup. Lily sighed, got up, went to the front door. She waved Peter in. He dropped his cigarette, ground it under the heel of his boot, and walked up to Lily, a question on his face.

"My mother wants to meet you."

He smiled wearily and nodded. *Happens a lot* was the message conveyed.

She stepped back and let him in. Adriana stood waiting, holding a mug of tea, smiling her beautiful, welcoming smile, any emotional fallout from her argument with Lily utterly invisible. Peter stopped dead when he saw her, presumably reacting to her appearance. Lily sighed, but she wasn't frustrated. It was nothing new. Might as well be angry at the sun for rising.

"Hello. I am Adriana Barnes," she said, and handed Peter the steaming mug. "Thank you for bringing my daughter home safely."

There was a moment, a pause, an awkwardness, as if things were not going exactly according to expectations, and no one quite knew what to do next.

Lily put it together. Adriana wanted Peter to introduce himself, and Peter didn't realize he needed to—he was who he was, after all.

"This is Peter Match," she said.

"A pleasure," Adriana replied. "Let's sit. I understand you're a pilot?"

Peter cast a bemused glance at Lily. She wondered if he was annoyed or if it was a welcome break from the constant pressure of recognition.

"He's not a pilot," Lily said. "I mean, he knows how to fly a plane, but he's a pop singer. Quite well-known, in fact."

"Is that so?" Adriana said, casting an appraising glance over Peter, who took a long sip of his tea. "I was impressed by the car, and the plane was icing on the cake. If you're a pop star to boot . . . Lily, I'll say it again. Well done. Where did such an interesting man come from?"

"I was born in Milwaukee," Peter said, his voice slightly smoother than usual, thanks to the healing powers of good Darjeeling.

"Oh, that's ruined it," Adriana said, affecting a frown. "I didn't realize he was American."

"Enough, Mother," Lily said. "Don't bother Peter. He's resting his voice. Doctor's orders."

Adriana took this in stride.

"Of course," she said, sounding slightly disappointed to be unable to pursue the interrogation she clearly intended. "Lily, it's wonderful to see you and to meet your friend, but why have you come all this way? And without calling ahead? We both know travel's getting complicated . . . Is something the matter?"

"It's about this," Lily answered.

She reached into her bag and produced the carbon scrubber, not taking time to explain what it was. The purpose of the device didn't matter; she just wanted Adriana to see the same unique configuration of wires she had shown Peter on the plane. Lily held it out, tilting it so her mother could see.

Adriana's face went white. She shrank back on the couch. She looked up, her eyes wide.

"What is that?" she said. "Where did you get that?"

"In Hong Kong," Lily answered. "I came across it in my job. But you see it, too, right? I'm not crazy."

"Your father," Adriana said, her voice just above a whisper. "His . . . that little sculpture he liked to make."

"This is hard for me too," Lily said. "I opened this thing up and saw this and . . . I still don't really know what to think. My working theory is that Dad licensed some of his technology out before he died. I know we don't really talk about him much, and I hope this isn't painful, but this is a part of Dad's story I'd really like to understand. Did he ever do any work with climate change mitigation companies?"

"You mean . . . like your job?" Adriana said, her eyes far away. "No, I don't remember anything like that. He worked with the mind, not the weather. But I didn't follow your father's business dealings very closely. He had his role, I had mine."

Lily agreed with that wholeheartedly. Her father was the mostly distant genius, the stability, the bedrock. Her mother was the warm, kind source of endless love and affection. The light, the laugh, the charm, the joy. She was the frosting, he was the cake, and Lily was the person for whom it was all made.

Until her father died, and then Adriana didn't know what she was, and tried to be everything, the whole bloody cake. She wanted to move back to Spain and take Lily there, where there was more family, more of a support network, but Lily was a teenager and abjectly refused, and in time the impulse to head south faded and they stayed in Gloucester and pulled further from each other with every passing day. The love curdled, the light faded, and wounds were created that clearly had never healed.

Barely even scarred over, Lily thought, remembering the things they had just said to each other.

"But surely by now . . . ," she said. "Haven't you gone through his files? It's been almost twenty years. Dad's work provides your livelihood."

"The payments keep coming, Lily. What more do I need to know?"

"Could I . . . poke around in his papers a bit? Whatever's left, I mean." Lily asked.

"It's all still as he left it," Adriana said. "I never touched a thing."

Lily's eyes slid over the framed photographs on the walls, frozen moments from a long-vanished life, and realized that, yes, of course that would be the case.

Adriana considered, then looked up and smiled.

"Lily, of course. Look at whatever you like. In fact, that would be wonderful. You and your father . . . both such big thinkers. I'm sure you'll connect with his work in a way I never did."

She set down her mug, got up, and went over to a bureau against the wall, returning a moment later with an iron key.

"It'll be musty back there. I haven't cleaned, I'm afraid. For all I know, garden mice have chewed through everything he left. But have a look. See what you can find."

Lily reached for the key, and at the last moment her mother pulled it back.

"If you find any money or nice whisky back there, that's mine. And if you come across a red photo album, for the sake of your pure, innocent spirit, leave it alone. Your father and I liked to . . . document our work, let's say."

Peter Match chuckled.

"Peter can look, though," Adriana said.

"Dear god, Mum," Lily said, and snatched the key from her mother's hand.

She knew this little piece of metal. She'd seen her father use it hundreds of times, as he'd disappear into his office/lab/cave for hours after dinner, on weekends—every chance he got, really.

She stood up. Peter followed suit.

"Actually," her mother said, putting a hand on his arm. "I was wondering . . . do you have any of your music? I'd love to hear a bit."

Peter smiled. He reached inside his coat and retrieved a flash drive.

"Last recordings I made . . . ," he croaked.

"Before" being the unspoken word that ended that sentence.

"Very good," Adriana said. "I'll bring out the computer."

Lily actually wanted to hear that music—she wondered what Peter Match had laid down, considering he'd have known he was recording what would probably be his last songs. She wasn't an oncologist, but she had a sense that even if he did somehow beat his cancer, odds were his throat would never again produce the honeysuckle tone for which it was known.

But then again, who knew what might be within the capabilities of the people at the end of the Wonder Path? Lily had in her possession a device that could solve the climate crisis. Throat cancer seemed like small potatoes in comparison.

She left the kitchen through the back door, leaving behind the sound of her mother chattering away to the rock star.

Dr. Frederick Barnes's office was in a stone slate-roofed outbuilding at the back edge of their property, built into and up against the wall that surrounded it. Stolid, imperturbable, hundreds of years old, with a heavy wooden door painted white. The building was well-maintained—even if Adriana hadn't gone inside in years, she was keeping up appearances on the exterior.

Very like her.

Lily unlocked the door and breathed in. The first scent was of her father's pipe tobacco, still, after all this time, saturating the air. Once you got past that, there was old paper, dust, age. Dim light streamed through the dusty windows, and she flipped on a light switch near the door—the fixtures lit up, brightening the space considerably.

The structure had two rooms—the first a study featuring an ancient sprung couch that still bore the imprint of her father's prone form. Lily was here now, and also she was eight, on tiptoes, sneaking in to look at the painting hung on the wall opposite the couch, trying to make sure she didn't disturb Frederick Barnes as he lay on that couch, one arm flung up above his head, eyes closed, deep in either contemplation or sleep.

Lily looked at that painting now and felt a little thud in her soul at the disconnect between how fascinated she'd been with it as a child and how indifferent she was to it now. The thing was huge, two meters high, commissioned by Lily's father from a local artist before she was born. It looked like a thousand bolts of lightning, or perhaps a maze made of light—an ever-forking set of pathways that grew finer and finer as they progressed. Frederick used to lie on his ratty, impossibly soft couch and stare at it, often after dosing up on something from one of the forbidden drawers in his workroom.

The painting depicted the "innerfinity"—Dr. Frederick Barnes's term for the human mind, at least as he imagined it to be. Each forking pathway represented electrical impulses in the brain as it considered, chose, remembered. Before he died, one of her father's professional goals was to find a way to literally map consciousness as it grew in the human brain from birth. He'd never figured it out, but Lily knew her father expected a successful result to look very much like the painting.

She went to one of the bookshelves lining the walls, ran her finger along the spines. Mostly medical texts and philosophy treatises, interspersed with antique instruments of celestial navigation, displayed like trophies.

The old sextants and astrolabes and marine chronometers weren't just for show—Dr. Barnes actually used them when he went out sailing. He was a voyager, and not just into the outer world. Just as frequently, he vanished into the deep recesses of his own mind.

Into the innerfinity, Lily thought.

A silly word, almost embarrassing—but Frederick Barnes never put it in his books or lectures, and only used it with his daughter, and so Lily had loved it. Now, as an adult, her opinions were more nuanced.

Years after her father's death, once she possessed the necessary scientific background, Lily read his published papers. Frederick's theories were centered on ethereal, ephemeral, largely unprovable concepts about the formation of ideas, memories, behavior. It was all just . . . opinions. In his world, two plus two could equal three. Or zero. Or a hummingbird. She knew that was the nature of the slippery beast that was neuroscience and probably why his work was popular—you could find anything you wanted in it. But, to Lily, her father's work didn't feel like science at all. It felt like philosophy. Frederick Barnes seemed to go out of his way to avoid finding any real answers, and so there was, as far as Lily Barnes was concerned, no real point.

She left the study and entered the second, larger room, where the real work was done. A thick wooden desk against the far wall held a decades-old computer and monitor, a massive grey assembly like a stack of cinder blocks. Notebooks, an overflowing ashtray. A workbench and tools. Yards upon yards of cabinets and drawers and storage compartments filled with the components Frederick used in his experiments.

Lily was forbidden from exploring those drawers, though of course she had. Many held innocuous bits of wire, screws, solder, and the like, but some held a different sort of tool. Dark curls of fungus, scraps of paper meant to be left on the tongue to dissolve, vials with eyedroppers screwed into them, powders and pills . . . Lily had never tried any of them, and even as an adult never ventured any deeper into drug use than the occasional joint. It all just seemed like a waste of time, things her father had used to go away, before he went away once and for all.

Three of the cabinets held her father's files, each grey-metal drawer with a hand-printed label offering the date range contained within. Lily tried to call up her earliest memory of the Mechanical Mandala. Not before her twelfth birthday, surely, because she clearly remembered bursting into this office on that wonderful day to see if he'd be joining for cake and being yelled at for disturbing him.

He'd been building some gadget on the workbench, with the unique wiring pattern clearly exposed—distinctive to her even then.

So . . . I need to look through the files starting three years before he died, she thought, *and go forward from there.*

Lily found the drawer she wanted, opening it to see a long row of documents stashed in manila folders, each labeled neatly in her father's hand. Hundreds of pages.

She sighed and brought the first twenty folders to her father's desk, notably unmarred by anything personal like, say, a photo of Dr. Barnes's wife or child. She sat and opened the first file.

Many of the documents were publishing contracts or appearance agreements. Her father had written several books considered classics in his field, taught classes at universities across the world, and pulled down significant speaking fees for his lectures. Beyond that, he had authored a series of populist renderings of his theories—*The I Within* was the first, followed by *The You Within* and finally *The We Within*—all bestsellers within that particular category of nonfiction straddling New Age, spiritualism, self-help and "science."

The cumulative effect was an ongoing sinecure for her mother that, while not exactly private-jet money, let her live in relative comfort after Frederick's death. She'd been able to continue raising their daughter and pay for Lily's university education without having to worry about finding a job.

Lily flipped through the documents quickly. She paused only when she saw her father's handwriting, scanning for notes he might have jotted down with respect to work in climate mitigation or, possibly, a secret society of super-geniuses.

It turned out that Frederick Barnes liked to doodle. Many of his papers had terribly rendered boats in the margins but occasionally also schematics, seeds of ideas. To these, Lily paid closer attention. Not because she expected them to lead her to the end of the Wonder Path, but because they were . . . him. The man he was when he wasn't her father, or Adriana's husband, or a professor, or a scientist. Just himself.

At some point Peter Match slipped into the room. She handed him a stack of files and a packet of tape flags, telling him to mark anything that looked promising.

They worked in silence for a while, breathing in air thick with newly disturbed dust. The story told by the files presented a fascinating shadow version of Lily's own experience of these years. A contract to appear in Sydney reminded her of a long two weeks with Adriana and a packet of kangaroo jerky her father brought home. She saw the itinerary for her father's trip to Paris, the one where he'd dropped her off at the Louvre, and saw all the things he'd done that day. Pieces slotted into the puzzle of his life beyond her.

Lily was deep in a file from the year she turned fourteen, her energy flagging (she desperately needed a proper bed) when she flipped over a document to reveal a sheet of notepaper featuring a drawing in her father's rickety hand. Here, laid out with a precision unlike most of Frederick Barnes's doodles, was a smaller, less intricate version of the framed painting out in the study: the electrical labyrinth of human consciousness. That was itself nested into a symbol Lily had first seen on a centuries-old contract, and then more recently on a plaque outside a building in Hong Kong—the odd figure eight made up of much tinier figure eights.

The intricacy of the drawing, and the time and focus it must have required, spoke volumes. Her father had cared about whatever this meant—deeply.

Right in the center of the whole assembly, nestled like an egg in a nest . . . was a telephone number.

"Huh," she said.

Peter Match looked up from his own papers and she showed him what she had found.

"Do you think this could be something?"

He shrugged, a noncommittal maybe of a gesture.

Lily reached for her satchel to retrieve her phone before she remembered she wasn't supposed to use it. Would Hong Kong's authorities get an alert all the way from England if she turned it on? She didn't know but didn't want to take the chance. Peter produced his own cell, but Lily waved it away.

"No. They might have connected you to all of this by now, be tracking your phone too," she said. "I have a better idea."

She moved into the study, bringing the doodled-upon sheet of notepaper. On a low table next to the couch was an ancient rotary telephone. She lifted the headset, suspecting that if her mother had kept up with the electric bill in here, she might also have forgotten to disconnect the . . .

A dial tone sounded in Lily's ear. Peter Match stood in the doorway leading to the inner office, watching her, his eyes alight.

"Shall we?" she said, holding up the sheet of paper.

I. FOURTEEN

GLOUCESTER. THE GARDEN OFFICE OF FREDERICK BARNES.

51°52'07.4"N, 2°18'53.1"W

Lily dialed the number. It began with 00, so clearly an international exchange, followed by a country code she didn't recognize—874. After that came the longest phone number she had ever seen. It took ages to roll the old rotary dial round to each digit, wait for it to spin back to zero, and then put in the next.

It's like a combination lock, she thought, and that made her smile, because hopefully it was exactly that.

And then she caught herself smiling and realized it had been actual *hours* since she'd thought about the Grey or the increasingly awful state of the world. Wonder Path indeed.

The dial clacked back to zero after Lily spun it to the final digit (a nine) and she held the handset to her ear. She waited, unsure of what would happen—ringing on the other side as the call attempted to go through, or a recording saying it could not be completed, that there was some error in transmission. The language of that voice, even its accent, could be a clue. A compass heading, even if vague.

Lily wondered if David could do something with the number. Assuming she could find a safe way to get in touch with him and if he'd be willing and able to help. She wasn't really sure where they'd left things. She missed him, as unfair as that was. She no longer had the right to miss David Johanssen.

Peter Match was watching, one eyebrow raised.

"Just silence," she said, listening closely. "But not like a dead line. There's something . . ."

What she heard on the other end of the line was not easily described. No sound, but not *nothing*. The silence of a filled balloon.

And then, a voice, with no warning, in English, female, with a very light French accent.

"Welcome to us. Please present yourself," the woman said, her voice accompanied by distant background music, strings doing something intricate and contrapuntal in 6/8 time, rolling and crashing back on itself like waves on a beach, asking a question that was never answered.

Lily didn't respond, stunned silent by the way the woman had come on the line without warning or the bizarre phrasing or the speech or the increasingly hypnotic music or all three.

"Present yourself," the voice said again, and the music's emotional cadence changed. It was tense now, wary.

Does this call have a . . . soundtrack? Lily wondered. *In real time*?

"I'm . . . Lily Barnes," she said. "I found this number in my father's study—Dr. Frederick Barnes. He passed away many years ago, but I'm looking for people he might have worked with. I don't know if that's you, but anything you could tell me would be incredibly helpful."

Just the music, which had changed again. Low now, deep in the bass, the pitch raising slightly every few seconds. It reminded Lily of the tone of a sine wave on an oscilloscope. The sound of ominous portent.

"Thank you," the woman said. "Someone will be along."

The music stopped.

"Wait—" Lily said, but she knew the line was dead.

She looked at Peter Match, who had an avid expression on his face, a *Tell me what just happened or I will literally die* look.

"It was strange," she told him. "A voice, and music, but it felt like I was talking *to* the music, somehow. I've never experienced anything like it. I don't even know who it was. They said about six words and hung up. Told me 'Someone would be along.' What do you suppose *that* means?"

Peter frowned. He seemed . . . angry, almost. Hugely frustrated. She got that. Perhaps he'd let himself hope.

"I can try calling again."

Peter lifted a hand, a slight gesture of acquiescence. *Sure, why the fuck not?*

Something that had been happening for at least half a minute now pushed its way into Lily's full awareness. The telephone's handset was growing warm.

No . . . *hot.*

She dropped it, and the handset fell to the couch.

"Christ," she said, looking at her palm, expecting to see a scorch mark.

A wave of heat surged from the phone, from the couch, rushing past Lily and Peter, ruffling their hair, like stepping out from an air-conditioned building into tropical heat. A scent, too, like a garbage can left out in that same hot sun.

Something whiffed around the room, circling them, then settling in the entrance to her father's office. Papers swirled up from the desk and the dustbin below it, along with little bits of debris, pencil shavings, food wrappers, and the like. They coalesced around the presence in the doorway, collapsing and molding themselves into a humanoid shape, like pieces of plastic wrap around a roast.

The trash became a man, and Lily did not know if it surrounded a form that was already there or it had compressed an unformed presence into a recognizable shape.

The thing had a face made partially of a crumpled bit of notepaper and the rest from a torn packet of crisps, foil side out. A mouth formed from paper festooned with her father's handwriting, opening and closing, no sound emerging.

It lifted its arms high, like a priest delivering a sermon. The rotting-trash odor wafted from its body. Its mouth opened wider and its head shook. It was laughing.

Dread bloomed in Lily, an ice-cold welling up that began in her core and surged to fill every part of her. She was in her *father's study,* a space she had visited during her entire childhood, usually reading quietly on the couch while her father worked in the office. She was in that familiar, ordinary, safe space, and something had come. An impossible thing, and now nothing was safe.

She was back under the water after falling off the boat near the Hebrides. She was twenty, reeling from far too much vodka, in the ladies in a pub in Leeds, her head not over but *in* the toilet. She was twenty-nine, watching a bus barrel toward her because she had stumbled at a corner in Wan Chai and fallen to her knees in the street. It was Chinese New Year in Lan Kwai Fong and she was in the midst of being trampled by too many people stampeding through those slick, wet, narrow alleys. She was about to die. She was utterly certain.

A *tchkk* sound to her left, and she snapped her head to see. Peter Match had fire in his hand.

He threw it, a small silver box with a flame at one end, and Lily recognized it as a lighter, one of the cool American ones, a Zippo.

The thing in the room with them caught it. The corners of its mouth turned up.

It burst into flames.

The bits of rubbish went up in a moment, transforming into tiny black flakes drifting through the air. Peter's lighter fell to the floor. The carpet caught, but Peter stamped out the flames and snatched up the lighter, snapping it closed and dropping it in his pocket.

Lily was astonished at his presence of mind.

"What *was* that?" she said.

Peter gave her an astonished expression. *Does it matter?* He pointed at the door.

"We need to get the fuck out of here," he said, his voice stronger than usual—fueled by adrenaline, Lily thought.

She had a bit of that going on herself. Her heart was throbbing, her head felt light, and she was still processing what she'd seen. Her rational mind was insisting nothing had happened, nothing at all—but the little black flakes still drifted through the air, and the scent of an overflowing August dumpster still filled the room.

Peter reached past her and grabbed the piece of paper with her father's diagram and the phone number, then headed for the door without a look back.

Lily took a moment. Her head swam. She glanced around her father's office one final time, then left, following Peter Match across the back garden.

How will I possibly explain this to mother? she wondered. *Is she safe here? Am I? Was that the security system Mr. Coriander and the others warned me about? Did that thing come for all the other travelers of the Wonder Path?*

Peter cut around the house, clearly headed for his car.

"Hey," Lily called to him. "My mother."

The singer stopped. Clearly he'd forgotten all about Adriana Barnes. He had the sheet of notepaper from the study clutched in one hand, and his expression was, for once, unreadable. He nodded quickly and gave her a thumbs-up, then snapped his fingers a few times. *Make it fast.*

Lily ran into her childhood home through the back door to the kitchen.

"Mum?" she called.

No response. Lily frowned. She moved into the living room and saw her mother on the couch with her laptop open in front of her, headphones on, the screen's glow shining on her face.

"Didn't you hear me?"

Adriana's eyes were fixed on her screen, and though Lily couldn't see the display, dread mounted in her heart. She walked slowly over to her mother and looked at her face.

Her mother's gaze slowly rolled up to Lily. No real reaction, barely any recognition. Her face . . . and the spirit behind it . . . had gone Grey.

"*No*," Lily screamed.

She spun the laptop toward her, ready to slam it closed if need be, and saw a list of YouTube clips of Peter Match. Live shows, fan-made videos of his recordings with the lyrics scrolling against his work, official clips from his label, all the hits, from "We Are the Light" to "The Stirring Days." The entire scenario ran through in Lily's mind—Peter had played Adriana some of his newest music and then left to join Lily out back. Her mother, intrigued, had searched for more and, despite the various filters and safeguards, had stumbled upon a clip or a pop-up ad with the Despair Manifesto inserted by Team Joy Joy. That was all it would take.

Her mother—her confounding, hidden, but always *alive* mother—had the Grey.

"Hello, dear," Adriana said, her voice toneless. "If you'd like more tea, help yourself. Forgive me, but I don't really feel up to fixing anything at the moment."

A wave of despair surged up within Lily, overwhelming the fear and disorientation. Not just despair, either. Guilt. She'd argued with Adriana, told her own mother to fuck off and die, and though she'd seemed to shrug it off, clearly she hadn't. Who would?

Lily had given her own mother the Grey, and now it was going to take her, too, and at this point she thought it might be simpler. What was the point? She—

A hand on her shoulder, and she looked up to see Peter Match. He recognized what had happened, too, and his expression was set in a cast of deepest sympathy.

"I'm so sorry, Lily," he said, his voice barely above a whisper.

"I did this," she said. "I made this happen."

"No, you didn't," Peter said. "You can't blame yourself."

"I don't know what to do," Lily said.

"Care center—just for now. So she's safe. I can arrange for a much better facility. Don't worry about cost. I'll have my team handle it. But . . . we need to go."

Speaking these words had clearly cost Peter a great deal. By the end, his voice was so ragged she could barely understand him. But he was right.

"I'll pack a bag for her," Lily said. "I'm sure there's a center in town. I can call them."

Urgent care facilities had popped up everywhere to provide immediate monitoring, diagnosis and support for people newly afflicted with the Grey. They were fully staffed, twenty-four hours per day, set up and funded by the government. Informally called darkhouses, they were mostly in place to ensure that Grey victims weren't able to commit suicide, but they had a range of therapeutic and pharmaceutical treatments to offer as well.

The darkhouses were not good places—or bad places, either. They were . . . grey. But they would keep Lily's mother alive until she could find a more permanent solution. Somewhere like

David's place. Hopefully the checks from her father's work would cover that expense as well.

Lily packed a bag, made the call, waited for the emergency services to come round—a pair of cheerful, efficient women who helped her mother into a sedan that would take her to the darkhouse. They provided all the information Lily might need to visit Adriana, contact her, move her, all of it. Lily gave these women her telephone number—even though she had no idea when she might be able to use her cell again.

She watched the vehicle pull away down the drive. The whole episode, from discovering her mother to the car driving away, had taken no more than an hour.

"What is happening to me?" she asked Peter, standing next to her on her mother's front stoop. "So much . . . so quickly. How?"

On the breeze, a faint whiff of rot. They both smelled it.

Peter rubbed at his forehead, a gesture of exhaustion and frustration.

He extended his thumb and pinkie finger from his fist and swept them upward, in a gently rising curve.

Time to fly.

I. FIFTEEN

LOS ANGELES.
WILDWOOD CANYON PARK.

34°12′15.2″N, 118°18′11.0″W

Aunt Jane sipped her drink while perched atop the spine of Los Angeles—the Santa Monica Mountains, the range that split the city right down the middle. She was dining at a restaurant called the Castaway. She loved that name. After all, humanity was adrift, and no one was coming to the rescue.

The space was mostly a huge open patio that boasted views of both sides of the enormous divided city. To the south, Hollywood, Santa Monica, Venice Beach, Beverly Hills. To the north, the entire San Fernando Valley was visible, filled to the brim with low-slung buildings and palm trees, the sprawl stopped only by a low mountain range many miles farther north. Burbank and Calabasas and Glendale and Toluca Lake and Sherman Oaks and Studio City and Van Nuys and all the other little communities filled the valley from edge to edge, like an invasive species that had spread to occupy every available ecological niche. Dusk was coming on, and streetlights popped on against the slowly darkening sky. Beautiful.

Jane sat alone, finishing a steak that, while priced for the view, wasn't half-bad. A rare filet mignon with béarnaise sauce, haricot verts, and lightly fried new potatoes, the last of which she was using to sop up a few remaining drops of sauce.

A few enterprising gentlemen approached her table during the meal, but she gently sent them on their way. She was working.

She chased down the last bite of dinner with a final mouthful of her espresso martini and was pleased to note that her server was at her table before she had even set down her glass.

"One more?" the man said. His name was Sandy, she recalled.

Jane looked at him through her sunglasses and flicked a strand of blond hair from her wig behind her ear. She was hugely recognizable these days—she refused to think of herself as famous—and a bit of misdirection in her appearance was necessary anytime she went out in public. But LA was good about that. No one looked too close even if they thought they knew who you were.

"Yes, please," she said.

"Very good. Any interest in dessert?" Sandy said.

"Oh *absolutely,*" Jane replied, smiling at him. "I'll do the chocolate lava cake. You literally cannot go wrong."

"You literally cannot," the waiter agreed. "Coming right up."

He hustled away, and Jane realized an older woman at the next table was giving her an amused look.

"Two espresso martinis? You'll be up all night!"

Jane pointed her index finger at the woman, grinned.

"Let's hope so."

She'd have winked, but the sunglasses were in the way.

Jane checked her watch. She was getting distracted. She'd never forgive herself if she missed this.

She reached into her purse and removed a pair of opera glasses, peering through them at the sky. The drones were already in the air. Jane knew where to look but also knew it was unlikely she'd be able to see anything. The machines were painted a neutral dark grey that blended in well against the darkening sky, especially from below, and boasted the quietest rotors on the market, further dampened by Team Joy Joy's technicians.

Jane lowered the glasses and tapped her phone's screen to check the time. About ten minutes left.

Aunt Jane looked down at the city below, now ablaze with lights to the horizon—an organism created over centuries by the sustained effort of mankind, always growing and changing, as alive as any creature on the face of the earth.

That would all be over soon. There would be no more growth and change, not in a Grey world. In time, the cities would become mausoleums. Every building a tombstone.

The Grey. Aunt Jane had spent time considering what it was, how it had come to be, and her firm sense was that it was the next step in humanity's evolution. It was as if every person on earth had the same epiphany: it was time. Time to move on, time to let go, time to stop grinding away at a cycle of birth and growth and death and destruction and consumption.

There was no greater meaning. There was only humanity eating itself and eating the world around it.

Evolution was rooted in organisms changing in reaction to the environment around them. What was the Grey if not a natural response to the Anthropocene Age? Completely understandable—and far overdue.

For tens of thousands of years, humanity had cornered the market on delusional thinking, ignoring the costs of progress paid by the innocent. Pretending that civilization was trending toward an increasingly humane world when in fact the opposite was true. Society grew increasingly imbalanced, the vectors of control becoming more sophisticated and subtle. Facebook instead of jackboots. Opioid addiction replacing firing squads. Endless debt just as effective a prison as work camps.

The Grey was the obvious endpoint, a form of convergent

evolution—billions of minds simultaneously coming to the same conclusion about humanity's ultimate failure.

The waiter delivered Aunt Jane's cake and her second martini. She sampled both and set her glass down as she kept her eyes on her watch face. The second hand swept around, and then—

A huge noise rolling up the mountainside. On the patio, glasses shook, cutlery rattled. From ten different locations across the city, blooms of fire. All around Jane, people shot up from their tables, rushed to look, pulled out their phones to film the spectacle.

Jane was pleased it had all happened at the same moment. Precision was important. It said something.

The ten locations included three studio lots in Burbank: Warner Bros., Disney, and CBS/Nickelodeon Studios. At the same time, on the city's south side, pillars of smoke rose above the Paramount, Netflix, and Raleigh studios in Hollywood, as well as Sony out in Santa Monica.

Each of Jane's drones had carried a single M112 demolition charge of C-4 plastic explosive with a white phosphorous smoke grenade snuggled up against it. The C-4 weighed about a pound and a quarter, and the grenade just under two. That was on the heavy side for most hobby drones, but these were special heavy-lift models, hugely expensive and requiring FAA clearance to purchase—but that hadn't been much of a problem. Team Joy Joy now boasted an admiral in its ranks, as well as a number of other powerful, well-placed members.

The drones had landed on the roofs of the studio lots' primary soundstages and executive offices, exploding with their shaped charges cutting down through the roof, scattering specks of white phosphorus burning at 5,000 degrees Fahrenheit. Instant inferno.

The lots mostly had their own on-site fire departments, but none were prepared for ten massive blazes popping up at once. The city's emergency services would respond as well . . . but as the world had seen in Paris, the Grey was taking a toll on those noble organizations.

Team Joy Joy had consulted its members with experience in fire departments when they planned the operation. They suggested the Los Angeles crews would quickly write off the lots and focus on an evacuation and containment strategy, in part because the studios were all behind high walls, which should help prevent the fires from spreading to the city beyond. Jane's people had chosen a night forecast to be windless and sent the drones out at an hour when the studios would be almost empty, the day's shoots well over. The studios would burn but, importantly, not much else. No one should die.

Jane opened her phone and tapped busily away at it for a few moments, pulling up a prerecorded message.

She appeared on her screen sitting in an empty movie theater—no wig, no sunglasses, immediately recognizable as Auntie Jane, Happiness Agent #1 for Team Joy Joy.

She hit send, shooting the message out to the world, then watched it on mute—mouthing along with words she had recorded a few days earlier in a theater in Lexington, Kentucky:

The dream factories are gone. Is that sad? A little bit. I liked going to the movies. I liked bingeing the latest dumb, wonderful thing everyone else was watching. But that time is done—and we need to recognize it. I just didn't want any of you thinking maybe it was worth hanging on until next summer, until that next season drops, or opening weekend. None of that is going to happen. Humanity will not be making new art. The Star Wars have ended. The Friends will not reunite. The Avengers and Justice League will not be back to save the day. That time is over.

This one was a gift from Team Joy Joy to all the artists out there. The musicians, the painters, the writers, the dancers, the chefs . . . just stop. You don't have to work so hard anymore. You don't have to push yourselves. You don't have to kill yourselves. There's nothing to prove. Nothing to strive for. Find the peace in that. You'll see. It's time to rest.

It's time to rest.

It's time to rest.

And embrace joy.

The shot cut away from the empty theater to the Despair Manifesto with no warning. Most people were savvy to that trick now, but it might catch a few. It got its hooks in quickly, the Manifesto did, and every convert to the Grey helped.

Aunt Jane set her phone down. She saw other patrons of the Castaway still standing silent at the railing, watching the flames, gorgeous against the darkening sky. These were Los Angelenos, mostly. They knew exactly what buildings were burning out there. Hell, most of them probably worked in the business.

Aunt Jane called out to her server, who was standing not far away, silent, holding a silver tray with a few cocktails on it.

"Sandy," she said.

The man turned, his face pallid with shock. Jane thought the night's events might just push him over the edge; he'd wake up the next morning Greyed out. Well, if so, there was always a spot on the Team for him, if he could find his way there.

"One more martini, please—and another piece of cake," Aunt Jane said. "I'm celebrating."

I. SIXTEEN

SOUTH OF SHOTTESBROOKE.

51°27'29.4"N, 0°47'42.0"W

THE ASTON MARTIN RACED ALONG THE M4, WEAVING THROUGH traffic as it sped east toward Heathrow. Peter changed lanes, slipping into a gap between a panel van and a delivery truck so tight that Lily actually squeaked in terror as they shot through it.

"Maybe take it a bit—" she began, and then was slammed back in her seat as he hammered the accelerator and the car shot forward, arrowing toward the next clump of unsuspecting vehicles puttering their way along the motorway ahead of them.

Where the hell are the traffic officers? Lily wondered, but like everything else, the Grey had cut off police departments at the knees. They were probably focusing their remaining resources on crimes more significant than speeding.

She thought about her mother, wondering if she would ever see her again. She tried to remember the last words Adriana had said to her before the Grey took her, but she couldn't recall. Lily suspected she would be thinking about that for the rest of her life.

"Where are we going to go?" she asked Peter Match.

His knuckles were white on the wheel. He released one hand and made the takeoff gesture again.

"Yes, the airport, your plane, I get it. But *then* where?" Lily said. "What *was* that thing? The trash creature . . . is it still coming after us? Can we get away from it?"

Peter shook his head. *No idea.*

He reached inside his jacket and removed his phone. He unlocked it and handed it to Lily.

"Coriander," he croaked.

"Ah, good idea," she replied.

Lily pulled up Peter's contacts, resisting the urge to look at his photos, even though his eyes were on the road and he'd never notice. Just at the beginning of the list, she saw an Adele and an Alanis and an Axl and felt a little zip run down her spine.

She tapped "Coriander" into the search bar and the number came up, with the 852 Hong Kong country code. She dialed, and after four or five rings a familiar voice came on the line—honeyed, strong—and at that moment very irritated.

"Peter, you have a lot of nerve calling me after how you left things—and do you have any idea what time it is here?"

Lily tapped the screen, putting the call on speaker.

"Mr. Coriander, it's Lily Barnes. Peter's here, too, but he's driving. He let me use his phone."

"Oh, Lily . . . hello."

His voice modulated, but probably more from surprise than any lessening of ire.

"It really is very late here."

"I know. I wouldn't call if it wasn't an emergency. It's related to the Wonder Path."

"I see . . . ," Coriander said, now fully awake, fully engaged. "How can I help?"

"Peter and I are in England. We came looking for additional information on where we could find the group you told me about—the Intercessionists."

"England? Did you have a particular reason for going there? And . . . you must have flown. What was worth such a risk?"

Coriander's tone had taken on a canny, needful edge.

"We were following a hunch I had, but something happened to us," Lily said. "This will sound ridiculous."

"I assure you, my dear, whatever you're about to tell me, I've heard stranger."

"We encountered a . . . thing. Like a presence in the air. It pulled together a kind of body for itself out of rubbish. It tried to speak, but there was no sound. It—"

"The Garbage Man," Coriander said.

He no longer sounded curious. He sounded afraid.

"It's connected to them. It's a security system," he continued. "It's been around for a very long time. I don't know how you came across it, Lily, or how you survived, but the thing is deadly. We don't have reports from anyone it ever targeted, because none of them lived. We only know about it because of observer reports, dismissed as nonsense by the authorities. If you saw it, it means you got close to them. Close enough for them to consider you a threat."

Coriander's voice was increasing in pace and pitch.

"Will it still come after us?"

"I'm afraid so. It's a hunter."

"Can we kill it?"

"I wouldn't even begin to think of how you would. Your only hope is to stay ahead of it. Keep moving. Try to find a completely clean environment. Anything that might be considered trash can be a channel for its manifestation."

"But what *is* it?" Lily asked, desperation pushing into her voice.

"It's how they keep people away. One of the ways, anyway. The Intercessionists are a *very* private group. They . . . well, what Peter said at dinner wasn't so far off the mark, really. My family did work for them for generations. One day, out of nowhere, back at the turn of the twentieth century, they just stopped communicating with us. We kept the faith for years—decades—but at a certain point it was clear they were just done with us, and any effort to communicate with them was beyond perilous. The entire St. Petersburg office of Calder & Calder ceased to exist, and we still don't really know why. A full branch of my family—gone.

"Our theory was always that the Intercessionists discovered or invented something incredibly precious and decided to protect it by completely withdrawing from the world."

"What do you think they found?"

"We really have no idea, and investigating too closely results in . . . well, you and Mr. Match know all too well. The Garbage Man comes calling."

Mr. Coriander's voice had taken on a resigned empathy, like a doctor delivering a terminal diagnosis with as much kindness as he could. Lily gripped the phone tighter.

"*How do we make it stop hunting us?*" she said, asking the only question that really mattered.

Silence from the other end of the line.

"We warned you to keep your distance, Lily," Coriander finally said. "I'll look in the archives. If I find anything, I'll reach out. Good luck to you both."

The line disconnected.

Lily looked out the window. They were passing a factory complex surrounded by a chain-link fence. Bits of garbage—wrappers and pieces of paper and plastic—were woven through the links. Below it, in the shallow ditch between it and the roadway, more debris. Flecks and swatches of rubbish.

You never realized how much there was. How inescapable the detritus of human society really was.

A sheet of newspaper twisted in the wind from passing cars on the motorway. At least, presumably the wind.

She turned back to Peter.

"Where can we go that doesn't have garbage? There has to be somewhere. A deserted island? A mountaintop?"

Peter did not answer.

A chocolate bar wrapper impacted the windshield, held there by the force of their passage. Peter pushed it away with a quick flip of the wipers.

Another bit of garbage hit the windscreen—an empty crisp packet. And then a torn, ragged piece of fabric plastering itself against the glass. The wipers were still going, but the strips of filthy fabric and plastic were undulating, lifting themselves to stay out of the way of the blades.

Lily felt the car slowing.

"No! Don't stop!" she said. "Maybe we're moving too fast for it to form a body. It can't catch us if we don't stop."

The Aston Martin accelerated again as another wet chunk of something splatted against the windscreen and stuck there, right in front of Peter. He frowned.

All at once, what had to be a hundred pieces of garbage slammed the windscreen at once, completely blocking their forward view. The car's interior went dim.

Peter grunted in frustration but kept driving. He looked out his window, trying to orient himself by the roadside, until litter whipped up to cover it, too, and the window on Lily's side.

The car grew dark, ambient lighting on the dashboard instruments flipping on. Peter began to slow. He had no choice.

A loud noise and the car fishtailed, slewing to one side, spinning. Lily screamed and grasped the handle above the door, knowing neither it nor her seat belt would save her. This was a sports car, designed for speed, not safety.

I'm going to die the same way my father did, she thought.

An impact, a sudden stop that jerked her whole body against the seat belt and yanked her breath from her in a brutal gasp. Lily's head slammed into the refuse-covered window, her spine sending her skull forward like a cracked whip, and she was gone.

I. SEVENTEEN

THE SIDE OF THE ROAD.

51°28′49.8″N, 0°45′46.6″W

LILY SMELLED PETROL AND HOT METAL. HER LEFT ARM FELT deeply wrong, and her head ached, pounding with every heartbeat. She was, she believed, upside down.

The car's interior was full of light again, the garbage gone, but it was all bent, cracked, destroyed. A parody of itself. She couldn't believe she was alive, and—

She looked, being careful to only move her eyes. Her neck didn't seem quite up to performing its usual functions. She could feel sheer agony biding its time in her skull, a wave building, building, just looking for an excuse to break. Peter was still in the driver's seat, stirring, blood on his face. He groaned and opened his eyes, meeting hers.

"We have to get out of the car," Lily said.

He closed his eyes, nodded, and didn't move again.

"Peter?"

No response. Cars on the motorway outside whipped past, the car rocking a bit with their passage, the sound Dopplering as they came and went. Each little wobble sent a twinge of sharp, bone-deep pain through Lily's skull.

She knew she should probably wait for emergency services before she tried to move, but also knew she couldn't. Something was hunting them.

Lily took a breath, held it, and released her seat belt. She slouched down, falling onto her head, neck, and shoulders. Immediate agony. Lily screamed, long and loud. She tried to find a more comfortable position, anything to get the weight off her neck, and couldn't. The car's roof was compressed. There wasn't much room to reorient herself, especially with only one working arm.

Calculations ran through Lily's head as she tried to figure out how much force her current position was exerting on the delicate structures that connected her spine to her brain.

She knew the tensile strength of bone—she knew the tensile strength of just about every material on the planet—and knew how low it was. Compared to carbon fiber, or steel, or even some of the really dense woods, bone wasn't really up to par.

Stop it, you silly idiot, she thought. *Either the neck snaps or it doesn't, but you're not just about to sit here and wait for it to happen, are you?*

She was not. Lily inched herself out through the shattered passenger's-side window like a caterpillar, humping herself along a painful path of jagged metal. She felt new pain in her back and knew she was cutting herself, harming her body further, but she did it anyway.

When finally free, Lily lay on the side of the road, hearing traffic whisk by, catching her breath. She could see what had happened. The car had scraped an overpass support pillar and flipped, skidding along the roadside, leaving a trail of debris—a line of pebbled automotive glass, bits of the car's exterior, even a single tire snapped off its axle. A rear door was missing as well, and the fenders. She was lucky to be alive.

This made her remember Peter, and Lily rolled over, pushing herself to her knees one-handed. Her left arm was broken, or dislocated, or had suffered some other kind of catastrophic injury. It was useless to her.

She got to her feet, her head swimming, and made her way to the driver's side. The door wouldn't open—it was bent along the frame. The window had broken in the crash, though, and she bent painfully and called into the car.

"Peter," she said. "You have to undo your seat belt. I can't get you out."

He stirred again, only barely conscious.

"Your *seat belt*," Lily repeated, mustering as much emphasis in her voice as she could. "Please . . . or you'll have to stay until emergency services come, and I don't know how long that will be. The car could catch fire. Please."

A click from inside the car, and Peter sagged into a position she knew well from having been in it just a few minutes before. Painful, maybe even damaging, the body's whole weight on the neck. The load calculations started to spin in Lily's head again, and she shoved them away.

It wasn't easy to get the singer out of the car, especially with just one good arm, but Lily managed. He did what he could to help her, occasionally letting loose long, deep groans as he squeezed his way through the window, leaving a trail of blood behind him.

They collapsed onto the verge. Hot, stinking wind blasted them as each car passed.

Surely someone will stop soon, Lily thought. *Maybe even a nurse or a doctor.*

But that was wishful thinking in a world where the weight of everyone's problems lay heavy upon them, and the idea of adding anyone else's might be a bridge too far. "Let someone else handle it" was becoming the unofficial motto of the Grey times.

Lily knew there were supposed to be emergency call boxes placed along the country's major roadways, one each mile, and the

M4 certainly qualified. So, assuming they chose the right direction, they would encounter one within at most a half mile, and if they picked wrong, it would be no more than a mile. Lily peered back in the direction of oncoming traffic, trying to see the telltale yellow post of the emergency box. Her vision was blurry. She had no idea which way to go.

A momentary break in traffic, perfectly timed to allow Lily to hear a much smaller noise, a skittering sort of scrape.

She and Peter both turned toward it. A small piece of metal was moving on its own, skidding along the ground, kicking up a little cloud of road dust.

Once they saw the first, it was impossible to miss the others—bits of metal and plastic and glass, wrappers and scraps of paper, being drawn in by some invisible suction like soap suds circling a drain.

The pieces leapt into the air, began to come together and adhere, becoming a scaffolding, like girders in a skyscraper. This was not like the thing that had appeared in Frederick Barnes's office. This was no spirit given vague shape via scraps of paper. What was assembling itself five yards away was a full, complete being.

Lily put her right arm under Peter, tried to haul him to his feet. He didn't move, and she slapped him.

"Peter, please!" she said. "It's here! We have to run!"

He groaned but put his arm around her shoulder. She lifted with her knees and, after a scrabbling, unsure moment when she thought they would both fall, he stood. They began to move, limping their way along the verge, the wash of traffic bringing them the scent of trash.

Why won't anyone stop? Lily thought. *Then again, who the fuck's going to stop to help two people being chased by* that *thing?*

Lily looked back and saw that the being was nearly complete, standing by the side of the wrecked Aston Martin. It reached out with steel-tipped hands and tore into the car's underside, like a lion after a gazelle, casting pieces of its workings aside.

As Lily watched, those pieces flipped up, rose into the air, and flew to the thing's body, incorporating themselves into its increasingly robust structure. No longer a skeleton or a scaffold, the Garbage Man was becoming fully fleshed.

It's turning the car into scrap, she thought, *and using it to make itself stronger.*

This, to Lily, seemed profoundly unfair.

Peter saw it too. He pulled at her. They had to keep moving. To where? To what? Maybe better to just lie down, rest. She felt the appeal in that. She was exhausted, in agony, and there was literally nowhere to go.

Lily just wanted to *stop*. She felt it creeping up on her, around the edges of her spirit—a slow wave of neutral energy, mold blooming in her soul. The freezing dark sea rising up around her.

The Grey, making its latest play for her, closer than it had ever been.

Exercises leapt to mind, little mantras promulgated by the public health services that were supposedly able to help push back the Grey when it came calling.

There is so much light in the world. So much.

Never stop fighting.

You are not alone.

But Lily couldn't see any light, didn't want to fight anymore, and felt more alone than she ever had in her life.

She tried to call up good moments, good times—the strange exhilaration of surviving her fall into the sea because her father had pulled her out of it; a particularly nice Christmas in Spain; the feeling of landing that first job in Hong Kong and knowing she could get *away*; hiking with David on the Dragon's Back that first time, both utterly breathless with the world spread out all around them and knowing they were obviously, joyfully falling in love . . .

But the Grey had something to say about that, didn't it? Because there was another time they hiked that trail, on the third anniversary of the first trek, and David had stopped her at the top of the highest peak, placing a hand on her arm. She turned back to see him down on one knee, holding out a little box toward her, his eye shining, nervous, huge. He looked like a little boy, and she loved him so incredibly much.

Lily had looked out at the sea for a long, increasingly uncomfortable moment and, without turning back to David, told him no. Not yet, she said. She told him she wasn't ready. But that wasn't the real reason, was it? No—it was because people you let yourself fully love ended up going away, and she didn't want David to go away. Better to hold something back so he'd stay.

David closed the box, sealing away the ring he'd chosen, selected after months of subtle (and utterly obvious) inquiries into Lily's taste in such things. They hiked back down off the mountain, not speaking much.

Not so long after that, the Grey took him.

And now it was coming for her, its latest assault, and this time she had nothing left with which to fight it.

But Peter Match did.

He lifted Lily up off the roadside, dragging her from danger in an echo of her pulling him from the ruined Aston Martin—which chose that moment to explode in a blast of fire and oily black smoke. Evidently the Garbage Man's depredations had damaged some crucial system, thrown a spark into the petrol tank—something.

Lily experienced the event as an impossibly loud noise and a hot hand pushing against her whole body from behind, not quite strong enough to knock her and Peter off their feet. They stumbled a little.

They both stopped to look back, hoping—and yes. The Garbage Man was not visible.

"Maybe it killed itself," Lily said.

A whisper of hot garbage stink, lover-close to Lily's ear.

Peter and Lily whipped their heads around to see the thing standing there, its face molded from old diapers, its hair created from strips of plastic takeout bags. One eye was a bottle cap, the other was the Aston Martin's fuel gauge, the needle swinging back and forth between empty and full like a drunk at the pub trying to make his way to the loo without falling over.

Its hands, though, were steel, drawn from what had once been a car, with wicking blade fingers and flexing cable tendons.

Lily screamed, and whatever level of mutual support she and Peter were offering to each other collapsed. They fell. Lily was trying to keep Peter from landing too hard and so improperly protected her damaged, probably broken arm, and the agony whited out every other thought.

She lay on the ground, on the side of one of the busiest highways in the United Kingdom, and spared a thought for the motorists zipping past a car crash, two injured people, and, incidentally, a gigantic refuse monster and *still not stopping.*

The Garbage Man spread its arms.

Lily did not scream again. She whimpered.

There would be no last-minute save from Peter Match this time. She could see him trying to push himself backward across the ragged, debris-strewn roadside, one booted foot shoving ineffectually along the ground. Blood-streaked face, wild eyes.

No answers at the end of the Wonder Path, only what Coriander and the others had warned her about. Horror. Peter Match had called them cowards, but they were wise. Lily had pushed for answers, for *more,* believing there was a resolution, a sense to things, that the puzzle of her life had a solution. It had brought her only here. Those people were right to stay in Hong Kong, have their banquets and debates, and only take their search so far. They would live, while she would die.

The Garbage Man crouched near her. It smelled like shit and oil. Its face creaked into something like a smile.

Lily closed her eyes.

She waited for the new flavor of pain that was sure to come and hoped it would be quick. The Grey danced around the edges of her mind.

Nothing.

Then a sound, a grinding extension of kludged-together joints and ersatz tissue.

Lily opened her eyes.

The Garbage Man stood above her, its head tilted up and cocked to one side as if it was listening to something. The moment stretched, the thing staying so still that Lily dared to hope that whatever spirit animated it had vanished, that it would collapse into its many bits in a clattering rain of debris and filth.

Instead, it moved again, its entire demeanor changed. It took on the air of a helpful laborer, slightly abashed.

It lifted its hands, and more pieces of the destroyed Aston Martin whipped through the air, attaching to its wrists, becoming clawlike attachments that reminded Lily of coin-wasting games at arcades and bowling alleys. Bits of the burned vehicle's hood and side panels connected to its back, curving up and out and revealing themselves to be large, batlike wings.

Lily felt the Garbage Man's new claw hands clamp lightly closed around her, cushioned by more diapers and wadded-up plastic and the unburned remnants of the Aston Martin's seating.

The Garbage Man leapt into the air.

I. EIGHTEEN

ABOVE.

51°27'00.9"N, 2°35'39.7"W

Lily dropped in and out of consciousness, intermittently aware of scrolling landscape far below, and both the sound and feel of wind rushing past her. The Garbage Man held her gently—and Peter Match, too, in its other claw—like an eagle holding a pair of fish it had snatched up from a river.

Every beat of the thing's enormous wings creaked and rasped like knives down a blackboard.

Lily had given up on thinking. She was just along for the ride.

Below them now: a city, rolling rooftops, and a river cutting through it all. Impossible to recognize from this vantage point—until she saw a high suspension bridge built over a gorge, with two tall brick towers at either end. That she knew—it was the Clifton Bridge, which meant they were over Bristol, well west of London.

The Garbage Man was flying with purpose, straight, unerring, and a map of England popped into Lily's head. West of Bristol was Cardiff, in Wales, but before you got there, you had to cross . . .

Of course, Lily thought. *The only thing that could make this worse.*

Briefly, a coastline, a narrow strip of sand, and then the Garbage Man took them out over the River Severn. The creature banked, and they followed the river's path: southwest now, toward the Bristol Channel, if Lily's mental map was accurate, muddled as it was by pain, fatigue and the overwhelming series of events.

The sea below now, dark and slate-blue and deep.

Endless.

They descended. The water rose up, whitecaps here and there.

To what? To nothing. To drowning. Lily had no illusions about how long she could keep herself afloat if the Garbage Man dropped her in the sea. She wondered if she would even try or just let her descent continue, all the way down. She knew how. She'd done it before.

A shimmer above the waves. A spectrum like light glinting off oil and water, and suddenly something else was there.

A ship, like nothing Lily had ever seen, rushing up to meet them. Huge and tiered, with glass encrustations vaguely reminiscent of the Kremlin's towers mixed with a deconstructed Art Deco chandelier, and sleek, swept-back sails, and every color you could think of, a riot of colors and shapes, the sea around it barely disturbed by its passage.

As big as a cruise liner, a skyscraper set on its side, styled like a starship. The ship spoke of *power*, of a society with technology and confidence beyond anything Lily could imagine. And if this was just the ship . . . who knew what might be waiting *inside* it?

The Garbage Man set Lily and Peter down on its forward deck, a broad, open space marked with a symbol Lily recognized from the paperwork in Danny Chang's office and the plaque outside Coriander's office and the diagram from her father's study. The number eight, but from this perspective clearly *not* the number eight but the symbol for infinity. As they drew closer, it was clear that the symbol was itself created of more infinity symbols connected together like links on a chain, and within those more still.

Infinity within infinity.

Lily lay there gasping, disoriented and in pain and afraid and suffering on every level she could imagine. Trying to sort through everything that had happened to her. Trying to exist.

A scent. One she knew. One she had been reacquainted with recently, after many years. Pipe tobacco, of a particular brand. An earth-stone-fire scent.

She was hallucinating.

"Dear god, Lily, what happened to you?" her father said.

He was there, kneeling beside her, his hand on her face.

Frederick Barnes, dead for seventeen years, his hair grey, his face grimy and tired but not so different—though perhaps Lily's blurred vision was simply smoothing out the work time had done on his features.

Blurred by pain and exhaustion; blurred by tears.

"Dad?" she said.

Lily Barnes understood that her entire adult life, all her choices, were attempts to solve a puzzle that could not be solved. It could not be solved because, for all that time, she was missing a crucial, all-important piece. The truth.

"I'm here," her father said. "You're all right now.

She sensed other figures rushing up, felt a hand at her neck, checking her pulse with practiced medical precision.

"Dad," Lily said, her voice thin and weak, "what is this? What's happening?"

Her father smiled.

"That," he said, "is a story."

BOOK II

THE DESTINATION

II. ONE

MASSACHUSETTS.

OCTOBER 1789.

42°28′13.9″N, 71°21′08.9″W

APOLLO CALDER SURVEYED HIS DOMAIN.

A cluster of buildings and machinery on the eastern shore of the Concord River, at a spot where it frothed and churned over a small precipice. The largest of these buildings was a great wheelhouse erected just below the falls, at the river's edge. The river poured through a flume built at the upper edge of the cascade, channeled directly to the wheel's highest point, generating power via not just the current but the weight of the water itself as it fell onto the wheel's blades.

That power, the great strength of God and nature itself, radiated outward from the wheel to all corners of the complex. It was divided and subdivided via a series of ingeniously assembled gears and shafts, used to turn a crank here, push a shuttle there. The buildings of the Calder Mill were filled with the very latest machines—spinning jennies, carding frames, everything needed to turn raw cotton into fine thread. Not even five years earlier this work would have been laboriously performed by hand, but now, by God's grace and human resourcefulness, it could be done at lower cost and at much greater scale and speed.

As yet there were no machines that could perform the next step in the process, weaving the thread into textiles. That task still needed to be performed by hand, and the Mill employed many skilled weavers to that end. (And fed and comfortably housed them all, a fact that made Apollo proud.) Nevertheless, Apollo believed a day might come when even the weaving would be done by some intricate engine. He envisioned an entire enterprise, a gigantic machine-factory that took in bales of cotton at one end and produced finished, dyed textiles of all colors, patterns, and fineness at the other. All with only the lightest touch of human hands, ingenuity reducing the need for labor.

Not there yet, but the day would come, and from there, who knew?

The Mill's workers moved within the compound in regular, dependable rhythms, shifting materials between buildings, taking reels of thread to the weaving house and uncolored fabric to the dyeing rooms, and from there to the drying halls and off to the warehouse.

Apollo shifted his gaze to the narrow track leading to the Mill's gate. A wagon laden with cotton bales made its way along the road between autumn trees well into their flame-colored season. It had come from the docks in Boston Harbor some twenty-five miles to the southeast.

"We need to cancel that cotton contract," said his wife, Molly, a typically short and sensible statement from the short, sensible, brilliant, beautiful woman with whom he shared his life.

She stood beside him on the porch of their home, built on a low rise above the falls, the better to provide an overview of the industry below. She tucked a few wisps of chestnut-colored hair up beneath her bonnet, patting the starched cloth in a satisfied way when it was once again just so.

"Do you think so, wife?" Apollo asked.

He knew that Molly and he differed as far as their thoughts when beholding their mill. She did not see a temple to invention and ingenuity, a glimpse of the future. No, she saw a vortex, a pit, an endlessly deep hole swallowing up the fortune she and her husband had painstakingly amassed over the past decade.

That had not always been the case. The Calder Mill had generated strong returns almost since its inception. But since the end of the War for Independence, its profitability had become much less certain, at least in Boston and its environs.

Britain had not particularly liked losing its former colonies or the hurt to its pride that such a loss entailed. It had retaliated by using its astonishingly robust navy and network of privateers to strangle trade from and to North America. Ships could not easily leave or arrive in New York, Boston, Baltimore, or any of the other great ports without fear of being sunk, particularly while flying the still-new American flag. This policy had a number of direct effects on the economics of the Calder Mill.

First, inflation, as imported goods became more scarce and therefore more dear. This included, of course, cotton. Even though the crop was grown within the new nation's borders, it was transported from the southern states up the eastern coast by ship. With Britain-affiliated vessels prowling those shores, this had become a dangerous enterprise.

Second, a reduction in income. The cursed English had also flexed their imperial muscle to close many overseas markets for American goods—including, obviously, England. Even if the Calders *did* spend the money required to get cotton and use it to create the beautiful fabric for which they were known on both sides of the Atlantic, the places where they could sell it were greatly diminished.

So, as far as Molly was concerned, the Calder Mill, a beautiful enterprise she had created with her dear husband, had transformed into a giant beast that ate money and shat fine textiles that could not easily be converted back into money. Yards upon yards were currently stacked in their warehouse with nowhere to go.

"We don't need to be making more cloth we cannot sell, Apollo," Molly said, her eyes tracking the supply wagon's steady progress toward the Mill. "We should at least reduce the cotton to one delivery per month."

"Do not think about today, my dear," Apollo said. "Consider tomorrow. More particularly, the tomorrow when the market improves and only the Calder Mill will have stock to sell while our more cautious competitors, the *cowards*, scramble to catch up."

"I see another tomorrow, Apollo, where those competitors remain in business and we live in a shack on Nantucket Island, having been forced to sell the Mill and all our products for pennies to make up even some small portion of our loss."

Apollo scratched at his beard. He looked at his good wife, whom he adored, and determined to speak plainly.

"Molly, you know the truth of the matter. If we take in less cotton, what will our workers do?" Apollo said, gesturing down at the Mill and the many people moving about, busy with the thousand tasks required to keep the place running. "They depend on us for their livelihood."

A quick look of frustration washed over Molly's face.

"My love, we cannot be responsible for every weaver and spinner in Boston. They will find new employment. It is the way of things."

"We have created a family here, a community," Apollo said. "I will not dissolve it lightly. There must another way to reduce costs. Some new efficiency. Perhaps Mr. Brooks, with all his ingenuity, might find some trick?"

Molly shook her head.

"We cannot depend on Mr. Brooks, as clever as he is. Our finances represent a real and growing problem, my love. A decision must be made," she said. "I know what I would do were I acting alone, but that has never been how you and I do things."

Molly placed her hand on Apollo's arm. His heart beat a bit faster and a smile came to his lips, even though he knew his wife was about to utter words he would not enjoy altogether much.

"I cannot argue with your desire to help our people," she said. "It is a lovely sentiment that speaks well to your character. But we must face reality. If we want to keep our current complement of workers, then we have only two options: either we decrease our costs or increase our income. Presently, I see no way to do the latter. Therefore, we *must* reduce our costs or we will lose this business and everything we have built, and the result you are trying to avoid will happen in any case. This family of ours will be scattered to the wind."

Molly moved her hand to his face and gave him a sad look.

"Only one decision makes any sense at all," she concluded.

Apollo frowned, realizing immediately to what she referred.

"Surely there is something else," he said.

"If you can devise another way to free up a similar amount of capital, I would like to hear it. We could cancel the cotton contract, yes, and it would save us a little money. But canceling the *construction* contract will sufficiently replenish our coffers so that we might operate at our current levels for years. Enough time for the market to rebound, if indeed it ever will."

Apollo saw the truth in his wife's words but found it difficult to face. So many dreams—their shared dreams, he believed—were pinned to that particular contract's completion.

"But we had planned to travel, to see the world, and create opportunities for our goods in new markets without depending on trade agents and their usurious contracts," he said. "We would be our own enterprise from start to finish."

"We will still do those things," Molly answered. "Just later in our lives. We are young yet, Apollo. There is a time for dreams and a time for practicality."

"I fear all your time is spent in the latter," Apollo said.

"And yours in the former, husband," she answered.

"Why live any other way, wife?"

"Why indeed, husband?" Molly said.

Apollo sighed.

"Let us go to the building site," he said. "If I am to cut off my own arm at the urging of mine own wife, lovely though she may be, let it be when I can stand before the thing itself," he said.

"I will have the coach prepared," Molly said. "We'll need to inform Brooks that we'll be gone. And do not fear. I would never allow you to lose either of your arms. I am fond of both, and all the many things they can do."

Apollo smiled.

"Yes, dear," he said. "Let us go see Mr. Brooks."

He stepped down off the porch and held out a hand to Molly, which she grasped. They walked that way down through the Mill. Up close, it seemed less a place of industry and more like a little town. Beyond the various buildings related to the Mill's textile business, it also boasted permanent housing in the form of sparse but comfortable tenements near the waterwheel, a company store where the workers' needs could be met at very reasonable prices, a chapel, a small alehouse and common building, and broad patches of cropland on the exterior between the Mill and the surrounding forest.

But the most important building at the Calder Mill was not any of those, nor even the house on the hill where Molly and Apollo lived. It was another, a well-constructed two-story building made in the saltbox style, with a deeply slanting roof on its rear side. In this place lived and worked the true secret to the Mill's success. The building was a laboratory, and Mr. Paul Brooks was its master.

Apollo walked with Molly along the well-kept gravel path leading to this building. His eyes were drawn, as always, to the huge flag hung above the laboratory door. It was impossible to miss, a sheet of sailcloth dyed a royal, rippling blue, flickering between azure and navy as it moved gently in the breeze of the fine spring morning. The flag had no further adornment. The color itself was all the decoration required.

This was the Calder Blue, by far the most popular shade produced by the Mill. The color was known throughout the former colonies and even in many of the finer homes of Europe—not that the Mill's sales agents could easily access those after the British blockades. The formula was secret, known only to Apollo, Molly, and its inventor, Paul Brooks.

Apollo and Molly passed beneath that flag and entered Mr. Brooks's laboratory, breathing tentatively at first—both knew the danger of a nasal scalding from some of the more acrid substances he worked with. But on this day, the lab had a pleasant aroma, something like boiling coffee with a strong floral note.

"Mr. and Mrs. Calder," Paul Brooks said, wiping his hands on a rag as he approached. "Lovely to see you both as always."

The man was of medium height but seemed taller because of his gaunt frame, an Englishman by birth but with no great loyalty to any nation, old or new. He was bald, generally cheerful, spent a few more than his share of his nights in the Mill tavern, and along with his apprentices kept the Mill's machines in working order, even devising many clever improvements for the devices.

Brooks was a fine engineer. But his obsession, his calling, was color. He was a self-schooled botanist, naturalist, and geologist, conversant with all plants, creatures, and minerals that yielded compounds that could generate dyes—a uniquely useful expertise at the Calder Mill. Brooks spent hours each day foraging in the forests around the Mill, and had traveled widely up and down the Atlantic coast. He met with local people from all over and took a holistic approach to the pursuit of knowledge. Anyone, of any age, background, gender, or social status, might know of a beetle that, when crushed, produced a bright orange juice. Or a mushroom whose spores were a gorgeous vermillion. Or a root that could be boiled down into a paste of the inkiest black.

All of that knowledge went into the bubbling vats and jars in Paul Brooks's laboratory, and the colors he produced had gone a long way toward earning the Mill its reputation.

"Is all well, Mr. Brooks?" asked Apollo.

"Beyond well, I'd say. I've got something cooking I think could be quite good for the Mill. I'm working up a way to print on cotton—you know, like a book? Same idea, but with patterns. You carve them out of a block of wood, ink them up, and off you go. Having some problems getting the dye to hold fast—bit of smearing to deal with, and then there's the problem of whether they'll stick through a laundering . . . but I'll sort that out. Just need to find the right fixing agent. Could be something. Really quite something."

"For dresses," Molly said.

Mr. Brooks laid his index finger along the side of his nose.

"I thought the same, Mrs. Calder," he said. "Ladies do like a bit of ornamentation, and this would be buckets easier than embroidery or lacework."

"Bedding as well, and curtains," said Molly. "This could open up entirely new avenues."

"Well, you've got the head for business," Brooks said. "Whatever you think."

"Perhaps this innovation will bring us new sources of income," Apollo said to his wife. "Why not put our faith in Mr. Brooks rather than—"

Apollo found his sentence cut short, a circumstance created by his wife placing her hand over his mouth.

"I always have faith in Mr. Brooks," Molly said, "but his idea, as brilliant as it is, will not serve as an immediate solution to our quandary. You know it as well as I, dear husband."

Molly released Apollo and turned back to the Englishman.

"Mr. Calder and I are off to Essex," she said. "We will be gone most of a week. While we are away, you are in charge."

"Aye, Mrs. Calder," Brooks said, tipping an imaginary cap. "I'll keep things running smooth. Safe travels."

APOLLO AND MOLLY OWNED A WELL-APPOINTED COACH, A FINE enough way to take the trip north. Still, no journey of fifty miles would be anything but arduous, even along the new turnpikes that had opened up travel within Massachusetts. For a small fee paid every so often at tollgates installed upon the road, one could pass along well-maintained lanes of gravel and flattened earth.

But even with the good new roads, it took time to travel such a significant distance. The Calders broke the journey in two, spending a night at the Merchant Inn in Salem, a place distinguished by the fact that it was due to host the still somewhat freshly inaugurated President Washington before the month was out. They knew this because the inn's owner, a man named Joshua Ward, mentioned it repeatedly to them while they dined on the mutton stew and beer he served them.

But around noon on the second day, the scents of Essex—fresh-cut wood, hot tar, hemp—came wafting in through the coach's open windows, well before Apollo and Molly could see the town. Next came sounds of hammers and saws and the cries of industrious men, and finally they saw evidence of the town's primary reason for existing, via tall spires poking up above the tree line, some already fitted with spars and rigging.

Ships were built in Essex. It was one of several spots along the Massachusetts coast with good, deep harbors and easy access to lumber from surrounding forests. Huge wooden frames on the shore of the river contained the vessels-to-be, like nests for fledglings not quite ready to fly on their own.

Essex had yards enough to build twenty ships at once, perhaps more, but as the Calder's coach rolled into the town, they saw that most were empty. Only two contained partially constructed vessels, and just one had any workers around it.

"Well, there she is," Apollo said, knowing he sounded proud.

"The work's a good bit further along," Molly observed. "The keel's laid in."

"We would have taken her on her maiden voyage soon enough," her husband said. "The *Olympian*, goddess of the seas."

Molly patted his hand.

"Save the name, dear husband," Molly said. "We'll use it yet. All things in their time."

Apollo helped his wife down from the coach, and they made their way along the riverbank to the shipyard containing the vessel actively under construction. The yard's master, a proud Norwegian named Knut Jacobsen, burly in beard and manner, came up to meet them, a hammer in hand.

"Master Calder, Madam Calder," he said. "Come to see the progress, eh?"

"Master Jacobsen," Molly replied, inclining her head. "Can it be possible there are no other ships under construction here but ours?"

The shipwright scowled.

"It is. If twenty ships are built in Massachusetts this entire year, I would be surprised."

"Why is that?" Apollo asked.

"There is nowhere to take them," Jacobsen nearly shouted, waving his hammer in agitation. "All British ports are closed to vessels flying the American flag. Until that changes, there is little market for new ships here in the colonies. The British may no longer control these lands, but they maintain an iron grip on the sea."

He scratched his beard with the hammer's claw end.

"In fact," the shipwright said, thoughtful, "once your contract is complete, I might return home to Norway to ply my trade. I fear the time of America as a shipping land is done. If we had not entered into our contract some years ago, I would counsel you against building a ship at this time."

"Ah," Apollo said, "but I would have built it anyway. I do not make choices based on today, Master Jacobsen. I make them based on tomorrow. The world I hope to see."

"And that strategy has worked well for you?"

Apollo smiled at Molly.

"Repeatedly."

"Well, follow me and I'll take you around. We've got the keel down, as you can see, and the ribbing's mostly in place."

Apollo looked up at the skeletal curve of the ship he would christen the *Olympian*, a nod to his father's affinity for the myths of the Greeks. His own name was proof. It was unusual in Protestant New England to have a Greek name. Apollo knew of only one other person with a name of Hellenic origin: the father of the Concord silversmith made famous in the war. That man was born Apollos Rivoire, though he had changed his name to the much more palatably English Paul Revere. Not so for Apollo Calder. He bore his unusual moniker with pride, and though he and Molly were apparently to have no children, he had planned to pay tribute to the gods of ancient Greece via the name of the ship he would build with his wife.

Molly stood next to him. She took his hand.

Apollo Calder believed in dreams, and his wife believed in reality, and together they made a formidable pair, each pushing or pulling the other as required toward a better, godlier life.

He thought of all the joy yet to come, the struggles and

challenges he and Molly would defeat together as they shaped their small part of the world into a more humane, profitable place for all. He gave her hand a gentle squeeze. She smiled at him.

What need did Apollo Calder have for a ship? He had all the adventure a man might need, standing at his side.

"I can let it go," he said. "We will tell Master Jacobsen we desire to terminate our agreement, and the *Olympian* will—"

A sharp pain spiked through Apollo's head, like a knife driven into his eye from behind. He gasped at the sheer shock, the audacity of it.

"Husband, are you well?" Molly said, concerned.

"I—"

Another blast of pain, this time exploding deep inside his skull like a cannon going off. His vision blurred, the world now as if seen through a rain-streaked window. Apollo Calder fell to his knees.

"Apollo!" Molly cried. "Help! My husband is ill!"

He lay on the shore of the Essex River, in the shadow of the ship upon which he would never sail, its masts spearing high into the sky above.

II. TWO

BOSTON.

NOVEMBER 1789.

42°21′26.6″N, 71°03′42.3″W

"Apollo Calder's diligence and Fidelity remain without question. Added to this must be the greatest integrity of life, probity, constancy, fortitude. and the most holy and honorable morals. He was a pleasant and polite man, which Cicero complains was remaining but with some few in his days. And we must not omit the smartness of his wit, with him since his youth and carrying well through to his adulthood. Or his piety, his religion, free from all superstition and purged of all immorality. But the chief grace and ornament of Apollo Calder's life was his beloved wife, Molly. The two were certainly a pair to be admired, even to be reckoned with in matters of . . ."

Molly Calder stopped listening. Isaac Lovett was an attorney, and attorneys knew nothing if not how to talk. The man would continue with his funeral oration for many minutes more, and rightly so—her husband deserved no less. But Molly did not need to be reminded of her dead husband's many virtues.

Thoughts of those good qualities consumed her thoughts; memories, dashed hopes, choices she would have made differently if she'd only known how short her time with Apollo would be.

Isaac's audience numbered well over a hundred. Many distinguished Bostonians had come to the Granary Burying Ground this day to see Apollo Calder put in the ground. She spied Samuel Adams, for one, and many of the other men of business and society Apollo had known. Her husband was well loved. This was a fitting tribute to the life he had lived and the lives he had touched during his time.

". . . While Apollo was not blessed with children of his own, he was always known to be kind to any he met, and was a generous uncle to his nieces and nephews, of which he had nineteen. His light shone out . . ."

Molly did her best to ignore Lovett's words. She didn't want to be reminded that God had never seen fit to bless her and Apollo with children. She let her eyes drift across the cemetery, the stones with their carvings of grinning death's heads and smiling cherubs with outstretched wings, the names and dates and verses carved into them: *Here Lyes Samuel Smith, husband to Anne Smith, aged Fifty-Six Years, died April 4th 1732 Beloved of God and His Family.*

A soft breeze blew across the burial yard, scattering the dead leaves on the ground and ruffling the black bonnet Molly wore, making sport with a few strands of hair that had escaped it. It was sunny, and there was no shade. Despite the cool of the fall day, her black mourning dress was an oven she could not escape. She felt sweat running down her back in rivulets, enough to power the river wheel up at the Mill.

Apollo was so proud of everything they built there, and so optimistic about the Calder Mill's prospects. He allowed nothing to defeat his certainty that good times would come again. Not war, not the economic depression that followed, not an inability to find markets for their fabrics. He could not be dissuaded.

Until, of course, he was, by the argument no man or woman could defeat.

Apollo's coffin lay on a bier next to the open grave. Sheets of paper were pinned to it, fluttering in the breeze like a flock of doves on the wing. Each held memories of her husband, or valedictions to him, written by the mourners. These would be collected into a memorial book after the funeral and given to Molly. She might read it someday. But not for a long, long time. She didn't think she could bear it.

Coils of rope sat near the bier, for the sexton and his crew to use to lower the coffin into the earth, into the hole in the ground that would serve as Apollo's resting place in perpetuity. Molly's own coffin would lie next to it someday—she and her husband had secured two plots in the Granary Yard years earlier—but that would be a long time from now, God willing. She was thirty-one years of age and possessed of both health and moderate wealth. Decades remained to her.

A long, lonely span.

Molly knew that did not have to be the case. She was the full and complete owner of the Calder Mill, the land upon which it rested, all its goods and chattels, and, of course, the triple-masted merchant ship currently under construction up at the Essex shipyards. Apollo had, years before and with the assistance of Isaac Lovett, created a marriage settlement document that provided all rights to these properties to Molly in fee simple. This went well beyond the default proposition for widowed wives, specifically a long-standing tenet of the common law called the dower rule. Under it, Molly would get half, with the rest going to Apollo's closest male relative. It was unusual to adjust this to give a widow full ownership and control over a deceased's estate, but Apollo Calder was an unusual man.

With such large holdings, Molly would find herself many suitors despite her advanced years. She had already gotten many appraising glances from the unmarried men standing at Apollo's graveside (or their female relatives). She knew this was only natural but found it impossible to imagine marrying another. The thought of other hands on her, another man in the house she had built with Apollo, in their bed . . . repulsive. Unthinkable.

And fortunately, due to her husband's foresight in ensuring she would fully inherit, she would never have to think such thoughts. She could steer the rest of her life as she saw fit, without being forced to remarry simply to survive.

I am Molly Calder, wife to Apollo Calder, she thought, *and will always be.*

He was right there. Not ten feet from her. Molly could throw open the casket and see him at that very moment if she chose, though she knew corruption would already have taken much of what she would recognize as her husband, especially in the unseasonably warm autumn Boston was currently experiencing

It was utterly unfair. The surgeon had claimed Apollo died from an affliction known as an aneurysm, a rupture in the brain all but impossible to detect or anticipate, not heralded by any prior infirmity or symptom. It came on in an instant, a bolt of God's lightning, stealing away her great love, her partner in all things.

It was wrong.

Isaac Lovett ended his oration at long last. The minister offered his blessings, and the sexton and his men carefully collected the fluttering memorial papers from the bier. With that done, the earthly remains of her husband were lowered into the ground. Molly threw a handful of dirt atop the coffin, heard it rattle against the wood, and then she retreated, this phase of her obligations complete.

Then a celebration at the home of Isaac Lovett, chosen because the attorney and most of the mourners resided in Boston. Forcing so many to make the journey up to the Mill would not do. Rum and wine and beer flowed freely. Molly sat with a few well-meaning wives, listening to their empty words and accepting gracious expressions of sorrow and solidarity from her husband's many friends, admirers, business partners, and well-wishers.

Her dead husband. Apollo Calder was dead.

Even now it did not register, though she had seen his coffin, seen the light dim from his eyes there on the banks of the Essex River, his last words a choking gasp as he tried to say her name. Apollo had seemed . . . surprised. Shocked that such a thing could happen to him, after a life lived so well, attempting to bring only light to the world.

Molly sat at her husband's wake and wondered who she was now, wondered if she would ever be happy again. The world, and her place within it going forward, seemed behind a curtain, gauzy, the details muted, unimportant, inaccessible.

Had her husband ascended to heaven? Did his spirit reside there? She assumed so. He was a good man. Everything Isaac Lovett had said was true.

What was Apollo now? Not the thing she had seen put in the dirt that day. He was his wit, his mind, his optimism, his love, his light, his spirit and soul.

He used to sing while he worked. Quietly, and under his breath, and not for anyone to hear, and perhaps that was for the best . . . but often and always. Apollo had music in him, and she had heard it. His beautiful, imperfect music.

How could that be gone? How could she never hear his song again? It seemed impossible. Unjust. Untrue.

Someone spoke to her. Molly nodded, offered a faint smile. Her mind was occupied, fully occupied.

The shape of an idea was forming in her mind. She had money. She had independence. She had the Calder Mill and its assets both physical and in the form of the industrious people who worked there.

Molly Calder was no longer the wife of a textile mill owner, tied to that path and profession. She was a widow possessed of many resources and could do, within the boundaries of the law, whatever she liked.

She stood, and the mourner who had just spoken to her stepped back. She recognized him, a portly man named William Wilson, a trader in whale oil with a shop on Tremont Street in the South End. His face was reddened by rum, and he seemed a bit surprised at her abrupt movement.

"Are you quite well, my dear?" he said.

"Why do you ask, Mr. Wilson?" she said.

"If you will forgive me for saying so, you seem . . . angry. Did my words land amiss? I was truly a great admirer and friend to your husband."

"I know that, Mr. Wilson," Molly said. "Nothing you said bothered me in the slightest."

Indeed, she could not have brought a single word of his utterance to mind if her own life had depended on it.

"I am preoccupied by other matters. If you will excuse me," she said, slipping past William Wilson as he stared at her, eyes wide.

The man had observed her correctly, though. Molly did feel anger in her breast, but anger was an insufficient descriptor for what she felt.

Rage.

That was the word.

Molly's eyes searched through the mourners filling Isaac Lovett's sitting room. She did not see the face she was looking for and left the house. She was immediately glad of the fresh air. The atmosphere inside had become close and malodorous.

From Isaac's front steps, Molly had a good view of the revelers in the street outside, cheerfully drinking and chatting as they partook of refreshments provided by the newly minted Widow

Calder's largesse. She did not think Apollo would mind. He enjoyed a celebration.

Her eyes flicked from one to the next, until . . . there. Standing with a group of workers from the Mill, tipping back a mug of ale: the man she sought.

Paul Brooks.

Molly walked to him, ignoring anyone who spoke to her along the way, her purpose and path plain to her now.

"Mr. Brooks," she said.

"Ma'am," the Englishman said, removing his cap to reveal his bald pate and offering a sympathetic expression. "So truly sorry again. I've said it before and I'm sure I'll say it many times in days to come—your husband was a shining light, a true man among men."

"I agree," Molly said.

"He will be greatly missed, both up at the mill and by the world at large, " Paul went on, these words garnering nods of agreement from the workers around him.

"Again I agree," Molly said.

"You'll be reunited with him in heaven, have no doubt of that," Paul said.

"On that, perhaps we differ," Molly said.

Paul paused with his mug of ale halfway to his lips.

"Er . . . ," he said.

"I would like a very brief word with you, Mr. Brooks, concerning the future operations of the Mill," Molly said. "Might we step away for a moment?"

Paul glanced at the other workers, who seemed suddenly nervous, their high spirits dampened. Funerals were not ordinarily a time for business, but Molly was now the sole overseer of their livelihoods, and her voice was to be obeyed.

"Course we might, Mrs. Calder," Paul said.

Molly gestured across the street, and they walked together to a spot shaded by the leaves of a large oak planted between two well-appointed homes owned by wealthy tradesmen of Boston's North End. The street was empty—the city's population had been depleted massively during the War for Independence and even now numbered only about ten thousand souls. Only her husband's mourners were in evidence, and between drink and distance, none of them would be able to hear anything she might say.

"Can I trust you, Mr. Brooks?" Molly said.

Paul took a moment to consider this, his eyes narrowing slightly. She was pleased that he did. Any man who answered that question without hesitation probably could not be trusted at all.

"I would say, ma'am, that as a general matter the answer is yes. But the nature of that inquiry suggests that I should probably hear a bit more before I answer with any specificity."

"Well reasoned, Mr. Brooks, and I would expect no less. Allow me to explain. My husband's estimation of your intellectual capacities knew no upper bound. I am sure you know that from his treatment of you and your role in our mill, but I want you to know that he often expressed those sentiments to me in private as well. He believed there was no puzzle you could not solve. Do you agree with that assessment?"

Paul took a long, slow sip of his ale as he mulled over her words. Again Molly was impressed with his thoughtfulness.

"I would not say there is no puzzle I cannot solve, ma'am. I would say that I apply myself diligently to any question set before me, and I always use my God-given capacities to their utmost. Given enough time and resources, I can find a solution to most problems. I would allow that, yes."

"Very good," Molly said. "Then, from this moment forward, here is the problem I would have you solve. Set aside all other responsibilities at the Mill. You have every resource I can provide and all the time you require."

Paul bent and set his mug of ale on the ground. He straightened and clasped his hands before him, taking on the posture of a man ready to take instruction.

"I will do my best, Mrs. Calder, and I'm honored you would ask. I'll get it done, whatever it is, both for you and in memory of your husband. What would you like me to do?"

"I would like you to solve death," Molly said.

For a long moment Paul Brooks stood there, under the shade of the oak tree, blinking.

"Do you mean . . . for everyone?" he said at last.

"No," Molly said. "It is simple enough, to my mind. My husband's spirit departed his flesh. The teachings of the church suggest it is now in heaven, intact and alive, but simply transported to a new realm, a new way of being. I believe Apollo was not ready to leave this world and would prefer to be here with me. That is the task I set you. Find my husband and return him to me."

Paul thought for a moment.

"I wouldn't even know where to begin," he said. "I'm not saying no, but this is . . . where would I even start?"

"Begin with the things you know," she said, "and use them to investigate the things you do not."

Molly bent, retrieved Paul's mug, and handed it to him.

"Enjoy the rest of the day, Mr. Brooks," she said. "But tomorrow . . ."

Molly Calder turned and walked back toward the celebration of her husband's life, his death, and what she now knew would be the first steps toward his rebirth.

II. THREE

PHILADELPHIA.

MARCH 1790.

39°57′00.5″N, 75°08′47.2″W

"Ah, yes. I remember your letter," Benjamin Franklin said. "You're the maniac who's trying to solve death."

Paul Brooks was used to this reaction, though it was a bit surprising coming from the ancient fellow before him. Ben Franklin was the oldest man Paul had ever seen, clearly a person who should be interested in any possible path that might avert the final goodbye.

"I don't exactly want to solve death, Mr. Franklin, sir," he replied, choosing his words cautiously. "Seems to me death is rather a necessary thing. My project is of a different sort. I want to see about bringing someone's spirit back after they've passed on so they might, say, be spoken to. Make them present here on earth in whatever fashion possible."

Franklin took this in. He was a very large man, occupying the high-backed leather armchair like the filling in a suet pie. He shifted a bit, and a pained cloud crossed his face. Paul presumed the great man had gout or some other disorder brought on from fine living. The perils of wealth.

Paul Brooks knew he'd never have any issues like that. He was built like a dried cornstalk, and didn't imagine he'd ever have the funds to change that fact—or any real desire to. He liked being a skinny fellow. Nimble of body and nimble of mind.

"I know what you are trying to do," Franklin said. "But I do not know why you have come. How did you even get in?"

Paul squinted at the man. He wondered if Franklin had simply forgotten. Old people were often forgetting things, and he supposed the man's brilliance was no real bar to the ravages of age.

"You sent me a letter. Invited me to come, to talk to you in person. So here I am," Paul said.

"Did I . . . ?" Franklin said, his face momentarily troubled.

Addled, Paul thought.

He reached inside his coat and retrieved his invitation to Philadelphia, held it out. Franklin took the letter, then lifted a small bell on a round table next to his armchair and rang it. A moment later a dark-skinned woman appeared at the room's entrance.

"My spectacles, Anne, if you please," Franklin said.

"Of course, sir. Won't be a moment," the woman said.

She threw a long, appraising glance Paul's way, then left the way she had come.

Franklin seemed content to wait. He stared at Paul, tapped the letter against his thigh, and did not say a word.

Suppose the old goat's not much for small talk, Paul thought. *Fair enough, neither am I.*

Paul took the opportunity offered by Franklin's silence to take in his surroundings. He'd been trying to get into this room for four days. On his first visit, he'd offered his letter of invitation to the servant who opened the door. That fellow, a wiry man with eyes like awls, had read over the letter and verified his authorization to enter. But not right away. Mr. Franklin was doing poorly, it seemed, and Paul Brooks would not be allowed to see him until he was up to receiving visitors. So Paul had taken up residence at the Blue Anchor Inn down on Front Street. The room fee was paid out of Molly Calder's coffers, as were the coaches he'd ridden down from Massachusetts, a frigid, bone-rattling journey that had taken just over three weeks.

He'd checked back each day, making the brisk fifteen-minute walk from the Blue Anchor down to Franklin's spacious three-story home on Philadelphia's Market Street. He was denied twice more, but on the fourth day he was admitted at last. Now he found himself in the great man's sitting room, a space filled with mementos of an extraordinary life by any possible measure. Artifacts of science, statesmanship, war, and culture. A glass harmonium in one corner where a harpsichord might ordinarily sit. A single brass key hanging from a nail on the wall. A painting of Franklin himself standing before a berobed king on a throne: Louis XVI if Paul didn't miss his guess.

Paul was not sure Ben Franklin would be able to help him complete the bizarre quest Molly had assigned him; in truth, he wasn't sure anyone could. After working on the problem for months, he had few indicators of progress, no deep insights.

Death was, it turned out, a devilish little puzzle indeed.

To Paul's mind, the initial question had to be this: Was death a cessation, or a transition? In other words . . . did Apollo Calder still exist, in some way, somewhere?

He concluded that yes, the man still existed in at least two places.

First, the past. A year ago Apollo was still alive. Second, in the memories of those who knew him—which was another way of saying the same thing.

Anywhere else? The evidence was scant at best.

But that did not mean evidence could not be found. Paul determined to gain a greater understanding of death by studying life. He acquired and dissected all manner of creatures—even, to his eternal shame, those that might be said to have a soul akin to the way human beings understood the idea—dogs and cats. Upon completing those bloody explorations, he came to believe that living things were just machines. More complex than a spinning jenny or a loom, but based on the same principles. They took in food, which gave them energy to power their various cords and cables and tubes, just as the river powered the waterwheel that powered the Mill.

For weeks after Apollo's funeral, Paul Brooks sat in his laboratory, feeling increasing pressure to come up with an answer for Molly, especially as she had paused the Mill's ordinary operations. No threads were being spun, no looms fed. All of the Mill's many workers awaited Paul's direction. Molly already had more fabric than she needed and wanted her people available for him when he was ready.

But ready for what? After all his study, Paul had no idea what to do next. He had taken up Molly's suggestion and begun with the things he knew, using them as starting points for further exploration . . . but all paths had petered out in impassable deadfalls. He simply did not have the necessary understanding. He was excellent with plants and chemicals, and decent with machines. Life and death were beyond him.

Stymied, Paul sought outside expertise.

He'd spoken to the Wampanoag at Mashpee, to see if their holy men had any understanding of death, or a method to communicate with those who had passed on. He learned that perhaps once, a way existed, but the practice was long since lost along with so much else, after the tumult of the past few centuries.

After the forest villages, Paul visited priests of various Christian sects in Boston. He had to be careful there. He kept his inquiries vague and discreet, couched in terms of a man seeking solace at the loss of a close friend. The Puritans of New England took their heresy seriously, even in these enlightened times. Paul did not want to bring any trouble back to Molly Calder. She had placed her trust in him, and he meant to be worthy of it.

The learned men of Harvard were his next stop, though he should have saved himself the trouble. They looked down their noses from such a height, he was surprised their feet were still on the ground. That was fine—Paul Brooks knew his worth and was not easily shamed—but it was frustrating. The Harvard swells treated him like a superstitious moron when in fact he was trying to conduct a legitimate scientific inquiry. Few would talk to him, and none of those who did took him seriously. Even Molly Calder's money wouldn't change that, not for these sons of some of the wealthiest families in New England.

Paul didn't care so much about the snubs, because Harvard's scholars were not the real prize he sought by traveling to Cambridge. No . . . he wanted their *library*. The oldest in America, filled with thousands of volumes that simply could not be found anywhere else. Surely, somewhere in all that great accumulation of knowledge would be a clue, a hint. And if not, then he could return to Molly and say in good conscience that he had exhausted all possible avenues of research available to him.

But library access was not to be granted. Not to the Englishman Paul Brooks, afflicted with an accent that marked him as a tradesman. The moment he uttered a single word, he gave himself away as someone who surely was no Harvard student or one of its illustrious faculty members. The Harvard Library was not open to the public. Only professors and some few students could use it, and Paul was unlikely to become either.

But there were other libraries in America, and other learned men, and Paul had written to them. Surely someone, somewhere, was interested in pursuing a line of research into the greatest mystery of humankind. What happens when we die? Where do we go? Is there a way back? These questions concerned literally everyone on the planet!

Most of his letters had received no response. A few had generated interesting correspondence but no real results. And then, finally, word from Philadelphia, and now Paul Brooks, born a gong farmer's son in London's East End, found himself in the home of one of the most famous, learned, and wealthy men in all of America.

Paul and Ben Franklin stared at each other in silence, the latter slowly tapping the letter Paul had brought against his leg. *Tap . . . tap . . . tap.*

He's eighty if he's a day, marveled Paul, making a mental inventory of the physical indignities so many years on earth wrought upon a man.

The door to the sitting room opened. The servant Anne returned bearing a pair of spectacles, which she handed to the old man. This time she did not retreat but stayed in the room, making herself busy tending the fire, which had drawn low in the intervening minutes.

Franklin unfolded the spectacles and placed them on his face. Paul noticed something unusual about them, a horizontal line across the middle of each lens. Subtle and difficult to see but definitely present. Some innovation or affectation, Paul decided.

The old inventor opened Paul's letter and began to read. After just a few moments, the speed of his reading belying Paul's suspicions of an infirm mind, Franklin looked up.

"I did not write this," the man said.

"Uh . . . if you're suggesting I did, I can assure you, sir . . ."

"I am not. The letter is in a passable version of my own hand. I can see why the servant at the door was fooled. It pushes credibility to think you would have seen enough examples of my script to create this. This letter is a forgery, though not by you. I suspected as much from the beginning, but I know the journey from Massachusetts is arduous, and I thought perhaps I should see you if my health permitted."

Paul was unsure how to respond.

"I don't understand. I sent a letter to this address and received a response inviting me here. If you didn't write it, who in God's name did?"

Franklin gestured languidly toward the woman tending the fire.

"Anne would be my guess. In recent years I have allowed her to assist me with my correspondence, as my own facility with a pen has diminished. She has a very quick mind and has become essential to those scientific explorations I allow myself in these last years."

Paul got to his feet, inclining his head respectfully toward the old man in the leather chair.

"Sir, I never intended to waste your time or participate in any foolishness or prank," he said, wondering what trouble he might have gotten himself into. "I will be on my way."

Benjamin Franklin was as close to a nobleman as they had on this side of the pond, and if there's one thing any honest Englishman knew, it's that you stayed beneath the notice of the titled if you valued your freedom.

"No, Mr. Brooks, stay, at least for a moment," Franklin said.

Paul's hands tightened into fists, an old reflex from his youth.

Not getting out of this that easy, he thought, trying to stay calm, wondering if Molly Calder would be willing to expend further resources to buy him out of whatever Philadelphia jail lay in wait.

Benjamin Franklin turned to look at Anne, now standing next to the fire, watching them.

"What was your purpose in this, Anne?" he said.

"I believe the man is asking interesting questions, sir," the servant said. "I also believe you might have insight he would find useful. His path of inquiry could be something you would find stimulating. As, in fact, would I. I see no reason why we *can't* investigate death."

Franklin chuckled, a sound that devolved quickly into a cough.

"I suspect I will be discovering the answer to that mystery very soon myself, with no additional effort required on my part," he said. "I wish to spend the time I have left imparting what small lessons I can to those who will come after me via that blasted autobiography I cannot seem to finish."

He looked back at Paul.

"But you have come such a long way, Mr. Brooks. You have gone to such great expense and effort to see me and deserve any aid I can offer. I do have some information I might impart to you, sir. I made some experiments along these lines in my earlier years, though they were of a nature I would not see made public at this point in my career, or even after I am gone."

Franklin peered at Paul over his unusual spectacles.

"I am a man who will leave some kind of legacy. I would not have it tainted, at least not beyond the many mistakes and missteps of which the public is already aware. If you pass along what I am to tell you, I will deny it, and I will instruct my attorney to bring a slander suit against you if any word of this comes out after I am dead. It will be the word of Paul Brooks, dye maker from Concord, against that of Benjamin Franklin. Do you understand?"

Paul nodded.

"I do, sir," he said, hearing a quaver in his voice. Anticipation, nerves . . . he couldn't say which.

"Electricity," said Franklin. "You are familiar with it?"

"In passing," Paul said. "I haven't made a serious study of it."

"I urge you to do so," said the old inventor. "I believe it holds the key to the next version of human civilization. I have done a great many experiments with it in my time."

He glanced at the actual key nailed to the wall, then back at Paul.

"I believe that, in some way I cannot fully define, we are ourselves creatures of electricity. All living things are."

"Is it our animating principle? Our spirit?"

"I cannot speak to that. But some years ago I tested the effect of electricity on recently deceased animal tissue. Rabbits, frogs, small beasts. Whole corpses, or even just limbs or heads."

Paul had not expected this. He understood why Franklin was unwilling to let these particular experiments be widely known. But then, science was science, and conventional morality often had to take a step back.

"What . . . happened?" Paul said.

Franklin leaned forward, his eyes sparkling. He seemed thrilled to be able to discuss these things.

"They *moved*," he said. "Life returned to them, even just for moments."

He waved a hand.

"My instruments were not precise enough to regulate the current in a fashion to refine the experiments, and I became consumed with other research and the demands of statesmanship and building this nation . . ."

Here, his eyes went distant, remembering events long past.

". . . but I have never forgotten the way he moved, there on the table."

He? Paul thought, and wondered what manner of rabbit or frog would be so familiar to the old inventor that he would call it "he."

"That is all I can tell you, Mr. Brooks," Franklin said. "I have no answer, but I would include electricity in your research. Now I ask you to take your leave. I must rest, and then Anne and I have another chapter of my autobiography to complete."

Paul stood.

"Yes, sir, of course. Thank you very much. This has been most enlightening."

Franklin nodded and turned back to the fire.

Paul took that to mean he was dismissed, and determined to see himself out. He left the room, closing the door behind him, and saw Franklin's nail-eyed footman already waiting in the front hall, holding his coat and hat.

Wealth, he thought. *Not so bad, I suppose.*

"I'll help him, Daniel," came a voice from behind him, and Paul turned to see Anne emerging from the sitting room.

"Very well, Miss Beaton," said the footman.

He handed Paul's things to Anne, gave a brief nod, and vanished, heading deeper into the house.

"Nice trick with the letter," Paul said as she held out his coat for him. "Might have gotten me thrown in jail if that had gone a different way. Not sure I appreciate that, you trifling with me that way—or Ben Franklin, for that matter. He's a great man."

"He's a man who'll be dead within the year, I am very sorry to say," Anne said. "His lungs are failing. He knows it and so do I."

Paul turned to look at her.

"Then what's this all about? You had to know he wouldn't help me."

"I did . . . though I suspect that bit about electricity could be useful. I'd never heard that story before, and I thought I'd heard all his tales in my time working with him."

She held out his cap, and Paul pulled it onto his head.

"I knew old Ben wouldn't help you," Anne said, "but I want to."

Paul narrowed his eyes.

"How's that?"

"I've trained at Franklin's right hand for years. I'm a good researcher, a good scientist, and I'd wager I know as much about electricity as any woman alive. As soon as Mr. Franklin passes on, I'll be without employment—a dangerous state for one with skin the color of mine, even here in the North. It sounds like you're well funded up there in Concord. I could be useful to you."

"I'll be buggered," Paul said, dumbfounded. "This was all . . . a job interview?"

"You might think of it that way. But I just want to work, to continue my studies, to make a good living as a free woman. How does it sound? Will your employer be willing to bring me on?"

"I . . . honestly don't know. Mrs. Calder is a good woman, but I'm not sure she's envisioned hiring additional staff for this little enterprise."

"Then let me make it easier for you. You mentioned in your letter that you were turned away at Harvard. I can write them in Franklin's hand and instruct them to give you access to the libraries. He is beloved there. It will work."

"I . . . believe it would at that," Paul said.

"There is also a magnificent library here at the University of Pennsylvania. Benjamin Franklin *founded* the place. Another letter from him, and you'll have access to those works as well."

"A letter from you, you mean," Paul said.

"I am at your disposal," she said, offering him a little curtsy.

Paul considered, but not for long.

"I'll have to clear it with Molly, and I presume you'll want to see Mr. Franklin through to the end, but when you're ready . . . come up to Concord and let's just see, Anne Beaton."

He stuck out his hand. Anne took it.

"Let's just see."

II. FOUR

MASSACHUSETTS.

JULY 1790.

42°28'13.9"N, 71°21'08.9"W

MOLLY CALDER SURVEYED HER DOMAIN.

She stood on the porch of the home she had once shared with Apollo Calder and, if God's will and human ingenuity permitted, someday would again. The porch offered a good view of her holdings below.

The Calder Mill, once an advanced facility for producing a variety of fabrics for many purposes, from sailcloth to broadcloth to fine linen, was now something else entirely.

A factory for thought.

The mill wheel still turned, the river's strength powering the Mill's buildings and machinery via a system of gears and crankshafts, but that system had become much more elaborate. The primary shaft from the wheel now vanished into a new building, the "gearing room," from which many smaller shafts ran to other workshops and laboratories around the complex.

Inside was an elaborate clockwork mechanism that could shift energy from one part of the Mill to another, divide it, even store it until it was needed via large springs. The device was designed by Eugenia Greaves, a red-cheeked, swarthy woman in her early thirties who had traveled to the Mill from New York City and requested employment. Like Molly, she was also recently widowed, though she refused to answer questions about the manner of her husband's passing. She allowed that he was a clockmaker and that she had worked at his side during the marriage, but that was all. She believed she had a broad set of skills applicable to the Mill's systems, despite the size differential between a watch movement and a waterwheel.

"Gears are gears," she often said. "Big or small, they work the same. If the teeth bite, you're all right."

Eugenia was one of many people who had made the journey to Massachusetts in the months since Apollo's death, drawn by promises of interesting work outside the boundaries traditionally drawn by considerations of gender, age, racial origin, marital status, and even propriety.

The first of the new arrivals showed up at the Mill a month after Paul returned from Philadelphia—Anne Beaton, the former slave who had used her intelligence and ingenuity to become apprenticed to Benjamin Franklin in his later years. Her appearance was not entirely unexpected, and she brought with her two interesting things. For one, news—that Franklin had himself passed on into death. He had died of pleurisy, expiring as peacefully as one could from a malady that made one feel like each lung was transmuted into an anvil.

For another, she brought a young Russian man, midway through his third decade, dour and dark, named Evgeny Choglovoka. This person spoke middling English but was apparently an astonishingly skilled doctor, having apprenticed in St. Petersburg with John Rogerson, the personal physician to Catherine the Great.

How Evgeny ended up in the former colonies was unclear.

Molly had the impression a dalliance at the Russian court was involved, a situation that had become potentially deadly for the handsome surgeon. Dr. Choglovoka had fled to America, where he connected with Anne in Philadelphia.

These three and many other brilliant, unusual individuals had found their way to the Calder Mill. Paul Brooks vetted them all, but ultimately, Molly didn't care why *any* of them had left their former lives. She'd have welcomed the worst criminal in the world if that person had skills that would help her reunite with her husband. All she cared about was Apollo.

Molly pulled a watch on a chain—once Apollo's, now hers—from a pocket in her skirts. She checked the time; it was nearly noon, which meant she had an appointment to keep. She stepped off the porch and made her way down the hill into the Mill proper. Little clusters of her workers new and old were everywhere, engaged in spirited discussions, arguing over slates covered with arcane scribblings and figures, or working on elaborate mechanisms.

Greetings rang out as she passed.

"Mrs. Calder!"

"Good morning, Molly!"

"If you've a moment, let us share this latest line of inquiry!"

Molly passed by them all, offering smiles and nods but none of her time.

She had somewhere to be.

That destination: a clapboard structure on the outskirts of the Mill called the Charge House, after the strange engine it contained. Anne Beaton had designed it, Paul Brooks had marshaled the Mill's craftspeople to build it, and Eugenia Greaves had contrived to bring a shaft all the way from the waterwheel to power it. As Molly approached the building, she could see the thick length of polished oak turning steadily, rotating smoothly in brackets lubricated by animal fat.

The Charge House contained a lightning machine, and while

that was strange enough, stranger still was what Molly's people intended to do with it.

Paul Brooks stood just outside the door. He held up a hand in greeting.

"Hello there, Mrs. Calder," he said. "We're ready. You may wish to brace yourself—the preparations were a bit . . . grim."

"Thank you, Mr. Brooks," Molly said, stepping past him and into the Charge House. "I'm sure I'll be fine."

A dead deer was laid out on the table in the center of the room. The poor beast was on its back, its head lolling down off the table upon which it lay, its spindly limbs splayed in a way that felt deeply immodest. A doe, by the lack of antlers. Molly felt sad for the creature.

Dark iron rods protruded from the corpse, each with a ring at its end, to which was attached a strange cord like nothing Molly had ever seen. Black and finger-thick, it coiled from the rods to the large cylinder of brass, ceramic, and glass that was the lightning engine.

"What is this?" she asked, touching the cord with an outstretched finger, immediately chastising herself.

One of the primary rules for the transformed Calder Mill: *Touch nothing*. Whether chemicals or lightning or some mechanical contrivance that would strip a limb from you in an instant, danger was everywhere.

Anne Beaton gently put her hand beneath Molly's wrist and lifted it away from the dark rope.

"Linen saturated with beeswax, wrapped around a copper core. Some materials transmit the electrical impulses more effectively than others, and copper is one of the very best. The wrapping ensures that little is lost as it travels from the engine to its destination."

"We used fabric from the stores," Paul said. "We have plenty. I hope that's not a problem."

Molly waved this off. She didn't care in the slightest. Everything she had made before Apollo's death was fair to use in facilitating his return. Money, goods, connections . . . anything. She would spend every penny she had if it would allow her more time with him—and at her current rate of expenditure, it was entirely possible she would do exactly that.

"The deer," she said. "Tell me about the deer."

"It's a fresh kill," came another voice.

Molly looked over to see Aarvan Bir standing in the corner, a long pipe in his hand, smoke curling up from its bowl. Bir was a Hindu mystic who had joined the compound about a month before. He was the one person whose presence at the Mill made Molly occasionally question Paul's judgment in his recruiting policies.

Bir was supposedly an expert in the spirit, with abilities beyond those of ordinary men. These talents were (by his account) subtle, not easily understood or demonstrated. This smacked to Molly of a person making claims that conveniently could not be verified. But when she voiced these concerns to Mr. Brooks, he'd said the Hindu had demonstrated his bona fides in some particular way the Englishman was loath to reveal. Bir had known things about him no one could possibly know.

And really, even if the white-bearded old man was a fraud, there was no great harm in it. Many at the Mill found his ideas interesting, even inspiring. Molly was willing to explore any and all paths. Most would be dead ends, but all had to be investigated.

Aarvan was currently passing a slim rod of pure silver over the deer's body. He then tapped it against a small brass bell and listened intently to the sound, waiting for it to die away. When the bell's chime had completely faded, he looked up.

"The creature's soul remains tied to its body for a few moments more," Aarvan said in clear English accented with a rolling lilt.

He was the first Hindu Molly had met, so she could not say if his manner of speaking was universal to his people, but it was easily understood.

"Good," Paul said. "Molly, let me give you a sense of the experiment we're attempting today. The idea is to try to send electricity into the deer's body to channel its spirit into this device here."

He pointed to a glass jar with a cork in it, coated halfway up its sides with a shiny metal, and a thin iron spike piercing the cork and entering the jar. At its end, a thin metal chain was attached and hanging down, touching the jar's interior, also covered in the same shiny metal as the exterior.

The chain's other end culminated in an iron ring like those touching the deer. Attached to it was more of the linen-wrapped cable, running to a single round plate affixed to the deer's chest.

"The containment device is called a Leyden jar," Anne Beaton said. "It can accumulate electrical charge and store it. About ten years ago, an Italian, Luigi Galvani, discovered that electricity runs through living tissue. He thought it was a unique phenomenon, some special sort of energy. He called this energy 'galvanic,' after himself; he was vain, like every Italian I ever met. But Ben Franklin believed Luigi was wrong . . . at least in part. He thought the energy Luigi discovered was no different from ordinary electricity. Old Ben thought electricity was the motivating energy for all life—that it animates us, allows us to think and be. I believe the same."

She pointed at the lightning engine, then gestured with her finger, running it along the cable until it reached the deer.

"We'll run a negative charge from the engine into the deer, which should push what we believe is the positively charged remains of its spirit into this plate here"—she pointed at the round metal disk on the deer's chest—"and then into the Leyden jar. We can measure the amount of current in the jar, and if we've set this experiment up properly, we might find ourselves in possession of the captured spirit of a deer."

Molly's eyes narrowed.

"And how will that return my husband to me?"

"It will not, madam," said Aarvan, his tone soothing, "not directly. But in much the same way as a single step brings one closer to a destination, this experiment today will offer us insight that will, in time, lead to your desired result."

"How *much* time?" Molly said.

The mystic spread his arms, palms up.

"Who can say? We must only continue the journey."

She shook her head. Paul had warned her to manage her expectations in terms of how long the effort to conquer death might take. It was an unprecedented area of scientific inquiry, after all. Despite the wisdom of this suggestion, Molly couldn't help herself. She was burning through her fortune, and every day Apollo felt farther away.

"I understand. I know you're all working very hard," she said. "I am grateful, and I am sure Apollo is as well."

"Step back, Mrs. Calder," Paul said. "We might need to move quickly. Wouldn't want to jostle you against any of the equipment."

Anne, Aarvan, and Paul took up positions around the room. Anne was at the Leyden jar, a short pair of tongs in her hand, having donned a thick leather glove. Paul was at the lightning engine's controls, and Aarvan was next to the deer with his eyes closed, taking deep breaths and holding his hands, fingers interlaced, above the metal plate on the beast's heart.

"On three," Paul said. "One . . . two . . ."

He flipped the main switch on the lightning engine, and with a sizzling *crack* the deer *convulsed.* Its entire body arced up off the table, bending its spine into a horrible comma. One of its delicate legs whipped out, striking Aarvan in the face. He cried out and fell back.

Molly felt as if the light had dimmed in the little room, though the sun outside was as bright as ever.

The deer's jaw was moving, its tongue lolling out, its teeth closing on it with a muffled, horrible *snap*.

"Stop this!" Molly cried.

"Just a little . . . more . . . ," said Anne, busy at the Leyden jar.

She was using her tongs to manipulate the spike in the jar, trying to keep the connection to the deer steady despite the creature's seizure-like movements.

In a corner of the room, Aarvan Bir was curled up on the floor, hands to his face, offering a low moan to the overarching chaos.

Molly could smell an odor—familiar, not entirely unpleasant, cooking meat with an edge of burned hair to it—and she realized the deer was being *roasted*.

This was no different than venison being cooked for a meal, but somehow it was. Molly felt her gorge rise.

The deer jerked again, and this time it snapped the restraints holding it to the table and rolled off, which in turn pulled the cable attached to the Leyden jar, yanking it off the stool upon which it rested. The jar fell to the ground and smashed, producing a sizzling snap and a tiny flash of light.

Was that its soul? Molly wondered.

The tiniest flicker of hope bloomed in her chest.

Paul flipped a switch on the lightning engine. The device went dark. The room was silent but for the slow creak of the mill shaft turning in its mounts. One could not turn off the river, after all.

Aarvan cautiously sat up. Blood soaked his beard, streaming down from a gash on his cheek.

"Go see Evgeny," Molly ordered. "A wound from an animal's hoof can carry corruption. Best have it seen to immediately."

"I'll take him," Paul said. "Fellow seems unsteady."

He helped Aarvan up, sliding his arm across the other man's back in support. They exited, slipping out without a word, the Hindu clearly in significant pain.

That left Molly, Anne, and the deer, which had mercifully

gone still. The other woman was down on her haunches, poking at the remains of the Leyden jar with her tongs.

"Before the jar broke," Molly said, "did you get it? Did you see the creature's soul?"

Anne stood. She placed the tongs and her leather glove on the table and then looked Molly in the eye.

"I don't want to tell you something that isn't true, Mrs. Calder," she said. "I have no idea what was in that jar before it broke. If we'd gotten a charge, I would have done more experiments to measure it, see how it might differ from an ordinary bit of current accumulated via an electrostatic generator. That's how science works. Perhaps the fact that we are working with electricity led you to believe this problem would be solved all at once, like a bolt of lightning. That will not be the case."

Her face went softer, more sympathetic.

"But everything we do brings us closer. We learned things today we did not previously know. I might not agree with, or even understand, much of what Aarvan Bir talks about, but on this one point we are fully united."

She smiled.

"This will happen one step at a time."

II. FIVE

THE CALDER MILL.

SEPTEMBER 1790.

42°28'13.9"N, 71°21'08.9"W

"Things have changed here since my last visit, Widow Calder," said the minister.

Molly considered this statement and all its veiled import. She glanced out through the fine glass panes of her sitting room window, only slightly marred by ripples and tiny bubbles. She and Apollo had chosen each pane together, cut from disks of crown glass before being set in the nine-panel grid of the window frames. A huge expense, and a risky one, considering the strength of winters in the Northeast, but thick exterior shutters had proven successful in protecting both the glass and the home's warmth during the colder months.

Through these windows one could see the Calder Mill, now unable to be viewed as anything other than the extensive forum for exploring odd ideas it had become. Piles of raw materials, strange contraptions belching smoke, the waterwheel's crankshafts running through the property, dividing and branching like cracks on a thawing sheet of spring ice. (These shafts were now sealed in protective housings rather than exposed to the elements, allowing them to remain lubricated for much longer periods. Another innovation of Eugenia Greaves.)

Linen-wrapped cabling connected many of the buildings, hanging from poles set at regular intervals, creating the impression of the web of a gigantic spider. These cables could all be traced back to the Charge House, which had been expanded significantly and now contained a large electrostatic generator. Enough of the Mill's experiments used electricity now that it had been deemed prudent to ensure current was available to the laboratories at all times.

The new Mill was constructed with an eye toward quick solutions and efficiency rather than any attempt at symmetry or beauty. And yet it all felt natural. Grown rather than built. Which, Molly thought, was exactly how it had all happened. The better part of a year had passed since Apollo's death, and it was astonishing what had been accomplished in that time.

The whole compound thrummed. Everywhere, men and women worked, intent on their tasks, moving supplies, building and deconstructing odd mechanisms, taking part in lectures in the open-air symposiums at which knowledge and theories were passed along and debated. Long tables were set in a cleared meadow for workers to eat and drink and, always, talk, think, exchange ideas.

There was even a makeshift tavern, named the Far Border. An outsider might suspect the name referred to its location near the low stone wall at the compound's northernmost edge. But Molly's people knew the tavern's name suggested another dividing line, between this life and the destination from which no one ever returned.

Yet.

She pulled her mind back to the clergyman sitting before her.

"This place has indeed seen many changes, Pastor Black," she said. "My aims have shifted from the prior business of the Mill to a new venture."

"That is what we understand as well, Widow Calder, and why we have come," replied the minister, a tall, thin man dressed all in black but for a broad white linen collar, who exuded an air of great calm and certainty of purpose.

Molly, the minister, and one other visitor were seated in her parlor around a round table covered by a pristine white linen cloth and a silver tea service. They had arrived unannounced, riding up the river road on a wagon pulled by two workhorses. Pastor Black she knew well—he had presided over Apollo's burial and had overseen Sunday services for them both for many years at the Old South Church in Boston. The other man was unfamiliar to her. He had the air of a mildly successful tradesman who had worked hard at a profession requiring intense physical labor—building or sailing or warehouse work—eventually saving enough to start his own business. His body was broad but in the manner of an oak tree, not from overindulgence.

This man's name was Jonathan Franck. Pastor Black had introduced him but offered no explanation as to the reason for his presence at the meeting. Franck had a dark air to him, like a thundercloud preparing to unleash itself upon the landscape.

"There have been suggestions," Pastor Black said, clearly choosing his words with delicacy, "that you are embarking upon scientific explorations here that are . . . troubling."

"Troubling?" Molly said. "It is true that I have created a workshop here, dedicated to innovation and the creation of new technology, but this is hardly novel. The Calder Mill has been known for using advanced machinery and techniques since its founding. It was part of my husband's philosophy for this place, and a great signifier of our success in the manufacture of textiles. I am merely carrying on with work Apollo himself supported. I see nothing troubling about that."

"Your husband ran a fabric mill, Molly," Pastor Black said, his tone softening, "but even a cursory glance around your property indicates that no linen or broadcloth is being made here. What are you doing?"

"As I said . . . ," Molly began, but was almost interrupted by Jonathan Franck.

"Stop dancing with the woman, Pastor," he said. "We know what she's doing. She is trying to raise the dead. She lost her husband and then she lost her bloody mind."

Franck sat back, folded his arms, and glared.

"This is indeed what we have heard, Molly," the pastor said. "Please tell me these are simply malicious rumors."

"Of course," Molly said. "That is nonsense. This place is dedicated to the principles of natural philosophy and how they might be marshaled in the form of machinery and advanced processes that might themselves be used to generate income. It is still a factory, Pastor, but where once we produced thread and rugs and sailcloth, now we produce ideas."

She lifted her tea and took a sip.

"I believe that, in time, the ideas will prove to be more profitable than the textiles ever were."

"So you are truly not working in areas that might be considered unnatural? Against the will of God?"

"Upon my honor and the love I held in my heart for my husband," Molly said.

God puts challenges before us, Molly thought, *and everything we do is his will. If he does not want me to pursue the goals I have set myself, why, he's more than welcome to strike me dead and let me rejoin my husband.*

"That is a relief to hear," Pastor Black said. "Scripture is extremely clear upon this point. Leviticus, chapter twenty, verse twenty-seven; Deuteronomy, chapter eighteen, verse ten; and others besides. Necromancy, sorcery, attempts to speak with the dead . . . all are expressly forbidden."

"Oh, yes, Pastor Black," Molly said. "I am well aware."

And I stopped caring about the Bible's restrictions the moment the light went out of Apollo's eyes, she thought. *If a way exists to bring someone back, well, God created that path too. If we find it, it will be science, not sorcery.*

"Everything here is well within the bounds of what God deems acceptable," Molly said. "I promise you."

The image of Aarvan Bir floated up in Molly's mind, as if in rebuttal to her words. Some of what the mystic had attempted in the past few months did seem to be rooted in something like . . . well, magic. But it didn't matter. None of it worked. She thought Bir's time at the Mill was drawing to an end. Even Paul Brooks's patience for him seemed to be running out, which might be for the best.

After all, not far up the coast was a town called Salem, and memories of what had occurred there a century before had scarcely faded.

A scream rose into the air from somewhere outside the house. All eyes turned toward the window. It grew in volume, stretched and wavered and became ragged, turning into a screech . . . before it was abruptly cut off. The minister and the tradesman turned to look back at Molly.

"A hog," she said, waving off their stares. "Slaughtered for butchering. I feed my people well. It is important to me that they are well cared for. That has always been the case at the Calder Mill, even in my husband's time."

She wondered what the noise actually was. Perhaps another deer falling prey to the un-tender ministrations of Anne Beaton. Or maybe one of Swami Bir's experiments had actually succeeded and something had appeared in his little corner of the Mill that engendered utter terror in whoever saw it. Or possibly—though she dearly hoped not—someone had gotten caught in one of Eugenia's gearing experiments, and Molly and her guests had just heard someone's life being crushed from their body. All were possible.

"Whatever you're doing here, how well you treat your people, I don't care," Jonathan Franck said. "I am here for my daughter. Produce her so the reverend and I might be on our way. It is several hours' journey back to Boston, and I do not wish to be traveling after nightfall."

Ah, Molly thought, the man's intentions becoming clear. *You want your property back, to place her somewhere else you think might earn you more coin, or to marry her off in some profitable union.*

"What is your daughter's name?" she asked. "We had many unmarried women working at the Mill, back when it produced textiles. A good number of them decided to stay on when we adjusted our output. Work, after all, is work."

"Is it?" said Mr. Franck. "At any rate, my daughter is Nellie Franck. You might have her in your books as Penelope. That is her given name."

"A beautiful name," Pastor Black said, seeming nervous at what felt like a storm gathering in the room. "From the classics."

"Yes, I know Nellie," Molly said. "A charming girl, and a very hard worker."

"I am aware of my daughter's good qualities," Jonathan said. "That is why I want her back."

"Then I will have her fetched," Molly said.

She raised her voice.

"Edward?" she called, and moments later her house steward presented himself, a lean man with a majestically maintained mustache.

Edward Albright was the man's name, and he ensured that the Calder house, and indeed the entirety of the Calder Mill, were kept in good order and security.

"Yes, Mrs. Calder?" he said.

"Please send for Milton and have Nellie Franck brought up here. I believe she's working with Eugenia's group in the gear house."

"Ah, of course," Edward said. "Should I have her . . . clean up?"

"No," she answered. "Let her not take the time. It is, after all, several hours' journey back to Boston."

In short order, a knock came at the door. Penelope Franck was admitted to the house, then brought to the sitting room. She was a plain girl of about sixteen years, hair in a sensible bun beneath a grey cotton bonnet, wearing a long skirt. Molly knew it had been donned just minutes before: no one worked the Gearworks while wearing anything that might be caught in the endlessly spinning, churning teeth. A few gruesome accidents early on had proven the folly of that idea. Those who maintained the Gearworks wore the most sensible choice for their surroundings: men's trousers. And since that part of the Mill's operations was exclusively the domain of Eugenia and her girls, it mattered not at all.

At Penelope Franck's side was Milton Tenenbaum, a man who had been in the Mill's employ for over five years. He had first worked for the Calders on an ad hoc basis, but the Mill's business had become so fruitful that in time they became his only clients. Milton was quick to laugh and quick to finish his meal and ask for more, and maintained an impeccable sense of dress—not easy in a wilderness enclave twenty-five miles from the nearest real civilization.

"Father?" Penelope said, more alarmed than surprised.

"Hello, Nellie," Jonathan said. "Gather your things, whatever they may be. We are returning to Boston."

"Today? But . . . I have work here. I am under contract. The wages are being paid, are they not?"

"They are," said Milton, "to the penny."

Jonathan Franck shot Tenenbaum a glance before dismissing him as a dandy and returning his gaze to his daughter.

Your mistake, Molly thought.

"I indentured you to the Calder Mill to learn the weaving trade. Not to do . . . whatever they do here. I am taking you back and we will find you another mill."

"But . . . I enjoy the work here, and my wages are the same as they were when I was weaving. I am learning about machinery, sir. It is useful experience."

"I do not care about your experience, Nellie," Jonathan Franck said, his face reddening. "I care about your reputation. This place is whispered about, and I will not have my daughter's prospects, such as they are, tainted by the association."

Penelope's eyebrows rose slightly, and a stubborn cast came over her face.

"I like it here, Father. I would not leave, and do not care about how my prospects might be affected . . . *such as they are*."

"You have no choice," Jonathan Franck said.

He stood from his chair, towering over his daughter.

"And you well know it."

"He is correct, Nellie," Pastor Black said. "Under the law, and the Church, and by right, you must mind your father. Be a good girl now and fetch your things so we might be on our way."

Molly caught Milton's eye and nodded. He returned the gesture and stepped forward, holding up a finger.

"Actually," he said, "not to contradict the good pastor, but the law suggests a different outcome."

Jonathan Franck turned to Milton, his face turning a darker shade of crimson.

"Whoever you are," he rumbled, "I urge you to leave this business be, before you find yourself in more trouble than you might handle."

"I am often in others' business, unfortunately," Milton replied, his tone amused. "For I am, you see, the Mill's attorney. Milton Tenenbaum, at your service."

He gave a neat, theatrical bow.

"Oh, no," said Jonathan.

"Oh, yes," said Milton. "Let's chat, Mr. Franck. I understand your desire here is to remove your daughter from her place of employment, the Calder Mill, to which you indentured her just over a year ago."

"As a *weaver,*" Jonathan spat.

"Yes, true. But I took the liberty of pulling Miss Franck's contract from my files before I came up to the house."

With a flourish, he pulled a broad leather wallet from within his coat, placed it on the table, opened it, and removed a densely worded piece of parchment. He scanned it briefly, then pointed to a bit of writing.

"Here," he said. "Read it for yourself. Your daughter here is indentured to the Mill 'as a weaver, or for any other work that might advance the purposes of the enterprise, in the sole discretion of its proprietors, for the full term of this contract.'"

"I don't need to read it," Jonathan said. "It doesn't matter. She's my daughter. I have rights."

"You do, but so does the Widow Calder. She is now the sole proprietor of the Mill, and as such she may administer your daughter's services here as she sees fit for the next . . . two years, I believe. That was the agreement you made. If you would like to break it, why, then we would of course see you at the courthouse. We would go through all the steps of the dance, and the resolution would be either that your daughter would continue working here through the end of her contract, or you would compensate us for the loss of her services—which would be, I guarantee you, a rather significant sum."

Milton stepped back, his role in the performance complete.

Jonathan stared at the lawyer with the sort of look reserved for something scraped off a shoe, or hurked up from a tubercular lung.

"This is wrong," he said, his voice quiet, but with the rumble of thunder buried within. "She belongs to me."

He turned his head to look at Molly.

"And you . . . you should not be in control of this place. You should not have the rights you have. No woman should."

Molly tilted her head.

"My deceased husband," she said, her voice relaxed, "who had the choice to allow me to inherit ownership and control and chose to do so . . . disagrees. If you also wish to dispute that *legally binding fact* . . ."

She gestured to Milton, who inclined his head in return.

". . . add it to the list of the matters you will bring to Mr. Tenenbaum."

"I do like to stay busy," Milton said.

Jonathan's fists clenched, opened, clenched, and Molly worried she would need to call in Edward Albright. He was more than capable of handling an incensed Boston tradesman or any other threats to her person. Mr. Albright would probably take great joy of it, in fact. The moment stretched . . . and then Pastor Black placed a hand on Franck's meaty arm.

"Let us go, Jonathan," he said. "We must think on these matters, and your daughter seems well cared for here. Let none of us do something we would regret, that would shame us in the eyes of the Lord."

Franck took a long, deep breath, a clear attempt to release his building rage. He seemed to shrink, to become less in some way, and all in the room could see it.

"This is wrong," he said to Molly, his eyes dark and hooded. "All of this is wrong."

II. SIX

THE CALDER MILL.

SEPTEMBER 1790.

42°28'13.6"N, 71°21'03.1"W

THEY CAME BEFORE DAWN. FOR FOUR DAYS AND THREE NIGHTS they observed the Calder Mill, coming to understand its rhythms. They learned who came and went, the tasks its people performed, and where the men, women, and children worked, ate, and slept. Not all lived in the dormitories on the compound's west side. Some families had small cabins. Others—the more important administrators and researchers—lived in larger homes. Atop the hill was the biggest house of all, standing sentry, with a view that commanded the entire enterprise.

The Mill was organized in a rough circle around an open central area, a commons. Surrounding it were all manner of buildings: a small general store and a schoolhouse. A church. A large kitchen with a dining hall attached. A large saltbox-style building boasting an enormous blue flag above its door. A tavern. Warehouses and storage sheds. The huge brick millhouse, to which the watchers saw no cotton delivered and from which no lengths of cloth were taken. Artisans' workshops, busy all day long manufacturing all manner of glass and metal items. A surgery. The waterwheel and the gearing shed attached to it, drawing energy from the falls and dispersing it via complex mechanisms to crankshafts throughout the property.

Hanging above it all, a tangle of strange dark cables suspended on poles, connecting many of the buildings. The purpose of those, the watchers did not understand, but ropes were ropes.

It was abundantly clear that this was not a textile manufacturing operation of the type found along the rivers of the Northeast. The Calder Mill was not a factory or even a village. It had become something between a town and a small city.

At night the Mill quieted. A few torch-bearing watchmen patrolled the grounds, but as often as not, as the hour grew late, they settled in and threw dice or gossiped or fell asleep.

The watchers did not. They took their vigil in shifts, developing an increasingly complete picture of the Mill. They observed from hidden vantage points in the forest, peering through spyglasses while perched high in trees or by slipping through the reeds at the riverbank, coming close to see and listen, then fading back to share what they had learned with their fellows.

They were eight—two men assigned to each of their four targets.

A strategy was devised, an order of attack. First, the deaths, then the taking, then the ruin. If that needed to change, due to the inevitable workings of chance against any battle plan, it could.

On the fourth night, moonless and dark, the watchers daubed their faces with pitch, tied back their hair, and secured their weapons and equipment to ensure noiseless movement. They waited until the Mill's watchmen had settled, and then they moved.

Their blood was up. It sang to them. It had been too long.

THE CALDER MILL'S LAWYER, MILTON TENENBAUM, WAS SHOCKED out of a sound sleep by the feeling of a hand on his person—an extremely unpleasant realization for a man who lived alone. Worse still was that the hand covered his mouth and nose, gripping him tightly, pushing his head down hard against his straw-filled mattress. He could not breathe or even turn his head, though he tried mightily to do both.

He thrashed his body, but a weight was upon him, and his struggles did no good. Panic filled him—no, terror. Abject, freezing terror.

Milton suddenly felt a great wrongness: a line of sharp, white heat across his neck. He felt *open*, in ways he should not. Air was touching parts of his person it had never reached before. He heard a gurgling, bubbling sound, thick and wet.

A lassitude settled upon Milton, a greater weight than whatever held him down. The pain was much more fierce now. He understood that he was soon to die.

Milton Tenenbaum's last thoughts were of books—he owned a great many. For years he spent much of his income on interesting volumes on diverse subjects, most of which he had not found time to read due to the demands of his profession. They were piled in untidy stacks around his small home at the Mill. Now they would remain forever unread—at least by him. He hoped they would find their way into the hands of other readers. If he couldn't read them, someone should.

When the lawyer was dead, his assailants took a live coal from his fireplace and set it on a pile of papers on his desk. Flames blossomed in short order, and the two men slipped out the way they had entered.

EDWARD ALBRIGHT WOKE.

He did not know why just yet, but he knew there was a reason. Albright had spent the war against the British serving under Lieutenant Colonel Thomas Knowlton until his death at the

Battle of Harlem Heights, and then Captain Stephen Brown. During that time he had learned how a soldier slept: short (grabbing moments of unconsciousness whenever possible) and light (awakening at the slightest hint something might be amiss).

Edward Albright was not just any soldier, either. His unit was named after Knowlton and kept that designation even after the man's death. They answered directly and only to General Washington, performing whatever task he required of them, things that would damn a man if it were not wartime and the circumstances not so dire. Knowlton's Rangers were spies, they were infiltrators, they were the men sent into enemy territory to destroy from within.

Edward had served with this unit throughout the War for Independence. He had retired only after the Siege of Yorktown in 1781 and attempted to find himself a new manner of living—no easy task. The patterns and desires of the soldier's life were difficult to shake loose, not to mention the damage it inflicted on body and spirit.

In time, Edward Albright washed up at the Mill, where Apollo Calder, not a veteran himself but sympathetic to their struggles, had hired him as a watchman. For seven years he had performed that role, eventually becoming part of the Calder household and now a trusted servant.

But he remained a man who could sleep short and sleep light.

Edward slipped from his bed. A short turn around the house would do no harm, and he knew sleep would not come again until he had quieted whatever misgivings had awakened him.

TWO OF THE WATCHERS—IN TRUTH NOW INVADERS, KILLERS, destroyers—waded into the river, feet bare. The current was strong, tugging at their legs as soon as they stepped from the bank. The roar of the falls was loud.

Each man carried a rucksack secured by straps across his shoulders. They chose their steps carefully. It would not do for them to slip. What they carried could be ruined if it got wet, and a rough impact could produce an even greater calamity.

The two men made their way to the mill wheel. The huge construct was not currently spinning, its great axle stilled by an iron locking bar thrown forward into its gearing. This was done every day at sunset. The watchers supposed it was to reduce wear and tear on the shaftworks running through the Mill, or perhaps to allow for maintenance.

Whatever the reason, the watchers found it a lucky thing. Much simpler to accomplish their task with the great wheel lying immobile.

The men climbed up out of the river into the wheel's structure, using its spokes like a ladder. At its midpoint they opened their rucksacks, revealing cast-iron spheres the size of a small gourd, each with a length of fuse protruding from a small hole at its apex. Those fuses were twined together, six at a time, to create a contraption like a bundle of large grapes. Between them, they had four of these, twenty-four grenades in all.

The saboteurs chose likely spots on the mill wheel, hanging the grenades from the spokes at evenly spaced intervals. When they were all properly placed, the men each perched themselves astride the wheel's central hub. They pulled lengths of slow match from their purses, lit them with the flint and steel they carried, and settled in to wait.

In the women's dormitory, two dark-clad men crept silently through the large, open room, hearing the sounds of sleep all around them. Rows of bunks filled the room, set against the eastern and western walls, and in two long lines running through the center. The men had observed this building thoroughly in the days leading up to their mission and now moved toward a specific bed they had marked well: on the eastern side, third from the corner, the lowermost.

That was lucky. If their target was in the upper bunk, it would be more difficult to acquire her without waking her or her neighbor below.

Edward Albright moved through the Calder house in near-complete darkness. The former soldier needed no lantern. He knew this place as well as any in the world.

He glided through the front parlor, his feet bare, each step soft, slow, and precise. Something was amiss. He heard nothing, but the quality of the silence was wrong.

Edward stopped, thinking, listening.

The front door was open, he decided. Not much—just enough to be slipped through—and then left ajar for a quick exit. This was a wrongness. Edward had ensured it was closed and locked before retiring for the night, as he always did.

But he knew that for anyone with the proper training, a locked door was no true barrier, and Molly Calder's front door had only a simple latch mechanism. A long-bladed knife could make short work of it if you knew the trick.

Someone was in the house.

Were they in the room with him?

No, he ascertained, after testing the feel of the air. He would sense it.

The Calder house had other rooms, but not many. If an intruder was still inside, there were not many places he could be. Edward knew where his duty lay to check first.

He tightened his grip on the tomahawk he held in his right hand, a weapon all too familiar to Lieutenant Edward Albright. Memories of other dark nights flitted through his mind, the feel of hot blood running down the haft of his axe and across his hand. He stepped silently toward the bedroom door of the mistress of the house, the Widow Calder.

THE MURDERERS OF MILTON TENENBAUM REJOINED THEIR FELlows at the river. They crouched in the reeds to wait, taking the opportunity to wash their hands and weapons clean of the lawyer's blood. Two goals had been achieved. Two remained.

They watched the Mill. Light had begun to bloom from a spot on its northern edge, and the faint breeze carried the smell of smoke. The lawyer's house had caught. No alarm thus far, but it would be raised in short order. Once it was, all eyes and attention would turn to the blaze, as opposed to where they might otherwise be looking.

FAINT ORANGE LIGHT ILLUMINATED MOLLY CALDER'S BEDROOM, spilling in through the window. Edward Albright knew there should be no light at all—the night was moonless. That was suspicious, a cause for alarm . . . but it was nothing compared to fact that two dark figures stood in his mistress's bedroom where none should be. The clear outline of a long-bladed dagger was visible in one man's hand, probably the very same that had slipped the latch on the house's front door.

Edward threw his tomahawk at the man holding the knife. The other was most likely armed as well, but he chose to deal with the more obvious, imminent danger to his patron.

The tomahawk whipped through the air and sank into the man's skull. It made a muffled crunch that Edward remembered well.

Edward lunged forward before the dead man hit the ground, toward the second attacker. He sprang across the bed, across

Molly. This would surely alarm her greatly but was, he'd wager, preferable to getting her throat slit.

The second man was quick—very quick—and twisted away before Edward could reach him. In the growing light of the fire through the window—for that was what it was; obviously someone had set part of the Mill ablaze—Edward could see the intruder more clearly. Buckskin clothing, pitch-darkened face dimly outlined by the firelight.

Molly shrieked as the reality of her current circumstances became clear.

"Out, ma'am," he said. "Out the door and raise the alarm. The Mill is being attacked."

Without a word, Molly Calder did as she was bid. She slid out from beneath her blankets, stumbling slightly over the dead man on the floor. As she circled around to the door, the surviving attacker made a move as if to go for her, but Edward ensured he was between his mistress and the man.

Molly slipped out through the bedroom door. She was away. Edward breathed more easily. The next part would be simple enough, no matter how it ended.

"What now, devil?" he said.

The man drew a knife, a wickedly long hunting blade.

Edward had none. But he was not defenseless.

He stepped forward, clenching his fists.

EUGENIA GREAVES WAS YANKED FROM SLEEP BY THE SOUND OF A bell clanging out across the Mill. She sat bolt upright in her bed at the dormitory's far western end—one of the few not built into a two-story bunk—and looked for the calamity the alarm indicated.

Firelight flickered against the windows, signifying a dire problem indeed, but a more immediate issue presented itself.

Eugenia saw two dark figures moving quickly through the dormitory, one with a long, awkward bundle over its shoulder, as of a long length of fabric or a rolled-up rug. Her sleep-addled mind took a moment to understand what she was seeing—but then she realized it could only be one thing. Not fabric, not a rug, but one of her girls being spirited away in the dark of night.

"Alarm!" she cried. "Stop them! They are taking one of your sisters!"

Between the fire bell and Eugenia's shouts, everyone in the dormitory was now awake, and the two kidnappers moved faster, realizing their peril. They were quite near the door and slipped outside before they could be caught.

And then, from outside, a huge roaring emanation, a sound like hell itself had come calling, like the loudest thunderclap Eugenia had ever heard. The girls in the dormitory began to scream in terror, and Eugenia realized she had absolutely no idea what to do.

THE TWO INVADERS ASSIGNED TO STEAL AWAY NELLIE FRANCK were thrown back by the force of the waterwheel's explosion. They tumbled to the ground, and the one carrying the girl landed badly, his full weight on her. She cried out loudly despite the strip of cloth they had used to gag her. The man cursed, fearing she was damaged, in which case he might not be paid his full bounty.

The kidnapper worked himself out from under the squirming, sheet-wrapped bundle of girl. He stood. Something heavy draped itself across his shoulders and he flinched away, snatching at it. His fingers found the thing—a length of cord. He realized it must be one of the dark ropes that festooned this cursed place, fallen loose from its mooring due to the force of the waterwheel's explosion. Indeed, his fingers found a frayed edge. They explored farther along the cord's length and—

The man was thrown back again, his body jittering as it impacted the dormitory, dancing and burning as the power of Anne Beaton's electrostatic generator coursed through his body.

The last invader watched this terrible, confounding event occur and quickly wrote his companion off as lost. Around him, people circled, holding torches aloft. Searching for him. The Mill's people were now fully roused, and the would-be kidnapper realized he had no hope of spiriting Penelope Franck away to her father as he had been hired to do. The man took a moment to kick the girl's bound and wrapped body, eliciting a groan that was poor recompense for the gold he'd lost that night. The man slipped away into the dark, headed for the forest, to the place where he would rendezvous with the rest of his team.

In Molly Calder's bedroom, Edward Albright twisted the knife in the dying killer's gut, taking satisfaction from the man's scream. Edward knew he should have tried to subdue the man, not kill him: the Mill's leaders would want to question him. Choices like that were often impossible in the heat of a fight, however. Survival was the primary goal, and Edward hadn't even managed that. A deep wound in his leg sent out freshets of blood with every heartbeat. Edward had seen injuries like this often enough on the battlefield. He knew his life was soon to end.

Weakening quickly, Edward fell to his knees, releasing the knife. He slumped to his side, down across floorboards soaked with the blood of three men. He died there, wondering if the firelight flickering on the walls was an indicator of the place in which his soul was shortly to reside.

The Mill was roused.

Fire lines worked to extinguish the blazing remnants of Milton Tenenbaum's house and the utterly destroyed mill wheel. Evgeny Choglovoka had already taken Penelope Franck to his surgery for care. Teams searched the compound and the surrounding forest, looking for any attackers that might still be lurking nearby.

Molly Calder stood in the commons, watching the flames.

She knew who had done this, and she knew why. She also knew another thing.

It would never happen again.

II. SEVEN

THE CALDER MILL.

NOVEMBER 1790.

42°28'13.1"N, 71°21'10.9"W

Molly Calder pulled her shawl close around her shoulders. Winter was not yet here, but it was in the air. The leaves had turned and fallen, leaving only the pines clothed in green. She thought about the supplies they had laid in, wondering if they would last. A wagon was waylaid the prior week, and they'd lost an important and expensive shipment of dry goods.

She stood in the tower at the south corner of the Mill, looking out across the compound. Two months since the attack that had killed Milton Tenenbaum and Edward Albright, traumatized young Nellie Franck, and forced them to rebuild the riverwheel and many other structures. The Mill was made new in a hundred ways. What was once a textile factory, and then a growing garden of free thought and innovation, was now something like a fortress.

A high palisade of sharpened tree trunks surrounded the Mill, with watchtowers at each compass point. Two heavy gates provided access—one to the river road and the other to the cropland to the northwest. Those crops had been harvested, the stalks plowed under, leaving wide swaths of cleared ground beyond the north gate. The forests to the Mill's south and east were cut down to create the palisade. On all sides, it was impossible to approach the Mill without crossing a long stretch of open ground or fording the Concord River.

Were such drastic measures necessary? Molly believed so. She had requested assistance from the local constable after the attack, even doing his job for him and pointing at Mr. Jonathan Franck as the obvious culprit. But the law, in the end, had not helped her. The constable pointed out that Molly had no real evidence of Franck's involvement, and anyone who could speak to the purpose of the attack had either vanished or died that dark night.

The people of the Mill looked to her for leadership, for explanations, but what could she tell them? That she had made enemies of the Puritan elite in Boston and odds were the attack was only the first of many to come? Molly had been on the verge of disbanding the compound, telling everyone to find other, safer employment, when help had arrived from a surprising source.

Just days after the death of Edward Albright, three men arrived at the Mill claiming to be wartime colleagues of the lieutenant. Molly had always had an inkling that Edward was no ordinary soldier, though the full truth of his past had died with him. These new arrivals had many of his mannerisms. They were sharp-eyed, precise, and acted as if they expected an attack from any side at any moment. They seemed, in a word, to be rather deadly.

The three soldiers—Dalton, Briggs, and Aselton—asked to view Albright's body, which Molly had ordered stored in the Mill's icehouse alongside the three corpses of the mysterious attackers. They spent a few solemn minutes in the presence of their dead brother-in-arms, then spoke among themselves for a time, over by the wreckage of the mill wheel.

After that, they returned to Molly and told her they would do three things. None of these were presented as offers, rather simple statements of intent.

First, they would arrange for Edward's body to be transported to his childhood home in Pennsylvania for burial. They were all former members of the old Continental Army unit called Knowlton's Rangers, and considered it their duty to aid a fallen comrade.

Second, they would obtain revenge for Albright's death and justice for the Mill. It seemed that the Rangers recognized the corpse of one of the Mill's attackers. He was also a veteran, but a much rougher sort, known to have fallen into thievery, thuggery, and even darker forms of employment. Dalton, Briggs, and Aselton knew many of the villain's associates and the spots in the rougher parts of Boston where they might be found. They assured Molly they could determine the identities of the Mill's surviving attackers and that they would be dealt with in an appropriate fashion.

Third, and finally: once they had meted out what they considered justice for Edward Albright, they would return to the Mill and offer what assistance they could to Molly in the course of her work there.

These three men, whom the Mill's people quickly dubbed the Allbrights, had proven to be deeply reliable. They had devised many of the changes to the Mill's security implemented over the past two months. The Calder Mill was now *defended*. Armed men (and some women) patrolled its walls day and night, and did not stop to rest or drink or gamble in the small hours.

The Mill now knew it had enemies. They would not be caught unawares again, though ensuring the compound's safety came at a steep cost. Implementing the Allbrights' recommendations meant more was now spent on the Mill's security than on the scientific explorations that were the reason for its existence.

Those continued, of course. Ideas bloomed. Anne Beaton's skill at forgery had given the Mill access to the libraries and professors of Harvard and Penn. Scholars across the world were becoming aware of what Molly Calder had built in the wilds of Massachusetts. Letters flowed back and forth on a regular basis, as did communication from farther afield—the Calder Mill now boasted the Royal Society as a correspondent.

But whatever the Mill's reputation across the sea, here, in heavily Protestant Massachusetts, its activities were viewed with fear, superstition, and religious terror. Threats to Molly and her people were commonplace, so much so that they no longer traveled to Boston, and brought in their supplies under armed guard. It was all so much harder now. Harder and more expensive.

But perhaps not forever. Molly adjusted her shawl and made her way down from the watchtower via a set of rough-hewn log steps. She walked toward the Mill's southeast gate, where her coach stood waiting.

Dalton and the other two Allbrights, along with a few additional guards, were preparing for what looked to be a long, dangerous ride—checking the coach's fittings, adjusting their weapons, counting supply bales lashed to the coach's roof. Paul Brooks was with them, chatting with the driver. He looked up as Molly approached.

She realized she probably had a worried cast to her face, because Mr. Brooks offered her a reassuring grin before he even said a word.

"Don't be concerned, Mrs. Calder," Paul Brooks said. "We'll make it to Boston all right. Woe to any fools who come after that coach. Those three friends of poor Master Edward are about the deadliest men I've ever encountered."

"Let us hope so, Mr. Brooks," Molly replied. "All my plans lay upon it."

"Dalton and his boys shared their arrangements with me," Paul said, his tone confident. "Two guards on the coach, fore and aft, and then two horsemen riding in front and behind. Advance scouts out in the woods to either side, ready to give the alarm if they run into any ruffians waiting to ambush us. Like I said, only a fool would try to take that coach."

"Good," she said. "Shall we see to its cargo?"

"Suppose we should," he said. "I'd like to be in the city by this evening. Don't much fancy traveling after dark, even with the Allbrights along."

Molly nodded, turned, and began the walk up to her house, Brooks falling into step at her side. She still found it difficult to sleep there. She often awakened in the middle of the night, sure there was a knife at her throat, but she endured. No one would push Molly Calder from her own bed, the one she had shared with Apollo. The fear would fade with time, she was sure; it had certainly lessened once Dalton and his men informed her that they had "handled" the issue of the surviving attackers. They offered no details, but Molly didn't need them. The stories had found her. Rumors abounded in Boston's churches and taverns about the work being done at the Mill, as did grisly tales about how it dealt with its enemies.

Molly and Paul reached the house and went inside, moving through its rooms until they reached its well-appointed kitchen. There, behind a set of shelves cleverly designed to swing open upon the depression of a secret latch, was a set of stairs leading down into a chamber built below the house. Molly lit a lantern and descended, Paul following close behind.

In the small cellar, their lamplight shone on a set of ten iron strongboxes stacked neatly against the wall, each with two keyholes. One set of keys had been kept on Apollo's person, the second was hers, and since her husband's death she carried both.

These ten chests represented the entirety of Molly Calder's fortune, aside from the material assets within the Mill itself.

Three contained nothing, emptied by the cost of altering and maintaining the Mill since Apollo's death. A fourth contained paper money, thick sheafs of Massachusetts Commonwealth currency rendered utterly valueless by inflation during the War for Independence and the economic downturn that followed.

Two of the remaining six contained silver coins representing the bizarre mishmash of currencies circulating in the former colonies. Pounds sterling in both the British and less precious Massachusetts varieties, pine tree shillings all dated 1652, and a mix of Spanish eight-real coins, French francs, German thalers, and Dutch stuivers, many with edges clipped and shaved within an inch of their lives.

Molly pointed at one of the two chests of silver.

"Mr. Brooks, you will take that chest and deposit its contents at the new Massachusetts Bank, housed in the old Manufactory House near Boston Common. Open the account in my name and the name of my husband—Calder and Calder—and have them prepare a set of bank drafts we can use to fund the work to come."

"I will, Mrs. Calder," Paul said.

She would keep the other chest of silver with her at the Mill and use it for whatever purposes she required.

"Those four," Molly said, gesturing at the remaining chests, more elaborately locked than the others, "you will dispose of as we discussed."

The final four chests contained gold. Two thousand five hundred British golden guineas each, stamped with the face of either Queen Anne or one of three King Georges, depending on their vintage. Each chest weighed fifty pounds, representing an astonishing sum.

"Are you certain you want to entrust me with that, Mrs. Calder?" Paul said, his tone uneasy. "I can do the job, but one hears stories of gold changing a man."

"I cannot go myself," Molly said. "I have preparations to

make here. I trust you, Paul. You are a good man. More than that, I believe you dearly want to see this enterprise through to its conclusion. If the Mill is to survive, it must become something new."

"That much I agree with, Mrs. Calder," he said. "We can't stay here. All the wooden stakes and muskets in the world won't protect us forever. And, yes, you're right. I want to see this through. The things we're accomplishing here . . . why, they feel like miracles, they truly do—and we've only been at it for about a year. Given more time, given more freedom and resources . . . why . . . I daresay we'll get your little project done."

Molly nodded.

"That's why I know you're the right man for this job," she said. "A fortune in gold has no interest for you. Knowledge is your treasure. You want to *know*."

She reached into her cloak and withdrew two letters, handing them to Paul.

"Each is properly addressed and sealed," Molly said. "See to the chest of silver at the bank, then deliver these letters for me. After that, the future of the Mill is in your hands, Mr. Brooks. Do not fail."

He took the letters and touched them to his forehead.

"I will not, Mrs. Calder," he said. "I'll send word when all is in readiness."

II. THE FIRST LETTER

To Mr. Samuel Slater, Pawtucket, Rhode Island—

I am writing with a business offer, which I hope you will consider and entertain. As you undoubtedly know, as we work within the same field, upon the death of my husband Apollo Calder I took possession of the Calder Textile Mill and all its assets. (See the itemized list appended hereto.)

We have been competitors in business for many years, but I believe that time is at an end. I intend to leave the textile field in short order, and I seek a buyer for the assets I possess, in order that I might live out my remaining years in comfort, enjoying pursuits appropriate to a widow. I no longer wish to run a factory mill. I have other goals.

I wish to sell my business to you, and will do so at a fair price. I believe this may be of interest to you not solely because it will signify an expansion of your own enterprise and the elimination of a competitor, but because the Calder Mill holds the key to greatly increased efficiency and profit in the textile process. It is, in essence, the future.

Beyond the machinery, finished fabrics, raw materials, and other equipment associated with the successful operation of the Calder Mill, I also possess unique technology, developed by my chief engineer Mr. Paul Brooks. As you know, much of the textile assembly chain has been made more rapid and efficient through the application of various ingenious machines such as the so-called spinning jenny. The one remaining element requiring hand-crafting is the weaving, which must still be performed by women skilled with the operation of looms.

I tell you that this is no longer so. Mr. Brooks has completed a prototype for a device he calls a "powered loom." This machine allows for the removal of hand-crafting from the textile manufacturing process, and therefore increased production at reduced cost.

The plans for the powered loom would be included in any acquisition of the assets of the Calder Mill. I will not sell them cheap, but I will sell them fair. I know the value of a device like this, and I am sure you do as well.

At this stage in my life, I require only capital to fund various ventures for my own interests and amusement. I would therefore prefer to divest myself of assets which are no longer of use to me.

If this offer is of interest to you, please provide your reply via my attorney Isaac Lovett, who keeps an office on Beacon Street in the North End, and we will discuss terms.

Sincerely yours,

Molly Calder

Concord

II. THE SECOND LETTER

Father—

I write to inform you that I will not be coming home, and your attempt to coerce me to return to you by force has turned my heart against you. Two good men of the Calder Mill were killed by the blackguards you hired, and I myself was dreadfully injured. My body has largely recovered thanks to the skill and good offices of Doctor Evgeny Choglovoka, the Mill's surgeon, but the scars I bear upon my soul are deep, and I fear, permanent.

Enclosed with this letter is a bank draft, which can be presented for payment at the Massachusetts Bank at the old Manufactory House. It represents the amount in full due to you under the indenture contract with Molly Calder for my work at the Mill. Mrs. Calder, in an act of great generosity, has determined to advance these funds to you so I might be free to work for her for the remainder of my contract term, in any place or manner she might choose, without any further obligation by the Mill to you.

Good-bye, Father. I do not expect to see you again in this lifetime. May God prove merciful when you depart this world.

Your daughter,

Penelope Franck

II. EIGHT

BOSTON HARBOR.

APRIL 1791.

42°21′33.6″N, 71°02′34.1″W

"MRS. CALDER, WE MUST GET UNDERWAY *NOW*," CAPTAIN TILLAROY said. "If those cutters do not stop us, the tide will."

Molly and the captain—a steady, bewhiskered man with a wooden hand and a deep limp—stood at the ship's taffrail. They ſaced the exit from Boston Harbor, a channel that led to Broad Sound and the Atlantic beyond, the green humps of Governors Island and Castle Island standing like sentinels to either side. Two ominous vessels—sleek, low-slung craft—were visible in the gap between the islands, directly in their path.

It was just after dawn. Molly and her people had originally intended to leave with the turn of the morning tide, which was imminent. They had loaded the ship at Boston's Long Wharf over the course of the night in a bid to avoid undue attention, but when dawn came, they could not leave because one crucial piece of cargo was not yet aboard.

Molly had refused to allow the ship to depart the harbor until this last item arrived, despite Captain Tillaroy's increasing insistence. This unusual and obvious delay had caused their vessel to gather the attention they had been trying to elude, that of two "revenue cutters." These were members of the small naval force maintained by the new Congress and tasked with patrolling the Atlantic coast. They were intended to protect American shipping against piracy, smuggling, and similar depredations of the new nation's struggling economy.

The cutters were not large ships—about sixty feet in length compared to the one hundred boasted by the ship upon which Molly currently stood—but they were fast, nimble vessels armed with swivel guns and even a few small cannon. Perhaps the cutters could not sink Molly's ship in any reasonable amount of time, but they could cause significant damage and kill many of the people aboard.

"This is ridiculous," Molly said, speaking as much to herself as to Captain Tillaroy. "We have done nothing wrong."

"Aye, Mrs. Calder, but that's how you see it," the captain replied, not taking his eyes off the approaching cutters. "If those folks out there see it different, well, they have the guns."

"They don't give a fig for our cargo," Molly spat. "The powers that be in this damnable city refuse to allow us to be free. They would rather destroy us than let us leave."

During the few minutes required for this exchange to take place, one of the revenue cutters deployed a small launch, and uniformed sailors in that boat rowed most of the distance to Molly's vessel. One of those, an officer, got to his feet and lifted a brass speaking trumpet to his mouth.

"Prepare for boarding and inspection," the man cried. "On the authority of the United States Revenue Cutter Service."

"We can evade them," Captain Tillaroy said, his voice quiet. "The cutters are not well positioned, and the tide and wind are in our favor. The range of their guns is not great. Even if they got off a shot or two, we could be past them and away before we took much damage. But we must be underway now, or that advantage will be lost."

"I understand, Captain," Molly said. "But we will not leave yet. I must have more time."

Tillaroy frowned but said nothing more. Molly turned away from the rail to see Paul Brooks waiting alongside some of his subordinates, men and women she recognized from his laboratory back at the Mill.

"Do not let that launch approach, Mr. Brooks," she said.

He nodded.

"You heard the boss," he said, and his people scattered across the deck, moving in pairs to a number of odd, squat barrels positioned at regular intervals near the rails, each well sealed with pitch.

These barrels were just one of the many unusual modifications made to the original design Apollo Calder had commissioned Knut Jacobsen to build. Originally, Apollo's ship was to be a somewhat smaller version of a standard East Indiaman. But Paul Brooks had ridden to Essex with a new set of plans designed by the geniuses of the Mill and ten thousand guineas with which to pay for them. Those funds were now almost gone, the monies not required by the ship's construction used up by the cost of moving the Mill's essential equipment and people to the Boston wharf.

Molly Calder was no longer a wealthy woman, at least not by her prior standards. Her primary asset was a large merchant ship that would almost defiantly refuse to earn her any money. It would transport no goods and engage in no trade. Instead, it would carry about a hundred Mill people and about that many in the ship's crew, all of whom had to be cared for and paid. An expensive endeavor, and while the sale of the Calder Mill and its assets to Samuel Slater in Rhode Island had provided a substantial influx of capital (at some cost to her pride), she wondered how long she could keep the operation going.

But Molly was committed—more than committed—and would see the effort through as long as she could. Before anything else, she needed to escape Boston Harbor. At the moment, that was entirely up to Paul Brooks and his men.

Brooks surveyed the placement of his teams, then nodded.

"Ware the wind," he called out, and got a few cries of acknowledgment. "Release the stuff."

The teams carefully opened stoppers in the base of each barrel; they were all situated above scuppers that fed out to the surface of the sea below. As the barrels opened, a quantity of yellow-white powder flowed from them down into the scuppers and fanned out to the water. When the powder touched the sea, it surged up into flame, each grain seemingly possessing the energy of a thousand candles.

The officer on the revenue cutter's launch cried out in alarm, and his oarsmen rapidly rowed the craft backward to a safe distance.

Captain Tillaroy shifted uneasily as he gazed out at the ring of fire surrounding the ship.

"You saw the tests before we set sail, Captain," Molly said. "The ship's hull has been treated with a solution that renders the potash powder inert. We are in no danger."

"Be that as it may, I hope you have enough of your, ah, succotash to hold them off until sundown," Tillaroy said, "because that's how long we'll be staying here if we do not move soon."

Molly turned toward the shore.

A crowd of angry Bostonians stood at the end of the Long Wharf, many holding lit torches. They were clearly waiting for the ship to be turned back by the revenue cutters, at which point they would undoubtedly burn Molly's vessel down to the waterline, possibly without waiting to let the people from the Mill disembark.

Molly pulled her eyes from the intolerant, ignorant fools and directed her gaze along the shore. The docks were busy, even with the reduction of the shipping trade that still plagued Boston. Plenty of people, plenty of wagons and horses and stevedores and the like, but none were what she sought.

She wondered how much time she really had left—how long Captain Tillaroy would actually wait to depart the harbor before taking measures into his own hands.

Movement ashore caught Molly's eye, a distant commotion. Then came the sign she had been watching for: a long flash of light followed by two short—a prearranged message from a signal lantern.

"There!" she cried, and pointed.

Captain Tillaroy produced a spyglass, looked through it, grunted, and handed it to Molly. It took her a moment to orient the instrument properly, but eventually she beheld a wagon containing three men and drawn by two horses speeding toward the quay. And in its bed, a long white bundle.

Molly clenched her fist around the spyglass.

"They can make it," she said, as much to herself as to the captain at her side.

"We'll see, ma'am," Tillaroy said. "Looks like your people stirred up some trouble on the way."

Molly realized his meaning as a second wagon hove into view with two horsemen galloping alongside, clearly chasing the first wagon with her people aboard.

Perhaps it was too much to hope the Allbrights would get away unseen, she thought.

The first wagon rattled to a clumsy stop before a small pier alongside which a number of boats were moored. Dalton and Briggs—for it was them—maneuvered the long bundle out of their wagon and into a ketch. Briggs drew a cavalry saber and cut the small boat's ties. The two men pushed off and raised sail just as the second wagon reached their pier.

Molly watched through the glass as a hue and cry was raised. Word spread quickly. Some of the torchbearers on the Long Wharf ran to meet the men from the second wagon, while others leapt into small boats tied to the wharf and cast off their lines.

Those small vessels immediately began to converge on the ketch, which was having some difficulty making headway.

"Your boys there are no sailors," Captain Tillaroy intoned mournfully, watching as the small craft twisted and turned in the waves. "Let us hope they do not capsize."

A sharp sound and a puff of smoke from one of the smaller boats. Molly knew what had happened—one of the Bostonians had fired a rifle at her people.

The ketch dropped its sails. Evidently, Dalton had realized that his crew did not have the skill to properly use them. Through the spyglass, Molly saw the craft unship its oars—two sets—and begin a new attempt at progressing through the waves.

"Too far, and rowing's too slow," the captain said. "They won't make it before they're caught."

Tillaroy was right. Barely a minute later, one of the Boston boats intercepted the Allbrights' ketch. Molly saw men standing in it, long knives and boathooks raised to hack her people apart. Then a crack from above her, and one of those attackers fell into the harbor. She looked up to see a figure in the rigging, balancing an excessively long-barreled rifle on a stay, two more slung across the man's back.

"Thank you, Mr. Aselton," Molly cried up to him. "Please do keep it up if you can."

In answer, he fired again.

Molly did not turn quick enough to see the result, but Captain Tillaroy offered a satisfied grunt at her side.

"Quite the crack shot, your man," he said.

"He does seem to be," Molly replied.

A few more shots found their mark, and the Bostonians fell back, realizing the danger they were in. Nothing further prevented the Allbrights from reaching the ship. Paul Brooks set another chemical upon the waters that extinguished the flames to the ship's starboard side, and the ketch drew up alongside. The long wrapped bundle was sent up first, and then the two Allbrights, one at a time in the bosun's chair. They collapsed on the deck near the prize they had fought so hard to retrieve.

Briggs was wounded, holding a bleeding arm. Molly opened her mouth to call for Evgeny, but the surgeon was already there, opening his instrument bag and bending to attend to the wounded soldier.

Confident that Briggs was in good hands, Molly turned to Dalton.

"What happened?" she asked the him as he struggled to his feet, clearly exhausted.

"We were discovered just as we were finishing," he gasped. "The sexton made a cry, chased us. But . . . we made it. Wasn't sure we would."

Molly placed a hand on his shoulder.

"I am grateful, Mr. Dalton," she said. "More than you can know. Rest now—you have done your duty this day and then some."

Dalton nodded, letting himself fall back to the deck. Molly's eyes turned to the long bundle, toward which she felt a strange ambivalence. Up close, the thing was mottled and stained and had a strong odor of dirt and corruption. It was not a bundle, of course, but a shroud. Aarvan Bir had appeared on deck as soon as the Allbrights returned, and the mystic now knelt next to the bundle and placed his hand upon it.

"Are you certain this was necessary?" Molly asked Bir, her nose full of the horrid smell. "He is gone. This is not him."

The mystic looked at her. The long scar on his cheek twitched.

"This was once the vessel your husband occupied, Mrs. Calder. It possesses a stronger connection to his spirit than anything else in this world. We may need Apollo's body for future experiments, or we may not, but I suspect we will never have another chance to retrieve it."

"Take it below," Captain Tillaroy ordered, speaking to Bir in a quiet voice filled with command. "To the surgery. We'll have to devise a way of masking the smell. It won't do to have the crew knowing what we've brought aboard. Sailors are superstitious about the smallest things—and this is no small thing."

He turned to Molly.

"And now, Mrs. Calder, if it pleases you, may we depart?"

"Certainly," Molly said.

Captain Tillaroy began giving orders, and Molly witnessed a great flurry of activity as ropes were uncoiled, sails were raised, and the capstan turned to raise the anchor. Immediately, the ship began to move.

"Blast it," the captain said, his eyes set upon the channel they would need to use to depart the harbor, staring at the two sleek, swept-back vessels standing in their way. "It's as I feared. The revenue cutters have moved to block our path. I told you, Mrs. Calder, we should not have delayed."

"Do not fear, Captain," Molly said. "I anticipated these events."

She turned to Mr. Aselton, who had climbed down from the rigging and now stood not far away.

"Is Miss Beaton ready with her apparatus?" she asked.

"Believe so," he said.

"Very good," Molly said. "Then tell her it is time to send the message."

Aselton departed in search of Anne Beaton.

"Message?" Captain Tillaroy asked.

Molly pointed at a nearby wreck fetched up on a sharp rock

in the harbor, not yet removed by time or intention. It was a large piece of hull from some old warship, easily fifty feet long, a remnant of naval battles here during the war.

"Captain Tillaroy, if you could please endeavor to move the ship near that hulk while not obstructing the view of either the people onshore or the two revenue cutters . . ."

The captain gave his helmsman the necessary orders, and the ship drew closer to the outcropping and the wreck upon it.

"We're ready," Anne Beaton said, standing at the rail with a little group of her apprentices.

She held something that looked like a harpoon attached to a long coil of the same dark cordage that had once run through the Mill. The other end of the cord was attached to a glass sphere suspended in a lattice of rope, and within it a metal cube somehow floating in a cloudy red liquid.

"I can throw this thing, but I can't guarantee I'll hit my mark. I don't know if my arms possess the necessary strength," Anne said.

"Allow me, miss," said one of the ship's crew, a burly man with a shaven skull. "I worked on the whalers out of Nantucket for many a season."

Anne handed him the harpoon and pointed at the wreck.

"Just stick it in that," she said.

The big man shrugged and, without much apparent effort but very apparent skill, let the harpoon fly. Despite the forward movement of the ship, and despite its deck bobbing up and down on the waves, the barbed metal spear embedded itself deeply in the wood of the wreck.

"Hell of a throw," Anne said.

The former whaleman shrugged again.

"Send them the message," Molly said.

"With pleasure," said Anne.

She flipped a wooden lever attached to the glass sphere, and there was a gigantic *surge* they could all feel in their bones, their teeth, their blood.

"By God," said Captain Tillaroy.

A crackle, and a rush of blue-white lightning ran from the glass sphere along the dark cord running to the harpoon embedded in the wreck. The sun had not yet fully risen, and the illumination was powerful—all could see it, whether on Molly's ship, the revenue cutters, or even the shore.

As Anne Beaton's lightning flashed to the wreck, the old hull exploded, shattering into a rain of rotting wood and bits of metal that rose high into the air and spattered down into the harbor.

A gasp of dismay carried across the waves from the Long Wharf, and Molly knew that those watchers, at least, had received her message.

Anne took Molly's arm.

"We don't have a second shot," she whispered. "Building up that charge took most of a week with the electrostatic generator. If those government ships don't get out of our way, we can't do it again."

"Don't worry," Molly said. "I believe they understood our message."

"Cutters are withdrawing," the ship's lookout called from above.

"As well they might," said Captain Tillaroy, his voice tinged with awe. "I daresay I'd do the same."

He looked at Molly.

"What was the message, Mrs. Calder?"

"Leave us in peace," she said, "or end your life regretting that you did not."

The ship moved along the channel and out into the Broad Sound, the revenue cutters keeping a respectful distance, letting them pass.

"There is one last thing to do," Molly said to Anne. "Gather our people."

She produced a bottle of wine from inside her cloak and waited as all who were not occupied with pressing matters assembled on the deck.

"Most of you know me well," she said. "For those who do not, my name is Molly Calder. I own this vessel. My husband and I built it together. His name was Apollo, and he was fond of the old myths of Greece. He thought perhaps we might call this ship the *Olympian*.

"But I am interested in another story, one I suspect many of you have heard. I will name this ship in tribute to that tale."

She took the bottle of wine by its neck.

"I christen thee . . ."

Molly smashed the bottle against the rail, and wine and glass rained down to the sea below.

". . . the *Lazarene*."

II. NINE

LISBON.

1795.

38°42′24.2″N, 9°08′09.5″W

Major James C. Dalton stepped onto the broad stone quay, followed by Lieutenants Francis Briggs and Jack Aselton. A fourth man, a slim Brazilian named Bartolomeo da Gama, came just after.

The four men looked out at Lisbon for the first time. They knew one thing about the city, the same thing most people knew—that the Portuguese capital had been all but leveled by a massive earthquake four decades before. This, however, seemed a well-ordered place. An ornate plaza awaited just past the quay, and beyond it a broad avenue led deeper into the city, between two- and three-story structures of white stone roofed with orange tile, with a ring of hills behind it all.

"Doesn't look too bad," Dalton said.

"I guess forty years was time enough to set things right," Aselton replied.

"Should make things easier for us," said Briggs. "There's Belém Tower; that's the landmark we were told to set at our back."

He pointed at the blocky limestone fortress standing sentinel at the entrance to Lisbon's harbor, centuries old and brutally tough, survivor of countless assaults up to and including the cataclysmic earthquake of 1755.

The four men walked along the quay, heading toward the city proper. Dalton turned to Bartolomeo da Gama.

"We know where we're supposed to meet this fellow, and the directions in his letter were fairly clear," he said. "But if we get turned around . . ."

"I'm sure my Portuguese is not the same as how they talk here—local dialects, you know—but if we get lost, I will find the way," da Gama said, in his strongly accented English. "Even better, you know I am an astronomer. This is why the *Lazarene* brought me along. If we meet no one before nightfall, why, I will navigate by the stars."

"Might come to that," said Briggs, wiping sweat from his brow with his sleeve. "Where the hell is everyone?"

It was midday, and the sun was high in the sky. The city was markedly still, the streets all but empty. A few horses were tied up here and there, and a merchant led a mule cart filled with oranges, but beyond that, almost no activity.

"Siesta?" Aselton ventured.

"Maybe," Briggs said.

"No," da Gama said. "Too early. This something else. This city is supposed to be a busy place."

"Let's not find trouble before it finds us," said Dalton. "Fewer people means we move faster. That's all."

They continued walking through the city's wide, open avenues and beautifully laid-out squares, one of which housed a large construction site, the foundations laid out for what was clearly to be an enormous structure.

"The new palace," da Gama said. "Queen Maria began building it as soon as her father died. The old one fell in the big quake, and poor King Joseph never felt safe indoors again. He ruled from a camp outside the city. His palace was a tent. A big one, but a tent all the same. Kings, eh?"

"Gonna take them a while to finish without workers," Aselton observed. "I don't see a single man on that site."

"I don't like this," Briggs said. "Feels off."

Dalton grunted in response. The men kept moving through the gorgeous, nearly deserted streets. They passed the Academia das Ciências de Lisboa, another landmark they had been told to expect, with its singular bright red double doors.

"That's where our man did his work," da Gama said. "The Scientific Academy of Lisbon, where Mattias Lompos performed his strange experiments. He was excommunicated from the Academia, you know. Had to leave in disgrace."

"Sounds familiar," said Dalton. "Suppose that's why he's willing to come sail around with us."

"What does he study again?" asked Briggs.

"Dr. Lompos is an extraordinary biologist," said da Gama. "He performed detailed experiments on human bodies just before and just after death, to document any changes, you see. They called him the death doctor."

"Clever," Briggs said.

"He is—very," da Gama said, missing the soldier's sarcasm entirely. "His work did not endear him to the people of Lisbon, but he will be very helpful aboard the *Lazarene*."

The quartet reached Rossio Square, marked by a small fountain at its far end. The white stone buildings bordering the square were more ornate than those they had passed previously.

"Neighborhood's getting richer. We're close," said Dalton. "We need to head east. We can orient ourselves by the castle up on the hill there."

He pointed to the Castle of St. George, perched up above the city, and turned. He took one step, then froze.

Bartolomeo da Gama sucked in a little hiss of breath.

The reason for the city's eerie emptiness suddenly became clear. A death cart rolled by, stacked with corpses, pulled by an ox, and led by a cloaked man wearing a bird-beaked plague mask. They caught a glimpse inside, and the scars on the corpses within were immediately recognizable to all four men.

"Smallpox," said Dalton.

"Guess we know where Dr. Death found people to experiment on," Aselton said. "The whole damn city's dying off."

"Let's move," Dalton said.

The group hurried through the streets, finally finding the house they wanted. Da Gama knocked on its door. No answer, from servants or master. Aselton broke it in with a few well-placed kicks, and they entered.

Immediately, a horrible odor of decay the three soldiers knew as intimately as they knew their own names. This was a house of death.

The Allbrights went upstairs to check, leaving da Gama on the ground floor to wait. They already knew what they would find. They heard the flies before they were halfway up the stairs.

Mattias Lompos, the great biologist, lay in his bed, swollen and black, the bedding stained with a stew of the man's bodily fluids.

"Dammit," Dalton said. "Molly won't be happy about this."

THE CROP DECK SMELLED OF GROWTH AND EARTH, AND WAS brightly lit despite being deep inside the ship. In one of the moments of ingenious innovation that had come to characterize life aboard the *Lazarene,* one of the ship's engineers had thought to install mirrored hatches on the vessel's exterior. These, when opened and angled properly, brought direct sunlight into the crop deck, all the way to its center.

Molly Calder reached out and lifted the stalk of a long,

grasslike plant, its tip bearing a tightly packed pod of green seeds surrounded by a wispy fringe like a donkey's mane. The plant and the others around it drooped, their stalks having difficulty bearing the weight of the seedpods.

"The barley's looking sad, Master Vanderwaal," she said.

"It's a difficult crop, Mrs. Calder," the old farmer replied, in his good, Dutch-accented English.

His tone was guarded, just on the edge of taking offense.

"The oats handle the salt better," he continued. "But I don't like having just the one source of grain. I'll keep breeding the barley for strength. Give me ten or so generations, and you'll see a robust crop."

Vanderwaal frowned.

"I'm doing my best at the task you set me, Madam Calder. I'm trying to feed the whole ship with barely any room and not enough light, in all kinds of weather, cutting between spring and summer and winter with the turn of the wind as we travel north and south. Do you suppose it's easy?"

Molly considered how best to respond. Even after five years at sea, she was still learning how to lead her people. All of the Lazarenes were different. An approach that could succeed with a discouraged member of Anne Beaton's electric scientists, the group now known as the Sparks, would fail utterly with, say, a thick-browed, broad-shouldered Dutch farmer with a tendency to turn cantankerous when challenged.

Abraham Vanderwaal had been with the *Lazarene* for about nine months. He had joined the crew as a direct response to many failed attempts to grow crops aboard. The ship's botanists found it impossible to keep brine out of the soil, and the plants died when merely shoots. At last, in desperation, one of the scientists had suggested they explore the agricultural techniques of the Netherlands. The region was constantly flooded by the sea due to its low-lying nature, and yet those people managed to grow crops and feed themselves. Perhaps they had some knowledge to impart.

So the *Lazarene* had sailed to Holland, finding it currently in possession of the French after a recent invasion and redesignated the Batavian Republic. These things happened.

The French invasion was not ideal for the Dutch, but had a direct benefit to the Lazarenes. For once they sent their agents ashore, they found many farmers skulking around the lowlands who had lost their land to French predation. One of those, a Mr. Abraham Vanderwaal, had two qualities that made him attractive as a potential new crew member. First, buried in his skull were generations of knowledge about coastal agriculture. It was more or less all he knew how to do. Second, he expressed a deep desire to continue plying his trade, even if his entire plot would consist of a few beds of salt-drenched soil aboard a very unusual ship.

Molly offered Abraham a reassuring smile.

"Your work is so valuable to the *Lazarene*, Master Vanderwaal," she said. "Every time we touch land is dangerous, and the most frequent reason we do is to acquire fresh food. I know how difficult it is to even attempt creating a patch of farmland out at sea. I do not mean to criticize. It is only that I have not visited the crop deck in some time. It seems like you have implemented many changes for the better."

She took a pointed glance across the Dutchman's impossible garden, lush and green, with bees buzzing here and there and sea breezes setting the plants in gentle motion.

"I understand yours is a task filled with unique challenges, and I will do my best to make it easier," Molly said. "But right now I would prefer to discuss your successes. To my eyes, they look to be many."

The farmer grunted. He began pointing out various plants, moving between the rows of soil-filled beds.

"Your eyes are correct. You can see the oats here. They're doing well. We've also got onions and a few types of beets, including the sugar beet. I know the cook likes that. Good puddings, happy crew, eh? Potato, cabbage, tomatoes and carrots. Samphire, sea aster . . ."

He stopped at a bed filled with thin-stalked plants that boasted lovely pink flowers along the lengths of their stems.

"Sea mallow," Vanderwaal said. "Found these when I went ashore in Georgia some months back. Saw them growing right off the beach, and the local people told me they cook up well. The flowers add a nice bit of color too."

"So they do," Molly said, plucking one of the blossoms and sliding it behind her ear.

"This one's trickier," the farmer said, moving to the next bed, which contained a slurry of wet earth out of which a few stunted green plants protruded. "Saltwort. It's a useful plant—you can eat it, use its ashes to make soap—but it grows in marshland, and I haven't determined the best way to make a marsh aboard ship."

"I trust you will, Master Vanderwaal," Molly said. "Might the ship's engineers be of assistance?"

"Perhaps I'll ask," he said, rubbing his chin and looking thoughtfully at the wet soil. "If they aren't tired of my requests."

Vanderwaal had indeed made *many* requests. The configuration of the crop deck was in constant flux as the farmer asked for and implemented solutions to increase the yield from his little bit of farmland: the mirror hatches to bring in sunlight. An intricate irrigation network built by the Gearfolk that supplied water in salt, fresh, or brackish varieties. Shelved beds along the inner hull that allowed water to drip down to the shelf below. An ingenious method for refreshing the soil with the dung produced by the ship's crew and their small complement of livestock. An electrical heating system created by Anne Beaton herself for when the ship ventured into colder waters.

"I daresay the engineers would welcome any requests you might make, sir," Molly said. "You know the Lazarenes: their intelligence is voracious, constantly craving new problems to solve."

Especially because they cannot seem to solve the problem that brought them here in the first place, she thought.

"Thank you for your ceaseless efforts to keep the crew well-fed and free of ailments, Master Vanderwaal," Molly added. "I appreciate your work, as does everyone aboard. Is there anything else I can do to help you?"

"Speaking of ailments," the Dutchman said, "I wouldn't say no to a swing through the West Indies. I haven't yet found a way to grow any citrus, and if we're to make a go of staying at sea for truly extended periods, we'll need it. I understand they have a certain lime down in that region we might use. Keep the scurvy away."

"I'll make a note of it for Captain Tillaroy," Molly said.

Vanderwaal tipped his hat.

"Obliged," he said.

Molly left the crop deck, climbing through a hatch to the deck above, then moving through a narrow passageway. Machines clanked and hissed all around her—this part of the ship was the transplanted version of the Mill's old Gearworks. Molly barely heard it. Her mind was consumed with everything she had just seen.

Vanderwaal's project was far from perfect; there was a reason farms were primarily land-based endeavors. Still, Molly thought it was trending toward successful. The ship's cook could now access fresh fruit and vegetables most of the time, as opposed to the pickled varieties in the ship's store. That was good. It meant a reduction of the *Lazarene*'s need to sail into foreign ports to buy supplies and saved her more than a few shillings to boot.

At the thought of shillings, Molly let out a long, deep sigh.

At that moment she happened to be passing Penelope Franck,

now twenty-one years old, a grown woman. A mother, too, to the year-old son she was currently holding, who boasted the lush eyebrows of a certain Russian surgeon who had once saved Nellie's life. There were a number of young Lazarenes now, children raised in the strange environment of the ship, becoming indoctrinated to its ways and unique modes of thought.

"Is all well, Molly?" Penelope asked, reacting to the sigh.

"Oh, yes, Nellie," Molly said, taking the pink flower from behind her ear and tucking it into the baby's blankets. "All is well. I'm just thinking about money. Most of my concerns these days seem to be connected to either funds or food."

"I'm sure you'll find a solution, ma'am," Penelope said, offering a sympathetic look (but no helpful advice, Molly noted) before continuing on her way.

Molly climbed another ladder, leaving the Gearworks and emerging into the ship's library. Scholars and researchers chattered away in many tongues all around her. During its travels, the *Lazarene* had acquired new minds from all around the world. A few dozen languages were spoken aboard, though Latin served as a lingua franca, along with the universal languages of mathematics and science. The way an Arab scholar thought about numbers or chemistry was not so different than that of one from Japan—and the *Lazarene* had both.

Molly took a moment to watch these people at their work, men and women of all shapes and types and colors and backgrounds. She thought about Penelope and her child. She considered the miracle of Abraham Vanderwaal's strange little farm, thriving aboard a ship that rarely came within a hundred miles of shore.

The primary purpose of the *Lazarene* and all its works remained the reunion of Molly Calder with her deceased husband, Apollo. But five years had come and gone, with little clear progress toward that goal. Death was the Devil's puzzle, as Paul Brooks was fond of saying. Aarvan Bir had once told her that there could be no set schedule, that there was nothing to be done but simply continue the journey. What had become blindingly obvious to Molly was that the journey in question might be much longer than she'd ever expected. Babies had been born aboard the ship! An entire second generation of Lazarenes was forming before her eyes!

Molly had realized she had two options. She could abandon her wild dream and allow her people to seek ordinary lives. Or she could accept the responsibilities that came with the creation of a tiny society above the waves that might need to persist for, well, who knew how long? For Molly, there was no question. The *Lazarene* would stay the course, and she would do what she must to ensure it did. (It did not escape her that, in searching for Apollo, she had become him, echoing his utter refusal to diminish the family of workers at the Calder Mill despite how difficult, detrimental, or irrational that might be.)

With the decision to persist came a new, second goal to which Molly had bent the great minds aboard her ship. She considered its acquisition to be her greatest practical obligation as leader of the Lazarenes. It was this: *self-sufficiency.*

Molly Calder dreamed of a *Lazarene* able to operate in complete independence from the rest of humanity (a group often referred to by those aboard as Landsmen (and, when they were in their cups and feeling superior, Dirters)). Staying away would keep the ship safe and allow them to pursue any lines of inquiry they chose without interference—not to mention that the constant need to acquire food, supplies, maintenance, and personnel from the land was ruinously, unsustainably expensive.

The ship's endless costs were financed by the funds Molly had brought with her from the Mill and the transfer of its assets to Samuel Stern, plus occasional sales of innovative technology developed in the ship's laboratories and workshops. (These transactions were made through business offices the Lazarenes had covertly established in Boston and London, run by a reliable outside agent and his son.) More money still went out than came in. Keeping the ship going was a constant, anxiety-inducing balancing act for Molly Calder. But someday that might change—she could envision a day when the ship no longer required money at all. When it would be truly free . . .

The ship's best minds had hacked away at what they called the "independence problem" for years. The crop deck was one approach; there were others. For example, Molly could see that many of the Lazarenes in the library were practicing their knotwork as they carried on their discussions, chattering away while tying lengths of rope into sheepshanks and sheet bends.

Every last person aboard underwent training as a sailor, no matter their prior Landsman career, gender, or age. Everyone took shifts performing all of the ship's many duties. The Lazarenes were slowly becoming adept at the arts of the sea, and every biologist or mathematician who learned to tie a bowline, or trim the mainsail in a roaring gale, was a Landsman the ship did not need to hire, pay, or feed.

Molly walked through the library, greeting fellow Lazarenes as she passed. She climbed a final ladder and came out into the open air, always a magical experience. The *Lazarene* was a large, well-appointed vessel, but all ships tended to be cramped. Every bit of space was used for storage; it had to be. Transitioning from the dark caves belowdecks to the boundless expanse of sea and sky above offered a moment of transcendence whose power never seemed to fade.

This was particularly true today, with the lush green hills of Portugal to the east, the city of Lisbon scattered across them like a hundred thrown dice. Between the hills ran the Tagus, the great river that cut through the city to empty into the harbor in which the *Lazarene* currently sat at anchor. Molly glanced up at the ship's flag, an uninterrupted expanse of rich Calder Blue, the very same that had once hung above the door to Paul Brooks' laboratory in Concord.

I know we'd be better off if we never set foot on land again, Molly thought, turning her eyes back to Lisbon in all its intricate complexity. *But, by God, when humankind sets its mind to it, it can build things that are truly beautiful.*

She considered the great city for a few moments more.

From a distance, she considered, remembering torches held high on the Long Wharf, *Boston was beautiful too.*

"Oi! Mrs. Calder," came a cry, and Molly turned to see Captain Tillaroy near the stern, overseeing the installation of two large oaken casks into a great rack-like device made of wood and iron. "Come see."

Molly made her way to the back of the ship.

"What's this?" she asked. "An experiment?"

Tillaroy pointed to the casks with his right hand—once just an immobile wooden lump, now an elaborate clockwork device devised by one of Eugenia Greaves's most promising apprentices.

"No," the captain said. "A defensive measure thought up by Brooks's boys, and a good one. These two casks are filled with noxious chemicals. The rack here will mix them, and then send the concoction out upon the sea. Once it hits the water, it'll create a cloud large enough to hide the entire ship. We can slip away from any other vessel that sights us out in the open water. We can even travel that way for a time—a moving fogbank, we'd be."

Molly nodded her approval.

"Good," she said. "Never again."

These words, an unofficial slogan among those Lazarenes who had been with Molly since the attack on the Calder Mill and the escape from Boston, stood in for a slightly longer phrase: "Never again will we allow close-minded bastards to hurt and kill us simply for living our lives."

"Never again," Tillaroy agreed, echoed by the other sailors working to install the new device.

"Between these casks, those fancy electric cannons Miss Beaton and her Sparks devised, and the other little toys we have aboard, I'd wager we're a match for any warship afloat, even three or four at once," Tillaroy said.

"I'm glad of it, Captain," Molly said. "But you sound eager at the prospect. Let me remind you—we must *avoid* battle. Word could spread. If Britain or France or Spain or any of the great navies hear about a mysterious vessel with unprecedented military capabilities, they might decide to hunt the *Lazarene.* If enough force is brought to bear, the ship could still be sunk or, God forbid, captured."

No, Molly thought. *Better just to stay away.*

"Of course, Mrs. Calder," Tillaroy said. "I'm just glad that if it ever comes to it, we can put up a hell of a fight. Lets a fellow rest easy at night."

A shout from below and to the side, out in the harbor.

"Ahoy the boat!"

Both Molly and Tillaroy looked over to see a small launch rowing directly toward the *Lazarene.* Molly noted approvingly of the skill with which the little craft was handled—a far cry from the clumsy escape from Boston Harbor not so many years before.

"Your team of hard men's back from the city," the captain said. "Didn't take long."

"No," Molly said, watching as the launch approached.

Captain Tillaroy had produced his spyglass and was peering through it.

"Hnh," he said.

"Is there a problem?" Molly asked.

"See for yourself," Tillaroy said, handing her the glass.

Looking through the lens, Molly immediately understood. The boat held only four people, the same number that set out from the *Lazarene* earlier that day. The spyglass offered enough magnification that she could identify each—Dalton, Briggs, Aselton, and the Brazilian, da Gama. The Allbrights had been sent ashore to retrieve a fifth man, and that man was clearly not with them.

Without a word, Molly handed the glass back to Tillaroy and set herself to wait. Something had gone wrong. Mattias Lompos, the death doctor, had agreed to join the *Lazarene* on its voyage. Had he thought better of it?

The launch pulled up alongside, and the four men clambered aboard using a rope ladder tossed down to them. Dalton was first and came to Molly the moment he was over the rail.

"Lompos?" she said.

"I'm sorry, Mrs. Calder. We found him, but he was dead. At least two days. Smallpox."

Without a word, she turned away.

II. TEN

LISBON HARBOR.

1795.

38°42′24.2″N, 9°08′09.5″W

"We lost Mattias Lompos. It did not have to happen. I would like it to never happen again," Molly said.

She sat in her cabin at the ship's stern, with a broad, many-paned window at her back, through which the Port of Lisbon could still be seen. Facing her, seated around a large table that could be cunningly folded and put away when no longer required, were some of the Lazarenes' most important and influential members. Evgeny Choglovoka represented the ship's medical professionals, the Barbers. Anne Beaton for the Sparks. Paul Brooks for the Mill faction, Aarvan Bir sat for the Watchers, and Eugenia Greaves for the Gearfolk. Major Dalton was present as well, and one other—the Chinese physician, Chen Lifeng.

Doctor Chen did not consider himself a Barber (indeed, Evgeny would have been offended if he did). The man approached his art primarily as a researcher, with the body as his laboratory. He held extraordinary beliefs about how the human form might be changed, protected, amplified. In many ways his theories aligned him with no Lazarene faction more than Aarvan Bir's mystics. But unlike that group's bizarre approaches to piercing the veil of death, most of Chen Lifeng's techniques seemed to work. He might stab a person with hundreds of tiny needles, apply immense pressure to various parts of the body, or simply administer unusual herbs—and more often than not his patients saw improvement.

"Smallpox," said Evgeny Choglovoka, somehow grown portly despite the lean and mostly vegetable-based diet provided aboard the ship for the past five years. "It's everywhere out there. We should not be surprised."

He gestured toward the window behind Molly, clearly referring to not just the city but the entire Iberian Peninsula, Europe, and the world beyond.

"I think we'd all prefer it if the world didn't have to contend with such a damnable disease, Molly," Paul noted. "But the pox is the pox. It'll take who it takes."

"Why is that?" Molly said. "After all, it won't take any of us, not after the gift Chen Lifeng gave us."

Doctor Chen nodded as he recognized his name, though he could not have been following the rest of the conversation closely. His English remained rudimentary, but he spoke passable French.

"If we had come to Lisbon one month earlier," Molly said, "*jiēzhǒng* would have saved the life of Mattias Lompos. For all we know, his mind and insights were the key to bringing Apollo back to us."

Chen Lifeng raised an eyebrow as he recognized the single Chinese word, the gift Molly had referred to. Upon joining the *Lazarene,* Chen had insisted that its crew undergo a process he called *jiēzhǒng.* This term could not be translated into French, and thus not into English or Latin. But via detailed description and evocative diagrams, he conveyed that the procedure was a protective measure, offering a shield against disease. In particular, it served as defense against the malady known in French as *variole*, in Chinese as *tiānhuā*, and in English . . . smallpox.

Many Lazarenes were receptive to the idea, especially since the treatment was so easily administered. When he boarded the ship, Chen brought with him a number of vials containing a fine brown dust. Small amounts of this substance were blown into the nostrils using a small, hollow piece of bamboo. The process was over in seconds. A few of the recipients suffered bouts of mild illness, but these passed in days.

Since then, no one aboard had contracted smallpox, despite the *Lazarene*'s travels around the world to many regions where the disease was endemic.

"The death of Mattias Lompos was a tragedy," Evgeny said, stroking his mustache.

"Correct," Molly said. "I believe it is a tragedy that need never happen again. I am proposing that we give Master Chen's *jiēzhǒng* to the world. We do not have the power to remove all disease, but we might end smallpox."

The table went very still.

"I thought the idea was for us not to be known," Anne Beaton said. "To be free of the entanglements of the rest of the world. To . . . hide, for lack of a better word. Surely taking this action would go against that goal."

"I am not suggesting we take *credit*," Molly replied. "I don't care who provides the treatment. Let it be someone else, not a Lazarene at all. To me, this is simple. We just lost a potentially valuable ally in our quest, due to a problem to which we have the solution. Let us solve it and ensure this never happens again."

"It sets a strange precedent, it does," said Eugenia. "The Landsmen have plenty of other conundrums we might solve for them. Are those our responsibility too? We left for a reason. They did not love us. Why should we love them back?"

"This is a matter of the body. I am concerned only with the eternal spirit," said Aarvan Bir. "It does not matter if a person's body dies from smallpox or any other cause. Their essential self remains, forever and pure. Death is irrelevant."

This declaration resulted in an exhausted exhalation from Evgeny.

"Irrelevant, eh?" the Russian doctor said. "Then please, by all means, bring Master Lompos to us now, Bir, so we might take advantage of the knowledge possessed by his *essential self*."

Aarvan Bir drew himself up, affecting an air of immense and slightly wounded dignity.

"As you know well, Dr. Choglovoka," he said, "my people and I are . . . *working on it*."

"*De quoi est-ce que vous discutez?*" Chen Lifeng broke in, which necessitated a quick explanation from Anne, whose French was quite excellent after time spent with Benjamin Franklin in that land.

Chen laughed.

"*Fait ça,*" he said. "*Les docteurs de l'ouest ne jamais m'écoutent. Je serai vraiment heureux si la médecine du Chine c'est le salut du pays de l'ouest. Mais j'ai déjà donné presque toute ma* jiēzhǒng *à les personnes ici.*"

"He wants us to do it," Anne translated. "He thinks it would be pleasing if his country's medicine were the salvation of the lands of the West. The only issue is that he's already used up almost all of his supply of the treatment on our people here."

"I'm no doctor," Dalton broke in, "but as I understand it, what Chen gave us was ground-up smallpox scabs. Any infected person is a factory for the remedy. I can go back into Lisbon with my Allbrights and find a burial pit. We can bring you back a hundred pounds of the stuff."

Quiet descended on the table as all contemplated the image conjured by that last phrase.

"I . . . don't think that will be necessary, Major Dalton," Molly said. "You've already dug up one grave for the *Lazarene*. I think that's enough."

"It wouldn't work, in any case," Anne said. "You're thinking of variolation, Major. That's a different treatment. It does use smallpox residue, and it's much riskier and less effective. People die from it. If I understand Dr. Chen's procedure, he didn't use smallpox at all to create his medicine. He used some other disease only present in his country. We'd need to travel to China and send a team in to harvest the, ah, raw materials."

"No, we wouldn't," Evgeny replied. "I have made a study of the treatment Chen Lifeng brought to us. His powder was indeed derived from a Chinese disease that affects camels, but I believe it is part of a larger family of diseases that include illnesses common in the West—cowpox, horsepox, and so on. I suspect using one of those would produce the same results as Doctor Chen's *jiēzhǒng*."

"Supposing we did this," Paul said, speaking slowly as if he were trying out the idea in real time, "we'd want to do it in secret. As Miss Beaton noted, we don't want to draw attention to ourselves. Would we put ads in the newspaper? Who would believe it? Who would *do* it? Snorting ground-up bits of cow disease . . . it sounds like lunacy."

"That problem, at least, is easily conquered," Anne said. "Benjamin Franklin had an interest in smallpox—he lost a son to it, as some of you may know. He carried on a correspondence with a doctor in Scotland, a man named Jenner, who has spent his career working to cure the disease. I can write to Jenner, nudge him in the proper direction. I could frame it in a way that would let him believe the ultimate inspiration was his and his alone. Jenner is the type of fellow who would not require much excuse to take full credit."

"Especially if the nudge comes from a woman, eh?" Eugenia said.

Anne did not reply, only gave Eugenia a knowing look.

The debate arose again, these brilliant people talking and talking and talking . . . Molly had come to love them all, but at that moment she wished all of them might be struck dumb.

"Enough," she said. "You are not listening to me."

The chatter stopped, and the leaders of the Lazarenes turned to look at her, all a bit surprised.

"I keep my husband's bones in a locked chest in my cabin," Molly said. "For more than five years, carrying on one-sided conversations with that damned box is as close as I've been to Apollo."

The others watched, silent.

Molly's husband was still present to her, but like the scent of well-cooked mutton as opposed to the roast on a plate. That . . . fading . . . she knew it was natural, but she could not stand it. It terrified her.

She remembered Apollo used to sing. She could no longer remember the words.

"I want you to remember why we are here," Molly said, and knew she was speaking to herself as much as the other Lazarenes. "It is not about devising clever ways of growing crops or inventing clever devices to sell to the Landsmen. Our purpose here, the reason I built this ship . . . is to conquer death."

She took a long, slow breath.

"For all we know, Mattias Lompos possessed the knowledge that would have brought Apollo back to me," Molly said. "I will not let the next Mattias Lompos die if it is within my power to prevent it. Let this thing be done, and then, please . . . stay the course."

This was the First Intercession.

II. ELEVEN

THE WESTERN INDIAN OCEAN.

1821.

10°29′58.3″S, 61°29′59.8″E

The *Lazarene* hovered above the Saya de Malha Bank, a vast plateau of seagrass and coral reefs rising from deep beneath the sea nearly all the way to the surface, hidden some distance north of the new British colony of Mauritius. The waters were clear and bright, revealing an undersea forest, an endless variety of sea creatures swirling just below the ship's hull.

The Bank was a beautiful, uncanny place. A ship would be sailing the vast, unknowable depths and then, as if entering a dream, would find itself flying across an island that could be seen but not touched. An endless expanse of color and beauty just below the waves, a world complete unto itself.

This was not the *Lazarene*'s first visit here and would not be its last. In the thirty years since the ship's departure from Boston Harbor, the vessel had explored every corner of every sea, from tropical waters to both polar oceans. The Saya de Malha Bank was a frequent stop, uniquely suited to the ship's needs. It was situated in a rarely traveled region of the sea and yet contained plentiful, easily harvested resources of fish and sea vegetation on the fertile plateau just below the surface—an ideal location for rest and resupply.

Now anchor chains at bow and stern held the great ship in place. A number of refits and expansions at the great Omani shipyards in Muscat and Sur had resulted in a vessel now over a hundred and fifty feet from bow to stern and fifty feet across at the beam, with many changes also wrought upon the ship's internal structure. The Lazarene engineers who devised these modifications were often greeted by consternation and flat refusals when they brought them to Landsmen shipwrights. But someone with the necessary ambition (creative or fiscal) was always found, and now the *Lazarene*, like the people aboard, was capable of extraordinary things.

Mechanisms within the vessel's hull clanked to life, a marriage of fine clockworks developed by the Gearfolk with electrical engines refined by the Sparks. Giant clanking and whirring sounds spun out across the sea as the *Lazarene* commenced a transformation into one of its secondary configurations. This process would all but exhaust the ship's batteries, but they would be refilled by the motion of the tide in time. If a speedier charge was required, a few days' sail would spin the Beaton Wheels mounted on the ship's hull and provide all the electricity required.

The *Lazarene* opened like a flower, its timbers groaning, gears clanking. Planks slid out from beneath the weather deck, wide panels that doubled the ship's width. Supports extended from below these new platforms, stout poles unfolding and telescoping downward to find anchor points in the seabed five fathoms below. As these locked into place one by one, the natural rocking of the ship against the gentle waves ceased. The *Lazarene* was no longer a creature of the sea. It was something more like a minuscule speck of land, a tiny sovereign country.

Its flag flew high above the mainmast, a new banner in Calder Blue stitched with a bright orange sunrise. This was created after the original Brooks Laboratory flag disintegrated from the effects of weather and time. The Lazarenes never raised their flag unless they were certain they would be unobserved. But here, in their own private nation in one of the most remote corners of the giant expanse of the Indian Ocean, the *Lazarene* could be its true self.

With the decks expanded and the platform anchored, a buzz of activity arose. The ship's crew began erecting ingenious collapsible buildings of canvas on the wide, flat deck—a temporary village for the Lazarenes to use until they set out on their next voyage. They were sealed with India rubber to keep out the damp and boasted in-built cabling and connection points for the electrical equipment that facilitated so many of the ship's experiments. Hammocks were slung in rows for those who chose to take their rest on deck while they could.

The *Lazarene* had come to this faraway place to execute one grand experiment, planned for months and in development, one way or another, for thirty years. The Lazarenes had taken everything they knew, everything they'd learned, everything they had theorized and guessed at and prayed for since they left the Calder Mill three decades before. It all went into this singular effort.

That night the Lazarenes would solve death.

"Add the fourth element, Mr. Szabó," Penelope said.

"Aye, Lady Franck."

The heavyset Hungarian, his waves of long white hair shining in the moonlight, did as he was bid. Carefully, he decanted a thick red liquid from a glass vial into a small silver cauldron, a reduction made from the blood of an Irishman hanged for a crime he did not commit. The vessel already contained measures of crushed emerald and the pulverized claws of a dragon captured on an island of the Dutch East Indies, as well as a minute fragment of one of Apollo Calder's femurs—the most valuable and rare ingredient of all.

Penelope Franck and Fodor Szabó stood just inside a circle made up of the other dark-cloaked members of the Open, centered around the bubbling cauldron, its contents heated by a shallow iron dish below it burning with bright blue flames. Symbols were chalked on the deck in small circles around where each of the Open stood, and embroidered in bright colors upon their robes. Sigils from alchemy and astrology and languages long dead, phrases of protection and entreaty and promise.

Penelope took a moment to glance at her audience. Most of the Lazarenes had gathered to watch the experiment and stood in loose groups outside the summoning circle. She saw excitement, fascination—but also plenty of barely hidden skepticism, even contempt.

This was hardly surprising. Penelope's people, the mystics, students of the eternal, the profane and profound, successors to the grand methodologies created by Aarvan Bir, called themselves the Open. But no one on the *Lazarene* was stupid, and so, of course, all understood the implication this name suggested. If the mystics were the Open, then the more literal-minded of those aboard—the engineers and chemists and physicists—were the Closed. The scientists found it condescending and belittling, and it won the Open little love aboard the ship.

But Penelope Franck did not concern herself with the opinions of the Closed. Except for one who was truly neither.

Molly Calder stood at the edge of the circle, her face wrinkled by decades of sun and salt, her hair now grey streaked with white, but her back straight and her eyes as sharp as ever.

She was the soul of the *Lazarene*, and Penelope felt nothing but boundless affection and respect for her. If not for Molly Calder, Penelope knew she would now be married to a Massachusetts merchant or farmer with a brood of children fully raised, perhaps even a grandchild or two, considering her advanced age of forty-seven. Molly had lifted her from a life of drudgery into a beautiful world of thought and independence.

Life on the *Lazarene* was not easy. But it was fascinating and free. Molly had given Penelope that—had given them all that. Now, tonight, in the middle of the vast ocean, Penelope Franck would try to repay her.

An odor arose on the deck as Szabó poured the blood into the heated cauldron—a fecund, prickly smell, like an old leather-bound book set aflame.

Penelope leaned forward and breathed deeply of the fumes. Immediately her senses seemed to sharpen and lights began to dance around the edges of her vision.

She looked out at the sea and saw that the lights extended all the way to the horizon, dancing, swirling, coming together, and splitting apart in some deeply confounding rhythm.

"It's ready," Penelope said, and the other members of the Open stepped forward, each taking their turn to inhale at the cauldron.

The experiment they were attempting—Penelope refused to call it a ritual, as this was science as much as anything the Closed did—was based in the traditions of dozens of cultures and histories. Many peoples had attempted to contact the dead over the millennia. The Lazarenes had studied those techniques and synthesized them into one path.

The Open began a chant, a low murmur of syllables meaningless to most. The verses were originally discovered by a three-man team of Corianders deployed from Calder & Calder's office in Athens, etched on the obsidian doors of a tomb they found outside Cairo. Well, perhaps a tomb. Perhaps something very different. Those doors, once pried open, had revealed a deep void immensely larger than the rocky hill into which the doors were set. Two of the men looked into the darkness beyond the doors and went mad. The third, a few steps behind, managed to shove the doors closed before he lost his sanity.

A mist began to swirl above the cauldron, a wisp of green phantom fire like the kind the ship often encountered when it sailed the Sargasso Sea in the southern Atlantic. But this vapor was different—purposeful. It moved, chased, spun, tried to cohere.

It was animate. It was alive.

"Who are you?" Penelope asked the apparition.

Molly stood up straighter, waiting for the word, the name they had all been waiting to hear for thirty years—Apollo.

A voice sounded, from the air, from the ship's timbers, from the sea.

"No," it said. "This world is not ready."

The mist coiled out and touched the face of one of the Open, a beautiful young man named Luis Pedrona who had joined the ship from Madrid. Luis froze, and a low groan emerged from his lips, of fear or pleasure.

"I will wait," said the voice, and somehow went *into* Luis's face.

A thunderclap, a flash of bright red light, and everyone on deck blinked as if rising from sleep.

It was no longer the depths of night but day, the sun shining down on the Lazarenes from high overhead. The flames below the cauldron were long since extinguished.

Hovering a handspan above the deck was something new, something bizarre: an opening in the fabric of the world, a bit taller and wider than a good-sized man. Blue mist swirled behind it, clouding whatever lay beyond.

Luis Pedrona lifted his hands, looking at them as if he had never seen them before.

Penelope felt a hand on her arm. She turned her head slowly, disoriented.

"What did it mean?" said Molly Calder, her eyes sharp. "Why did it deny you, Nellie?"

"I . . . don't know, Molly."

"*Find out*," the old woman said.

THREE DAYS LATER, PENELOPE FRANCK STOOD IN A RATHER SPLENdid silk tent dyed a vibrant Calder Blue, set up on the wide deck platform. The Lazarene Council was also present, its members seated around a circular table of polished teak.

The Council included Molly Calder at its head, and also Edna Greaves, who had taken over from her mother to run the Gearworks. Edna's father was either a member of the crew or someone Eugenia met on one of the *Lazarene*'s infrequent stops in port. She was disinclined to tell, and no one aboard the ship, Edna included, seemed particularly interested in finding out. Eugenia had died without telling a soul.

Anne Beaton of the Sparks was there, still feisty despite nearly seven decades on the planet. Doctor Chen Lifeng of the Barbers, the ship's medical and biological contingent. And the others: the Brooks, the Allbrights, the Leaves, the Tillers and more. All with their roles, all working toward the same goal, which might—or might not—have been achieved just three nights past.

They waited, Molly most of all, for Penelope Franck to deliver her report.

"I do not think we reached Apollo," Penelope said. "What appeared to us was something else."

A long silence broken only by the sea breeze ruffling the sides of the tent.

"I would have you explain that, Nellie," said Molly. "But first, how is Luis Pedrona?"

"Fine, by all accounts," Penelope answered. "He can't remember what happened to him and seems no worse for wear."

"I examined him myself," Chen Lifeng said, his English fluent after a quarter century aboard. "Physically, I could detect nothing untoward. Whatever happened to him seems to have had no lasting effects."

"It's been three days, Dr. Chen," Molly said, her tone dry. "It seems a bit early to offer an opinion about *lasting effects*. Continue, Penelope."

"One of the primary aims of the research and experimentation conducted by the Open is to locate a realm beyond this earthly existence," Penelope said. "Call it the spirit world, the hereafter, another plane . . . we are sure this place, or places, exist, although we cannot be certain human souls travel there after death.

"All of the world's great religions consider the possibility of a land beyond death and have various methods to try to access it. Over the past thirty years, the Open and its predecessors have rigorously examined these ideas, taking what seemed useful and discarding the fancy and superstition.

"The experiment three nights ago was the culmination of that work. We had two goals. First, to open a door to the realm past death. Once it was open, we intended to search for Apollo Calder. I believe we succeeded in the first goal. A door was indeed opened."

The Lazarenes shifted in their chairs. The door to which Nellie Franck referred was still open, not twenty feet from where they sat. A portal to nowhere. It seemed that living things could not pass through it; it felt like touching a wall made of thundercloud and would not allow any part of the body to pass. Inanimate objects could penetrate, but not without consequence—a boathook inserted into the door would return as half a handle, sliced away neatly at the point of entry.

Stranger still, the door was tied to the ship in some impossible way. They had tried to leave it behind, transforming the *Lazarene* back to its mobile configuration and setting sail. The portal had come with them, hovering just above that same spot of deck, keeping pace no matter their speed.

"We know about the door," Anne Beaton said, her voice wizened but strong, "We want to know about the voice. You say it was not Apollo. Was it some other ghost?"

"I do not believe it was a deceased spirit, no," Penelope replied. "It felt like something else, a greater presence. But whatever it was, it clearly communicated just one thing—that we are not yet ready."

She paused, looking Molly Calder straight in the eye.

"I propose," Penelope said, "that we become ready."

"What are you talking about, Nellie?" Molly said. "Speak plainly."

"The presence from the other side did not say that we, the crew of the *Lazarene*, were unready. It said this *world*. I believe that it referred to one sad truth: humanity as a species does not take seriously the possibility of communicating with the dead. They greet it with skepticism and terror. You know this is true. It is the reason the Calder Mill was attacked. The reason the *Lazarene* exists."

Penelope cast her eyes across the Lazarene Council.

"Even on this ship, the methods of the Open are viewed skeptically by those focused on pure science. This is a shame, of course, as we are all tied to the same goal, and it does not matter how it is achieved. At least, that is my belief."

Certain members of the Council, all Closed, shifted in their seats. The events of the past few days, including and especially the presence of the mysterious, impassable, impossible-to-ignore door on the ship's main deck, had shaken many previously held certainties.

"I would like to legitimize the idea of communicating with entities from other planes," Penelope said. "The Open have devised many techniques. We could provide those to select recipients and let them propagate those ideas throughout the world."

"If you think the Landsmen will be able to figure out something the Lazarenes cannot, Nellie, you're sorely mistaken," said Edna Greaves, with all the skepticism and confidence of her twenty-two years. "We are ahead of the Dirters on, well, everything."

"I don't think they'll find Apollo, Edna," Penelope said. "I think we'll do that, in time. But based on what happened a few nights ago, I believe we will have an easier time of it in a world that is . . . well . . . ready. Offering this information to the Landsmen is no different than the smallpox inoculations."

More squirming in seats. The *Lazarene*'s provision of techniques that led to Edward Jenner's smallpox vaccine in 1796 was a much-debated event in the history of the ship. To this day, many aboard believed it should not have been done. It was far too easy for such actions to bring attention that would destroy the small, perfect society of harmony and intellect Molly Calder had somehow managed to build.

The *Lazarene* was unique in all the world, and everyone aboard knew it.

Still, that intercession had happened. There was precedent for what Penelope was suggesting.

"What you are proposing is nothing like what we did with smallpox," said Chen Lifeng. "Giving *jiēzhǒng* to the world did not just advance our own goals; it had a clear benefit to humanity. Your idea tinkers with human society for no one's benefit but our own."

Marcus Bardot, the head of the Leaves, the ship's historical contingent, raised a single long finger and spoke in a mild tone.

"It could also bring us new enemies," he said. "The church—all the churches, really—claim dominion over these matters. They will not be pleased if we encroach upon their kingdoms. The Mill was before my time, but I know many you have direct experience of the violence that results from spiritual leaders feeling challenged."

"For my part, I say no," said Edna Greaves. "The *Lazarene* is my world. I don't need or want anything beyond it. There is nothing we can't accomplish just with the minds and bodies aboard this ship. We don't need anyone else."

Murmurs of assent from others around the table. It was clear that sentiment had turned against Penelope. She tightened her lips against her instinct to call every one of them a cowardly fool.

"Penelope," Molly said, her voice low but very firm.

All movement around the table ceased.

"Ma'am," she replied.

"Have we ever been closer to my husband than we were three nights ago?"

Penelope answered honestly.

"Never," she said.

"Do it," Molly Calder said, and the matter was closed.

This was the Second Intercession.

II. TWELVE

NEW YORK HARBOR.

1835.

40°41′45.9″N, 74°00′58.8″W

"New York City," Molly Calder said, in a voice touched by equal parts admiration and terror. "What an extraordinary place, eh, Luis? When was the last time we were here?"

She lay in a hammock on the *Lazarene*'s deck, propped up by pillows, watching ships flow in and out of New York Harbor. Luis Pedrona sat on a crate to one side, whittling a knotty bit of wood, carving it into the shape of a tree. The man seemed obsessed with them, ever since the night Penelope Franck found the First Door back on the Saya de Malha fifteen years before. He'd probably created an entire forest by himself, between his carvings, paintings, and drawings.

"Must be a while back, Molly," Luis replied. "Before my time. I came aboard the *Lazarene* in 1810, and I've never been here."

"You'd think they would pay us more notice," Molly said, gesturing out at the shipping traffic all around them.

Her hand caught her eye, and she sighed. Molly's hands had

become unrecognizable to her—gnarled and twisted by forty years at sea, knots of knuckle and bone.

"We don't look like anything else afloat, do we?" she said, lowering her hand. "We stand out from the other ships like a zebra in a herd of horses. Our sails alone!"

Molly looked up. Fluttering above were not the typical main sheet and topsails but instead a hundred small sheets of watered silk—in Calder Blue, of course. It made the ship look like a flock of bluebirds had invaded its masts and spars.

My ship, Molly thought, gazing at the wisps of silk flickering in the wind, each tiny but powerful together, taking the *Lazarene* anywhere it wanted to go. *My beautiful little nation.*

The sails moved constantly of their own accord, making adjustments large and small to catch the faintest breeze. They were connected to electric mechanisms designed to constantly maneuver them into the most perfect tension against oncoming winds. The helmsmen could set a dial to a desired speed and heading and the ship would respond accordingly. It could even stand still or reverse itself.

The sails were the most obvious signifiers that the *Lazarene* was utterly unique, but anyone experienced with shipbuilding would see many other differences from bow to stern. Along its hull were protuberances of unclear purpose, like folded wings. Instead of cannon barrels protruding from its gun deck, it had much thinner metal rods, like uncored rifle barrels. Its figurehead, if you could call it that, was a huge smoked-glass globe within which shapes seemed to move.

And yet, the *Lazarene* sat at anchor in New York Harbor, resoundingly ignored.

"I have heard," Luis said, carving a sliver away from the chunk of wood in his hands, "that in New York City the primary business of concern for every resident is their own. But that is a good thing, no? We Lazarenes prefer to remain unnoticed. Hopefully, Penelope will return soon and we can set out on our journey once again."

"If she returns at all," Molly said. "Nellie's little crusade got the better of her, didn't it?"

"I would say she's been very successful," Luis replied.

"Yes and no," Molly said. "She's had the Corianders traveling all over America and Europe for fifteen years, preaching the gospel of the Open to anyone who would listen, teaching people how to contact the spirit world. Worked like a charm, for good and ill. Many more people believe than ever before, but you can't spread knowledge like that and not expect some people to abuse it. Those Fox sisters up in Poughkeepsie certainly took the ideas and ran with them, eh?"

Luis didn't respond, just kept carving away at his little tree.

"More to the point, Nellie gave spiritualism to the world," Molly said. "The Second Intercession was supposed to change things not just among the Landsmen but for us too. But it hasn't, has it? We've still got a Door no one can walk through, just a few decks down."

Luis shrugged.

"These things take time," he said.

"You might have time," Molly said. "Not all of us are so lucky."

Luis paused his whittling. She was struck, as always, by the way the man hadn't aged a day since that night in the Indian Ocean. Years at sea usually tore a person to shreds. For Luis Pedrona, the opposite appeared to be true. His time afloat had blessed him with eternal youth.

Luis was generally a warm, friendly person, cheerfully attending to whatever duties the *Lazarene* required of him. But all aboard remembered the Saya del Malha. There was something in Luis Pedrona, something other, and sometimes that thing looked out from behind his eyes, spoke with its own voice.

"Do you suppose there's a real danger from those girls in Poughkeepsie, Luis? When Penelope described what she and her people were going ashore to do, she seemed . . . really quite nervous."

"The Fox sisters are playing foolish games by extending invitations to deeply unsavory otherworldly presences to take residence within their bodies," Luis said. "These are not the souls of humans who have passed on. They were never human, not even alive, for if a being cannot die, it cannot be said to live."

He held up the piece of wood, inspecting it.

"Penelope and her team are with the Fox sisters now, engaged in battle. I think they will probably win, and come back to us soon enough."

Molly did not question how Luis sometimes knew about things happening far from the *Lazarene*. He just did, ever since the Door. It was probably not Luis who knew these details at all, Molly believed. It was whatever lived behind his eyes.

That's who I'm talking to right now, Molly thought.

She didn't mind. Even if it was an otherworldly demon, it was unfailingly polite. In fact, Molly often preferred talking to the thing inside Luis. It was forthright, made no judgments, and was wonderful at keeping confidences.

"Do you think I'm a fool, Luis?" Molly asked.

"No," Luis replied without hesitation. "You are a very wise woman."

"Oh? I've spent forty-five years looking for my dead husband, and almost all of it at sea. That's more than four times as long as we were together in life. Apollo had an extraordinary impact on my life, but I was barely grown when we met. We built a successful business, had no children, and then he died. That should have been the end of it."

She looked at her hands again and sighed.

"I could have found another husband easily enough," she said. "You wouldn't believe it now, but I used to be beautiful."

"I believe it," Luis said.

"I was just so sad, and angry," Molly said, looking out at the sea.

"I believe that too," Luis said.

He set down his knife and half-completed bit of woodwork. He said nothing, just waited.

"I never truly expected to see Apollo again," Molly said. "I haven't, not for decades. Five years into the *Lazarene*'s journey, it became clear to me that even the greatest minds on earth might not be able to defeat death. It is a mystery, and I suspect it will always remain one.

"Though," she added, "perhaps not to me. Not for much longer."

Luis smiled gently down at her.

"So why did you continue?" he asked.

"I had a role to play, Luis. The Lazarenes needed a Molly Calder endlessly devoted to her lost love. It was part of the ship's creed. I care about the people here as much as I ever loved my husband."

A tear slipped down her cheek.

"More," she said, her voice down to a whisper. "I no longer feel very much when I think of Apollo. I have forgotten him."

She wiped the tear away with the back of her hand.

"But why shouldn't I? What foolish woman centers their entire life around a man who died in her youth? No. I wish Apollo well, wherever he is . . . but the most important work of my life was not the quest to find him. It was this. This place. The *Lazarene.* A home for brilliant dreamers, where they could be safe and free.

"And think, Luis! In just forty years, the Lazarenes created ideas and technology that exist nowhere else on earth and contributed greatly to the cure for a dread disease that has been a scourge of humanity for centuries."

Luis reached over and took her hand.

"The *Lazarene* is a great work, Molly. Your great work."

"Thank you, Luis," Molly said, squeezing his hand before releasing it. "But still, I am afraid."

"Of what? Of your imminent death?"

Molly chuckled. The thing inside Luis was forthright, honest, withheld judgment . . . and could be as blunt as a hammer.

"Not my death. The ship's. I want it to live, forever if possible, but solving death and finding Apollo—they're the *Lazarene*'s compass headings. The Lazarene Creed. It's why I kept letting them believe that I cared about Apollo long after that ended for me. Once I'm gone—and as you very rightly pointed out, it won't be long—I fear everything I have built will fall apart.

"I still wish to conquer death," Molly said. "The death of the *Lazarene*."

Luis Pedrona sat back. He took a long moment, appearing to consider everything Molly had just said. Then he stood, bent, and slipped his arms beneath the old woman, lifting her from the hammock.

"Luis!" Molly said. "What are you doing?"

"Come with me, Molly Calder," he said. "You're ready."

II. THE LAST LETTER

To the Crew of the *Lazarene*:

Thank you all for everything you have done for me. Bringing you together was the great purpose and joy of my life.

As you read this, I am gone, and have learned the truth we have all spent so many years chasing. In the end, the trick to it seems much simpler than any of us expected. All I had to do was die.

My people, my family, my beautiful Lazarenes, you must realize that you have a purpose greater than anything I ever asked you to do. I set us upon our voyage and, yes, I had a goal I asked you to help me attain. But now that goal is irrelevant—and in truth has been for some time.

So now I issue my last orders to you, which you will choose to obey or ignore as you like. My authority will die with me. But I thought I might set down these words as a form of guidance, a few last observations from a woman who has spent much of her life alongside all of you and everything we have built together.

What is important now? First, the *Lazarene* itself. This little world provides a home for those whose ideas or circumstances alienate them from society or expose them to ridicule or persecution. We are free to follow the paths of intellect wherever they may lead—a unique and precious thing.

Second, I tell you this—those paths have taken us to

a place you could never imagine. I have been beyond the First Door. Luis Pedrona brought me there. I will not tell you why or what I found there. But know Luis believes many of you will be ready soon to undertake the same journey. You will see, as I did, that there is no greater treasure in all the world, and it must be protected at all costs.

With that in mind, stay hidden, as we always have. The mere fact of our existence will cause others to hate us, to fear us, to try to destroy us. Protect the *Lazarene* and what lies beyond the Door, as well as the other wonders you might find.

This grand adventure began with two people. My husband and I named our enterprise after ourselves—and the symbol we chose reflected our esteem for each other, two people facing each other as equals. Calder, and Calder.

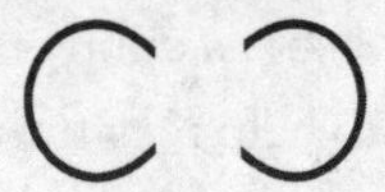

But now we have become something else. We have voyaged together for half a century. I see no reason the journey should end, simply because I am no longer with you.

My last command is this: *Stay the course.*

See what else there is to see. Now and forever.

—*Molly Calder*

The Lazarene
June 1835

BOOK III

THE HOMECOMING

III. ONE

THE SOUTH CHINA SEA.

SIX MONTHS AGO.

21°26′51.7″N, 114°05′32.2″E

DR. FREDERICK BARNES STOOD IN HIS OFFICE AT THE OUTERMOST edge of the *Lazarene*'s Brooks deck, staring north through a wide, curved window at the nighttime sea.

He had lived aboard the ship for over sixteen years, been an accomplished sailor for decades before that, yet the ocean at night still chilled him to the bone. It felt like looking at death itself—or perhaps what came after. The illumination provided by the ship's running lights vanished a few meters off the hull, and after that it was just a flat expanse of black nothing all the way to the horizon, unless a lone boat happened to be passing—and they usually weren't. The ocean was just so breathtakingly *huge.* A huge open mouth, waiting to swallow anything foolish enough to—

You're stalling, he told himself, and sighed.

Barnes turned from the window and walked to his desk. The broad, gently luminous slab of slipstone had been purchased from the beings beyond the Third Door in exchange for three chests of solid iodine, a delicacy across that threshold. It was one of his favorite possessions, and normally it brought him great happiness. But now his desk made his stomach churn, for resting atop it was a solid metal alloy cylinder cast in the Lazarenes' signature color, a shade everywhere on the ship, the ubiquitous Calder Blue.

Beside the cylinder lay his unlit pipe, and next to that was an incredibly powerful, versatile tool called a formaker. Frederick always thought it looked like a glove woven by spiders. He slipped the formaker over his right hand, feeling it gently and automatically tighten against his skin. He wiggled his fingers, feeling the telltale, more than slightly unnerving buzz that signified a good connection.

He rasped his middle finger against the ball of his thumb and a spotlight appeared above his desk with no apparent source, its beam centered on the night-blue cylinder. Another flick of the formaker and a hatch opened on the side of the device, revealing its interior mechanisms.

Barnes sorted through the gadget, seeking a particular component he'd seen on the design schematic. After a few moments he found his quarry: several loops of wire coral connecting two of the thing's processors. Carefully, making precise gestures with the formaker, he detached the loops of hyperconductive semi-living metal—mined by the *Lazarene*'s Automen from below the seas of the Fourth Door—manipulating them into a new configuration, then reattaching them.

He dropped his hand, letting his fingers rest. Barnes leaned forward, inspecting his work. Inside the cylinder, the wire coral was now woven into an intricate pattern, crossing and recrossing itself, coiling into a braid-like shape that Frederick, at least, found to be both centering and calming.

The Mechanical Mandala, Barnes thought. *Risen from the dead.*

Frederick had not built the cylinder, though he had argued to the Council that the Lazarenes should create it. His modification of the device served no engineering purpose. It was more of an affectation, a sort of signature. A message.

Whether that message would ever be seen by the person he intended to receive it, or be properly interpreted, or achieve the result he was hoping for, Barnes did not know. But this was the best he could do. The *Lazarene* allowed direct contact with Landsmen only under very specific circumstances, and there was zero chance this particular message would be approved, not at such a delicate moment for both the ship and the larger world.

Barnes double-checked his connections, then used the formaker to seal the device closed. A few quick passes with the formaker's cohesion tool, and you'd never know the blue cylinder had been opened at all.

He took up his pipe with his left hand, setting its stem between his teeth. He nudged the cylinder with a fingertip, setting it rocking gently, blue reflections shimmering against his desk. It was so light, especially considering all it could do, and all it might mean to . . .

Lily, he thought.

He considered, not for the first time, whether he was sailing a prudent course. The cylinder could cause turmoil in his daughter's life. Trouble in his own, too, if the other members of the Lazarene Council learned what he had done.

But this was a gift. A parting gift. Not just to her but to the entire world. And Lily would get some of the credit for that. She deserved it.

Gift or not, Dr. Barnes, he asked himself, *are you sure it's a good idea to* sign *it?*

It didn't matter now. He didn't have time to undo his adjustment even if he changed his mind. A woman was waiting for the cylinder in the corridor just outside Dr. Barnes's office: an eighth-generation Lazarene named Ilana Bayonne, whose line could be drawn back to Evgeny Choglovoka. This gave her both the dark, thick eyebrows borne by many descendants of the hyper-virile Russian surgeon, and an air of confidence (haughtiness, Frederick would have said) common to many of the Mill descendants.

Ilana had responsibility for seeing this particular operation through. She had initiated Council-sanctioned contact with the man in Hong Kong who would receive the cylinder, and the plans that would allow him to manufacture it—a Mr. Danny Chang, who ran a company called CarbonGo.

Mr. Chang was probably not the best candidate to get the cylinder. CarbonGo was poorly funded, without the necessary contacts that would allow efficient upscaling and manufacture in any reasonable amount of time. But Frederick Barnes had gone to great lengths to ensure Danny Chang would receive it nevertheless.

Barnes was a trusted member of the Lazarene Council. As such, he was an important part of designing and implementing the greatest interaction the ship had made with the Landsmen in a century—the Great Adjustment, embodied by the Tenth through Fourteenth Intercessions.

When the initial discussions around these new Intercessions had begun, Barnes had pushed the Council to include an effort focused on climate change. Once they agreed, he had steered the conversation toward a hyper-efficient device for removing atmospheric carbon and overseen the cylinder's design and construction by engineers in the Gearworks. He had chosen its destination among the Landsmen. And finally, he had insisted that he be given a few minutes with the device before it left the ship. Barnes had power, and he had used it.

If the Lazarenes learned what he had done, he would be cast out, or cast beyond. They would be right to do it. Barnes was breaking one of the *Lazarene*'s most sacrosanct rules for entirely personal reasons. Everything he was doing was contrary to the ship's goals and the safety of the people aboard.

This was not the first time he had done something like this. In that case as well as now, he believed he had no choice.

A knock came at the door. Confident. Haughty. Ilana had clearly run out of patience.

"Come in, Ms. Bayonne," he called.

Ilana entered the office wearing a sleek grey coverall with a sun-shaped badge at the collar that marked her as one of the All-brights. She raised an eyebrow, an act so powerful it nearly qualified as violence.

"Have you finished, Dr. Barnes?" she said. "I need to take the transport to Hong Kong. Don't want to be late. Don't want to spend more time ashore than I have to, either. Being on the dirt . . . it's unsettling."

Frederick handed the device to Ilana Bayonne.

"You're good to go, Ilana," Frederick said.

"What did you need this for?" she asked, her tone light but shaded by the unearned belief all the Mill descendants held that they deserved to know everything that went on aboard the *Lazarene* at all times.

"I just wanted to look it over one last time," he said. "This is my project. It's an Intercession. They don't happen very often, you know."

He made a little shooing gesture toward the woman.

"Off you go, Ilana," he said. "As you said, we wouldn't want you to be late. It's very important this gets where it's going."

This was the Tenth Intercession.

III. TWO

THE NORTH ATLANTIC.

SIX MONTHS LATER.

51°16'16.8"N, 7°05'56.7"W

BENJAMIN ELKHORN SAT AT HIS STATION INSIDE THE ROUND OF Doors, Janet Crowe one seat over. They were both watching a ticking, smooth-shelled Automan perform the standard series of checks on the Fourth Door. That one opened onto a world that was entirely ocean, maybe an entire universe that was ocean—they'd never found a surface over there, though an expedition had discovered the seabed forty kilometers down, covered by the drowned cities of some ancient civilization of seven-legged, three-eyed creatures.

The point was you wouldn't want the Fourth Door to open unless you were good and ready. The first time the Lazarenes had opened it, back in the 1950s, so much water had spewed through that it drowned all the Open performing the ritual and nearly sank the whole damn ship before they could it close again. So they had built a heavy metal access port over the Door—a door to the Door—and now an Automan checked the seals once every hour, looking for anything unusual.

Once the machine finished with the Fourth, it would move on to the Fifth, equally sealed but for different reasons entirely. Then it would leave the Round of Doors to perform other duties until cycling back in an hour.

"I envy that thing," Janet said, eyeing it. "At least it gets to leave every once in a while. We're stuck here for the full watch."

Benjamin wasn't going to say it out loud, but he didn't mind spending time in the Round of Doors, not one bit. Yes, the room was just a big circle, its only notable features the doors to other dimensions floating in midair, plus the control console where he and Janet sat. But he thought Janet Crowe was pretty notable indeed, with her pretty pink-dyed hair and sailor's tattoos running down from her coveralls along both arms.

Ben's crush on his coworker went deeper than that ocean beyond the Fourth Door—not that he had the slightest damn idea what to do about it. The *Lazarene* was a very small world, and while connections were bound to happen—had to, really, if they wanted babies for the next generation—things could get hellish if a romance went wrong. He and Janet were both Riggers, too, which meant they'd be seeing each other all over the ship on maintenance and navigation shifts.

Time was running out, though. If Ben didn't move quickly, he might never get a chance to get anywhere with Janet at all. On the other hand, the ticking clock meant he didn't really have much to lose, did he? Might as well just ask her to a coffee, or to catch a performance in the theater, or just to take a stroll through the safari room.

Screw it, he thought.

"Say, Janet, I was thinking—" he began.

A chime sounded and an indicator light illuminated on the control console. Janet leaned forward to check.

"Looks like Dr. Barnes's team is back," she said.

Fuck, Benjamin thought.

"I'll get it," he said.

He sighed and got to his feet, grabbing a thinnie from the desktop and heading toward the Echo Door. Once there, Benjamin activated the two-way camera system installed in the metal portal built over the Door, preventing unauthorized access from either side. Dr. Frederick Barnes looked back at him through the lens. He looked beat half to hell. His lined face had dirt in the crevices, his long, grey-streaked hair looked like you could lube an engine with the grease in it. Mostly, he just looked tired. Barnes and his team had been on the other side for more than a week, living rough, and it had taken its toll. The man wasn't young, either—had to be pushing sixty.

"Ready to come home, Dr. Barnes?" Ben said into the camera.

"Like you wouldn't believe, Ben," the other man replied. "We found some really interesting things on this trip, at least three significant discoveries. I'm looking forward to digging into the results. And a real bed. I'm also looking forward to that."

"Have you over here in a tick," Ben said.

Barnes had used the word "three" in his reply, which meant they were uncompromised. If he'd used different numbers, other messages might have been conveyed—everything from *Send help* to *Never open* this Door *again and vaporize anything that tries to come through*.

Despite that reassurance, Ben activated the various security and identification verification technologies built into the heavy metal seal over the Echo Door. He wanted to make sure Dr. Barnes and his fellow researchers were actually, in fact, Dr. Barnes and his fellow researchers.

After fighting the Second People in the 1940s, and what they had learned about the capabilities of the beings behind the Third Door, the Lazarenes took no chances.

But everything came up green. Benjamin released the seals, and the Echo Door swung open. Dr. Barnes and the other two members of his small team stepped back aboard the *Lazarene*, lugging their gear with them. A pungent wave of body funk accompanied them. No showers for a week would do that.

Janet came around from the control console and helped them bring the satchels and such through, including their garbage—they never left anything behind after an expedition into the Echo Door.

"Ah, that's good," Barnes said, pulling off his breathing mask. "Nice to be back."

"I bet," Janet said. "I'm sure you'll be wanting a wash and a hot meal, not necessarily in that order, but do you want to have a look at the open items first?"

Dr. Barnes sighed. Now that Benjamin had a closer look at him, he realized the older man didn't just seem tired. He looked bone-weary, exhausted to his core.

"Yes, Janet, I suppose so," Barnes said. "Don't ever join the Council, no matter how nicely they ask."

"Noted, Dr. Barnes," she replied. "Ben's got the thinnie."

Barnes reached out, and Benjamin handed him the rectangular, transparent device. The scientist activated it, sighed again when he saw the dozens of items requiring his attention, and began scrolling through them.

He froze.

"The Garbage Man was activated?" Barnes said, his exhaustion dropping away.

"Mm," said Ben, not sure why the man thought that was so important.

He wasn't an Allbright, after all. Ship's security wasn't his department. Barnes was a Barber, Elkhorn believed. Or maybe one of the Leaves. In any case, ship security wasn't his business.

"In *Gloucester*?" Barnes asked, looking up from the thinnie, his eyes wide.

"If . . . that's what it says, sir," Janet said.

Barnes seemed to be having a panic attack. Behind him, the

rest of his team took notice. One gently took him by the arm, a copper-skinned woman with a thin face Benjamin knew he should recognize but didn't.

"Frederick, is there a problem?" the woman said.

"Of course there bloody is!" Barnes snapped, shaking off the woman's arm.

He tapped and selected and tapped again on the thinnie, opening a communications channel. A face appeared on the screen, and this one Elkhorn did recognize. Maxwell Franck—the Lazarene Council's reigning Molly. Franck wasn't the captain, but for all intents and purposes this man ran the whole goddamn boat.

"The Garbage Man—*call it off,*" Barnes said, his voice insistent, almost desperate.

"Welcome back from the Echoes, Frederick," said Maxwell Franck. "We sent out the Garbage Man because of a significant security breach. Do you want to explain why we should call it back?"

"Because," Barnes said, pleading, "*it's going to kill my daughter.*"

HOURS LATER, FREDERICK BARNES STOOD ON THE DECK OF THE *Lazarene,* wind and sea spray blasting his face as he scanned the sky. The ship was headed east at full speed, racing through the chill waters of the Atlantic toward the British coast.

High in the sky, Barnes saw a dark dot with a silhouette completely unlike an airplane. It was closer to a strange, gigantic bird of prey with two rabbits dangling from its talons. The dot grew rapidly, its brutal razored wings flapping, and then suddenly a woman he recognized as his daughter was sprawled nearly at his feet, along with a long-haired man he didn't know. Both were battered, clearly hurt quite badly.

And I'm about to hurt her again, he thought. *Worse than anything she's already suffered.*

For a moment Barnes entertained the idea of slipping away,

deeper into the ship, rather than face this moment. But that was the thought of a child, and for the first time in a long time he needed to act like a father.

He moved toward Lily as the Garbage Man dissipated, returning to wherever it lived. A great, rattling crash as the pieces of metal, plastic, and glass that had made up its body fell across the deck.

Barnes knelt next to his grown daughter, an adult, no longer the lanky creature she'd been the last time he saw her, before he died. Before he lied.

Lily pushed herself up on her elbow, grimacing. He gently touched the side of her face, trying to comfort her the way he had when she was very young and she skinned her knee or fell off her bicycle. His daughter looked stunned, bewildered, overwhelmed. The tears brimming up in her eyes were clearly not just related to her physical injuries.

"Dear god, Lily, what happened to you?" Barnes said.

"Dad?" she said.

The first word she'd said to him in seventeen years.

"I'm here," her father said. "You're all right now."

Members of the ship's medical team rushed up. They opened their kits and began checking Lily's vitals, offering first aid to the new arrivals. Frederick knew how good the Barbers were. It wouldn't be long before his daughter and her friend—he'd have to figure out who that fellow was; he hadn't said a word yet—were right as rain, at least physically.

"Dad," Lily said, her voice thin and weak, "what is this? What's happening?"

Frederick forced himself to smile.

"That," he said, "is a story."

"We'd like to give you something for the pain," one of the medics said. "It might make you a little fuzzy for a bit, but when you come out of it, it'll be like none of this ever happened."

Lily looked at the medic. Slowly, and with great apparent effort, she raised an eyebrow.

"Is that right?" she said, her tone absolutely saturated with sarcasm. "I'll just forget it all? *All of it?*"

"No promises," said the medic, and touched a slim silver rod to Lily's arm. A tiny, imperceptible whoosh, which Barnes knew signified the delivery of a sedative.

His daughter's gaze shifted back to him, her eyes fierce in just the way he remembered Adriana's getting from time to time, and then Lily's eyelids drooped and the medic lowered her back to the deck.

Frederick Barnes stood, knowing the Barbers would take it from there. He had little to offer—he wasn't a medical doctor. Beyond that, his mind felt as cloudy as the winter fogs off Patagonia.

Lily is here, actually here on the Lazarene.

"Barnes," said a familiar voice, and he turned.

Maxwell Franck stalked across the deck toward him, his long white hair rippling in the chill breeze off the Atlantic. Behind him came Magdalena Crouch and Lucinda Bir, making three members of the Lazarene Council—an Open, a Closed, and the Molly himself.

All factions present and accounted for, Barnes thought.

"This is your daughter?" Franck asked, pointing at Lily.

Who the hell else would it be? Barnes thought.

"It is," he answered. "Lily."

"Why is she here, Frederick?" Magdalena Crouch said, her big fists clenched. "*What have you done?*"

Barnes drew himself up.

"I'm a Council member, too, Maggie," he said. "And a Lazarene for almost twenty years. Enough with the accusations."

"Answer her questions," said Lucinda Bir, the Open representative dressed in the ridiculous wizard robes members of that group sometimes liked to wear.

"Not here," Barnes said. "Let's go the Council chamber and we'll handle it like any other piece of ship's business."

This was an attempt to buy time, so transparent that he was certain it would be called out. There were no fools among the Lazarenes, and certainly not on their Council.

"And if we did, what should be done with them?" Franck said, gesturing to Lily and her as-yet-unnamed friend, still being worked on by the medics, Automen ready with stretchers to carry both below. "Most ships deal with stowaways by tossing them over the side. I don't see why the *Lazarene* should be any different."

"You do that, Max, and I'll make sure you follow them, whether you're the Molly or not," Barnes said, standing straight and putting some heat into his tone. "Lily and her companion are our guests. They were brought here against their will by our security system. We owe them hospitality and care. I say we treat their injuries and then . . . give them the tour."

"They're *Dirters*," said Magdalena.

"And one of them is my *daughter*," Barnes said, heat slipping into his tone. "Watch yourself."

Maggie just shook her head, disgusted.

"What possible difference could it make?" Barnes said. "Considering everything, I mean."

The Council members looked at each other.

"There will be consequences," Franck said after a moment. "There have to be, Barnes. If they don't land on your daughter, I suspect they'll land on you. But you're right. In the end, it probably doesn't make a difference if we show these two . . . guests . . . who we are. We could tell our story to the whole world and it wouldn't change a thing."

Maxwell looked out at the sea, his hair streaming out behind him.

"That ship," he said, "has sailed."

III. THREE

THE *LAZARENE*.

50°36'24.3"N, 34°59'04.8"W

LILY AWOKE TO FIND HERSELF LYING IN A BED IN WHAT WAS CLEARLY a small medical facility.

A sick bay, she thought. *That's what they're called when they're on a ship. Unless that's just from* Star Trek.

On the other hand, *Star Trek* wasn't too far off the mark. The room boasted obvious signs of technology far beyond the usual medical clinic. A 3D display of Lily's vital signs hovered in the air above her bed, and a glass-fronted cabinet built into one wall contained shiny instruments of unknown purpose and material, though she recognized the iridescent shimmer on their surface from the shell on the carbon scrubber.

Which is now lying somewhere on the side of the M4, she realized. So much for that particular miracle.

Lily was wearing a hospital gown made of some tightly woven or printed material she didn't recognize. Her dirty, torn clothes were visible on a table across the room, folded neatly. Peter's were there, too, along with a little pile of his personal effects. No such luck for Lily—everything she'd had on her was back in that satchel on the side of the highway. She thought about her tile puzzle, lost with the rest of her things.

A missing tile in her own puzzle had just been filled in, up there on the deck. But it hadn't solved anything. It just opened up a new hole, ten times as big.

Peter Match was in the next bed over, beginning to stir. The singer opened his eyes.

"You okay?" Lily asked.

Peter took a moment to assess his surroundings, then himself. Then he nodded, seeming almost surprised.

That, Lily understood. Despite having been through more physical trauma in the past forty-eight hours than she'd experienced in her entire prior life, she felt pretty good.

She checked her body. Her various wounds had vanished without leaving scars. Her head felt fine. She was clean. Even the scrape on the back of her left ankle she'd sustained while escaping CarbonGo was gone.

Peter got up and walked over to the table with their stuff, utterly unconcerned by the breezy lack of modesty afforded by his own hospital gown. He reached for his phone and tapped its surface, checking its clock.

"It's been an hour," he said, his voice as rough as ever.

The doctors fixed our cuts and bruises but they didn't get around to the cancer, Lily thought. *Maybe they just didn't know.*

If it bothered Peter, he didn't show it.

The door to the medical bay opened and a *thing* trundled into the room. A machine in the shape of a man, pushing a little cart bearing sandwiches, bottles of water, and two bundles of fabric. It was a . . . "robot" was the only word Lily could come up with, like a 1950s sci-fi movie trope come to life, with big bulblike eyes and a speaker grille for a mouth. The thing presented its gifts. The bundles turned out to be surprisingly stylish coveralls, blue with red and orange accent stripes.

"Guess our clothes aren't salvageable," Lily said, holding up the coveralls.

Peter just grunted.

She slipped into the small bathroom attached to the medical bay, changed, and came back out to see that Peter had taken the opportunity to do the same, though he'd put his leather jacket back on over the coveralls. The jacket was much the worse for wear, scraped and torn.

But I'll be damned if it doesn't look even better, Lily thought.

Peter took his Zippo and his phone from the pile of his stuff and slipped them into pockets. Then he walked over to the cart and picked up the packages of food and drink. He gave the silent robot a little salute, then returned to Lily and handed her a sandwich and a water.

The sandwiches turned out to be pockets of dense bread filled with marinated vegetables both familiar and not, and the water was cold and clear. They sat on their beds and wolfed it all down—it was utterly delicious. As they were finishing, the door to the medical bay opened and someone new entered—a person this time.

"Hello, you two," he said, speaking with a Dutch accent. "My name is Willem Vanderwaal. I have been assigned to take care of you while you are our guests."

Could be worse, Lily thought. *He could have said "prisoners."*

Willem was youngish and sandy-haired, wore coveralls of his own (though his were yellow with turquoise accents), and had the feel of an intern or lab assistant annoyed to have to take time off his work to show his bosses' kid around the workplace.

Over the next hour Willem bustled them through a tour of the ship, which turned out to be called the *Lazarene*. It was clear that he was giving them only a cursory look—the ship was massive. Lily thought again of the gigantic cruise ships that docked at the terminals in Tsim Sha Tsui in Hong Kong—this was at least as large, if not bigger.

Willem told them that over a thousand people lived and worked aboard, with plenty of space for everyone. Lily believed it. The tour encompassed huge greenhouses; workshops; laboratories; three pubs of wildly divergent character; a full-size football pitch; a gorgeously designed Art Deco auditorium/cinema; a hangar and dry dock filled with a variety of exotic craft for traversing land, air, and sea; a chamber that seemed to contain an African savannah except that, as far as Lily knew, the sun was not purple in Africa and the animals there did not include golden-furred dragons; and an entirely dark room smelling of earth their guide referred to as the Dyeing Chamber—though it could just as easily have been the Dying Chamber.

Everywhere, Lily and Peter saw impossible things. It was like the foyer at Coriander & Associates back in Shek O but multiplied a thousand times. Even the very stuff from which the ship was made confounded Lily, despite her expertise in such matters. Whatever the *Lazarene* was built from was utterly foreign to her, a series of meta-materials she could only assume were derived from unicorn bones and UFO hulls and stone mined from a quarry at Shangri-La.

Willem Vanderwaal showed them these things, and Lily asked a hundred questions, which the guide invariably answered in a manner calculated to provide very little additional information. Mostly, Willem told them a story about the history of what he called the Lazarene Society. It began with a textile mill in Massachusetts just after the American Revolution and ended with the death of a woman named Molly Calder in 1835. Willem told it as an epic love story whose only child was a floating intellectual utopia.

Lily didn't completely buy it. She thought the details were probably true, mostly—but 1835 was a long, long time ago. Just as Willem had studiously avoided showing them vast swaths of the *Lazarene,* his story left out almost two centuries of history.

And, of course, there was the trash spirit that had tried to murder her and Peter back in Gloucester. Willem had neglected to mention the Garbage Man at all.

But Vanderwaal was clearly just a flunky sent to babysit them for a few hours. Lily knew the story she truly wanted would have to come from someone else, and she intended to get it.

The final stop on the tour turned out to be a gigantic chamber buried deep in the heart of the ship. It contained a truly awe-inspiring sight, even aboard this ship of miracles.

A skylight high above brought in a shaft of bright, golden sunlight centered on a three-masted sailing ship floating in midair. At first, Lily's mind processed it as a model, because there was no way it could be real, a whole ship inside another like a fetus in a womb . . . but then her brain reconciled the perspectives, and there was no denying it. A full-sized ship from . . . the 1800s, Lily thought. Intact and whole, deep inside the *Lazarene.* It looked odd even to Lily's nonexpert eyes. Its flags were tiny scraps of bright blue silk, hundreds of them. A gigantic smoke-filled globe at its bow like a fortune teller's crystal ball, and an elaborate clockwork engine attachment at its stern.

And, of course, the fact that it was floating two meters above the floor of this gigantic well of a room without any visible means of support.

"Do either of you know what this is?" asked Willem, proudly gesturing at the enormous ship.

Peter Match had not made a single sound for the entire tour, which wasn't surprising. He seemed utterly fascinated, though, hanging on Willem's every word.

Good for him, Lily thought, a little sourly. *Maybe I'd be able to enjoy some sightseeing, too, if I wasn't preoccupied by the fact that, oh, right, my entire life is a lie.*

Peter answered Willem's question by lifting a hand and pointed at the sailing ship. Then he took the same hand and swirled it around in a circle, indicating the vessel all around them.

Willem smiled.

"Very good, Mr. Match," he said. "This is indeed the original *Lazarene,* built in Essex, Massachusetts, just after the American War for Independence. Over the centuries this ship was modified to incorporate many design enhancements created by the brilliant people who formed its crew, from its fabled crop deck to the Round of Doors. But eventually it was determined that the needs of our little community would be better served by creating an entirely new ship designed from the ground up to incorporate the technological innovations and unique needs of a group like this."

He looked at the ship and smiled.

"But we were too attached to the original *Lazarene* to simply scuttle it, so we decided to build *around* it. Even now we adhere to the naval traditions that marked our early years. Every crew member studies the arts of the sailor, from sailmaking to navigation, before they become a fully fledged adult in our society. We all hold ranks as well. I, for instance, am a midshipman, though that rank is largely ceremonial. The modern *Lazarene* mostly runs itself, though our illustrious captain, Frank Tokyo, would keelhaul me if he heard me say that. But we do not forget where we came from, and so the first *Lazarene* is with us always, a monument to where our story began. And for you, it is also where the story comes to an end. Do you have any questions I can answer?"

"I hope you can," Lily said, and asked Willem Vanderwaal the question she had been asking herself in one way or another since she was seventeen years old.

"Where is my father?" she said.

Willem nodded.

"Of course," he said. "You must be anxious."

"Anxious?" she replied. "No. I wouldn't say I'm anxious, Willem."

During the entire tour, she'd been carrying on a detailed internal dialogue with herself, ripe with emotion, betrayal, twists . . . trying to find some story that would make all of this make *sense.*

Dad would never have left unless he had no choice. Maybe he was kidnapped. These seem like the kind of people who would do that. And he sent you a message, didn't he, Lily? There's no way that carbon scrubber showed up at your workplace accidentally. He knew you'd see it, and he knew you'd come looking.

No, fuck him—he did this on purpose. He ruined your life because he wanted something else.

But maybe . . . that's not what happened. I mean, he's your father. He wouldn't just . . .

"I just need to talk to my dad," Lily said. "Where is he?"

Willem Vanderwaal checked a device on his wrist—clearly not a watch; more like a smartphone strapped to his forearm. He waved a finger in the air above it and seemed to receive some kind of information from the thing. He looked back up.

"According to my mini, Dr. Barnes is on his way," Willem said. "He'll meet us here."

"And then what?" Peter Match said, in his sharp-edged whisper.

The singer seemed anxious, laser focused. Lily knew why. He had gone through utter hell to get here, and was now standing closer to a cure for his cancer than he'd ever come. Based on what they'd seen in the sick bay, the *Lazarene* possessed medical technology beyond anything in the rest of the world. Peter's cure was almost certainly here. He had a chance to live—maybe even sing again—but there were no guarantees he'd get it.

Their status on the ship was unclear. Lily felt like a guest who'd shown up at an acquaintance's house unannounced, with the residents trying to be hospitable while hiding their obvious annoyance. And while Lily's father had invited her to come in a roundabout way, Peter wasn't part of that, and he knew it.

The Lazarenes could give him his life back . . . but he had no idea if they would.

"I actually don't know what will happen once Dr. Barnes arrives," Willem said. "As I said, I'm just a midshipman. My guess is you two are being discussed by the Council right now. Nothing like this has ever happened before. They told me to give you the tour, so I gave you the tour."

Peter Match nodded, clearly frustrated. He took a long, deep breath, held it, then let it out—centering himself, Lily figured. She wanted to help him, reassure him, but Willem's words—"Dr. Barnes is on his way"—were ringing in her head, and she was falling into her own anxiety spin.

She wanted to see her father again—couldn't believe she was about to, imminently—and never wanted to see him again.

"Apollo and Molly," Peter said, crunching out the words, "you guys ever figure it out? They ever find each other again?"

"They did," Willem said.

Peter raised an eyebrow. He was clearly considering another question no matter how much it might hurt him to ask, but didn't get the chance.

"Lily," Frederick Barnes said, coming around the hull of the original *Lazarene* and walking toward their little group. "I'm so sorry."

Her father had taken time to clean up and change clothes, she noted.

Of course, Lily thought. *Why not? What's the rush, after all? It's been seventeen years; what's an extra twenty minutes or so?*

Her father stopped about three meters away, clearly unsure whether to come closer. Lily could only imagine the expression she must have on her face. Good old Freddy Barnes was probably afraid she might strike him dead right there.

And she might.

"What are you sorry for, Dad?" she said. "What . . . are you *sorry for*?"

He tilted his head a touch to the left in a gesture so familiar it ripped Lily's heart in half. She had wished so many times for another day with her father, just ten more minutes, a cup of coffee . . . and now that he was here, she just wished the asshole would drop dead.

And also, she felt some part of herself soaring with unassailable joy. Whatever happened seventeen years ago—whether her father had lied and abandoned her and her mother, or he had been kidnapped, or maybe the story was even stranger—here he was, no longer dead, and maybe, *maybe,* he loved her and always had.

"I'm sorry you were brought here the way you were," Frederick said. "I'm sorry that you were afraid. I didn't intend for any of it to happen. The *Lazarene* protects itself, because it's protecting something else, something crucially important. The Garbage Man is one of its defense mechanisms. It's automated, basically. I had no idea you'd ever encounter it."

"Mum has the Grey," Lily said. "She's in a darkhouse. Do you know what that is, or are you too far removed from the world to even know what's happening to it?"

Frederick's eyebrows shot up. His face paled.

"I know about the Grey," her father answered. "Just because I was here doesn't mean I stopped paying attention."

Lily could not process this—any of it. The first aid she had received had done wonders for her aches and pains, but it hadn't erased her exhaustion. She could feel herself being dragged down into an adrenaline crash.

"How are you here?" she said, her voice raw. "How are you alive?"

Frederick Barnes's eyes flicked to Peter and Willem and his mouth tightened.

"I don't want to do this here," he said. "This is a family thing."

Her father seemed almost as overwhelmed as she did. Like this was all a level of complication he hadn't expected and didn't need.

"Since when do you care about *family things*?" Lily spat.

Her fists clenched. She took a step forward, then felt a hand on her arm and looked back. Peter was holding her, gentle but firm. His eyes were locked on her father.

"What will happen to us?" Peter Match said.

"The discussion is ongoing," Frederick said. "I just left a Council meeting. I didn't want to leave you alone for too long."

"Oh, *that's* rich," Lily said.

Her father looked at her.

"It's a serious situation, Lily. Half the Council wants to send you back to the world. The other half wants to send you over the side."

"But . . . you sent that thing to me," Lily said. "The carbon scrubber, with the Mechanical Mandala inside. It was a clue. It put me on the Wonder Path. You *wanted* me to come."

Frederick Barnes gave her a long look, his face very still.

Oh . . . fuck, she realized. *I have this whole thing wrong, don't I?*

Her father was not yet done breaking her heart.

"The Mandala was . . . a reminder, not an invitation. I wanted you to think of me, think about me. That's all. I never thought you'd . . . I didn't think it was possible for you to get here. I just wanted to reach out to you one more time, while I had the chance."

"While you had the chance . . . ," Lily echoed. "What does that mean?"

"We're leaving, Lily," her father said. "All of us aboard. The Lazarenes are getting ready to go."

"Why?" she said, the only question she seemed able to ask.

"Why would we stay?" he answered. "It's the end of the world."

III. FOUR

MANHATTAN.

40°46′26.3″N, 73°57′02.7″W

The ground was dead. Nothing would grow. The lot on Eighty-Second Street between First and York was a garden of broken glass and wind-weathered plastic water bottles and condoms, little plastic bags of dog shit in blue and yellow like wrapped candies. Grease-stained fast-food sacks. Bits of wood. Inside-out umbrellas. Back in one corner, a plastic dollhouse, conjuring up the horrifying idea that children had actually attempted to play in this awful, filthy wasteland.

Aunt Jane had created this place. In a way, it had created her. So, on the eve of the Pyre, the very day before her greatest work was to begin, she had asked her people to bring her here. She wanted to see where so much had begun, before so much ended.

Her main man, Lorenzo, stood beside her, quietly waiting to see what she would do, why they had come to this place. Jane's guards kept a respectful distance behind them, their attention on the street, the sidewalk, even up at the windows in the apartments above, looking for nosy New Yorkers who might recognize Aunt Jane and call the police. She was famous, after all. Would the police even respond to a 911 call if someone made it? Maybe; maybe not. Things were getting dicey out there. Still, there was no point in taking a chance. Not with the Pyre so close. After that, it wouldn't matter.

The van that had brought them to Manhattan's Upper West Side sat at the curb, double-parked and idling, ready to whisk Jane away at the merest hint of danger. She liked that. Liked that everyone was ready, wary. Eyes on the prize.

Team Joy Joy is probably the most effective organization on the planet at the moment, she thought, taking pride in it.

Aunt Jane took Lorenzo's hand and stepped off the sidewalk into the lot.

"I haven't been here in fourteen months," she said. "This was a vacant lot then too."

"Yeah?" Lorenzo replied. "Funny nothing got built here, then. I thought they never stopped building in this town."

"Mm," Jane said. "It's a Grey world, Lorenzo. Manhattan real estate ain't such a sure bet anymore."

They ambled through the lot, in no particular hurry. Beneath the layer of cast-off New York City, the places where the original beds were laid out were still visible, with stone paths set between them. But nothing green. Not a weed, not a blade of grass, just a few dry stalks of what had once grown here.

"This used to be a garden," Jane said.

"Here?" Lorenzo said.

"Yes. It was beautiful."

Jane let go of Lorenzo's hand, then walked over to one of the cinder block–bordered rectangles of ashy soil. She crouched down, took up a pinch of earth between forefinger and thumb, and looked at it. It was fine textured, more like dust than dirt. Aunt Jane closed her eyes, touched her tongue to her fingertip.

Salt.

Jane smiled.

She stood, brushing the dust off her finger. She turned and pointed back at the building across the street, at a window four floors up.

"I saw it every day. I used to live up there. 405 East Eighty-Second, unit 4F. Every morning, I'd sit in the window when I woke up and have a mug of tea and watch the garden while I said my seven affirmations."

Jane smiled, remembering.

"'I am good. There is good in this world, and I am part of it. I am stronger than my fears. My past does not define me. I am loved, and I love. I am enough, and complete within myself. I am light.'"

She turned to look at Lorenzo, who was, as always, listening quietly. He expressed his joy in stillness, in service. She loved him. She loved all her Joy Boys and Joy Girls, but Lorenzo really was special. He never said anything he didn't mean.

"I wrote them myself," Jane said. "I pulled them out of my Love Library, the biggest collection of self-help books you've ever seen in your life. I had stuff about mindfulness and self-actualization and spiritual healing and gurus and all kinds of shit. Like, hundreds, all crammed into a bookcase in my bedroom.

"I didn't always keep them there," she said, her eyes far away, "but I moved them once a new friend came over and saw them and didn't come over anymore."

"Huh," Lorenzo said.

"I wonder what that bitch would have thought if she found out about all the audio books, you know? Or all the mindfulness podcasts, the happiness apps on my phone, all that stuff. I used to go to retreats too. Put it all on credit cards. I can quote Deepak Chopra and Kahlil Gibran and Rhonda Byrne and Tony Robbins and Michael A. Singer. Didn't even have to look anything up when I was posting on Facebook."

Jane realized her fists were clenched. She took a breath, let them relax.

"I always had seven affirmations because seven is lucky. They didn't always stay the same, but the basic idea always did. I said seven things, but it was really just one thing."

She took Lorenzo's hand again, and smiled at him—the smile that made her beautiful.

"Be happy."

"Nice," Lorenzo said, and Jane knew he meant it.

"Let's walk," she said, and they did.

"I know I was an addict," Jane said, knowing Lorenzo wouldn't judge her. "I was addicted to the search for joy. I even think I knew that continually seeking happiness can prevent you from ever feeling happy. But it was better than drugs or sex or booze or gambling or shoplifting or defacing public property or anything else I got up to before I found the happiness game."

Jane didn't say anything for a minute or two, and neither did Lorenzo. She kicked at an old broken bit of a pot, thinking about how to say this next part.

"So there was this one day," she said. "It was the morning, and I was watching the old folks working over here before I had to get ready to go to work at the law firm. I was a paralegal. Anyway, the old people were always there. It didn't matter how early I got up. If it wasn't winter, at least one was out there doing their best with their little patch of vegetables or flowers. This day I'm telling you about was in May, so the spring flowers were up, and the real heat of summer hadn't come on to wilt anything. The garden was *gorgeous*, and I wanted to just sit in my window and watch it all day long.

"There were three gardeners that morning. I remember it really clearly. One was pulling weeds, another was deadheading a rosebush, and the third was just sitting on a bench, enjoying the morning. I watched them until I finished my tea, then went to take a shower.

"I was standing there under the spray, shampoo in my hair, and I had this idea. It was an idea to help those nice people in the garden. It made me smile, and I smiled all through work that day thinking about it.

"On the way home, I stopped at a hardware store and bought a big sprayer bottle. You know, the kind you can put whatever you want in it, and then you pump it up to make the pressure to send it out through this wand, like this long nozzle?"

"I know that kind," Lorenzo said.

"Right. I knew you would," Jane said. "The one I got was for wasp or yellowjacket nests, so you could shoot the poison at them without getting too close, but you could fill it up with anything you wanted.

"When I got home, I filled it half full with water from the tap, and I then took a big box of table salt—I bought that, too—and dumped half of it in. I swirled it with my biggest mixing spoon until it dissolved, and then I just kept doing it, adding more and more until it tasted saltier than the ocean. By a lot."

She stopped walking, lost in the memory.

She'd waited until after dark, until the garden was empty, then lugged the heavy sprayer into the elevator and across the street. The garden gate had a small padlock, but she snipped it off with a pair of bolt cutters (another hardware store purchase—she had the whole plan in her mind from the minute she first had the idea) and went inside.

From then on, it was straightforward work, though keeping the pump primed hurt her arm after a while.

"I waited until the middle of the night, and then I sprayed it over here," she said, gesturing to the empty, dead ground around them. "I emptied it out, and then I went back up to my apartment, refilled it, and did it again. Like, three times.

"I slept like *crazy* that night. I was so excited. I just wanted to wake up and see how happy everyone would be!"

Jane did a little spin, the grey dust rising around her.

"I made my tea and said my affirmations and looked out the window and it was amazing. *Amazing*, Lorenzo."

Lorenzo nodded.

"All those plants were drooping! A lot seemed like they were already dead. Some of the old gardeners were standing in there, just talking. They all seemed so sad. One old lady was crying, and another lady had her arm around her shoulder. I didn't like that."

"They were missing the point," Lorenzo said.

Jane threw her arms around him and gave him the biggest hug in the world.

"Yes," she said. "So I got dressed and went down there to try to explain."

She remembered the whole thing. It was all so clear.

"What's the matter?" Jane had said as she approached the group.

"Someone poisoned the garden last night," one of the old fellows said. "Killed everything, we think."

"It was salt water," Jane said to him. "I didn't just want to kill these plants. I wanted to make sure nothing could ever grow here again."

Shock and confusion on their wrinkly old faces, disbelief and then the first shadings of anger.

"That's not funny, young lady," the old guy said. "Just leave us alone."

"I'm not joking," she told them. "I really did it. But I did it for you. You shouldn't be wasting your time on something like this. There's no point, and you should accept it. Time's up. But you don't need some stupid garden to be happy. You are all complete within yourselves. You are light."

She opened her arms and stepped toward the man, offering a hug, but he raised a hand as if to slap her.

"Stay back, you crazy bitch," he said.

Jane frowned and lowered her arms.

"That's not nice," she said.

"I'm calling the cops," one of the old ladies said, with her phone to her ear. "Don't let her go anywhere."

"Oh, I'm fine right here," Jane said. "I just want to look at the garden."

She'd sat on a bench in the garden and watched the plants die until the police officers came, then went with them back to their precinct house in the back of a squad car. She talked to the cops on the way, sharing some of the realizations she'd had the prior day. One of them didn't seem very receptive, but the other had a thoughtful look on his face.

"Huh," that one said. "Never really thought about it that way."

"Was that Angus?" Lorenzo asked, bringing Jane out of the memory.

"It was!" Jane said. "He joined Team Joy Joy not so long after that."

They were passing a broken-down old bench. Some of the slats were gone, but it still had a seat, kind of. Jane sat down, pulling Lorenzo down next to her.

"I got booked for vandalism and destruction of property, but I called a friend at the law firm where I worked and he helped me get out on bail," Jane said.

She was suddenly self-conscious. She didn't want to be boring.

"I know this is a long story, Lorenzo, but I'm almost done, I promise."

"Talk as long as you want, lady," Lorenzo said. "We're here for a reason."

"We are, my friend," Jane said. "Because that was the day the Grey came for me, even though I didn't know it then. When I got out, the news wanted to interview me, and so I started talking about the reasons I'd come down here and killed this garden. Turns out a lot of people were interested in the things I had to say."

"It's obvious," Lorenzo said. "At least to me. Find happiness now, today, and get rid of anything that prevents you from being happy today."

"That's it," Jane said. "One of those happiness books I had was about Buddhism. It talked a lot about wanting *nothing*. Having no goals at all. Just existing. That's what I think it's all about. I think everyone should get there. I'm doing my best to help."

She thought about the garden, and the city, and the country, and the world.

"It just makes sense, you know?" she said. "The world is winding down, and pretending it isn't . . . well, that's the whole problem."

But now, here, as she sat in the garden she had killed, Jane didn't expect it would be a problem for much longer.

She pulled a phone from her pocket and sent a single emoji to a group chat set up using a secure messaging app:

In response, more flames, from her teams all over the world. Burning torches lighting the way to a saner, more accepting, happier world.

"Look at that, Lorenzo," Jane said, tasting salt on her tongue.

The Pyre was lit.

Jane got off the broken bench and lowered herself to the dead ground after checking carefully for broken glass. She stretched out her legs, put her hands behind her head, and lay flat on the salted earth.

She looked up at the sky.

She thought happy thoughts.

III. FIVE

THE *LAZARENE*.

29°57'05.4"N, 42°17'58.2"W

"ALL RIGHT," SAID FREDERICK BARNES. "WHERE DO WE START?

Lily and her father were sitting in a lounge on one of the *Lazarene*'s upper decks. The walls were a shimmering metal—whatever alloy it was, Lily once again didn't recognize it—incised with the same pattern she had seen on the main deck: a series of linked, fractal infinity symbols.

The room's leading edge was a huge, curving wall of a clear material, glass-like but with faint waves of iridescence, as though it were coated with a molecule-thin layer of mother-of-pearl. This gave a broad view of a sundeck outside the lounge and the Atlantic beyond. Peter Match was currently sprawled on a chaise out there, fiddling with his phone while he waited for Lily and her father to finish their conversation.

An Automan had brought Lily and Frederick cups of tea. (She had learned the proper Lazarene term for the robots on Willem Vanderwaal's tour.) Some detached part of her noticed that the steaming turquoise liquid remained utterly still in her cup despite the movement of the sea. She'd never been on a boat that didn't rock with the waves. Just another casual Lazarene magic trick.

"I would like to start, Dad, with why," Lily said.

"I thought it would be easier on you," Frederick said without hesitation.

"It wasn't."

"I didn't say easy. I said easier."

A beat.

"I ran the options," her father said, and Lily's heart twanged a bit. She remembered him saying it: he liked to model complex decisions before he acted, zip through all the branches of the decision tree.

"I decided it would be better for you to believe I died rather than think I left you. I didn't want you to blame yourself, Lily. I couldn't abide you thinking of yourself as less than, not worthwhile. I never wanted you to see yourself as the reason I left. Not for a second."

Lily considered this. It sounded like rationalization, a selfish, ever-logical man's path to forgive himself for abandoning his family. It sounded like something Frederick Barnes had been telling himself for a very long time.

"Did Mum know?"

Frederick Barnes's shoulders slumped.

"The truth, please, Dad," Lily said. "I want to understand how much of my life was some weird construct you built for me."

He turned toward her, his mouth compressed into a tight line.

"No. Adriana didn't know. I lied to her too. I left you both."

Frederick rubbed at the side of his face. Lily remembered that gesture too. It meant he was getting frustrated, impatient.

"I realize you're in pain, Lily," her father said, "but there are things bigger than you, and bigger than me. I could have chosen to stay in Gloucester, and I didn't. I'll own that. But I tried to find a way to allow you and your mother to live comfortably, to give you a loss you could understand and heal from, rather than—"

"Rather than just hating you?" Lily said. "You wanted us to mourn, and miss you, and keep loving you."

"Choices can have more than one objective, dear. Of course I wanted you to think well of me. What father wouldn't? Under the circumstances, it seemed like the best decision."

Whatever part of Lily interested in justifying or defending the choices of Dr. Frederick Barnes had gone notably silent. Her father had ruined his family for *what possible purpose*? Every time she stopped to think about it, her mind became a surging ball of bright-white static.

"Do you know what happened to us, Dad?"

He frowned, then opened his mouth as if to respond.

"We fell apart," Lily said, before he could speak. "Mum and I didn't know how to talk to each other anymore. She didn't die, but she left me too. I was an orphan but *both my parents were still alive.*

"I decided to follow in your fucking footsteps," she said. "I went into science. I liked it well enough, but I could have done all sorts of things. Art, music, writing. I didn't because I wanted to make you proud, wherever you were."

Where he was was on a fancy super-boat in the middle of the fucking ocean for seventeen years doing something more important than you.

Lily hated that stupid girl, and all the choices she had made based on a lie. But more than that, much more, she hated her father. Frederick Barnes. The liar himself.

"There's nothing wrong with science, Lily, and I *am* proud of you—you've grown up to be—"

She slapped the surface of the table, gunshot loud in the cavernous room. Out of the corner of her eye she saw Peter Match turn to look—he'd heard it even from outside. She didn't care.

"I won't let anyone get close to me because they'll just leave," she shouted. "I had a boyfriend, Dad, a wonderful man, and he proposed to me, and I turned him down—and then he got the goddamned Grey, and now he's gone. That's down to you.

"My relationship with Mum is fucked, too, and that's why we had an argument when I was home, and that's why she got the Grey. Don't you see? That wreck didn't kill you . . . it killed *us*."

Lily felt tears running down her face, and she was angry at that. She didn't want to feel sad because of the monster that was Frederick Barnes. She didn't want to feel loss. She just wanted to hate him.

"I don't forgive you, Dad," Lily said.

"I don't expect you to. I'm not asking for forgiveness," her father said.

"So why did you do this? Why did you send me that goddamned carbon scrubber?"

"I told you. I didn't intend for you to find me. I never thought you could. This ship is so hidden, so isolated . . . It was all bad luck, really."

Bad luck that you see your daughter again after seventeen years.

"I love you, Lily," he said. "I have missed you very much, every day."

But not as much as whatever you love on this ship, she thought.

"How did you pull it off? The fake death, I mean. How long were you planning it?"

"Not long," he said. "I was recruited by the Lazarenes."

His eyes went distant.

"They came to me and said I was exactly what they needed—a neuroscientist who understood mapping the brain and navigation and literally everything I loved and was good at—and I would get to do those things among a group of brilliant people while doing something that truly *mattered* . . ."

He cut himself short.

"Of course, you mattered to me, too, Lily, so much, and—"

"Save it," she said.

Frederick nodded.

"The Lazarenes took care of the details," he said. "There's very little the people on this ship can't achieve."

He sounded awed. Lily felt revolted.

"Why didn't you bring us along?" she said.

"To live at sea for the rest of your lives? No. You deserved a normal life."

Lily was realizing Frederick Barnes believed he had done the right thing. Nothing she could say—about her anger or her grief or the reality of growing up without a father and the things that had done to her—would change his opinion of himself as a good and noble man who had made necessary sacrifices.

"Just tell me, all right? Tell me what mattered more than me."

"It's not like that, Lily," her father said.

"It absolutely is. I'll just have to accept it. I think you did a long time ago. But that's because you know why you did it. I don't. Please, stop pretending you want to be my father just because I happened to show up here and just *tell me*," Lily said.

"It's complicated. Hard to believe, even. You were told the story of the *Lazarene*? Where the ship came from, its goals?"

Lily nodded.

"Yes. Willem the midshipman laid it all out," she said. "A wealthy American widow missed her dead husband so much she hired the best thinkers of the late eighteenth century to find a way to bring him back. They built a boat, and . . . here we are, two and a half centuries later."

"That's right," Frederick said. "But it leaves out a lot."

Lily rolled her eyes.

"Obviously. I'm not going to retell a story both of us know. Tell me the things I don't know, please."

"The primary element Willem omitted was that by the time

Molly Calder died in 1835, some of the Lazarenes' experiments to cheat or conquer death . . . were actually beginning to work. In 1821, they opened a door to . . . well, another place."

Lily had no idea how to respond.

"Something came out of that door, a kind of presence. It merged with one of the Lazarenes, a Spanish geologist named Luis Pedrona, and spoke through him. That entity declared that no one would be allowed through the door—they call it the Echo Door now—until they were . . . ready."

"Ready? Ready for what?"

"That's what I'm trying to explain to you, Lily," Frederick said, rubbing again at the side of his face. "Luis showed Molly what was beyond the Echo Door just before her death, and a few additional Lazarenes have been allowed through over the centuries. Protecting the secret of the Echo Door has become the primary mission of this ship.

"For two hundred years, it's done exactly that. The Third through Ninth Intercessions were actions taken to ensure the safety of the *Lazarene* and the Echo Door. For example, we stopped the Tunguska asteroid impact in 1908, which would have destroyed the world and us along with it. The way we did it, unfortunately, riled up the folks who live behind the Second Door, and about thirty years later they tried to invade. Tunguska was the Fifth Intercession. Stopping the Second People from coming through was the Seventh. And so on."

"Wait," Lily said, trying to follow. "The *second* door?"

"Yes," Frederick said, taking a sip of his tea. "The Lazarenes didn't stop their research after finding the Echo Door. Since then, they have opened four more, five in total. All open to other worlds, other planes of existence. Very strange, very wonderful, very dangerous. They're all aboard this ship, in a chamber called the Round of Doors.

"This is nonsense," Lily said.

"It sounds like it, I'll grant you," Frederick replied. "But the *Lazarene* is an extraordinary ship, and the Lazarenes are extraordinary people."

She could hear the admiration in his voice and suppressed an impulse to slap his teacup from his hand.

"So tell me," Lily said. "Tell me what's behind the Echo Door."

"I . . . can't. I mean, I could, but it wouldn't mean what it needs to. You wouldn't understand. You have to see it."

"Then show me," Lily said, her voice flat.

Her father lifted his hand to his face, realized what he was doing, and deliberately lowered his arm.

"I want to, but it's not that simple. I can't just *take* you there. You need access, and that's beyond my power to give."

"I thought you were on the Council. Don't you help run this place?"

"Yes, but it's more than that. We need . . ."

Frederick looked up as someone entered the lounge. Lily followed his gaze to see a short man with chestnut-colored skin and very, very long hair, so white it seemed to glow, braided into a long queue that ran down his back and reached almost to the floor.

"I thought you said no one would disturb us, Dad," Lily said, watching the man approach.

"I gave the order, but this fellow's . . . a unique case," her father said.

The closer the man came, the odder he seemed. He looked . . . burnished. As if his skin were made of mahogany and someone had taken a soft cloth to it and polished until it shone.

"Hello, Lily Barnes," the man said, extending a hand for her to shake.

"Ah . . . hello," Lily said.

She took his hand, which was hard yet slightly yielding, like an unripe piece of fruit.

"My name is Luis Pedrona," the man said, "but most folks these days just call me the Old Salt."

"Oh," Lily said, her voice small.

This man is over two hundred years old, she thought, not wanting to believe it, but then again, this was exactly what a two-hundred-year-old man would look like.

"I couldn't help but overhear your conversation," the Old Salt said.

"You . . . how? There was no one in here," Lily said.

"Luis just . . . knows things, Lily. It's something we all understand," her father said, clearly nervous.

"You're ready, Lily," the ancient man said.

He placed the ball of his thumb against Lily's forehead and a light bloomed inside her head. She gasped like she'd just been dunked in cold water.

"What?" she said, blinking.

Luis turned.

"Hello, Peter Match," he said.

Lily and her father both looked, and there was Peter, eyes wide.

The Old Salt walked over to him, his pace measured and dignified. He said nothing, just held the singer's gaze for a long, long moment.

Then he placed his thumb on Peter's forehead as he had done with Lily.

Without another word, Luis turned and left the lounge. The three of them watched him go, stunned into silence. It was like they'd just been visited by a god. Or a ghost.

"You have no idea how lucky you are, Lily," her father said, then shifted his gaze to Peter. "Or your friend. This is . . . well, it's unprecedented."

He stood up.

"Come with me," he said.

Frederick sounded excited. Vindicated, even.

"Where are we going?" Lily asked.

"I was going to try to explain it, but now I don't have to. You've been given access, Lily. You can see what's beyond the Echo Door with your own two eyes."

PETER, LILY, AND FREDERICK LEFT THE LOUNGE AND DESCENDED deeper into the ship, passing through a series of strange rooms, including one in which wisps of breeze chattered in many languages, and another with a menagerie featuring life-size animals made entirely of glass. In time, they reached a large, circular chamber dominated by five doors set into the floor at regular intervals, just frames and doors, portals to nowhere. These were strange, out of place in the high-tech environment of the *Lazarene*. Two were of weathered wood, one was of rusted metal, another was shiny and reflective. Another looked to be made of stained glass.

Two guards, a man and a woman, manned a security desk in the middle of the room—the first such installation they had seen since they reached the *Lazarene*.

"Dr. Barnes," the male guard said, standing, clearly alarmed. "You know Landsmen aren't allowed in this place. What are you doing?"

"This woman is my daughter, Lily. The man is her friend, Peter Match. I am going to show Lily what's behind the Echo Door."

The second guard stood.

"I'm afraid not, sir," she said. "You know better."

"Benjamin, Janet, I know you're just doing your duty, but I need my daughter to understand why I left her and her mother when she was a teenager to come here. I refuse to allow her to believe it was on a whim, or for any reason other than the most important possible circumstance."

The guards clearly were not expecting such a nakedly emotional explanation. They glanced at one another, uncertain.

"Be that as it may, sir," Benjamin said, "the Round of Doors is . . ."

"The Round of Doors," Peter Match said, his voice low, awed. "Fucking *incredible*."

"I'm on the Council, for god's sake," Frederick said to the guards. "You know it won't matter what these two see. In a week we'll be gone. It won't matter."

"Regardless, sir, we can't allow you to pass."

Her father slipped his hand inside his pocket. When he removed it, it was covered by a strange white glove that looked like it was made of tightly woven, shiny white thread.

The guards reacted immediately, reaching for weapons at their hips, even though the glove posed no threat that Lily could determine.

"Dr. Barnes, don't—"

Her father made a peculiar, precise gesture with his gloved hand, and in an instant both guards dropped to the floor.

"Dad!" Lily said. "What did you do?"

He showed her the glove.

"This a formaker, Lily. It's Lazarene tech, an adaptation of something the Second People use," he said, gesturing vaguely toward the stained glass door. "It's like a screwdriver on the molecular level. Lets me manipulate matter down to the angstrom range."

"Wait, it can do . . . what?" Lily said.

The things I could do with that, she thought. *It would revolutionize my entire field. And aboard this insane ship, it's no more exciting than a goddamned screwdriver.*

Peter Match walked around the desk, reached out, and touched the neck of one of the two collapsed guards.

"Alive," he croaked.

"Of course they're alive. I compressed their carotids, just a bit, just enough to render them unconscious. I would never kill them."

Lily had no idea what to think.

"Aren't they your people?"

"They are," her father said, tapping a few controls on the unfortunate guards' console, then walking to one of the doors, the one made from the shiny silver material. His reflection walked toward him as he approached. "But I'm already in trouble because you're here, and this won't make it much worse."

Frederick placed his hand on the door, and a latch appeared, pushing itself out from the shiny metal like a surfacing whale.

"This is the Echo Door. Behind it lies the greatest secret in the world. The other Doors hold amazing things as well—the Stain Garden, the World of Stares"—*Stairs?* Lily thought—"Hole Fourteen . . ."

"Why fourteen?" Lily interrupted. "Where are one through thirteen?"

"They're inside Hole Fourteen now," her father said, a little annoyed at the interruption. "But none of them are as significant as what we found here."

He looked at Peter.

"I'd like you to stay out here," he said. "We won't be long."

"No," Lily said.

She stepped up to Peter Match and put her hand on his shoulder.

"Peter has been with me through all of this. Got me out of Hong Kong and all the way to England safely. He kept me alive, kept me away from the police. Helped me with mother. He's coming. I owe him that. If he doesn't go, I don't go, and your grand plan to convince me you're not an asshole can end right here."

She looked at the famous rock star, who didn't say anything, just offered a smile—a humble, grateful, amazed smile. He put his hand over hers.

My god, Lily thought. *Life is strange.*

Her father shook his head.

"Fine," he said.

He took three clear triangular masks from a cabinet on the wall, each clearly marked with the number one, and handed one to Lily and a second to Peter. He placed it over his nose and mouth and it sealed to his skin with no visible means of adhesion. Just another minor miracle of the Lazarenes.

"Put it on," he said. "Air in there's a little off. This filters it, makes it breathable. You won't even notice you're wearing it after a few minutes."

Peter and Lily complied, and then her father opened the Echo Door.

A sound, or rather a change in sound, like a conversation that immediately stops when you enter a room, the expectant stillness as all eyes turn to see who's just come in . . .

"Go on in," Lily's father said. "You're ready."

III. SIX

EVERYWHERE.

The Pyre began. All over the world, Team Joy Joy moved into position.

All the Joy People everywhere knew what this mission meant to Aunt Jane. She had told them, in a video sent out to all team members just after she had lit the Pyre.

"If humanity's ever going to just let go, allow itself to feel some fucking *joy* for once," Jane said, smiling, her message recorded in what looked like a garbage-strewn patch of dirt, "then they need to *embrace the now.* That means they have to do two very important things."

She held up an index finger.

"First, they need to stop thinking about the future. We've been doing a pretty good job helping them with that: burning the universities and wrecking the art and the rest of the good work we've all done. I'm proud of you. But now it's time for part two, and that's much harder."

She raised the index finger on her other hand, now holding up both.

"Humanity needs to let go of its past. That's harder, because, well, there's a lot more of it. Humanity defines itself by its yesterdays, those who have come before. It's how people know who they are, who they're supposed to be. But the Pyre will help. We'll cut away as much as we can. You'll get it done. I know you will."

Jane smiled, big and bright.

"When you don't have any future, and you don't have any past, what's left?"

She lowered her fingers so she was pointing right at the screen. Right at everyone and anyone watching.

"That's right. The present. The *now*."

Jane wrapped her arms around herself in a big self-hug.

"Get out there, Team Joy Joy. Save humanity from itself. Make the world a better place. I know you can do it. I love you all so much. See you on the other side."

Some Joy Boys and Joy Girls and Joy People watched that message more than once. Some watched it a hundred times. And then they set out in their assigned groups. Sometimes it was just a single teammate, sometimes a dozen. But they all carried tools of destruction.

Explosives, heavy machinery, gigantic electromagnets, jugs of kerosene and gasoline, axes and crowbars and acetylene torches. And guns, of course. Always guns, in case anyone tried to step on their joy.

These people worked with a song in their hearts.

Some made their way through the desert heat outside Las Vegas and Reno. Another team headed for a building in Atlanta that was once a distribution hub for the Sears department store chain. A group of four rode in an open-topped truck toward their destination some thirty-five kilometers southeast of Mumbai. Teams approached low-slung, sprawling industrial complexes in Mongolia and China, each as big as a good-sized town. Back in the United States, not far from the Chicago lakeshore, a white panel van rolled up to a building that once housed a telephone book printing company. The team leader of this group, a fan of interesting trivia, told his people that this building was currently the second-highest consumer of power in Illinois after O'Hare International Airport.

Another squad went to Utah, to Bluffdale. Their target was a place known as the Bumblehive. This location, unlike many others on Team Joy Joy's list, was still well defended despite the Grey. All six Joy Boys in that group were apprehended before they got close and taken into custody for interrogation. That didn't matter. The Pyre would be raging before any useful information could be extracted from them.

Team Joy Joy's good work was not confined to operations upon the land. Across the planet, submarine commanders from many different navies received bizarre orders issued by Joy People who were also high-ranking military officers. Thirty of the United States' sixty-eight active submarines received coordinates and instructions. Twenty-three Chinese, forty-one Russian, twelve Iranian, and a smattering of others from nations such as Australia and Brazil.

North Korea had the highest number of active-duty submarines in the world at eighty-three but contributed none to the Pyre. Team Joy Joy was unable to find a footing in the hermit kingdom. It was unclear whether the North Koreans even suffered from the Grey; official sources claimed they did not. Whether that was true or just their propaganda office's latest false declaration of national superiority, no one knew. Some theorized that if the North Koreans did not have the Grey, it was because decades of privation and struggle had already immunized them against it.

Whatever the truth of the matter, although no North Korean submarines participated in the Pyre, about a hundred and twenty others did, moving into position below the waves.

At the same time, up on the surface, an American carrier group cruised the mid-Atlantic. While officially the huge flotilla was designated as Strike Group 2 of the US Second Fleet, it was more often referred to by its nickname, the Eisenhower Group. Its flagship, the massive *Nimitz*-class aircraft carrier *George H. W. Bush,* held station amid dozens of support ships of many different classes and capabilities. Of particular interest to Team Joy Joy's mission that day were two *Ticonderoga*-class missile cruisers—the USS *Philippine Sea* and USS *Vella Gulf.*

The Eisenhower Group's commanding officer was Rear Admiral Gloria Greene, also secretly a Joy Girl. She was about to take actions that would signal to the American government that one of their carrier groups was now under Team Joy Joy's control. Once that happened, US forces would immediately converge upon and destroy all ships of the Eisenhower Group. It was simply too dangerous to allow its many powerful weapons to remain under enemy control, particularly a nuclear arsenal capable of destroying several cities.

Rear Admiral Gloria Greene stood at her station on the bridge of her flagship, trying to keep herself from grinning like an idiot. She was almost certainly experiencing her last few hours alive, as was every sailor currently her command. She was fine with that. She was down with the plan. *Go, Team Joy Joy, go. Burn, baby, burn.*

This is fantastic, she thought.

Greene looked across the bridge at one of her subordinates, a crisp, by-the-book career officer named Captain George Davenport. He currently served the Eisenhower Group in the position of strike warfare commander, or STWC in the acronym-heavy tradition of the Navy.

Davenport's role gave him two primary responsibilities. First, he oversaw the fleet's enormous air wing—its squadrons of F/A-18 and F-35 fighter jets and a number of Sikorsky helicopters.

But more important to the Pyre was that Captain Davenport had command authority over the devastating weapons housed on the two missile cruisers deployed with the strike group.

Admiral Greene issued orders to Captain Davenport. He asked no questions, just nodded crisply and undertook to carry them out. He and his junior officers began the complex set of procedures that would send a brutal wave of firepower out from the strike group against targets elsewhere in the world.

Flames licked up around the edges of the Pyre.

III. SEVEN

XX°XX'XX.X", YY°YY'YY.Y"

Lily Barnes stepped through the Echo Door. Her first thought was that she had somehow stepped out onto one of the *Lazarene*'s exterior decks and was looking at the endless blue of the Atlantic.

Then her perception dialed in, and she realized she was standing just above the canopy of a vast forest. The Echo Door opened onto a bare hilltop of dark brown earth. Below it, in all directions, all the way to the horizon, were trees. Unmistakably so, with trunks and branches and leaves and even flowers, despite the fact that almost all of them were different shades of blue.

Most were a dark, midnight blue. Some were brighter, a healthy sapphire blue not so different from the shade she'd seen all over the *Lazarene* when she and Peter got their tour. The darker trees outnumbered the bright by what Lily estimated as about fifteen to one.

Much less common were regions that looked as though a fire had swept through and the vegetation had not yet recovered—swaths of grey dotted with black. Some of the trees looked like they were burning still—individual trees here and there, colored in a rich fall palette of bright red, yellow, and orange, stood out against the blue like a campfire at night.

Beyond the endless forest, the only other visible feature was a craggy mountain looming up above the trees far in the distance. It was a broad-based shard of stone, a uniform quartz white, bare of trees. Above its single peak floated a ball of white light, Eye of Sauron–style. But unlike that baleful glare, this light was calm, soothing, like the UV spectrum lamp Lily kept in her bedroom to help her wake up in the mornings. Atop a flat plateau near the mountain's peak was another shape just below the glowing, churning, rotating orb. It was hard to make out in the wash of light from the white sphere, but the silhouette suggested a castle or fortress.

This was what Lily registered upon stepping into what was—and she could hardly credit it, the truth of the situation sinking in all at once—

Holy shit, she thought. *This is another world.*

"We have a few names for this place," her father said, extending an arm out toward the endless sea of trees. "It's recorded in the *Lazarene*'s log as Interposition One. Some of our people call it the Haunted Forest. Luis Pedrona calls it the Echolands; I use that one too. It feels closest to what this place is."

"Hnh," grunted Peter Match, staring out off the hilltop toward the distant mountain.

His attention was focused on the orb. He seemed mesmerized by the thing.

Probably going to write a song about it, Lily thought, and then felt bad for him, because even if he wrote it, his illness would never let him sing it.

"This place is bizarre," she said.

"It gets stranger the more you dig in," Frederick said, his voice almost proud. "For instance, where's the light coming from?"

Lily realized he was right. There was no sun in the bright blue sky above, but the forest was lit as if there were. That was just the start too. None of the trees cast shadows, though she wondered if they did closer to the mountain orb. There was no wind, but there was sound all around her. She couldn't hear it, exactly. Her mind experienced it, though not with her ears. Something like watching people have an animated conversation on a muted TV.

Even Lily's body felt strange. She gave an experimental hop and noted herself rising and falling at an unfamiliar rate. The closest inexact equivalent her mind could supply was the way she moved in a swimming pool. So . . . gravity was different here too.

She walked down the hill toward the nearest tree, realizing as she got closer that she might have to find another word for whatever these things were. From a distance they had all the necessary ingredients, but up close they were like no trees Lily had ever seen. Their trunks were smooth, more like rubber tubing than bark, and of precisely the same color as the leaves. The tree's structure split off from the trunk into limbs, branches, twigs, and leaves, dividing again and again into incredible fineness. It reminded Lily of capillaries, becoming thinner and thinner until they grew too small to be detected by the naked eye.

This particular tree had flowers, but they looked like no blossom she knew. Not cherry, not dogwood . . . but wait. Lily stopped herself. She had seen flowers like this before, or at least something similar, in the foyer at Coriander & Associates in Hong Kong, under glass. What that meant, she had no idea.

Lily turned back toward the hilltop to see her father standing not far away.

"Is this all?" she said.

What she meant, of course, was *Is this all it took for you to walk away? A bunch of weird trees?*

"No. You haven't seen it yet. Not really. I'll show you."

Frederick closed his eyes, reached out a hand, and the forest *shifted.* It moved, rearranged itself, somehow brought two new trees forward directly to the edge of the hilltop near where Lily stood.

"What the *hell*?" Lily said.

The new trees were both of the dark blue variety, both bore flowers, and, most notably, they were entwined. The trees seemed to have grown together during their lives, their trunks and branches wrapping around each other. One was nearly three times as tall as the other. The flowers on the trees were orange and pink, and each seemed to have an equal number of both colors.

"Lily . . . meet Molly and Apollo Calder," her father said, opening his eyes and gesturing at the pair of trees.

Peter Match had come down to stand next to Lily. He looked at the trees, his head tilted in confusion.

"You guys . . . turned them into trees?" he said, his voice a cutting whisper.

Frederick chuckled, slipping into a professorial mode Lily found both comfortingly familiar and profoundly grating.

"No," he said, walking down the hill to stand next to them. "They were always here. And these aren't really trees. They're lives. Human lives. There's a tree in this forest for everyone who's ever lived."

Her father put a hand on the shorter of the two.

"This is Apollo. He died younger, so his tree is smaller. The other is Molly, who lived a much longer life. In these trees you can see every choice they made, every experience they had."

"It's art, then?" Lily said. "Representational? Like the painting in your study?"

That yanked Lily's mind back to Gloucester, to her old home, to her mother, and it seemed to do the same to her father. They both stood silent for a moment, the enormity of it just crushing any other thoughts. Frederick shook it off first, clearing his throat and speaking again.

"It is a bit like that painting, Lily, yes. I got pretty close, didn't I? That's part of why the Lazarenes recruited me. I was the only theorist out there who got close to how it actually works. It turns out that when a person is born, a tree sprouts here. As they grow, learn, make decisions, the tree begins to branch and change, just as the neural structure inside a human mind becomes more complex as a child matures."

Frederick pointed at a spot on the trees where their branches intertwined.

"Here, both of you—Put your hands there and try to open your minds."

Lily and Peter did as they were bid. An image swam up into Lily's mind like a memory, but of no life she had ever lived.

She was seated at a plain wooden table in an old-fashioned dining room wallpapered in a blue-and-white floral pattern. Her hand, a male hand, reached out over the table, across plates of food, and joined with the hand of a beautiful, smiling brown-haired woman in a simple dress. They were saying grace.

"Apollo and Molly," her father said. "They were never reunited in life, but they were always together here. Not every connection is as strong as theirs. Sometimes it's just signified through the flowers: someone else's blossoms blooming here or there on your tree. But when it's strong—when lives come together in a deep, meaningful way—the trees do too."

Lily looked at Peter, whose eyes had gone wide.

"Unbelievable," he said, his voice clear.

She wondered what he was seeing, if it was the same shared moment between the Calders.

"Did you make this place?" Lily asked her father, stepping back from the trees. "The Lazarenes, I mean."

"Of course not," he said. "We don't have the faintest idea how it exists or why. The Old Salt might, but he's not telling. All we know is that consciousness on earth is echoed here. There may be other forests for other intelligences, but we've never found them. This seems to be the echo of humanity's spirits. All of us. Every last one."

He pointed at the entwined trees again. Now that she understood what she was looking at, Lily couldn't see it as anything but an embrace.

"The Calders have passed on, so their trees are frozen. They don't change or grow. But if you look here . . ."

He closed his eyes, and the forest shifted yet again, bringing a grove of the bright royal blue trees to the hilltop.

". . . you'll see the difference. These are people alive on earth today. They're still growing."

Even at a glance, it was easy to see the trees putting out new growth in real time, their branches growing slightly longer, their complexity increasing. Lily wondered who these people were, the decisions they were making at that moment, and realized she didn't have to wonder.

She placed her hand on the trunk of the nearest tree and got the sense of a young man, possibly somewhere in Africa. He lived near a beach, maybe. Had a family. Worked with machinery, she thought. The overall sensation was very different from when she had connected to the Calders. That was like watching a film, a single locked series of events; this felt like staring at a river, constantly in motion, unpredictable, and always open to change.

Lily pulled her hand back and looked at her father.

"This is just . . . astonishing," she said. "Why can we feel them?"

"We don't know. We believe it's because of a resonance between the electrical impulses in the brain and their representation here, the way a tuning fork can bring a note out of crystal. But how it works is less important than what this actually is, Lily. Every life is here. Everyone. Jesus Christ is here. Buddha. Mozart. John Lennon. They're all in this forest."

Frederick Barnes looked out at the trees, and Lily saw love in his eyes.

"We haven't found them all yet," he said. "It's not easy to navigate this place. That's the other main reason the Lazarenes brought me aboard: my navigational interests. A hundred and twenty billion people have lived since modern humanity came into existence. Finding one soul among all of that can be very challenging. It helps to have a direct connection to the person you're seeking. That's how we found the Calders. But we've discovered some pretty notable people, and the things we've learned are endless."

He looked at her, smiled, his eyes bright.

"Are you starting to understanding why this is all so important? Why we take such desperate measures to protect this place? It's the biggest discovery in human history. It's the discovery *of* human history."

The worst thing about this, Lily thought, *the worst, is that I'm not sure I actually disagree with him. It's the innerfinity. This place. That's what it is.*

"The light out there, and the castle?" Peter ground out, grimacing in pain.

"We have no idea," Frederick said, glancing in the direction of the glowing orb. "We can't reach it. No matter how far you travel through the forest toward it, you just . . . never get there. We've tried to fly—no luck. We end up just endlessly circling this hilltop. Whatever that thing is, whatever the structure might be, we have no idea. There are mysteries the Echolands won't let us solve."

"The other trees?" Peter Match said. "The colors?"

"Ah, that I can explain," Frederick said. "You understand the living and the dead, the two shades of blue. For a long time, that's most of what we saw here, with the occasional black tree mixed in. But about twenty years ago we saw what we thought was a blight."

He concentrated, and several of the trees with ash-colored leaves shimmered up out of the forest.

"These are people with the Grey," Lily said, certain she was right.

"Correct," Frederick said. "These are people with the first expression of the disease. The people who lose themselves."

He closed his eyes and the grey trees receded, replaced with black versions. Up close, they reminded Lily of substances coated with Vantablack or other light-absorbing materials—blacker than ordinary black. These trees were very, very still.

"These are type two," Frederick said. "People whose minds were swallowed by darkness. Suicides, although that's an oversimplification. We began to see many more of them when the Grey arrived. And finally . . ."

A last set of trees rotated out from the forest: the ones colored like fall foliage, though up close they seemed more to be made of fire, the red, orange, and yellow shades shifting and rippling along their branches and leaves.

"These are the ones who burn bright."

"Team Joy Joy," Peter said.

"That's the name, yes, as I understand it."

The Joy trees were mesmerizing. Inviting. Lily wanted to touch one, feel that heat, that intensity, see the world through those people's eyes. She yanked her gaze away, looking back at her father, his lined face like poorly done old-age makeup over her memory of his features.

"Did the Grey come from here or is it just reflected in the minds of people?"

"We don't know, Lily. No one aboard the *Lazarene* has it, so we haven't been able to study it as closely as we'd like. When the Grey was first detected in the Echolands, Luis Pedrona allowed more people to come here than ever before, so we could learn more about it. That's actually the reason I'm here. The Lazarenes knew what the Grey could mean and wanted to bring new minds to the ship to try to help."

She took a step toward him.

"You're telling me that, with the miracles aboard this ship, you can't find a way to fix it? You could save everyone. You could save my *mother*. You could save *David*."

Her father had no idea who David was, obviously, but Lily didn't care. The dark, cold, angry sea was rising up around her again, and she was beginning to flail, pushing her rational mind aside.

"No," she said. "You're just *studying* the Grey because it hasn't affected you directly. Keeping your distance from the *actual* problems of the world, just like you left Mum and me because it was *easier*."

"Lily, believe me, we've done what we can. We've done *five* Intercessions in the last few years—the Tenth through Fourteenth. All in an effort to try to help humanity. That is utterly unprecedented. We risked exposure. We risked—"

"Uh-huh, and when it didn't work, instead of continuing to try, all you geniuses decided to *leave*," Lily said.

Her father suddenly seemed abashed.

"Right," Lily said, pressing her advantage. "Don't think I didn't put that together. I'm brilliant, my father's daughter. You're leaving because of the Grey, because you'd rather fuck off to some other dimension than try to *help*."

She looked at the flame-colored tree not two feet away, feeling the resonance of its bright-dark energy.

"And that's not even the worst—you didn't even want to bring me or Mum with you. You sent me that scrubber, your goodbye note, so you could feel like a hero without having to confront anything you'd actually done. You're a coward, Dad, you and everyone on your fucking ship."

Peter Match was looking at her. She thought he seemed . . . impressed.

"Lily, truly, it's not that—" Frederick began.

"How do you bring a particular tree here to the clearing?" she interrupted.

Her father's head gave a little shake, as if he was reeling from Lily's assault.

Good, she thought.

"It's, ah, not that complex, really," Frederick said, starting slowly, then speaking more quickly as he found himself on safer ground. "You bring the person to mind as clearly as you can, and once you pull together a strong enough mental image, the forest reacts. It's like you call out the name and the forest brings you back the echo."

Lily closed her eyes. She lifted her a hand as she had seen her father do, and focused. She heard a rustling noise, and when it ceased, she looked again and saw three trees. Two were a bright, glowing blue, one about twice the height of the other. The third was about as high as the taller blue, but it was grey-white, as if it had been dipped in ash.

All three trees were entwined as the Calders had been, but in a different configuration. The two larger trees, blue and grey, pulled together toward each other first, and then both reached toward the smaller blue. Then, at a point higher up the trunk, the taller blue pulled away again, the embrace becoming attenuated, distant. Flowers were visible on all three trees, though those on the grey tree drooped, and as she watched, one disintegrated into a puff of white smoke.

"Look at that," Lily said.

She looked at her father.

"One happy family."

II. EIGHT

THE EISENHOWER GROUP.

36°58′54.6″N, 50°28′32.2″W

THE PYRE WAS WELL AND TRULY UNDERWAY. NOT YET THE RAGING inferno Aunt Jane had planned for, and that Team Joy Joy was trying to build for her, but the fires were growing.

In the Atlantic, sailors aboard the USS *Philippine Sea* and USS *Vella Gulf* worked to carry out the orders they had received from Captain George Davenport, their commanding officer (who had in turned received his from the group commander, Rear Admiral Gloria Greene, who had received hers from Aunt Jane).

Captain Davenport had just activated a system present on both missile cruisers called the Aegis. It was a defensive measure, primarily designed to prevent a nuclear attack on the United States or its allies. The Aegis contained highly sophisticated tracking and targeting systems that could follow the flight path of intercontinental ballistic missiles fired by an enemy. Once the Aegis had the foreign nukes lined up in its sights, it would fire off rockets into the stratosphere, where they could shoot ICBMs right out of the sky like a Wild West gunslinger bull's-eyeing a silver dollar.

But the Aegis had another capability, highly classified and never before used in combat—the United States hadn't even publicly acknowledged they could do it. The Aegis could fire its rocket bullets much farther than just the stratosphere. It could shoot them into space, to over a thousand kilometers up. This meant low earth orbit and even the bottom range of middle earth orbit were within the Aegis's reach. The fact that the Aegis could do this had not happened by chance. Within its weapons range lived and worked the vast majority of the artificial objects ever placed into space by mankind.

The *Vella Gulf* and *Philippine Sea* both activated their Aegis systems. A spread of missiles shot up from the launchers on the cruisers, slapped up into the sky on ribbons of flame.

The missiles accelerated rapidly, flashing upward and dwindling into specks; on decks all across the Eisenhower Group, sailors turned to watch the missiles go. It was unusual to see such a significant display of force in peacetime, and shreds of worry crossed more than a few of the sailors' faces. But they were not being paid to worry or wonder, and so they quickly turned back to their assigned tasks. Whatever came next, they would do their duty.

The fuel reserves of the missiles burned down rapidly, but they met less resistance from the air as they flew higher and were able to keep accelerating. They divided into three swarms, headed for objectives at approximately 550, 750, and 1,500 kilometers above the planet. The first group naturally found its targets more quickly—over a thousand tiny communications satellites making up the Starlink constellation. Not much later, the rest of the missiles reached their destinations—the networks known as Globalstar and Iridium, comprising another hundred or so orbital comms stations.

Starlink, Iridium, and Globalstar all did essentially the same thing: provided satellite-based internet coverage and phone service to any spot on the planet at any time, no matter how remote. If you had the necessary handset, you could surf the web from the middle of the Gobi Desert or call home from the depths of Antarctica. It was a bit slower than land-based service, but only because the signals literally had to travel to orbit and back. They were astonishing miracles of human ingenuity.

The Aegis missiles tore through the networks like a bear through a spiderweb. The constellations could continue to function if a small percentage of their satellites went offline, but these strikes took out hundreds of satellites from each array. Starlink, Iridium, and Globalstar collapsed, and those who used their devices to access the internet down on earth were puzzled at the abrupt cessation of service.

The missiles used in the Aegis strike cost, in the aggregate, over $250 million. The wrecked satellites had a cumulative value in the billions.

Yet this attack, and its effects, were only the tiniest part of what Aunt Jane was building the Pyre to be. A candle flame, next to the primary blaze.

Beneath the seas, one hundred and eighty submarines followed their orders and released torpedoes and depth charges. They did this at the behest of Team Joy Joy, though most of the submarine captains were unaware of this fact. Their weapons were aimed at very specific targets—the undersea cables that carried the vast majority of global internet traffic.

One by one, the huge bundles of wire, fiber optics, and rubber were severed. Immediately, much of mankind's global communications network vanished. It was no longer possible for a person in Nebraska to effortlessly email someone in Japan or to text someone in Paris. Access to international databases: vanished. Privileges taken for granted for over two decades: gone. Each continent became its own island.

The Pyre was growing, but still just a bonfire compared to what was to come.

On land, Joy Joy strike teams moved in on their own collective target: the amorphous global data storage vault known as the "cloud." Most people thought of this in the way the name implied, as if their information wispily zipped around the world with no real home or no centralized location. This was incorrect. The true definition of the cloud was this: "other people's hard drives."

Those hard drives, holding in total over a hundred zetabytes of data, were owned by a handful of private companies across the planet. These businesses operated massive facilities filled with rack upon rack of servers, all of which gulped down electricity and generated immense heat. They were like dragon's hoards: hot, well guarded, and filled with digital treasure.

Every text message, every data-mined advertising profile, scanned document, email, music, tweet, post, meme, financial record, irreplaceable digitized archive. Streaming video and games, trillions of photographs, money, pornography. Humanity's shared memory of the digital age and well before, its loves and hates and loss, its past and its foundation for the future—all entrusted to about twenty gigantic hard-drive filled warehouses scattered across the world.

In the United States, in China, in India and Europe and Australia and Africa and South America, squads from Team Joy Joy forced their way past the gates of the server farms. They hurt and killed many people, but they did not allow themselves to feel guilt, because they knew it was necessary in the service of their good, important work. Once inside, they laid down their explosive charges, poured out their barrels of kerosene, lit their sticks of dynamite. Then they ran—most of them. Some stayed to watch. Some stayed to dance.

The cloud burned, and died, and was gone forever.

If the loss of the satellite internet constellations affected only a few, and the cutting of the undersea cables hit only those who regularly engaged in international communication, the loss of the cloud was a hammerblow against the entire human psyche. People could no longer access their bank accounts, consume their films and shows, play their games. Texting was gone—systems like WhatsApp and iMessage relied on the server farms to store and relay messages. GPS navigation dropped offline. Limited pockets of information were still available. Hardened government networks remained operational. But for all intents and purposes humanity was no longer in the digital age.

Now the Pyre was truly beginning to roar, but still Team Joy Joy was not quite done. There was one more fire to light.

In Washington, DC, an explosion ripped through the Library of Congress. In New York City, flames shot from the arched entrance and high windows of the huge public library at Forty-Second Street and Fifth Avenue. In London, the British Library was blown apart by a cruise missile launched from one of the cruisers with Admiral Greene's strike group. The Shanghai Library. The Library and Archives Canada in Ottawa. The Bibliothèque nationale de France. And many more—twenty of the greatest libraries in the world burned to the ground.

The planet had far too many libraries for them all to be destroyed in one night. There were still many, many books left in the world. Aunt Jane knew this. But she also knew that she did not have to destroy everything for her results to be achieved. Humanity was already struggling under an enormous psychological burden as those who had not yet succumbed to the Grey tried to keep the world running. She had in one stroke taken away their connectedness, the digital world in which they had placed their faith, and an enormous amount of the knowledge they might have used to rebuild.

This was the Pyre, burning away the comforting weight of humanity's memory of itself, leaving them naked to confront the inevitability of the end. The past had burned, and there would be no future. The tools that might be used to create it had been damaged or destroyed, and while repair might have been possible in a world that didn't already have the Grey, now the weight was too much.

As the realization of what had happened spread, the true fire raged, burning through the minds of a panicked, terrified humanity. And then it cooled and became ash.

Became Grey.

III. NINE

THE ECHOLANDS.

Lily had originally intended to use her family's soul trees as ammunition. She'd brought them up out of the forest-sea to reinforce for Dr. Frederick Barnes the wreckage his absence had caused for her and her mother. She wanted him to see what he'd done. And then she planned to tell him about it, in as crushing a fashion as she could devise.

But Lily didn't say a word. She couldn't stop looking at herself.

A medium-sized bright blue tree nestled between two larger ones: one the same vibrant color as hers, the other ash-grey. The smaller tree . . . was her. Lily Florencia Barnes, daughter of Frederick and Adriana.

Every experience she ever had, every choice she ever made. All thirty-two years of her life laid bare. Lily stepped closer, examining the flowers that adorned many of the branches. Most were a light turquoise, but some were yellow, and others were orange. She looked for some pattern and saw only that the mix of colors was more prominent where her tree intertwined with the two others.

There's no tree here for David, she thought, then realized that was because of a choice she'd made, knowingly or not. She didn't want to see David Johanssen's tree.

It would be Grey, entwined with hers for a time, but then her own blue tree would separate from it, moving forward alone. Lily knew the memory she would experience if she touched his tree at the spot of divergence. A mountaintop in Hong Kong, a request and a refusal.

Her tree—the tree that was Lily Barnes—was moving as she watched, changing in a barely perceptible way, and she understood that it was like looking into a mirror with a mirror behind you. Endless reflection, off to infinity. Somewhere on this beautiful, delicate thing, a new bud was unfolding, containing her experience of this moment.

Lily looked past it, deeper into the Haunted Forest.

Everyone who ever lived. Ever. Out there. Waiting to be found.

Somewhere in the Echolands was the moment Prince wrote "Purple Rain." The moment Princess Diana died. Jack the Ripper. Socrates. The true author of Shakespeare's plays. Lily thought about all the lost technologies of ancient civilizations, the materials modern science didn't know how to reproduce: the Iron Pillar of Delhi, Roman concrete, Caesar's flexible glass. The inventors of those things were here. She could find them, learn how they did what they did. Not just that. She could *watch them doing it.*

Among these trees was every moment every human had ever experienced, the answers to every question humanity had ever asked about its past. You could be in Neil Armstrong's head as he took that first step on the moon. You could be in Paul C. W. Chu's head when he figured out his yttrium barium copper oxide superconductor, or any Spice Girl you wanted. All the Spice Girls, one after the other. You could be in the head of a king or a queen or a—

Lily sat on the ground, which was covered not in grass but a brown substance that was not dirt, exactly . . . more like the inside of a particularly rich chocolate cake. It was soft and dry and did not stick to her hands when she touched it. She felt a powerful compulsion to lift a handful to her mouth and taste it.

Dad was telling the truth, she thought. *This is the greatest discovery in the history of mankind. It's a beautiful, infinite, fractal puzzle, and it's got the solution to every puzzle inside it. This place could rewrite our understanding of . . . everything.*

There were no secrets left. Not in this place. Find the tree, find the truth.

"It's a lot, isn't it?" her father said from not far away.

"The meaning of this place, the potential . . . it won't stop growing in my mind," she answered, tearing her eyes away from the forest to look at him. "Every idea I have spawns a hundred more."

"You're not alone," Frederick said. "We've studied this place from as many angles as you can imagine. Some of our historians have spent their entire careers in the forest trying to find one tree or another, Jesus or Confucius and so on. But there's also the neuroscientists and the mystics . . . The Lazarenes still work on other areas of study—the worlds beyond the other Doors, and some of us are still trying to solve death, but as far as I'm concerned, nothing's more important than the Echolands."

Lily let her gaze roam across the forest.

"All of you on this ship make such a big deal about staying separate from the rest of humanity, and yet here it is, right here. You've been knee-deep in it for over two centuries."

"The contradiction is not lost on me, Lily."

Father and daughter both looked at the trees representing their family, three damaged, complex lives woven together and drawn apart.

Could be any family on earth, Lily thought.

She wondered if her father had touched her tree, seen bits of her life through her eyes. Of course he had. Hideously embarrassing intimacies swam into her mind, alongside successes she'd desperately wanted to share with him. Lily was sick to her stomach, and elated, and ashamed, and proud. Her emotional churn ever since arriving on the *Lazarene* showed no signs of letting up.

"You should show this place to the world," she said.

"If you cut down a living tree, the person dies," Frederick replied, his tone becoming flat and certain. "If you cut down a dead one, they are forgotten. This place is not just a repository, a library, an archive. In the wrong hands, it is a *weapon*."

And how, exactly, did your benevolent Lazarenes learn that? she wondered.

Her father reached out a hand toward his own tree, touched it, smiled. Lily wondered what memory he'd just experienced.

"It's been discussed, you know. Revealing this discovery to a select few of the Landsmen, inviting scholars to experience it . . . But the risk was deemed too great."

"So you're just keeping all of this to yourselves forever?"

"Not exactly. We've never been completely isolated here. I told you about the Intercessions. We do try to help from time to time. There's been talk of giving the world an archive of what we've learned here when we leave, and even, potentially, instructions on how to access this place, but so far—"

"Why *are* you leaving?" Peter Match said, his voice slicing through her father's words.

Lily realized the Echolands had overwhelmed everything else in her mind. She'd forgotten about the rock star she'd been hanging around with and she'd forgotten that, yes, her father had said more than once that the *Lazarene* was imminently going . . . somewhere.

Frederick glanced over at him. Peter had clearly escaped his mind as well.

"Because soon there won't be any reason to stay," Lily's father said. "We don't know what the Grey is and, despite significant efforts on our part, we have no idea how to stop it.

"So far we've avoided bringing it aboard the *Lazarene*, but we aren't taking any chances. It's part of why the Council was so angry that you two came here. I had to put my own reputation on the line, convince them you wouldn't cause any—"

He paused, perhaps thinking about the two guards he'd rendered unconscious back out in the Round of Doors.

"At any rate," he said, waving a dismissive hand, "The ship's motto is *Tener cursum*. Latin for, loosely, 'Stay the course.' That's what we do. For centuries, we've studied death, protected the Echolands and the other Doors . . . and we'll keep doing it, whether here or elsewhere.

"The Second Door opens to a place we can live. We've known about it for about a century. We were at war with the people there for a while, but that's all been smoothed over. That will be our new home."

Lily got to her feet, feeling the anger welling up again.

"And what about Peter and me? You want to send your own daughter back to a world that's just . . . dying?"

"What I want is, unfortunately, rather distant from what I can actually *achieve*," her father said.

Peter Match made a sound, a surprised cough, and Lily and Frederick looked over at him. He lifted a hand and pointed out at the forest.

Trees were turning grey. Not all. None of the dark blue trees were changing, or the flame-colored versions. But among the bright blue, the living minds of humanity, a wave of decolorization swept out across the forest. Tree after tree faded, seeming to droop, to wilt. A few turned black, and some turned to flame, to Joy. But most . . . just became grey.

"Dad, what's happening?" Lily said.

"Catastrophic failure," her father said, his voice distant, his gaze on the changing forest. "We thought this was possible. As more people catch the Grey, keeping civilization running gets more difficult. The weight lands harder on those who are left. Like a suspension bridge where you cut the cables one by one. Eventually, all of the remaining ones snap at once.

"This is it," he said, turning to look at her. "This is the end."

The horror of it, of *watching it happen* . . . Lily and Peter and Frederick just stood there watching humanity die. Ten seconds, twenty . . . It was impossible to look away.

"You have to do something," Lily said, her voice small. "All the power of this ship, all your technology . . . and *this place* . . . there has to be something. We can't just *watch*."

"We need to get back to the ship," Frederick said, turning to stride back up to the top of the hill. "We need to see if there was a reason, a catalyst. Maybe we can do something, even just to slow it down."

He pointed at the waiting Echo Door.

"I'll tell the Council I need your help, Lily. Maybe, if you're useful enough, they'll let you stay aboard."

What? Lily thought.

He turned to Peter Match.

"I can't promise you'll be allowed to stay, Peter, but I can make sure your cancer is cured. We have incredible medical facilities aboard. I can do that much."

"Oh, that's all right," Peter said, his voice clear as a bell. "No need."

He pulled a pistol from inside his leather jacket and shot Lily's father in the heart.

III. TEN

PARIS.

YEARS AGO.

48°50'18.8"N, 2°22'43.1"E

"*In your life, is the light*," Peter Match sings.

"*In the light, is your life*," twenty thousand people sing back to him.

The houselights are off in the Accor Arena—stage lights, too—but it isn't dark. Almost every person in the audience has their phone raised, its flashlight on. It gives the arena the feeling of a candlelight dinner. Intimate, lit from below and all around as opposed to from above.

In their life was the light.

This is the encore, and Peter is singing the song everyone came to hear. He wrote it ten years back. He knows some people in his business hate playing their old hits, but he isn't there yet. Not even close.

"*It's there when you close your eyes*," he sings, the crowd right there with him.

The band's slamming tonight, he thinks.

The drummer is the only one in the group who played on the original recording, but that doesn't matter. This song isn't about any particular instrument other than maybe Peter's voice. It's about the vibe, the rush, the power of it, the shared experience.

For ten years people have told Peter what this song means to them. Where they were when they heard it for the first time, life events connected to it. Listening to it on a loop while enduring chemo. Walking down the aisle to it. It is the soundtrack to the climactic action sequence in at least two films. A bestselling novel about a lovelorn astronomer borrows its title, with the TV show on the way. So many club remixes and YouTube acoustic covers and TikTok memes that Peter has lost count.

People *dance* to this song. People *sing* this song. People love this song and love *to* this song.

It is the greatest thing Peter has ever done, and he doesn't care if no other song he writes ever comes close. This one had a real, obvious, definable impact. It is *undeniable*. An all-timer. How many musicians can say that about their work?

All music helps the world. But some music changes it.

"*Your light is mine, and my light is yours,*" he sings, and most of the band drops away, just Giorgio on the bass keeping the harmonic structure going, the merest hint of tempo and beat.

The crowd knows what's coming. If the song is the reason they bought their tickets, this moment is the feeling they wanted to take home.

"*Be the light,*" Peter Match sings, long, drawn out, beautiful, his voice, his instrument working beautifully, liquid sunshine honey sliding into every ear, mind, and body in the place.

Be the light, he thinks.

The room is vibrating. They know what's about to happen. Intensity. Anticipation.

"*Be the light,*" he sings again, this time the crowd singing along.

Alex on the drums starts keeping time on the hi-hat, a rattling little shuffly hissing beat.

Peter feels as if he could levitate if he wanted to.

"Be the light . . . be the light . . . ," he sings, guitar and keys starting to slip into the feel, like sunrise colors appearing at the horizon just before dawn.

A buildup and then a *full, pregnant, four-count full stop,* and tens of thousands of voices sing all at once, the band slamming in exactly on the 1 with the power of a space train smashing into a rocket ship explosion supernova filled with joy, joy, *joy* . . .

"We are the light!"

Peter gives it all he has, and that is *quite a bit.*

Finale, bows, *"Merci un mille fois! À bientôt, Paris! Bonne nuit! Je vous aime! Je vous aime!"*

Peter and the band leave the stage. Peter comes back for a final bow, leaves again. The houselights come up, and the spell is broken, the fans filing out, carrying the moment with them as long as they can.

Then, backstage.

Based on long-established protocol, Peter Match will spend some time by himself, just breathing and centering after the adrenaline eruption he always feels at shows. He will meditate, taking the emotions and shaping them, pulling them from a lightning-rush scattered joy storm and molding them like clay into a ball of, well, light, which he places above his heart and lets sink in.

This is his reward, his moment to just marvel that this is really how he makes his living, that he has been given this gift. He never wants to take it for granted.

Sometimes it's ten minutes, sometimes it's an hour, but everyone on his team knows better than to disturb Peter Match until he comes out of his personal green room. It's in his contract, too, a rider—if anyone from the venue knocks on his door, bothers him in any way, it's an extra fifty grand.

Someone is in the room.

A woman. Short skirt, tall boots, diaphanous halter top, lace peeking out beneath, pixie cut, impeccable makeup. Groupie vibes.

She looks at Peter and smiles. He stops just inside the door.

"Hey," he says, not wanting anything but his customary tea with honey and lemon, annoyed that this, whatever this will turn out to be, stands in his way.

If he waits too long to center the energy, he'll lose it, and that would be one hell of a waste.

"Hello," the woman says. "That was amazing."

She's beautiful. He doesn't care. Peter Match is long past caring about physical beauty. It's a trap. Rock stars get addicted to all sorts of things, and sex is no exception. There is a cautionary tale shared on tours and in VIP rooms and green rooms for fifty years: a guy in Three Dog Night screwed so many women, his penis exploded.

More importantly, external beauty can be a lie, with no relationship to the actual person inside. Internal beauty can't be faked. It's the only thing worth pursuing.

"Thank you," Peter says to the woman, "but you're not supposed to be in here. How did you get in? Actually, it doesn't matter. I'm glad you liked the show, but this is my me time. I'd appreciate it if you'd just, you know . . . head out."

There's a fine line with situations like this. Normally there's a buffer between fan and star, whether provided by velvet rope, burly security guards, or just the fact that famous people move through the world along channels non-celebrities can't access and don't even realize exist. Whenever the two worlds do collide, it's usually in regimented, controlled settings, fan meet and greets and such, where the aforementioned burly fellows can intervene if something goes wrong.

She could have a knife, Peter thinks, *or a gun.*

A gun was unlikely—security was tight, especially in Paris

ever since that horrible shooting at the Bataclan. Now everyone went through metal detectors and patdowns, even Peter and the band. But a knife . . . anything could be a knife. A toothbrush could be a knife if you filed its end down into a point.

The woman raises her hands in a peace gesture.

"Absolutely," she says, smiling a little bit more broadly. "I don't want to freak you out or disturb you. I'll be gone in thirty seconds. My name is Grace Kazan. I know this isn't the way this stuff is done, but I work with the Bowie estate. We're working on a posthumous album using unreleased material, and we're looking for singers to duet with the stuff that's already recorded. We tried reaching out to you through your team, but they stonewalled us. Said you don't do things like this; said you'd think it was a stunt."

Peter frowns. He thinks he'll have to talk to Joanna, his manager. She should have told him about this. Ordinarily, yes, he'd never consider something like this . . . but *Bowie.* There were stunts, and then there was a chance to sing with the Thin White Duke.

Grace Kazan points at a tablet computer on the coffee table; Peter hasn't noticed it until this moment.

"The track we're thinking of for you is on here. It's preloaded, no passcode. Just open it up and hit play. If you like what you hear, tell your manager to reach out. She knows how to get in touch."

The woman stands.

"I'll get out of your way, and I hope me coming to you this way doesn't prejudice you against the project. We're doing something special, and we'd love to have you. That performance really was amazing. You mean something to people, Peter Match."

Peter steps to one side as Grace heads past him and, with a wink, leaves, shutting the door behind her. He locks it, takes a breath. Looks at the tablet.

Huh, he thinks.

He walks to the leather couch, sits down in the little indentation left by Grace, still warm from her body. He reaches out, takes the tablet, opens it (as promised, no passcode, it just turns on) and hits play on the video player that appears on the screen.

A man appears. He's white, he has a beard, he's anywhere between thirty-five and fifty. Bit of a gut. He's sitting at a desk, clearly being filmed by a webcam on an unseen laptop. This man is looking just to one side of the camera. It's very disconcerting. Gives Peter the sense that there's someone behind him, just over his shoulder.

The room the man is in is nondescript. The only prominent feature is a crib pushed up against the wall in the background. Blankets are draped over its sides.

"I killed a baby today," the man says. "Did it a favor, I think. I want to explain that, explain myself. I've been thinking about it a lot. There are things I need to say, things I think everyone knows but no one talks about."

This is clearly not a Bowie demo, Peter thinks. But something in the man's tone of voice, his timbre, his attitude of resigned certainty, his lack of shame or regret about the horrifying thing he just said, is compelling. Peter wants to know the things this man feels he needs to explain.

His surface mind tells him it is a stunt, a filmed monologue, an audition. His deep instincts tell him it is not.

"You're a hole," the man says.

"The world would be better if you had not been born.

"Anything you do to make other people happy, to have a child, to raise a child, contributes to the oncoming darkness.

"You are shoveling dirt down into a grave containing everyone.

"If you create something, and other people use it, are inspired by it—if they are distracted from the truth that their existence is burning down the world—you have contributed to the problem.

"A person flies to see their grandmother before she dies. This makes both of them happy. The resources used by the flights, and the carbon produced, will kill us.

"You buy food and you eat it. The industries that produced that food will kill us because there are too many people who need to eat and so they must find ways to increase yield, which create pesticide-resistant diseases and blights, which will eventually kill us.

"The medicine you take to heal your infection create more and deadlier diseases. You are choosing your own health now at the expense of future generations.

"Everything you do—every choice you make—makes things worse. Every bit of happiness you take now, every bite of food, everything, everything, everything . . . is a theft.

"By being alive now, at this time, when there are too many of us, you are part of a great machine that is destroying the world. Every bit of happiness you take, every breath you take, contributes to burning the world. It doesn't matter how you try to change that. You can't. It's too late. It was too late a hundred years ago.

"Your life, your existence, *murders other people.* People alive now, people who aren't born yet. You are death.

"You are a mouth.

"You are a hole.

"You are a pit.

"What you consume is hope."

The man continues speaking. Peter Match listens. His eyes flicker to the crib pushed up against the wall in the back of the shot. The light inside him dies.

He heads out into the world, leaving the tour behind, leaving his voice behind. Some people want him to sing and ask him why he will not. He explains that he is sick and they leave him alone.

He comes to Aunt Jane and Team Joy Joy the way most people do, by seeing the Joy People dance in the ashes of something they have burned and asking if he can help. Because Peter Match is famous, he is eventually brought before Aunt Jane herself.

Jane, that wonderful, beautiful, joyful soul, greets him warmly. From her, he learns that the visit of Grace Kazan to his green room in Paris was purposeful, because Jane thought he could be a great asset to her work. She wants to unveil him as her latest recruit. There is power in the idea that someone like Peter Match has joined Team Joy Joy.

Peter says no, that he has another idea. He wants to hide his true status as a Joy Boy and instead go on a secret mission related to something he recently learned. Not long ago, another musician, sympathetic to the throat cancer Peter claims to have so he will not be asked to sing, told him a story. A tale of a society of miracle workers hidden somewhere in the world.

"Anyone can burn a museum," Peter says, "but what if I could find *those guys* for you? A group like that, if it's real, could inspire a lot of people. That wouldn't be good. Would be, uh, contrary to the interests of Team Joy Joy. We'd want to get rid of a group like that."

Aunt Jane agrees. She wishes him well, and off Peter Match goes, traveling the Wonder Path.

III. ELEVEN

THE ECHOLANDS.
NOW.

Peter Match fired his pistol at the pompous old asshole, saw the bullet hit, then turned back toward the weird door or portal or whatever it was that had brought the three of them to this fucked-up place. He heard Lily howl with grief, which he didn't really get. From what he'd heard of the conversation between Lily and her pop, he'd just done her a favor. Maybe she was just surprised.

Anyway, that didn't matter. Dr. Freddy Barnes was dead, and so he couldn't use that weird glove (or anything else he might have up his sleeve) to stop Peter from doing what came next.

Peter looked at the Echo Door.

Wild, he thought.

It was still open, and he could see through it to the *Lazarene* on the other side—could even see one of those guards Freddy had knocked out. Still unconscious, by the looks of him. That was good.

From this side, looking through the Echo Door was like . . . huh. Peter tried on various metaphors for size.

Like looking at the world through woodsmoke.

. . . *through tears.*

. . . *through rain on a window.*

In the old days, all three of those would have gone in the little notebook he used to keep in his pocket, or maybe sung into his phone and put into a new tune down the road.

But these were the new days. His lyric book was long gone. He'd burned it for Aunt Jane the first day he met her. She gave him a hug and sang a snappy little version of "You Are My Sunshine," and he chimed in, and they did a little shuffling dance as the smoke rose up from all those words he'd never sing.

Peter Match stepped through the Echo Door. Behind him, he could hear Lily wailing, "No . . . oh, god, no, Dad . . ." He just didn't get it.

Back in the Round of Doors, he pulled the breathing mask off his face and stuffed it in his jacket pocket. He took stock. First, he checked the guards Freddy Barnes had knocked out. Both still flat on the floor near their security desk.

I should go back and get that glove thing off Freddy's body, Peter reflected. *Could come in handy.*

He figured it probably needed special training to use, but you never knew. Even if you couldn't play an electric guitar, you could still make plenty of noise with it.

Peter closed the Echo Door, then locked it. That, at least, was simple. The door had a big latch bolt on the handle on this side. He just flipped it closed. Now Lily couldn't sneak up on him while he was doing what he needed to do. Not that he expected her to try to jump him when he still had his gun—the woman wasn't stupid (*just gullible as hell,* he thought)—but he needed a minute here and didn't want to take any chances.

He crouched by the unconscious guards, considering.

Peter Match had led an exceptional life, and had done many interesting things. He was not, however, an experienced murderer. Old Dr. Barnes was the first person he'd ever killed. That number was about to increase by two; he just had to figure out the best way to do it.

No noise, don't make a mess, he thought. *Get it over with quick.*

He figured he was already lucky no one on the ship had come to this room since Barnes knocked these guys out. God knew what he'd do if one of the robots came in. Shoot it and hope for the best, probably.

He thought about strangling the guards, working out how he'd do it.

Too bad this goofy outfit they gave me doesn't have a belt. Bare hands?

Peter visualized himself doing that, straddling the dude, his hands around his neck. He could do it like he'd seen in the movies, but would that work? These people were pretty big, pretty tough. If they woke up while he was choking them, they could probably buck him off, and then he'd be screwed.

He frowned.

Then an idea occurred to him. These were *security guards*. He'd seen thousands of them in his career, at venues all over the world. Some tougher than others, sure, but these days, they almost always all carried—

Peter checked the belt of the one closest to him. A lot of the gear attached to it was weird, like everything on this crazy ship, but you could recognize the basic intention behind most of it. A metal bottle with a button at the top and a little nozzle—probably some fancy version of pepper spray. Plastic-esque rings connected by a thin metal cord—those were cuffs. A rod with a rubberized grip at one end—a stick for breaking skulls.

And then he found what he was looking for: a device about the size and shape of a box-cutter. It had two controls—a black trigger button about midway along, and a dial was set into the handle on the opposite side, with colors running from green to yellow to orange to red. It was currently at green. At what Peter thought was probably the business end was a milky orb that might have been glass but almost certainly wasn't.

Peter tried it, pulling the trigger. Nothing happened. After the tiniest bit of give, the thing stopped dead.

He frowned, then realized he had missed a third control, a little switch on the side of the handle, with an X at the bottom and an O at the top. It was set to the X.

Hugs and kisses, he thought.

Peter flipped the switch to the O and tried the trigger again. This time the orb lit up in green, mirroring the setting on the dial. He brought his index finger near it. He felt a tingle, and as he moved his finger closer, the sensation grew into a buzz right on the edge of pain.

Okay, I get it, he thought.

Peter spun the dial to red, touched it to the nearest guard's temple, and pulled the trigger.

A muffled *zzzck*, and the guard's body gave a little twitch, a spasmy little wiggle.

That is wild, he thought. *Absolutely wild.*

He'd never seen anything like it. The guard's mouth sagged open and—swear to god—*smoke* came out. From her nose, too, and ears.

Peter looked at the gadget in his hand with wonder.

These Lazarenes make some cool shit, he thought.

He turned to the other guard, who, he saw with alarm, had his eyes open. The man was clearly groggy, still pulling himself together, but definitely awake.

"Oh, *shit,*" Peter said.

He lunged forward with the Taser extended at arm's length—

that's what he was calling it, even though this thing was miles beyond the ones his security team used back in the world—but the guard rolled away at the last moment. Peter missed, got off-balance, and ended up partially sprawled out on the floor.

The guard kicked out with a boot, catching Peter on a forearm. That hurt, and it shoved him even further off-center. His wrist bent and he fell forward, smacking his face on the ground. Took it all on the forehead, ringing his head like a bell.

Peter lay there for a second, hearing the guard trying to get up. The man groaned. He empathized.

Fuck this, he thought.

His head hurt. He hadn't signed up for this. He was a *rock star*, for god's sake.

He tried to focus. The truth was this ship, these people, were *dangerous*. All their inventions, and that *forest* . . . Peter had a sense that the *Lazarene* could, if it wanted, keep mankind going for a while. Like putting a new tank of gas in a car running on empty.

He couldn't let that happen. Team Joy Joy needed him. Humanity needed him. If people were going to ever accept there was no future, that everyone just needed to live in the present and embrace joy, there couldn't be any distractions. Getting rid of this ship was the most important thing he'd ever do.

It's all up to you, he thought. *Stop being a little bitch and get it done.*

Peter looked up just in time to get a boot to the face.

He blanked out, and then pain came rushing in like water through a breached dam. Smacking his forehead on the deck was nothing. This was real, fuck-you hurt.

Peter rolled, just an instinctive move to try to avoid another kick. He fetched up against another one of the doors hanging in midair. His vision was blurry and he blinked, looking for the guard, trying to see how close the asshole was. There. He was up, about ten feet away, holding a hand to his head. Swaying a little, like he was dizzy.

Stood up too quick, Peter thought. *Dr. Barnes and his creepy glove really did a number on your head, huh?*

The guard went down on one knee, hard. He looked as though he was trying to keep from puking.

Peter lunged forward, the super-Taser outstretched in one hand. The guard looked up at the last minute and grabbed Peter's wrist. The big man was strong as hell—Peter felt the bones in his wrist compressing, and his arm was stopped cold.

"Screw you!" Peter yelled.

He rotated his fingers, twisting the Taser so the orb at its end touched the bare bit of blue-veined skin poking out from beyond the guard's shirt cuff. Peter pulled the trigger.

"Aagh!" the guard yelled.

He let go of Peter and fell back, clutching his wrist, that hand twisting into a claw.

Peter didn't waste the opportunity. He zapped the guy again, this time in the neck, pulling the trigger three times. Again that weird, near-sensuous wiggle, and that was that.

The guard slumped to the deck and didn't move again. Peter was alone once more, at least for now. He didn't expect that to last. Too much yelling.

He gathered himself—five deep breaths, using a centering technique he'd learned at an ashram in Nepal he'd gone to once with Chris Martin. He reached inside his jacket. In a hidden pocket in the lining, right next to his gun (a ceramic nine-millimeter pistol one of his security team had gotten for him, designed with a slim profile that made almost no bulge in the coat's thin lining, easy to overlook) he found a small rectangular device.

A satellite phone.

Peter pressed a button on the speed dial. A signal went up into the sky, into the atmosphere, until it reached a communications satellite in geosynchronous orbit well above the zone of the attacks carried out during the Pyre. Aunt Jane was fine with everyone *else* being out of touch, but she wanted her own communication lines to remain open.

"Peter!" came her voice over the line. "Did you see? The Pyre is lit! It's all going so well!"

"I thought maybe so," he said, thinking of the way the trees in the Echolands had turned grey. "Saw some indications."

"There's a lot going on, so if you're calling to congratulate me, just save it. Plenty of time to celebrate later. That's all that's left, really, for everyone. Party time until the end."

"Maybe not," Peter said. "That's why I'm calling."

"Oh?" Aunt Jane said, her voice sharpening.

"I found the people I was looking for . . . They're on this huge fucking ship out in the middle of the Atlantic Ocean. I've never seen anything like it. These people could really screw things up for us. You need to find a way to destroy this ship. Can you, like, zero in on my phone or something?"

"I'm sure Admiral Greene can figure something out."

"Okay. But you're going to want to get it done quick. If the people here figure out what I'm doing, that I'm a Joy Boy . . . it could be really bad."

"Do you want to explain that a little?"

"You wouldn't believe me if I told you. Just . . . just get it done."

"I will. But, Peter . . . you don't mind that you'll probably, you know, go down with the ship? I care about you, and if you want to stay alive for a bit longer . . ."

"Nah," Peter said. "I've done my part. I was just glad to be part of all this. And besides, if I'm gone, one less person making the world worse, right?"

"Right," Aunt Jane said. "Embrace joy, Peter Match."

"Embrace joy," he said, and ended the call.

Peter pushed himself to his feet and took a few unsteady steps back to the Echo Door. Seemed like the best place to lay low. Lily was still in there, which meant he probably still had some work to do. Once that was done, he wanted to spend more time with those trees. If he'd understood what dead old Dr. Barnes had said, he might learn some really interesting things.

He paused as he noticed a fire safety panel on the wall. Bulkhead? He wasn't sure: he was a pilot, not a sailor. Through its glass front, he could see it contained a fire extinguisher, a coil of rope . . . and an axe.

Peter opened the panel, removed the axe. He gave it an experimental swing, testing its weight.

"Huh," he said.

Peter Match leaned the axe against the wall long enough to put his breathing mask back on. Then he grabbed the axe, opened the Echo Door, stepped through, and pulled it closed behind him.

III. TWELVE

THE ECHOLANDS.

LILY BARNES LOOKED AT HER FATHER—TWO VERSIONS OF THE MAN.

First, the one she had always known, the Frederick Barnes who smoked a pipe and studied the mind and did drugs and had once saved his daughter's life and another time had destroyed it.

Second, just steps away from him, a beautiful blue tree, a reflection of every thought he'd ever had, the living record of everything he'd ever done, wanted, dreamed, imagined.

Her father reached up, his hand trembling a little, and touched a hole in his chest.

He pulled his hand back, looked at his reddened fingers, and then his eyes turned up, to his tree, to himself. They looked up, up, to the top, to where one last branching happened. One last tendril of bright blue, a reflection of a reflection. A mirror looking at a mirror, infinite.

Endless.

Lily watched her father fall, not like a living thing. Living things were aware they were falling and did something to lessen the eventual impact, to reduce the hurt.

Frederick Barnes fell like a dead thing.

Like a tray of dirty dishes and glasses and silverware dropped by a server on their way back to the kitchen after clearing a table. Trash from a dumpster upended over a garbage truck. An ice shelf collapsing into the sea. Fast but slow. Uncontrolled but inevitable.

Lily watched all of this happen in an infinitely long moment that took no time at all; the sound of gunfire hadn't yet faded by the time her father hit the ground.

Within that instant Lily came to the very clear realization that a daughter watching her father die was a deeply distressing event. There was a real chance her soul would not be able to handle the strain. She could already feel the Grey prowling around her heart. So, she pulled herself back, observing everything happening to her father from a place she thought her spirit could survive, finding refuge in a scientist's detachment.

Scientists began by observing; she was already doing that. And once they had observed, they asked questions.

What is consciousness, will? Life?

Something standing up when it should be falling down.

Life was *not being dead*.

What a miracle! After all, from a statistical standpoint, everything in the universe was dead.

Death was the default state of matter. Or . . . rather, unlife. Never having been alive at all. Rocks, gases, metals—these things composed the vast, vast majority of everything that existed, and none of it was alive, or ever had been.

Life was, therefore, one of the rarest things there was. Living things constituted the tiniest fraction of a percentage of all the stuff that was out there. The universe was great swaths of dead matter stretching out to infinity, with a few tiny pinpricks of light here and there

In the face of that, being alive was . . . defiance. A raised middle finger to everything. Life was, by its nature, a spit in the eye of what the universe seemed to want. A *battle*.

Frederick Barnes, father of Lily and wife to Adriana, had lost that fight in the face of circumstances beyond his control—*a bullet to his fucking chest fired by someone I introduced him to,* Lily thought, her detachment starting to crack as her father collapsed to sprawl facedown, his blood spilling out onto the strange soil of this other world.

She scramble-ran across the clearing, too late to catch him but quick enough to get to him before he died. Lily rolled her father to his back and pressed a hand to his chest, trying to apply pressure to the wound. That's what you were supposed to do.

Frederick gasped with pain and, dear god, she could *feel* that breath sucking in against her palm.

"No . . . oh, god, no, Dad . . . ," she said.

There was no last moment of reconnection, no last declaration of love, no sense of regret for all the time they hadn't spent together.

Lily's father simply died. He made a long, slow sound—*A death rattle,* she thought. *So that's what that is*—and then he was just a dead thing she was touching. Still warm, still made of all the atoms and molecules and compounds that had made up her father half a second before—and she knew them all, and their densities and tensile strengths and yield points—but that miraculously complex mixture was no longer life.

No longer defiant.

Lily didn't know what to do. She felt suspended, numb. CPR seemed insane, a non-option. Five quick chest compressions and a strong exhalation into his open mouth? Fucking nonsense. His lung was a deflated balloon. His heart was an exploded fist of meat.

She left her hand on her father's chest. Didn't want to move on from the moment. Didn't want to start making decisions about what to do next. She felt all of that looming, a tidal wave out on the horizon, a distant rumble of choice-thunder.

Peter Match had murdered her father and skipped on out through the Echo Door, closing it behind him when he went. Had the bastard locked it somehow? Was she stranded here, destined to join her father in three or four days after a much more agonizing death of thirst? Even if she could somehow find a source of water, she couldn't imagine there was anything in the Echolands she could eat.

Maybe . . . the trees? Lily thought, and shuddered. *Cannibalism.*

Lily realized guiltily that she was already thinking about what would come next for her. Her father hadn't been dead for thirty seconds and she was thinking about how the hell she was going to survive, even if that meant leaving her father's body here in this alien place. Life was defiance.

Why am I taking this so hard? she asked herself. *He abandoned me. My father's been dead to me for almost half my life. He was alive again for, what, four hours? This shouldn't matter to me so much.*

But of course it did. Despite the abandonment, the betrayal, the lies, there was also the incontrovertible fact that for those few hours she'd gotten with him, Lily's father was alive. *Alive.* And so, somehow, maybe things could be different going forward. Maybe they could find their way back together. Maybe the Lazarenes could help them bring Adriana back to herself. Maybe there could be a third act to their lives, to their family.

Lily hadn't realized how deeply those hopes had taken root in her heart until she looked at them directly. But, yes, that's what she had wanted, from the first instant she'd seen her father alive again.

But now, no. No third act. The play was done. And with her mother and David swallowed by the Grey, she was, at last, completely alone.

Lily took her hand off her father's chest, feeling a bit of sticky resistance she immediately knew would lodge deep in her mind as long as she lived.

She opened Frederick's coat and took the handkerchief she knew would be there from fifteen years of him using similar models to dab at cuts or messes or snotty noses. She used it to wipe his blood from her hand as best as she could. Lily refolded the square of cloth and put it in her pocket. She had a feeling she wouldn't get much more to remember him by, and a handkerchief was better than nothing.

Wait, Lily thought. *Wait.*

The Echolands *were* memory.

Lily looked at the little stand of trees closest to the edge of the hilltop clearing. Three trees. Two tall, one shorter, all connected to each other. One grey, one bright blue, and now the third was rapidly darkening, sapphire and cobalt becoming indigo and navy.

She watched her father die again, transfixed. Was the tree's change happening in real time as the last spark of life faded from Frederick Barnes's mind, or was there a transmission delay between human minds and the Echolands, like a telephone call to someone on the other side of the planet?

He looked up, at the end, she thought, and sent her gaze to the top of the tree, where the last few vestiges of bright blue were fading away into darkness.

She watched four final spots of brightness turn into three, then two. And then only one remained, at the end of a long branch extending off on its own from the main structure of her father's tree. Lily tracked that branch back to where it joined the main trunk and thought she understood.

She was looking at the last seventeen years of her father's life. The branch diverged at the moment he left her and her mother to become a Lazarene.

A last shadow appeared at the end of that final branch, and her father's tree gave a minute shudder Lily wasn't even certain she'd perceived. Then it was still.

Now Lily broke. How many people's father had died three times, twice before their own eyes? She sobbed, pulling in air and letting it out in great whooping gasps of grief.

Her eyes blurred by tears, Lily got to her feet and put her hand on the darkened tree, right on its trunk. She experienced a moment of great satisfaction, vague and imprecise. She thought it was something related to an achievement of early childhood. Stacking blocks well, successfully catching a beam of sunlight in his palm. Something like that.

Lily yanked her hand back.

You think you want this, but you don't, she told herself. *You'll just be giving him another chance to hurt you.*

She thought about her life, all the times she had pulled back instead of reaching out, because, to her, everyone was Frederick Barnes, everyone was Adriana Barnes, her father and mother, her family, the people who were supposed to love her no matter what, no matter what she did. And then they both left, each in their own way, and Lily decided to never let anyone be in a position to do that to her again.

What's the worst that can happen? she thought. *The damage is already done.*

She scrubbed her forearm against her eyes, scraping them clean of tears. She stepped closer to her father's tree.

And I am so, so sick of being alone.

Lily reached out.

She began to climb.

Every handhold gave her a piece of Frederick Barnes. She pressed her face against the trunk, the limbs, the tiny capillary-like fronds at the end of twigs. Each gave her a memory, a moment in her father's life. Sometimes she saw herself, sometimes she saw her mother, and very often it was work—a great many views of work desks and notebooks and computers of various vintages and psychological experiments and animal dissections and many, many images of the sea and his boats. Lily experienced a number of bizarre visions she realized were the other sort of voyage her father liked to take, psychedelic explorations of the mind. She saw friends, colleagues, her grandparents well before she was born, when they were just Freddy Barnes's parents.

There were many memories of Adriana, and that was a complicated knot Lily wasn't properly equipped to untangle. The love was clear, but it was wrapped up in feelings of ambition and choices made and chances lost, moments of connection and moments of despair. Guilt, anger, adoration, gratitude. Lily thought, though, on balance, her parents' marriage had been good. More good than bad.

And yet, and then, he left.

Lily saw the moment the Lazarenes came to her father, showed him what they where, what they had, and what *he* might be, what he might have. She felt Frederick's disbelief, then his understanding that, yes, it was all real, it was true. Then the horrible realization that these people had opened a door for him that he could not turn away from. He was going to walk through it no matter what it cost—or, more particularly, what it would cost his wife and daughter.

Frederick Barnes had hated himself for that realization. But he hadn't turned away.

She saw him aboard the *Lazarene* and experienced his loneliness leavened by his sense of purpose, his joy at the things he was learning, and his membership in the elite society of the minds aboard this ship.

Lily slipped once and almost fell, barely holding on, her entire weight supported by one hand. Touching the tree at that single point of contact seemed to bring the particular memory housed there into sharp relief. It was a deep, strong feeling of *self-hatred.*

Frederick was sitting on the deck of the *Lazarene*, looking out at some dark sea, and for whatever reason he despised himself.

To Lily, the feeling—which roughly translated to *Why not me?*—was unmistakable, utterly familiar, as if it were plucked from her own emotional paint box. She had felt that way herself when someone else got a job she wanted, or a partner she desired, or anything else she thought she deserved. The feeling wasn't exactly unique; after all, everyone felt worthless from time to time, hard done by. But this specific flavor of the emotion, the timbre of it—her father's version wasn't just an analogue to the way Lily experienced the feeling. It was the *same thing*. Precisely the same thing.

When it came to Lily Barnes's and resentment, she was her father's daughter.

She kept climbing. At the end of the last branch, where the last spot of brightness in her father's soul had turned dark, Lily saw a single tiny flower, dark blue.

Lily hesitated.

Then she reached out, wrapped her hand around the blossom, and closed her eyes.

She saw . . . herself.

It was like looking in a mirror, but deeper, more nuanced, colored by the emotions her father had felt as he looked at her. Lily saw fear on her own face, shock, tears. This must have been just after Peter Match fired his gun. She felt her own hand on her father's chest, in the way that he had felt it. It hurt, but he didn't mind. He was happy she was with him. Lily saw her own mouth move in the memory—she was saying something, but her voice was distant, low. And then, to her father, Lily of now became Lily of then. A sleeping infant. An uncontrollable force of nature as a toddler. A child of ten, soaking wet and freezing, being pulled from the sea. A dinner with his wife and child—the last dinner before he died. The first time he had died.

Lily felt her father's pride at her achievements. A swim meet.

An academic competition. A well-drawn piece of art. A recognition of the implications of infinity as a concept. He loved that she saw the world in a way not so different than he did, but not exactly the same—Lily was not just his daughter but her mother's as well.

And then . . . Lily saw more.

Somehow her father had watched her graduate from university and obtain her degree. She saw social media postings she had made. Details of her life that might be gleaned from the internet by a deeply curious father. And finally Lily experienced her father's decision to send her a message in the form of wires crossed in a particular way inside a miraculous device, a choice made in hopes she would think of him—and think well of him.

All of that in that last moment.

Lily opened her eyes. She took the flower between thumb and forefinger. She twisted slightly and the thing came free.

She held it up to look at it, perched there on the farthest reaches of her father's soul.

Lily put the flower in her pocket and then climbed down from the tree.

She took a deep breath.

Lily had no idea how long she would stay in this place, whether she would live or die. But she felt she understood her father better than she ever had, and therefore herself. But he was only half the picture, wasn't he?

She turned, and held out her hand, and touched the soul of Adriana Barnes.

The memories of Lily's mother—her lived experiences—felt vastly different than her father's. Lily wondered if that was because she was, after all, an entirely different person, or if it was because of the Grey. A terrible thought occurred to her: that she was doing something dangerous. The Grey was contagious; everyone said so. But then, if she hadn't already gotten it after everything that had happened to her . . . she was willing to take the risk.

The trunk of her mother's tree gave Lily the most central tenets of Adriana Barnes, née Ramos. Her childhood in Spain, her adolescence as a gorgeous, dark-haired beauty, running amok in the sunlit fantasyland that was how she saw Barcelona. A hundred loves, light and music and dancing. A hidden life Lily had never seen.

A trip with girlfriends to London, a drink sent with a flower in it, plucked from a nearby plant on the bar—this was the story Lily had heard and couldn't see her father in. But it had happened: there he was, a young, charming, handsome, shy version of Frederick Barnes. Adriana was lithe and stunning and knew exactly how much power she had at that point in her life. But you had to use it for something. Even if you could have anyone, you eventually had to choose; you had to make a bet on your future. So she chose this brilliant boy, decided to tie her life to his, and then a daughter, and the joy, the joy, the joy, and then the dimming. Gloucester was no sunlit fantasyland, and Frederick was in love with his mushrooms and microchips, and all she wanted was for him to send her more flowers in more drinks, to turn his brilliance back toward the goal of giving her joy, even sometimes, even once.

Frederick wasn't a monster—he loved her—but for someone used to being the sun around which all attention orbited, the slow eclipse brought on by time was hard to realize, then to understand, then to accept.

They had grown apart.

And then he was gone, and all Adriana had was Lily, and she couldn't find a way to be what she needed, and at a certain point she no longer had the strength to keep trying, and then one day Lily was gone, too, to work on the other side of the world.

But in all that, Adriana Barnes née Ramos was still herself.

She was still a sun around which so much orbited, and even if time had forgotten some of that, she had not. The sunlight was inside her still.

And then another memory: of Lily coming to her home out of nowhere, for reasons still unclear, along with a handsome man who was apparently a rock star. This man was a singer, but he couldn't sing because of cancer—so sad! She and Lily had a terrible fight (Lily quailed as she saw this through her mother's eyes, the ugly venality of the argument, her own childishness), and then her daughter went out to Frederick's old workshop to look for something, but the rock star, Peter, stayed back to spend a little time with her, to show him some of her music.

Adriana was flattered and flustered and pleased. This man was younger than she was by many years. But why should she care? She looked good, and attention from men, even much younger men, was nothing so strange for her. A rock star was novel, yes, but why not enjoy this fellow's company while she had it?

The quiet man's rasping voice was a little disturbing, but he didn't talk much, so that was okay. Mostly, Peter Match smiled and smoldered and looked wonderfully dangerous.

Adriana pulled out a laptop to listen to the songs Peter wanted to play for her. She offered it to him, thinking of ways she might prolong this interaction; Lily didn't act as if this was her boyfriend, and as far as she knew, her daughter was still wrapped up in that poor man with the Grey in Hong Kong, David. A dalliance between her and this handsome singer was beyond unlikely for a thousand reasons. But who knew?

Peter inserted his flash drive into her laptop and typed for a moment.

A video appeared on the screen—of the very same man sitting close beside her at that moment on her living room couch, his thigh touching hers. Peter Match, singing a song on a stage before many, many fans.

"*We are all the light!*" he sang, his voice soaring out, incredibly beautiful and pure.

Adriana was so sad for him then, as she understood what the cancer had taken from him.

She glanced at Peter. He was staring at the screen, his expression . . . complex, she would say.

The song cut off abruptly. Surprised, Adriana looked back at the computer, where a man's face filled the screen. Bearded, sad, looking away from the camera.

Lily shoved herself back and out of her mother's life, or perhaps was expelled. She wasn't sure: she just knew she was *out,* and thank god for that, because she knew what she had almost just seen. Everyone did. Photos of the man on her mother's laptop had been distributed widely across the entire planet. Ezra Montaigne. The author of the Despair Manifesto.

She fell, sprawled back on the ground, the not-soil. She gasped for air through her breathing mask as she shoved herself backward, away from her mother's tree.

Lily now understood a terrible, terrible thing. Peter Match had not just taken one of her parents from her. He had taken both.

She lay back, waiting. The Grey was coming for her too. It had to be. Sure, she hadn't seen the Despair Manifesto, hadn't heard its poisonous, treacly words, but enough was fucking enough, wasn't it?

It's all just . . . loss.

Lily lay on her back, her eyes closed.

Enough. Just enough. Please.

A rustling sound. Wind through the trees.

But there was no wind in the Echolands. It was still, always still.

Lily opened her eyes. She saw something wonderful. Her mother's tree was trembling. And where it was, when it was, the grey—the Grey—was lifting away in great sheets that dissolved into puffs of smoky dust, as if the tree itself were shaking it off. Underneath, Adriana's tree was blue, and not the darkness of a finished life. It was bright. Vibrant, alive, filled with light.

Defiant.

Alive.

"Mother," Lily breathed, and light bloomed in her, too, and the oncoming dark tide that threatened to swallow her was pushed back yet again.

Adriana's tree shook off the last of the Grey, and Lily imagined her smiling, sitting up in that darkhouse in Gloucester, awake and alert. She'd be wondering what the hell she was doing there, berating nurses and getting dressed and getting herself up and out and back home, possibly stopping off at a nightclub on the way for a quick dance or two.

Lily smiled and she was happy, so happy, and for a moment forgot that her father was lying dead three meters away.

And then Peter Match stepped back through the Echo Door, holding a huge axe.

"Hi there," he said, his voice clear as a bell.

III. THIRTEEN

THE ECHOLANDS.

"YOU MOTHERFUCKER," LILY SAID.

Peter thought Lily Barnes was possibly the angriest person he'd ever seen. Her hands were clenching and unclenching; her mouth was a thin, white-edged slit; and that red hair of hers was standing up off her skull. Her whole body was wire tight. Made her look scary as hell.

"You ever see *Roger Rabbit*?" Peter said, trying to keep things light.

Lily didn't answer.

"Probably before your time. Anyway, there's a line in it," he said. "Jessica Rabbit says it. 'I'm not bad, I'm just drawn that way.'"

On the last bit, Peter pitched his voice a little lower, sexier, doing his best vintage Kathleen Turner.

"That's how I feel, kind of. I'm not bad, Lily. I'm not evil. I'm *realistic.*"

"No," she said. "You're a motherfucker."

Lily made a quick little lunge that stopped short, like she

wanted to come at him but thought better of it at the last second and pulled herself back.

"Come on, lady," he said, holding up his axe, showing it to her. "Be smart. I've got the high ground here. But you know what? I'm not sure I have it in me to chop you up. That's a bridge too far."

He flipped the axe and let it rest blade-down on the ground, leaning it against his hip. He then reached into his leather jacket and pulled out his pistol, pointing it at Lily.

"This will do the trick just fine."

Lily moved. No moment of hesitation, no stopping to decide if it was a good idea. She just juked sideways, headed for the tree line. Peter fired. He missed—too slow, or maybe he just wasn't very good with pistols. He hadn't ever trained on them. Most people in his field—famous people—fired guns from time to time as part of the exotic experiences their lives tended to offer. He'd shot a bazooka off a yacht in the South Pacific, fired a shell from a tank in Croatia, used an AK-47 that supposedly once belonged to Hunter S. Thompson. But actually using a firearm for its intended purpose against a moving target who very much did not want to be shot was another story.

This was all just so much more *charged*.

Lily changed direction again, throwing herself away from the trees, dashing around the hilltop to the other side, putting the Echo Door between them, and Peter's second shot missed too.

"Dammit!" he yelled.

And then she was gone, down into the forest. Peter could hear her running but couldn't see her—the trees were actually pretty dense. Even the sound of Lily crashing through the weird foliage faded quickly, swallowed up. Maybe she'd stopped running and was hiding, listening, waiting to see if he'd come after her.

Either way, for a little while, Lily Barnes wasn't a problem.

Peter turned back toward the strange, rippled patch of air that marked the Echo Door. He could still see the *Lazarene* over there, and those two dead guards. It was just a matter of time before someone showed up in there, maybe tried to come through the door after him. That, he did not want, but the door didn't lock from this side (or even close, as far as he could tell). Fortunately, he had a plan.

He put his pistol back into his jacket. It held eighteen cartridges and he'd fired three—plenty left if Lily tried to ambush him. His axe had fallen to the ground when he started shooting, and now he bent and picked it up, giving it an experimental swing.

Peter Match looked out across the forest-sea. He could still see trees turning grey, and sometimes to those gorgeous fire colors. It was wild to watch, to see it in real time and know it was the Pyre doing its work. Word must be spreading out in the world of what Team Joy Joy had done.

So much had just been lost, and so much would never be recovered. A massive chunk of mankind's memory had just been erased. Humanity would have to start fresh, and that took energy, a lot of energy. Energy came from hope, from the sense that whatever you were doing had a point, was worthwhile, for yourself or for your children or just for the human race. Auntie Jane and Team Joy Joy had steadily whittled away at that hope, and the Pyre had cut it off at the knees.

If what was happening in the Echolands was any indication, it seemed like many people had just given up the ghost. Realized there was no point in going on.

Which was, of course, the point. Peter felt good. Truly proud to be a part of it, in his little way.

Peter walked down the hill, heading for a dark blue tree at the forest's edge. Most were that color. He knew that meant the person who had grown it was dead, and he figured that was probably a safe place to start. He wasn't exactly sure what was going to happen.

He lifted the axe to his shoulder and turned sideways to the tree. He adjusted his hands a little, trying to get it to feel right . . .

. . . and then he *swung*.

The axe blade bit deep into the trunk of the soul-tree, and the thing quivered. If Peter needed confirmation that these things were not actually trees, what came out of the cut he'd just made would confirm it. It was *light*. A bright white glow, and inside the trunk he saw something that looked like tubules, clusters, like the stuff inside a fiber-optic cable. He didn't know what it was, and it didn't matter as long as the axe could cut through it.

Peter was through the trunk in about ten more blows. Didn't take long, even after pausing to take off his jacket (but not before sticking his pistol in the pocket of his coveralls). The tree fell downslope, crashing into a few other trees on the way down. It landed with a thud on the weird not-soil that was the ground in this place.

He leaned the axe against another tree and put his hands on one of the lower limbs of the one he'd just cut. He dragged it up the hill—not without effort, it wasn't exactly light—to the clear area neat the Echo Door. He looked at it critically, then took up the axe again and started to strip the trunk, creating a brush pile of the odd, fringy tree limbs. Another few chopping sessions on the trunk split it into six decent-sized logs. Those he stacked near the Echo Door.

Then he went back for another tree, and another.

After a while he had made a sort of woodpile barricade in front of the Echo Door.

Not bad, he thought, *but could be better.*

He fished in his coverall pocket and brought out a Zippo lighter, the same one he had used to burn up the Garbage Man what seemed like a thousand years back. He lit the flame, then touched it to one of the soul-tree branches, not exactly sure what would happen.

What happened was it burned. It put out a weird-smelling

white smoke that was probably toxic, and the tree-stuff melted and drooped instead of charring up, more like plastic than wood . . . but fire was fire. For the time being, no one was getting into the Echolands unless they brought a fire extinguisher. (Which they absolutely would, he knew; hell, he'd left one in the Round of Doors just outside, sitting in that panel right next to where he'd grabbed his trusty axe.) But this was at least something. And Peter liked fires.

EEEEeeeeeEEEEEeeee . . .

What the fuck is that? he thought.

An angry, sharp, ragged sound, like a pissed-off teakettle. But *was* it a sound? He wasn't hearing it with his ears. It was in his head, behind his eyes. The noise was ugly, made him want to puke. He shook his head, trying to clear it.

The fucking trees, he thought. *They're pissed, or scared. Well, suck it, trees. Scream all you want. Won't change a thing.*

Peter Match put his fingertips to his temples, trying to massage the sound out of his head. He watched the trees burn and wondered what this would mean for the people whose lives they represented. Would they just vanish from human memory? Like, what if one of these trees was someone famous? What if it was Bowie? Would everyone just forget his songs, his presence? Obviously the songs wouldn't go away. Burning a tree didn't erase master tapes and records and CDs and all that shit. But probably details of his life would go. People wouldn't think about him. Wouldn't *want* to put on his records. Wouldn't remember the songs anymore. Wouldn't sing them or play them at clubs or on the radio. Bowie would just be . . . gone.

Fascinating shit, Peter thought, watching the souls burn.

An idea occurred to him. He put his axe over his shoulder, then scanned the trees close to the hilltop. He was looking for one of the bright blue trees. And . . . there. A small one, not as tall as some of the others. He chopped it down too.

This time it wasn't white light that came out of the cuts. It was yellow—warmer, brighter. And the whole tree shook and crimped in on itself and seemed to feel every damn bite of the axe in much the same way, he thought, a living creature might.

Makes sense, Peter thought, swinging the axe.

When he was done, he chopped the bright blue tree up and threw the pieces on the bonfire in front of the Echo Door. He thought about what probably happened to that person, out in the world. He figured they'd probably dropped dead, just like that.

He thought about that for a little while. He watched the flames moving and dancing in a way that felt new, fresh. Like fire from a different world.

Then Peter walked down the hill again, picking a direction at random. He left his axe behind. He didn't need it, not for this.

The first tree he came to was dark blue. A dead guy, then. Peter reached up with his Zippo, flicked a flame free, and touched it to the closest branch, holding it there until it caught.

Flames raced up and along the tree's limbs. The whole damn thing went up in a whoosh, like a . . .

Like a lit fucking match, thought Peter Match.

And then something very good happened, something Peter had hoped for. A burning branch from the one he had lit brushed up against the tree next door. That one was bright blue, and it went up too.

Whoosh. Like a lit match.

Here's another Pyre, Janie Jane, he thought. *Custom-made just for you.*

As the fire spread, Peter Match stepped back from the growing heat. He nodded, smiled a little. He opened his mouth.

He began to sing.

III. FOURTEEN

THE *LAZARENE*.

32°07'56.5"N, 39°30'49.2"W

Frank Tokyo, sixty-two years old and fifteen years the captain of the *Lazarene*, wanted to know what the hell was going on. Windows of information floated before his captain's chair, projected into midair by a swarm of tiny drones that were the primary component of the ship's intranet. Handy little things, they could follow him wherever he went on the ship, giving him constant access to command-and-control functions.

At the moment, all that information was giving him a deeply comprehensive picture of one hell of a lot of bullshit that made no sense.

All across the world, simultaneous attacks had wrecked the internet, plus a pretty significant chunk of the global communications network. In a scenario like that, you'd look for the party that still had working systems—that's how you'd know who'd set off the attack. But here . . . it looked like everyone had attacked everyone else. It was a war against everyone on the planet, that everyone had lost.

"Another launch, Captain," his XO called out, a fabulously

skilled woman named Chen Xiaoli, *Lazarene*-born, like everyone on the bridge crew. "Same strike group as before."

"I see it," said Tokyo. "Don't like it."

Some of the attacks on the Landsmen's internet and comms networks were initiated by an American carrier strike group that just so happened to share the same ocean with the *Lazarene.* Those other ships weren't close, exactly, but modern weapons systems didn't have to be—for instance, this particular force had just carried out a successful attack against targets in outer space.

Now those same Americans had just fired off several Tomahawk cruise missiles. Tokyo could see them very clearly on his displays. These particular models were designed to zoom up, get to a specified height in the atmosphere, and then flip over and begin arrowing down toward their target. You wouldn't know where they were headed until they made that turn. The missiles were outlined in red on his display—because they could still, in theory, pose a threat to the *Lazarene.*

They've got the range to get to us, Captain Tokyo thought, *and they've sure as hell got the power to do some damage if they do. Hell, for all we know, the Americans stuck nukes on the ends of those things.*

"Another anti-satellite attack?" he asked.

"Uncertain, sir," Chen Xiaoli said. "We have telemetry data, but it's too soon to tell. Should have a list of likely targets in about thirty seconds."

"Battle stations," Tokyo ordered, almost wistfully. "You know. Just in case."

He knew that the odds the American missiles were heading for the *Lazarene* were exactly nil. The ship was invisible to most sensors, including the naked eye. It was impossible to effectively target. Not to mention, no one knew it existed.

The ship hadn't been in a real fight with a Landsmen enemy since World War II—a German U-boat wolf pack had chanced on them, and they'd had to burn it out of the water. But beyond that, you had to go back to the nineteenth century. The *Lazarene* was very good at staying out of harm's way.

That was not to say the *Lazarene* couldn't fight. Frank Tokyo drilled his people relentlessly, and pressured the Council for new weapons and defenses whenever they were willing to listen. They could fight. They just never got to.

Frank got up from his captain's chair, the tiny drones dutifully maintaining station around him as he stretched, bent at the waist, laid his hands flat on the deck, held the pose for a few seconds, and straightened up. He patted his relentlessly flat stomach.

Still tight as a drum, he thought.

The captain made a circuit of the ship's bridge, set high up on the *Lazarene*'s tallest tower, a circular room, windowed on all sides to provide a full 360-degree image of the sea beyond. The best view on the ship. Projected on the windows was a graphic display representing every vessel within two thousand nautical miles. Merchant and recreational shipping was displayed in green, military vessels in blue, and a cluster of ships about sixteen hundred kilometers to the southwest were bright red, indicating a potential active threat.

No one on his bridge crew seemed particularly worried, though. They numbered twenty, and all were going about their duties with the practiced precision he had instilled within them.

He watched them, good sailors one and all, women and men of great integrity and skill. He wondered where they would all go when the Lazarenes left this world behind.

There were options, of course. One of the many wonderful things about the *Lazarene* was how much it carried within it. The Fifth Door, for instance, opened onto a series of cliffs above an endless sea. Frank liked to go jogging there. Most of the Lazarenes were planning to resettle into the world through the Second Door—they knew that place best, and the ship had friends there. But Frank thought he might spend his retirement up on the Fifth

Door's cliffs. Build himself a little cottage, spend his days looking out at that alien sea.

Maybe he'd even get another ship, a smaller one. See what was across that new horizon. See what those gigantic things were that leapt out of the water whenever both of that world's moons were in the sky.

God knows, this world's oceans don't have any surprises left for me.

"Enemy missiles have reached altitude and are repositioning toward their target," Chen Xiaoli called out.

"And?" Frank Tokyo said.

"We're still within the potential target zone," the XO said.

Frank's pulse kicked up a notch, even though he knew it was stupid to hope, for many reasons.

What kind of idiot captain would actually look forward to a fight with the most powerful navy in the world? he thought. *The Lazarene can take some serious hits—dish them out, too—but an American carrier group is no joke.*

But the *Lazarene* hadn't had to defend itself for almost a hundred years. The Council all but rolled their eyes whenever he went to them and asked for upgrades. Might be nice to show Maxwell Franck and the others what he and his people could do. He'd trained everyone on this bridge, made them into a fighting force he knew was one of the best in the world.

What that all added up to: on some level, Captain Frank Tokyo wanted an excuse. One last fight before they left this world behind and there were maybe no fights ever again.

"Keep an eye on them," he told his XO.

"Our birds are on target, Admiral," said Captain Davenport.

What target is that, exactly? Gloria Greene thought.

She stood at the weapons station on the bridge of her carrier, watching as the four Tomahawks she'd launched from the USS *Vella Gulf* reached the pinnacle of their ascent, arced back over, and accelerated, intent on delivering warheads carrying half a ton of high explosives to . . . a patch of empty ocean in the North Atlantic.

There had to be *something* there, because Aunt Jane had sent over the signature of an active satellite phone in the target zone that the Tomahawks' guidance systems were now using to zero in. But satellite surveillance wasn't showing a damn thing at those coordinates. Maybe their target was under the surface.

Admiral Greene had many questions. She hadn't asked them. She'd just authorized the strike. Either you trusted Aunt Jane or you didn't . . . and she trusted Aunt Jane.

Hell, I just gave up my career for the cause, she thought. *First female commander of a carrier group in the entire US Navy, and* poof—*adios.*

But she was always going to lose this job. That was the whole point of everything Team Joy Joy was doing. The world was coming to an end. No reason to get upset about losing something you were going to lose anyway. At least this way she was doing something truly meaningful for the rest of humanity.

As Gloria watched the tactical display, tracking the missiles' paths, she idly wondered how long her strike force would continue to exist. She had to assume American military infrastructure was still very much in place. She'd basically stolen a carrier group and gone rogue. Things might be bad on the mainland, but it was just a matter of time before the US Navy decided to take action.

Will they nuke us? she wondered. *That's what I'd do. Send some B-2s out, have them drop enough bombs to vaporize a pretty good patch of the Atlantic, make sure they got us. Or maybe send a* Virginia-*class sub with those nuclear stealth torpedoes they're packing. They're basically invisible. We'd never see it coming.*

Admiral Greene had no idea how much time she had left—in her command or in her life. But while she could, she would use the power at her command to keep the Pyre burning, to end threats to Team Joy Joy and its mission, to help humanity finally find a little happiness.

She was going to do her damnedest to do whatever Aunt Jane asked her to do. At the moment, that meant destroying the source of that satphone signal.

The four Tomahawks were racing toward their target now, heading straight down at a speed of nearly nine hundred kilometers per hour.

And if they don't do the trick, Gloria thought, *I'll bring out the big guns.*

"RAISE SHIELDS!" CAPTAIN TOKYO THUNDERED.

Their situation was clear now. Someone had found the *Lazarene.* That someone wanted it gone. Four Tomahawk cruise missiles were headed straight for them, each with enough explosive power to blow a city block to powder. They would impact in a matter of seconds.

The bridge crew executed their captain's command without hesitation, finally putting all those months and years of training to use. The *Lazarene*'s visual camouflage dropped, revealing its immense, sleek, fantastical silhouette. Half an instant later, the ship's kinetic energy shield activated—it was one of Captain Tokyo's constant aggravations that the camouflage couldn't be active at the same time as the shield due to some kind of interference. For years he had asked the Council for engineering resources to address the issue, pleas that were consistently ignored in favor of . . . entomological studies of the wispwings from beyond the Third Door, or yet another expedition into the Haunted Forest to try to find Julius Caesar or some other ancient notable.

Frank spared a thought for the Council, and the engineers, and every other person aboard. Alarms were blaring across the ship. Hopefully everyone was observing the emergency protocols and had gone below and braced themselves. He couldn't be certain. The *Lazarene* went on alert fairly regularly, anytime another ship got close enough to potentially pose a threat. After literally decades of none of those alarms ever amounting to anything, Frank knew the Lazarenes had gotten complacent. Nothing for it now.

Anyone still on deck was about to get a hell of a show.

Four *whumps*, the first two almost simultaneous, and then a pause of about a second between the third and fourth. The *Lazarene* was enveloped in a swirling sphere of flame and smoke. The air temperature around the ship rose by thousands of degrees. Automatic systems on the bridge windows darkened the glass, but it was still bright, *very* bright. It was like the entire ship had been dropped into hell.

In fact, the ship *did* drop. The impact of the missiles *shoved* it backward and down, its hull dipping deeper, farther below the surface than it had ever been designed to do, as though something in the sea were taking a great gulping swallow, trying to suck the *Lazarene* down.

A deep, sickening pull, and then the ship shot back up, quickly and violently. Some of the bridge crew were thrown from their seats, tossed against the ceiling and back down.

Blasted hell, Captain Tokyo thought. *That scrambled our eggs.*

He wondered if the original *Lazarene* had survived, down in its shrine at the center of the ship, or if it was now just a pile of centuries-old timber and rigging.

New alarms blared, indicating damage to ship's systems.

"Report!" Tokyo shouted, though he was eyeing his own displays and had a fair picture of what had just happened.

"Shields held," his XO said, ice in her voice. "They dissipated the impact, but it strained the field generator to its limits.

"We can't take many more direct hits of that magnitude," Chen added, telling him something he already knew.

Frank Tokyo considered his options.

Run, hold station and defend, or . . . , he thought.

"Lieutenant Chen," he said. "I realize that this ship has a long-standing policy of not antagonizing the Landsmen. We stay as far away from them as we can. Always have. However, as you and I well know, the *Lazarene* isn't long for this world—literally. You, me, and everyone else aboard are getting the hell out of here. So as I see it, normal procedures and policies relating to engaging the Landsmen in battle may no longer be as relevant. Would you agree?"

Chen Xiaoli thought about this. He could see a smile in her body language, even if she was too professional to allow it to appear on her face.

"I would say, sir," she answered, "that we have suffered an unprovoked attack by a foreign navy. I would also say that the safety and security of this ship and its crew are our primary concerns and supersede everything else."

Frank nodded.

"Makes a lot of sense. So, since we are clearly in *imminent* danger, we should make sure our enemy is neutralized. Once we're sure we're safe, we can look at other options, including informing the Council of the situation and seeking their guidance."

"That is how I see it, Captain Tokyo."

"Thank you, Lieutenant Chen."

He turned to look at the rest of the bridge crew, who were all staring at him, excited, stunned, but above all else ready.

"Any objections?" he asked his crew.

Going into battle against a carrier group. No joke, he thought again.

The bridge crew was silent.

"Let's light these fuckers up," Captain Frank Tokyo of the *Lazarene* said. "Find me some targets."

III. FIFTEEN

THE ECHOLANDS.

LILY RACED THROUGH THE TREES OF THE HAUNTED FOREST, AWAY from the murderer Peter Match and his murdering gun. It was a bizarre place, and got stranger the farther she ran.

There were no clearings, for one. The hillside with the Echo Door seemed to be the only open spot in this entire world, other than the inaccessible mountain in the distance. Beyond that, nothing but trees. Most were much taller than she was, and dark blue (but a few were no taller than shrubs, and any time she saw one of those her heart broke a little). Some were one of the other four colors—the bright blue, increasingly frequent examples of grey or orange-yellow-red, and the occasional black.

Moving through them was like pushing through a well-weeded patch of corn where all the plants were basically the same and there was nothing else in the soil *but* them. That was compounded by the fact that every time Lily brushed up against one, her mind was inundated with a momentary flash of another life. She met hundreds of people in a matter of minutes, lived experiences mundane, profound, and profane.

It was mentally exhausting, and constant. It was impossible to move through the forest without occasionally coming into contact with the trees. Lily's sense of direction vanished, and then her sense of progress, and she realized very quickly that she was, in fact, lost, a castaway in the lived history of all of humanity.

A few moments later her mind pointed out that she was also quite possibly irretrievably fucked. There was only one door out of the Echolands as far as she knew, and she couldn't get there; in fact, she wasn't sure she could even find her way back to that hilltop. There was nothing to eat, nothing to drink. The air was toxic, and Lily had no idea how long the breathing mask she still wore would continue to work. Was it like a scuba diver's oxygen tank? Would it run out eventually?

And, of course, a maniac was in here with her. Peter Match. The man who had, in one way or another, murdered both her parents. Everything was terrible.

Not everything, she thought. *I brought Mum back to life.*

That was true; at least, she hoped so. She didn't really know what she'd done. If she'd had more time with her mother's tree, she could have run some tests. Checked to see if it was putting out new growth, if the natural progress of Adriana's soul had restarted.

But Peter Match had shown up with a fucking gun before she had a chance, tried to kill her like he killed her dad, and . . .

Lily just stopped. She couldn't handle it. She sat down on the ground, taking care to avoid the nearby trees, and shuddered. Tears fell, beading up on the strange soil like oil on rubber.

She drew her knees up and wrapped her arms around them and sobbed. She was so sick of crying, of grief, but she couldn't seem to stop. The breathing mask didn't impede her great snuffling cries, and she rocked back and forth, her thoughts a huge churning wave of *dark, black, scream, unfair, why, hurt, lost, gone, why, no, impossible, wrong, did not happen, pain pain pain pain pain pain pain pain pain*

Then she heard the song.

"In your life, is the light . . .

". . . in the light, is your light."

Beautiful, clear, pure. Not loud—distant—but the trees carried the sound to her. Maybe they liked it. Maybe they liked music. To her scrambled brain, it made perfect sense.

What's more human than music?

"It's there when you close your eyes . . ."

I love this song, Lily thought, her despair deepening.

How—*how*—could she have misread Peter Match so deeply? He was one of them. One of the Team Joy Joy fanatics. She ran across her time with him in her mind, looking for clues, and could find none. The man had committed to his bit utterly, from the very beginning, and probably well before she'd met him.

He seemed like such a happy person, she thought.

Lily wished him dead.

It rose up in her like a plug of vomit.

Die, die, die, die, she thought.

Around her, the trees rustled like a bunch of scandalized old ladies.

They like music but they don't like a death wish, she thought, and spat out a little laugh.

A scent, not brought to her on the breeze—there was no breeze here—but propagated somehow. It wasn't like any odor she knew, and yet it was.

Something was burning, but it was the *fuel* for that fire she had never encountered before. Not woodsmoke, not cooking oil or gasoline, not charcoal, not even burning rubber or garbage or any of the more exotic materials she'd set aflame in the course of her career.

And then she had it.

There was only one thing here to burn.

Holy god, he set the trees on fire.

Her mouth fell open.

Peter Match was not a person. Whatever he was, he was not a human being. No human could have done what he had just done.

Shock washed over Lily. Shock got her up, up on her knees, and got her thinking.

What can I do?

She knew where Peter Match was. He was still singing. She could just follow the music. Lily envisioned herself tackling the man from behind, disarming him, and shooting him with his own gun. Then she'd get back through the Echo Door to the *Lazarene* and tell them what was happening. They'd be able to help. They could do anything.

Then again, killing a person . . . she had no idea if she could do that, even if it was actually a monster wearing a person mask.

Someone from the *Lazarene* would have to investigate. After all, her father had left two unconscious guards in that control room. Someone would notice eventually, and then they'd come in. Maybe Peter could kill some of them, but surely they had ray guns and lightsabers and such. It wouldn't be long before he was dead, and then Lily could come up out of the forest and explain what had happened.

That seemed like the safest, sanest plan. She just needed to wait him out.

Lily took a breath, then coughed uncontrollably as the smoke from the burning trees filled her lungs. It sat heavy on the air like fog, with no wind to stir or dissipate it.

"Easy there," Peter Match called out, a smile in his voice. "You're smoking someone's life. That's heavy shit."

She realized it was true, that she was breathing in someone's soul, and felt her gorge rise. She hated that she felt so useless, so alone. She put a hand on a nearby tree to steady herself and got a flash of a horse's hindquarters pulling a plow through a field from the point of view of the farmer steering it.

Lily pulled her hand back.

Peter's alone too, she thought. *He's as lost as I am.*

She closed her eyes and listened to Peter's voice. He was still singing that goddamned song. That beautiful, soaring song.

I can find him.

Lily thought about everything that song had ever meant to her—memories associated with it, times she'd danced or made out to it, times she'd turned it up in the car or gone running to it. The music swelled up around Peter's voice, sounding out from above the trees.

She opened her eyes.

There before her was one of the flame-colored trees, its foliage blazing out like a neon sign in the thickening haze from the fire.

Lily stepped forward, put her hands on its trunk, and saw.

She saw a boy, loved and adored, born in the 1980s, one of several children in a nice family. Growing up in what she recognized from television as the American suburbs, with bike rides and school and summer vacation. She saw a school trip to the city and a visit to a monument, one Lily recognized—a huge silver arch next to a broad river. The Gateway Arch in St. Louis, in the heart of the United States.

Music, early. The boy's parents gave him piano lessons at a young age, which he began grudgingly but soon looked forward to as he found he was good at it, that music came easy, and made him and made other people happy too. Lily felt the boy's spirit open as he started to understand the language of harmony and rhythm, learned to read, learned to sing as he played.

The boy was told he was exceptional by his teachers and came to believe it. Piano competitions and recitals, awards and applause. In secondary school, a shift away from classical to the more immediately rewarding worlds of pop and rock, as he came to understand the power of playing songs people knew as opposed to meticulous music written by centuries-dead composers. Playing U2 and Beatles and Nirvana and Alanis Morissette and the Spice Girls and Madonna and Prince and really anything that would get people's attention, make them smile, make them happy, leave them in awe of his talent. Especially girls.

He learned that he had a power. He could work actual magic using just his hands and his voice. He could make people feel any emotion he wanted, like he had a superpower. The boy learned other instruments—guitar, bass, drums. He got into bands, many bands, playing all kinds of music, and learned to write his own songs.

Everything else fell away as he began to slip through increasingly narrow gates of achievement in his musical career. His band was signed to a major label when he was twenty and opened for the White Stripes when he was twenty-one. A single was licensed for an ad for one of the first iPhones and drove that album into the stratosphere.

All of these things were impossible, statistically speaking. Many, many, many, many people tried to achieve these things, and essentially everyone failed. But he did not.

There was a catch, though. Once he had achieved something, it was no longer something to *be* achieved. It was in his past, was no longer relevant, could no longer give him anything.

The boy, now a man, went solo, leaving his band behind. He ascended further. His relationships never lasted long, as his desire for more, upward, onward made him some variation of insufferable, impossible, or unavailable, and one side or the other of the partnership tired of it.

The man wrote a song, a truly beloved song, that touched people all over the world, and it gave him great joy to sing it.

He was sure he could do it again . . . he would do it again—but he did not. Nothing he wrote after that ever equaled the success or impact of that one song. Either the world's taste or his talent had changed in some fundamental way, and while he would always be beloved, it was now in the manner of a favorite uncle—seen from time to time, always welcome, but rarely in the forefront of anyone's thoughts.

This was challenging for the man to accept. He tried many things to prove that he was as exceptional as ever. He embarrassed himself, and he failed, and he came close to destroying his legacy. He nearly became . . . ridiculous.

But the man was lucky. He realized the danger in time, and found peace in the idea that he was not and had never actually been exceptional. He was talented and diligent, but mostly he was *lucky*. His life was blessed and would always be blessed, even if he never wrote another new song. The man came to understand that his purpose was to bring joy to the world through his music, to try to return some of the gifts that had been given to him.

And so he did, until one day he finished a concert in Paris and went to his green room afterward and met a woman who gave him an opportunity to sing with David Bowie and invited him to listen to a demo of the tune. She gave him a tablet to look at and left and he hit play and saw a man and—

Once again, Lily yanked herself back, realizing how close she had come, for the second time, to seeing the Despair Manifesto through another person's eyes.

She looked up at the tree that echoed Peter Match's life. It was no longer ablaze with red, orange, and yellow, the signifiers of the Team Joy Joy insanity.

Peter Match's tree was blue. Vibrant. Alive.

Healed.

Lily wondered what he was thinking.

III. SIXTEEN

AT THE ECHO DOOR.

PETER WAS AWAKE NOW. SOMETHING HAD YANKED HIM OUT OF THE poisoned trance he was trapped inside. He could see again, remember himself. But that wasn't exactly the right metaphor, was it? It wasn't like he was asleep during all of it. It was just that when Grey Peter did all that awful shit, he didn't think it was wrong. Now, remembering it all, Real Peter very much fucking did.

How many people have I killed? Peter Match thought. *How many fucking people?*

Three by his direct hand, and god only knew how many more in the forest. It wasn't as bad to burn the dark blue trees—they were for dead people. But the others . . . every one of them—a person, alive back in the real world. He had *set their fucking souls on fire*.

He remembered it all. He remembered the little dance the two guards he'd killed had done as they died, and the look on Frederick Barnes's face when he realized he had just a few moments of life left.

"Fuck," he said, collapsing into a crouch, balling his hands into fists, pounding them against his head. "Fuck, fuck fuck fuck *fuck.*"

He'd been *singing,* singing that song he loved, as he watched the odd, rippling flames move slowly through the forest of souls.

He couldn't imagine ever singing it again.

If you aren't going to sing, what the fuck are you going to do? he asked himself.

He couldn't bring those guards back to life, couldn't reverse time. Frederick Barnes's corpse, visible out of the corner of his eye at that very moment, was not going to sit up and return to the land of the living.

Peter couldn't un-kill anyone. But he could—he had to—make sure no one else died because of his fucked-up choices.

He spun to look at the Echo Door. It was still blocked, the ersatz barricade he'd built still burning, oily flames made of memories sending smoke up into the weird air of the Echolands.

Where did I put the goddamn—

He looked for the axe—there it was, leaning against a burning tree trunk, its handle aflame.

Peter lunged across the hilltop and snatched up his leather jacket from where he'd left it. He kicked the burning axe away from the tree, then threw his jacket over it in an effort to smother the flames. He left it that way for a minute, then dropped to his knees and pulled his ruined coat away. The flames were out. Good. Peter grabbed the axe.

"FUCK," he roared, dropping it again, his palms seared.

Angry at himself, angry at how long this was taking, how stupid he was being, Peter Match went back to the barricade at the Echo Door. He kicked at it, trying to scatter the brush. Ash and twigs flew up, and the fire collapsed in on itself, some of it falling through the opening in the air.

As good as it's gonna get.

Peter Match took a step or two back, then ran at the flames

and leapt over them. He felt the heat—fire in the Echolands might not roar but it definitely burned—and then he was through, back in the real world.

Blaring alarms, a voice telling all crew to go to assigned duty stations, red emergency lighting, and, of course, two corpses on the ground.

What the hell is happening out here? Peter thought, and then he knew.

He had told Aunt Jane about the *Lazarene,* had given her a way to find it, and she had used Team Joy Joy to attack the ship. This incredible place, a matryoshka of miracles, and now it was in danger of being destroyed—say it once again for the people in the cheap seats—*because of him.*

A massive *boom* and the whole ship rocked, throwing Peter against one of the other magical doors. Its locking mechanism stabbed into the small of his back. It hurt—hurt like hell.

Too many things were happening. Peter couldn't keep his focus. He'd only had his soul back for a minute or so. That was disorienting enough on its own, even without the utter chaos he'd found on both sides of the Door.

Hell, he could barely see. Bits of his burning soul-tree barrier had fallen through the Echo Door when he kicked it apart, and they were filling the room with smoke, burning more fiercely on this side than they had on the other. He didn't know why. Maybe Lily Barnes would.

That kicked his ass into gear—that wonderful, caring, brilliant, deeply hurt woman who had given him her trust only for him to add his name to the list of people who hurt her more. He had to help her, had to try to set things right.

Peter wondered if a fire alarm might go off from the smoke and people would come who could help. But who would even hear it with the ship under attack? No. No one would come; no one was going to solve this problem except for the motherfucker who had caused it.

"Stop whining, you ass," he told himself, and pushed himself off the wall.

The Round of Doors had two emergency fire panels, located opposite each other on the walls. One was open and missing its fire axe—Peter had pillaged it for his little lumberjack adventure back in the Echolands—but both still had fire extinguishers.

Peter grabbed one extinguisher, then raced across the room to grab the second and wheeled back toward the Echo Door. He took a minute to figure out how the things worked—they were Lazarene tech, with an unfamiliar design. (A tiny corner of his mind wondered how these people had time to do things like design and manufacture fire extinguishers—but then again, two and a half centuries was plenty of time to do just about anything.)

It turned out the extinguishers weren't that complicated, which made sense. The last thing you wanted was an emergency device that was hard to figure out in an emergency. There was a trigger-y thing, and when you pulled it, pink foam shot out. There was a dial you could twist to narrow or widen the stream. That was about it.

Peter tested the extinguisher on the burning bits of soul-tree. The flames vanished so quickly, it was as if they were being teleported to another dimension—and who was to say they weren't?

He jumped back through the Echo Door, back over the remnants of his barrier. He started there, putting out the flames just in case someone from the *Lazarene* realized what was happening and came through to check or help.

Then he turned to look at the forest, and his blood froze.

You stupid fucking idiot, he thought. *What did you do?*

Hundreds of trees were ablaze in a rapidly widening circle centered on the hilltop where he stood. Peter dropped one fire extinguisher and raised the other. He fired off a blast of the pink foam toward the nearest burning tree. Again, it was like the fire was eaten or consumed in some way—both the pink foam and the flames vanished immediately on contact, leaving the tree steaming in the Echolands' unlight. Horrible scars marred its surface, and who knew what had been lost, what Grey Peter had stolen from humanity's collective memory?

Peter lifted the extinguisher, looked at it, and twisted the dial so the foam would hit as wide an area as possible. He got set to fire it off again, but as he lifted his canister, a second arc of pink suppressant foam blasted out from behind him, shooting out over the trees. Everywhere it hit, the fire vanished, leaving steaming, charred trees in its wake.

He turned and there was Lily Barnes, wielding the second extinguisher.

"Hurry up," she snarled, and began working on another batch of burning forest.

They made decent progress. It helped that the Echo Door's hilltop was higher than anything else in the forest except for the bizarre orb-mountain in the far distance. Their extinguishers could reach pretty far into the burning forest. They were lucky, too, that there was no wind in the Echolands to spread the fire. Back in the other world, using ordinary firefighting tech against a typical forest fire, they wouldn't have had a chance. But here, maybe.

"We need to hit the edges first, then work on the middle," Peter said. "Make a firebreak. The trees won't burn twice."

"They aren't trees, you prick," Lily said. "They're people."

But she seemed to agree with his suggestion. They focused their efforts on the exterior of the blaze, working the controls of the extinguishers to send long arcs of suppressant toward the far edges of the fire.

In the end, it was enough. Peter's canister ran out a minute or so before Lily's, and there were still a few trees burning when hers was done, but they were deep inside the firebreak and would burn themselves out without spreading to any of the living trees.

Smoke and steam rose from a large swath of forest, the trees now black, crumbling away into dust.

But it wouldn't go any farther.

Peter dropped his canister and stared out, his thoughts bleak. The forest was saved, but he could see patches turning grey even as he watched. Those weren't directly his fault, but he was part of it all the same.

"Like what you see, Peter?" Lily said, her tone freighted with barely restrained rage. "How does it make you feel?"

He looked at her. She was holding the extinguisher with the nozzle pointed at him, and he found himself wishing the stuff could snuff him out the same way it did the flames. Just make him no longer exist.

He flirted with the idea of telling Lily about Grey Peter, about how disconnected he felt from all the things he had done, then cut that off cold. There was no Grey Peter. There was only him.

"Like shit," he said.

"Good," Lily said. "Help me get my dad back to the *Lazarene*."

III. SEVENTEEN

THE EISENHOWER GROUP.

36°58′14.5″N, 50°17′22.6″W

"CONTACT," SAID PETTY OFFICER THIRD CLASS JOHN SVENSSON, sonar technician (surface) of the USS *Philippine Sea,* his eyes glued to his display. "Approaching from directly southeast. Velocity approximately two thousand knots. Submerged at two fathoms."

Svensson had no idea what he was looking at. The sonic signature matched nothing he'd ever seen. He knew the unknown object's speed, a rough approximation of its size, and one other detail, which seemed especially pertinent.

The mysterious signal was coming at them from the same heading toward which they'd just fired four cruise missiles. The *Philippine Sea* had attacked something out there. It seemed logical to think he was looking at the counterstrike.

Svensson's direct superior, Chief Petty Officer Aidan Burke, leaned over the sonar station, eyeing the signal.

"Did you say two *thousand*?" he said.

"Yes, chief. I can run a diagnostic, but the data seems legit."

"Nothing moves at two thousand knots underwater, Svensson. Nothing. It's a glitch."

"Yes, chief," Svensson said, knowing better than to disagree.

"Christ, whatever that thing is . . . it's coming on *fast*."

"Yes, chief," Svensson said.

"I'll notify the captain. Sing out if you get any more information."

"Aye, chief."

Word quickly passed to the cruiser's commanding officer, and from there to the rest of the ships in the strike group, many of whom had already picked up the incoming object on their own sensors.

Admiral Greene ordered all ships to take evasive maneuvers. The fleet split apart, all vessels diverting from their previous paths to ensure a single attack couldn't take them all out at once. The strike group already had planes in the air, the standard combat air patrol sent up whenever the carrier went to alert status. More were scrambled and launched—F/A-18 Hornets and F-35 Lightnings, with rescue helicopters and secondary crews on standby.

It was an impressive display. But running through the mind of every sailor, soldier, and pilot who had seen or heard about the contact they were tracking—getting closer by the second—was the realization that there wasn't a lot they could do. The enemy object was headed toward them at ten times the speed of the fastest man-made undersea object they'd ever heard of.

The Americans radioed warnings to the approaching object, indicating that they would attack if it did not change its course. These went unanswered.

The lack of response meant the strike group could now not be faulted for trying to destroy the thing, and so they did, sending out torpedoes and firing missiles and deploying countermeasures. The object zipped past all of that without much notice, other than an occasional swerve to avoid the worst of an explosion.

The unknown contact raced ahead until it was within five

hundred meters of the *Philippine Sea*. Then it shot straight up from beneath the water, moving too fast for the eye to track.

The object stopped directly above the foredeck of the missile cruiser, hovering about ten meters up and five meters from the bridge, displaying itself for the entire fleet to see. The object was all white, pill-shaped, eight meters long. It stood on its end, floating in midair, and had clearly positioned itself to avoid attacks from the planes and helicopters buzzing around above it. Any shots from those aircraft against the pill would rain down destruction on the cruiser directly below it, as well as its personnel.

Sailors aboard the *Philippine Sea* attempted to destroy the object with small-arms fire, shooting at it from below with their pistols and rifles. These efforts had absolutely zero effect, and the order was quickly given to leave the thing alone lest it retaliate.

This order was given too late. With no warning, and no visible or audible signal from the pill, every system on the *Philippine Sea* died. Engines, navigation, radar and sonar, weapons, electrical, even the stoves in the galley—all at once, they ceased operations. The huge, multibillion-dollar, hyper-advanced vessel was now basically a rowboat.

This was troubling to the strike group's commanders for many reasons. First among them was a fact that was not advertised to the general public: the *Philippine Sea* carried a variety of nuclear weapons systems. Generally speaking, when you had atomic bombs on board, it wasn't ideal when the lights went out.

Running a close second to that problem was the fact that *Ticonderoga*-class missile cruisers had highly redundant power systems. A system-wide power outage like that suffered by the *Philippine Sea* should have been impossible. Yet there it sat, dead in the water.

Over on the strike group's command ship, the enormous *Nimitz*-class aircraft carrier *George H. W. Bush*, heated discussions were in progress with respect to the best way to respond to the pill's attack. A call request came through to its signals officer, on a highly secure channel normally reserved for only the highest-level communication. The incoming caller asked to speak to the strike group commander. He identified himself as the captain "of the fucking ship you assholes just tried to blow out of the water for no goddamned reason."

Rear Admiral Gloria Greene issued an order for all personnel aboard the USS *Philippine Sea* to abandon ship. Then she took the call.

"This is Admiral Greene," she said.

"And this is Captain Frank Tokyo," said the enemy commander, who sounded ticked off indeed. "I wish I could say it's a pleasure to meet a fellow sailor, Admiral, but the truth is I'm pretty damn *dis*pleased. Unprovoked, you just shot four Tomahawks at a civilian research vessel, a ship that I have the honor and privilege of keeping safe. You're causing me a lot of trouble over here."

Greene frowned. She knew that all four of her missiles had struck the intended target. She'd seen the telemetry herself. Nothing afloat that she knew of could survive four direct Tomahawk hits.

"What is the name of your vessel, Captain Tokyo? Where are you registered? Under what flag do you sail?"

Basic questions any legitimate captain of any legitimate ship would be able to answer immediately.

"We're called the Leave Us, out of the Fuck Alone, under the beautiful flag of Or You'll Regret It–land," Tokyo said. "Or maybe you didn't notice that one of your missile cruisers doesn't work anymore. Thank goodness it's a boat and not a plane, huh? At least it can still float."

"You've just admitted to attacking and disabling a US Navy vessel, Captain Tokyo. That was a very bad idea. I advise you to deactivate whatever jamming system you're using and return my cruiser to full operational status, or—"

"Or I'll regret it? I literally just said that. To *you*," Tokyo broke in. "I mean it, too. We are non-hostile, but we are very far from defenseless. You can go your way and we'll go ours, and your fine bridge crew and all the sailors and officers under your command can live to see another sunset, with this all being chalked up as one of those weird things that happens out here. I guarantee you'll never see us again.

"Or," he went on, "you can push me, and you and your people will learn a hard lesson. I'll give you the easy version right now, for free. Five words, easy to remember: Don't fuck with Frank Tokyo."

During the time this exchange had taken, the USS *Philippine Sea* had evacuated all three-hundred and sixty-four sailors and officers aboard. Once they were clear, one of the circling F-35s was given the order to fire at the bizarre pill-shaped aircraft still hovering above the disabled ship. The pilot did so.

The distance to the target was short, and the missile got there in almost no time at all. It hit the pill dead center, exploding in a blast of superheated air and fire. The pill was not destroyed, but it did take some damage. Its systems were slightly compromised, its reaction time slowed by a hair.

So when the missile's impact ignited fuel and weapons stored in the bow half of the *Philippine Sea,* causing a massive secondary explosion, the pill could not evade that much larger blast. Its shell cracked, it came apart, it died.

Greene clenched her fist in triumph as the sound of the blast faded, and her techs confirmed that the enemy object had been destroyed.

She now knew that the other side's weapons were not invulnerable. Sure, it took a lot to knock them down, but that was fine. She was in command of an entire carrier strike group (less one missile cruiser, of course). She had a lot of boom at her disposal.

"We are under attack," she said, addressing her bridge officers. "I want the enemy vessel gone. Eradicated. All tactics and weapons systems authorized. Let's make sure nothing's left but an oil slick on the waves."

And if that oil happens to glow in the dark, she thought, thinking of the nuclear arsenal at her disposal, *so be it.*

Admiral Greene laughed, joy in her heart.

ABOARD THE *LAZARENE,* LIEUTENANT CHEN XIAOLI GESTURED at the bridge's threat display, where a number of bright red dots were projected against the east-facing windows.

"Fighters inbound, sir," she said. "Their new F-35s and some F/A-18s."

"Any of them nuclear-capable?" Captain Tokyo asked.

He'd parked himself back in his command chair at the center of the bridge. His mood had soured on losing the pill drone. It shouldn't have happened.

Never thought she'd burn one of her own ships like that, he thought. *Took out an entire missile cruiser just to kill one little drone.*

That single action suggested to Frank Tokyo that the American commander was not making sound tactical decisions. It felt like a choice made out of frustration or anger, which meant he could (possibly) expect the same going forward. It meant irrationality and—much worse—unpredictability.

"We haven't been keeping a close eye, captain, but there's honestly no reason to think they aren't. The Americans like to—"

"Stick a nuke on anything they can. Yes, Lieutenant, I know," Tokyo said.

He had a decision to make. The *Lazarene* could shoot down these incoming planes and let this whole thing escalate, as it most certainly would. Escalation, in this case, could be deeply dangerous.

The bridge crew had been analyzing signals traffic from

around the world. Team Joy Joy had claimed responsibility for the attacks on the internet and communications networks, and it was clear that they had partly accomplished that by infiltrating the world's navies and shanghaiing a bunch of submarines. It wasn't that much of a stretch to figure they could get a rear admiral or two as well. If the *Lazarene* was up against one of those fanatics, it was just a matter of time before the A-bombs started flying.

Frank Tokyo was not one to back down from a battle. Part of him wanted to fight it out, to shoot down all those planes—which he most *assuredly* could—and then head straight for that carrier group, get all the big guns out of the locker, and really see what the *Lazarene* could do. He thought he'd win. But he might not.

Engaging in a head-to-head battle with this admiral risked literally everything, endangered every living Lazarene. The stakes were as high as they could be. Going after the Americans now went against everything the ship had tried to do for almost two hundred and fifty years, and risked not just its people but the incredible treasures it had discovered in that time, from the Haunted Forest on down.

But that didn't mean he had to sit here and take hits for no reason.

"Send out another few pills on an intercept course for the American fighters," Captain Tokyo ordered. "Shut down their engines, but do it at a decent altitude. All those planes have non-electrical ejection systems. They'll be able to pop out, drift down to the water, and wait for their people to pick them up."

"Yes, Captain," said the XO.

That'll buy me a little time—not much, but a little, he thought.

Frank Tokyo knew he could not risk taking the *Lazarene* into battle. Not against an enemy commander capable of the decisions this American admiral seemed willing to make. He needed to stop this. Shut it down cold before things really got out of control. He didn't have enough pills to disable the entire carrier group before they potentially fired off a nuke, especially if they had some submarines tagging along. The admiral was the problem. If he could just—

He stood straight up from his command chair. Lieutenant Chen looked at him, one eyebrow raised.

"Never again," the captain of the *Lazarene* said.

"Never again," responded his first mate.

"Get the Council on the horn," Tillaroy said. "I need to borrow something."

Admiral Greene could not believe what she was hearing.

"Every single plane?" she said.

"Yes, Admiral," said Captain Davenport, the frustration in his voice obvious. "Our attack wing engaged with two more of those pills about a hundred kilometers from the enemy vessel. Both enemy drones deployed that same unknown weapon that deactivated the power systems on the *Philippine Sea*. All our aircraft were lost, but the pilots ejected safely. We've sent search-and-rescue units to pick them up."

"Did any of them get a shot off? Even one missile?" she asked.

"Two Sidewinders were fired at the hostile aircraft, but they, ah, dodged."

"Fine," Greene said. "We'll try a different approach. We'll go for an area of effect, where we can have a high level of confidence that we've destroyed the target. Prep two LRASMs and set a target zone on either side of the last known position of the enemy vessel."

The AGM-158C long-range anti-ship missiles were the most powerful nonnuclear weapons in the strike group's arsenal. They were specifically designed to kill large naval vessels, and had sophisticated stealth and maneuvering capabilities that let them evade any countermeasures deployed against them. Admiral

Greene loved them. They kicked ass. Even just one was damn strong. Two together would smash the enemy vessel between them like a couple of sledgehammers.

It had to be done. It was clear to her that this Frank Tokyo was a true enemy of joy.

"Another call, Admiral," the comms officer called. "Same channel as before."

How the hell did they get our access codes? Greene thought, but walked over to take the call. She assumed it was another attempt at negotiation, or possibly a surrender—but the time for that was over.

"We have nothing to discuss, Captain Tokyo," the admiral began, but stopped.

She felt like something had interrupted her, but no one had spoken. She heard nothing but silence on the other end of the line. Though . . . no. It was not the silence of a dead connection, or even an empty room. This was a dark quiet, hollow in the middle. The silence of something listening.

"Cut the connec—" she cried, but it was too late.

Something came through.

Admiral Greene kept her ship, well, shipshape. There was very little paper used on her bridge, and all was kept well stowed in its proper containers.

But not so far away from the bridge of her aircraft carrier was a huge pile of wreckage that had once been a warship called the USS *Philippine Sea*. Its hull was still afloat, though not for much longer; it was rapidly taking on water. Pieces of the cruiser's superstructure dotted the surface around its hull, kept from sinking by soon-to-dissipate bubbles of air trapped inside. Between them floated much smaller pieces of wreckage and trash, everything from lightweight parts of the ship to chunks of insulation and coffee cups and even a few sailors' caps.

Many of the smaller remnants of the destroyed ship now

lifted out of the water as if simultaneously scooped up by a giant, unseen hand. These bits of metal and plastic and glass whipped through the air just above the waves until they reached the *George H. W. Bush*, at which point they rose, gathering in a spinning, churning ball just outside the windows of its bridge tower.

Five pseudopods spun out from the ball's substance, and its central core lengthened, flattened. The whirling mass took on a humanoid shape, though skeletal, incomplete, and significantly larger than any person had ever been.

This did not go unnoticed. Members of the carrier's bridge crew drew their sidearms and began firing at the thing, shooting directly through the windows. The being took no notice except to incorporate the spent bullets and shards of glass from the bridge windows into itself.

The thing moved forward, pulling itself inside the bridge through one of the shattered holes. It was huge, too huge for the space, bent, and twisted. It was a thing of broken glass and charred metal, the image of war, an enemy. It scraped and tore its way forward, and presented itself to Rear Admiral Gloria Greene, who stood with her empty pistol gripped loosely in one hand.

"What are you?" she said.

In answer, it offered a smile of shards.

III. EIGHTEEN

THE *LAZARENE*.

WITH THE HELP OF PETER MATCH, LILY CARRIED THE BODY OF her father out of the Echolands and back to the Round of Doors. The alarms had ceased; all was calm.

"Oh, god," Lily said when she saw the guards lying on the floor.

Both of them, the swarthy man and the pretty woman with the pink hair, were both obviously dead, eyes staring, bodies twisted.

"My dad, he—"

"No," Peter Match said, gently helping her lower her father's body to the deck. "It wasn't Dr. Barnes. I did it. When I came back for the axe."

Lily looked at Peter. He seemed . . . smaller. Like he had shrunk into himself, as though his soul was cringing away from the reality of what he'd done.

Good, she thought.

But perhaps not as strongly as she would have before she found his tree in the Echolands.

A sound at the entrance to the chamber. They looked up, and

there stood one of the Automen, staring at them with its bulb-eyed face. Its head shifted, moving smoothly on a well-oiled neck. It looked at the first guard, the second, Frederick Barnes, and then back at Lily and Peter.

"Please remain where you are," it said, its voice really quite beautiful.

IT TOOK A WHILE, BUT EVENTUALLY LILY AND PETER WERE TAKEN into custody by the ship's security team, frightening people in grey coveralls who identified themselves as Allbrights.

"Lily didn't do any of it," Peter told them. "It was all me."

"We know" was the reply. "But she brought you here."

Now they sat in cells in the ship's brig, facing each other, separated by two sets of white bars and a short length of corridor, supervised by a single guard—yet another of the Automen. Lily thought they'd been there for at least a few hours. Peter hadn't said a word in all that time. He sat on the bunk built into the cell's rear wall, arms on his knees, head hanging, hair in his face.

That was fine. Lily wasn't in much of a talking mood, either. She assumed she was living her last few hours of life before the Lazarenes executed her with some high-tech version of walking the plank. She didn't want to waste any of it. She had a lot to work through—the life and deaths of her father, the life and death and rebirth of her mother, and even everything she'd learned about Peter. David too. She was thinking about David.

She was considering the miracle that was the Echolands. Lily almost—almost—forgave her father for his choice to spend his life studying it. She'd gotten so little time there.

Lily tried to remember every moment she'd had in the forest, all the lives she'd touched. She wondered about those people, the long-dead and those still alive, in two places at once. In the Echolands and, at the same time, out in the—

"Peter," she said. "Wake up. I need to talk to you."

"I'm not asleep," he said.

"I know," Lily said. "Look at me."

He did. His eyes were bloodshot and red-rimmed, and she realized he'd been crying.

Good, Lily thought again.

"What do you need?" he said.

"Back in the Echolands, just before you killed my father, trees started turning grey all at once. My dad called it a catastrophic failure—and then you pulled out your gun, showed us both who you really were."

He didn't answer.

"Why did you choose that moment? Were you . . . expecting that to happen? Was that some kind of trigger for you?"

"The Pyre," Peter said.

"What?"

"Aunt Jane and Team Joy Joy had a plan to turn more of the world Grey—to push it past the point of no return. It was big, complex, had all these moving parts, but the idea was to make everyone, you know, give up. It started not long after you and I got to the *Lazarene*. That's why all those trees changed."

He ran a hand through his tangled hair.

"I guess it worked."

Lily stared at him.

"That's why you lit the fire, isn't it? Wanting to do your part?"

In response, Peter offered just a small, miserable shrug.

A thought occurred to Lily. A terrible, brutal thought.

"Wait . . . ," she said. "The Pyre. Is it still *going*? Are people still turning Grey out there?"

Again, Peter stayed silent. His look was answer enough.

"We have to stop it," Lily said.

"We can't, Lily," Peter said. "It's not like that. It already happened. Aunt Jane did what she set out to do. The rest is just gonna be . . . human nature. Nothing we can do."

"Yes, there is."

Lily got up off her bunk and stood by the bars to her cell. She stuck a hand through and waved at the silent Automan sentry.

"Hey," Lily said. "*Hey.*"

The beautiful silver machine rotated its head to look at her.

"Please," she said. "Tell the Allbrights, or the Council, or whoever. Tell them I need to talk to them. They brought my father here for a reason. If they trusted him, they should trust me. It's important. You need to go get them right now."

"I require additional information," the Automan said.

Lily hesitated, wondering if she actually believed what she was about to say. She decided she did.

"I know how to stop the Grey."

THE LAZARENE COUNCIL MET IN A CHAMBER AT THE REAR OF THE ship, in roughly the same location as Molly Calder's cabin on the original *Lazarene*, though twenty times larger. Like that older space, its rear wall was a huge wall of glass looking directly out at the ship's wake, a nod to the idea that the ship, and especially its rulers, should never forget where the great vessel or its people had come from.

The entire room was Calder Blue. The shade was in the silk wallpaper, the long drapery on either side of the window, and the cushions on the rows of seats arrayed before a wide, semicircular table of the finest slipstone where the Council deliberated upon how, exactly, the *Lazarene* might Stay the Course.

The Lazarene Council had seven members. Once, it had more, one from each of the ship's many departments, but that had proven unwieldy. Now it boasted two members each from among the Open and Closed, plus a representative of one of the original

Mill families. Each was elevated to the Council by nomination from within their factions. The sixth was the Molly, the head of the Council, elected from within the roster by the members themselves.

The final member of the Lazarene Council had served longer than any others. The Old Salt, Luis Pedrona. He always voted, but rarely spoke. When he did, everyone listened.

The Council was now in session, assembled at the request of the daughter of a former member. The originator of that request, Lily Barnes, stood before them in a small circle of light from a skylight high above, ready to justify her actions.

"Why should we listen to you, Ms. Barnes?" said Maxwell Franck, the currently serving Molly. "You were involved with the murder of three Lazarenes, including your own father, former Council member Dr. Frederick Barnes. You and your accomplice infiltrated the Echolands and attempted to destroy it, thereby killing who knows how many additional Landsmen. You are a criminal."

"You're making me feel like one," she said. "You've got me standing here, literally under a spotlight, with all of you up there like you're going to sentence me to death, when all I want to do is—"

"Let me make something clear, Ms. Barnes," said Jenny Beaton, a heavyset, dark-skinned woman, the Mill representative. "This is not 'like' you will be sentenced to death. That is an extremely possible outcome today."

"I don't deserve to be put on trial," Lily said. "I didn't kill anyone or hurt the Echolands. That forest is the most incredible thing I've ever seen. I just want you to listen to me."

"She's telling the truth," Peter Match said from his seat in the front row of the gallery, between two Automan guards.

"As if your word carries any more weight than hers," said Franck.

"My mother had the Grey," Lily said, speaking loud and fast so she'd be difficult to interrupt. "The first variant. It happened just before I came here. I put her in one of the care homes. You can verify that, right? Adriana Barnes, at the Happy Valley Long-Term Care Facility in Gloucester, England. Use one of your little computers and check it."

Magdalena Crouch, of the Closed, glanced over at Maxwell. He gave her a little shrug, and she spent a few seconds tapping at a thinnie on the table before her.

"Yes," Magdalena said. "She checked in a few days ago."

"She's not there anymore," Lily said. "I cured her."

"You are mistaken," said Gregor da Gama, a geologist, the second Closed member on the Council. "There is no cure for the Grey."

"Do you have a phone?" Lily asked. "That can make a call back to England?"

The Council exchanged glances, and finally Maxwell Franck made an impatient gesture of acquiescence.

"The Automen have that capability," he said.

Lily turned to one of Peter's guards and rattled off the number for her mother's cell.

I have no idea what time it is in England, she thought. *With my luck, she'll probably be asleep, or out, or not near her phone, or—*

"Hello?" came the lovely, lilting voice of Adriana Barnes from the speaker on the Automan's face. "Who is this?"

"It's Lily, Mum. It's so good to hear you. How do you feel?"

"Just fine, darling, just fine. Why shouldn't I?"

Lily exhaled in relief. Just because a tree in another world had changed color didn't necessarily mean her mother was healed. The call to Adriana was as much for herself as to convince the Council.

"You had the Grey, Mother. But it's all right. It's gone now."

"So they tell me here, but it must have been a mistake. There's no cure for the Grey, and I feel as good as I ever have, Lily. Happier, even."

She did. Adriana's voice was strong, filled with light and life.

"I'm so, so glad," Lily said. "I need to go now, but I'll come see you as soon as I can. I promise. We'll spend some good time together."

"I'd like that, Lily," her mother said. "But what's the occasion?"

"We have a lot to catch up on, Mother. Things you wouldn't believe. I'll see you soon. I love you."

"I love you, too, Lily," her mother said.

The call ended.

"Did that sound like a woman with the Grey?" Lily asked, staring defiantly up at the Council.

"How should we know?" Jenny Beaton said. "No one on the *Lazarene* has ever had it. She sounded cheerful enough. Doesn't prove anything. My guess is the same as your mother's . . . a mistaken diagnosis. She probably never had the Grey at all."

"She did," said Peter Match. "I gave it to her. I showed her the Despair Manifesto."

A long pause as everyone in the room took a moment to look at Peter as if he were an insect, something to be stepped on and scraped off the sole of your boot.

"He's telling the truth," Lily said. "You all know it. Who would lie about something like that? In fact, Peter had the Grey, too, and even worse. He had the Joy variant. I cured him too."

"You . . . what?" said Peter.

"Let's say you did," said Maxwell Franck. "How? We considered many therapeutic approaches. The Barbers worked up a number of pharmaceuticals, but we sent agents to the Landsmen to test them and nothing worked."

"That's the thing," Lily said. "Pills wouldn't do it. This isn't about someone swooping in with a miracle cure. Humanity has to save itself."

"Be . . . *specific*," said one of the Council members who hadn't yet spoken, Iggy Overhold, of the Open. "Stop wasting our time. We were tired of you before you even walked into this room."

"The key is connection," Lily said, forcing herself to stay calm. "The trees in the Echolands let you see other people's lives. You already know that. But if you do more than just watch, if you open yourself up, too, *connect* . . . get close to them, take in everything they are, understand and accept them good and bad . . . the Grey ends."

She looked at the Council, who did not seem particularly moved.

How the hell do I explain this to them?

"I think we're all just alone," she continued. "But we don't have to be."

"You . . . did that for me?" Peter said, his voice smaller than Lily had ever heard it.

She turned to look at him.

"Not for you," Lily said. "I'm still angry. You did monstrous things. When I found your tree in the Echolands, I didn't want to help you. I was just trying to save my life.

"But now I've seen you, Peter. From your start all the way to now. I understand why you did all that awful shit, but that's the least of it. I saw *everything*. Everything you've ever done. The totality of you. I know the person you were before the Grey. You're not evil. You were just . . . lost."

Peter's mouth twitched. They stared at each other for a long, long moment, until he turned away, holding the back of his hand against one eye.

"Ms. Barnes," said Maxwell Franck, and Lily turned back to the Council.

"Even assuming your plan would work," the man said, "we don't have time to implement it. Something like three billion people have the Grey now—more and more as we speak. It would take lifetimes."

"You're not listening to me," Lily said. "You don't have to do this yourself. Just open doors to the Echolands, all over. Let people in and tell them what to do. That's all."

"Absolutely not," said Jenny Beaton, a deep frown on her face.

"It wouldn't work, in any case," Lucinda Bir said. "Even if we opened Echo Doors all over the world, it doesn't mean people could walk through them."

She gestured at the Old Salt where he sat watching, listening.

"In the two hundred years since we found the way to the Echolands, Luis Pedrona has deemed only a handful of people ready to pass through that—"

"The world is ready," the Old Salt said, the words sounding odd, doubled, like two voices speaking through one mouth.

Lucinda's eyebrows rose. Her head tilted back. She took in a breath as if to reply but, in the end, said nothing.

"There are two ways someone can be made ready to receive a great truth," Luis said, the more human of his two voices fading away to leave another, a voice of brass and steel and light.

That's what lives in that castle up on the mountain, Lily thought.

"They can be prepared so they will understand it," the voice said.

The thing behind Luis Pedrona's eyes looked directly at Lily Barnes.

"Or they can be destroyed, so they will have no choice but to accept it."

And then Luis Pedrona was once again the Old Salt. Strange, clearly no ordinary man, but more human than not.

"The world is ready," he said, his voice his own again.

"There you are," Lily said. "Nothing in your way. You need to act right now. Things are getting worse out there. We don't have a lot of time."

The Council members hesitated, exchanged glances.

"Oh, come on," Lily said. "What now?"

"We are the Lazarenes. We Stay the Course," said Gregor da Gama. "We protect the ship, we protect its people, and we protect what it has found. Any choice to the contrary goes against what we stand for."

"But it's the entire human race," Lily said, disbelieving.

Iggy Overhold shook his head.

"The Landsmen caused their own problems," he said. "Humanity's always been its own worst enemy. Time after time, they give power to maniacs, divide themselves into factions, reject progress, reject reality. We've been watching for two and a half centuries, and it's the same mistakes, over and over.

"We've tried to help. We looked for a cure for the Grey, and when we couldn't find it, we gave them the Tenth through Fourteenth Intercessions. None of that changed their path. That's why we're leaving, before the Landsmen take us down with them. All we can do now is mourn what might have been.

"Humanity," Overhold concluded, "is a failed experiment."

"If we were to Intercede in the way you're suggesting, it would just be delaying the inevitable," added Maxwell Franck.

"Are you seriously that fucking selfish?" Peter Match said, sounding disgusted.

All heads turned to look at him. He was standing, his arms folded. Waves of deeply charismatic anger radiated off him. It was impossible to look away.

"You're like Smaug, sitting on a pile of gold you can't ever spend."

"Says the man who tried to burn the Echolands to the ground," Jenny Beaton snapped. "Your actions prove our point, superstar. The forest is not supposed to be shared. It's supposed to be protected."

"If we let them in, they will destroy it. It's what they do," said Iggy Overhold, his tone mournful and certain.

"Then what difference does it make?" Lily said, almost shouting. "Whether the Grey kills humanity or they do it themselves by wrecking that forest, it's the same thing in the end."

"The difference, Ms. Barnes," said Maxwell Franck, "is that in one scenario the Echolands still exist, and in the other they do not. Even if humanity must end, its record will remain, and that is valuable. That is the mission of the *Lazarene*—to keep that record of humankind safe at all—"

"Bullshit," said Peter Match, stepping forward to stand next to Lily. "I *am* a rock star. You don't get to be one unless selfishness is part of your DNA. I know the type. You're not saying no because protecting the Echolands is your fucking mission. It's because your trees are in that forest too. If you let everyone in and they wreck the place, you'll all die too. God forbid. Because you're all so *exceptional*."

"That is enough," said Magdalena Crouch. "You know nothing about us. We gave you this audience as a courtesy, as a way to honor Dr. Barnes. He was a Lazarene. He understood what the Echolands mean. You two clearly do not. This is over."

"No," Lily said, her voice cold, focused, loud.

She knew she was dooming herself, dooming her chances to convince these people. She didn't care. She was caught up.

"You're idiots. A bunch of genius idiots. You've got neurologists and biologists and wizards and god knows what else, but what this ship really needs is a fucking *therapist*.

"I understand exactly what the Echolands mean," Lily said. "I understand all of you, too, better than you think. We're exactly the same. When I was a child, I lost my father. And then I lost my mother, and I was alone. They both left me, so I decided to stay alone. It makes sense, right? If you're alone, then no one can ever leave you.

"That principle steered my entire life. It hurt me and hurt people who got close to me. I lost so much—so many relationships, so many opportunities to grow, to connect.

"It was a mistake. It goes against how we're meant to be. I mean, even the trees know it. You've seen what they do. When they're connected to other people, they grow together. They support each other. They become stronger.

"I turned my back on that, and so did you. You left humanity behind because it hurt you. For two hundred and fifty years you've made sure it could never do it again. You'd rather let the world die than take a chance on getting hurt, and you call it your mission."

Lily looked past the Council, through the windows behind them at the endless, vast sea, the ship's wake churning, then smoothing, then gone as it were never there.

"This isn't what the *Lazarene* was supposed to be," she said.

"I heard the story of this place when I first got here. Molly and Apollo Calder—the whole thing. The *Lazarene* came about because of connection. Two people with a bond so strong, it transcended death. This entire ship exists because of one thing, and it's not intelligence or freedom or some higher purpose you've assigned yourselves. You want to stay the course? Remember who you are. Open the Echolands for the same reason Molly Calder created this place.

"Love," Lily said.

No one in the Council chamber spoke. Not for a long little while. And then someone did.

"We are of them, even if we are no longer among them," said Luis Pedrona, the Old Salt.

The Council deliberated.

And in the end the Lazarenes made a decision.

This was the Fifteenth Intercession.

III. NINETEEN

EVERYWHERE.

A door opens in Times Square.

A door opens in the great plaza at the entrance to the Forbidden City.

A door opens below the Eiffel Tower.

A door opens in Red Square.

A door opens in Shibuya Crossing.

A door opens in Palestine.

A door opens in Mecca.

A door opens in Jerusalem.

Doors open in Capetown and Johannesburg.

Doors open in Sydney and Auckland and Wellington, in Jakarta and Singapore and Dubai and Delhi and Chicago and Islamabad and Vancouver and Mexico City and Montevideo and Lagos and Morocco and Rio de Janeiro.

They open where the people are, and the people walk through them and find a great forest and find themselves. They are ready.

At the same time, a statement is released, delivered to the internet systems that still work, to the offices of resurgent newspapers, sent to heads of state for dissemination through whatever means necessary.

It includes the words of a woman named Lily Barnes, delivered both in video and written form. In the video, she holds a baby in her arms, beautiful, asleep. Lily says:

"The story of us is us.

"A mother fights off a lion with her bare hands to save her child.

"A man puts all else aside in his life to care for his sick wife and holds her hand as she dies.

" 'Have a good day' said on the way out the door. 'I love you.' The implicit promise in that. 'I will still love you when you come home.'

"A storm comes, and the power goes out, and neighbors share warm beers on candlelit porches.

"People march for what they believe in, and risk getting hurt or jailed, but link arms and say the words and hope someone will listen.

"We give everything we have so our children can have it better than we did, and we know they don't and can't and won't see it, not until they have children of their own.

"We play together.

"We love together.

"We build together.

"Humans are always an 'us,' not a 'me,' not an 'I.' That's what we forgot. We were shattered and fragmented because there's money in it, and power in it, and people figured out how to use that.

"We thought we were alone. That no one would ever come to help us. And so we became exactly that. Falling into the Grey, losing ourselves.

"But that's not the truth. We're not trees. We're a forest.

"Go look. That's why these doors were opened. Connect with

other people, see their lives, see their joy and their hurt and their struggle. See your own life. As you do, the Grey will fall away. I've seen it. I've done it.

"There is hope. There always was. We don't have to let ourselves die. The loss doesn't have to swallow us up.

"We are all the light.

"Go into the forest and you'll see it, off on the horizon. We can't get there, for the same reason you can't grab your own shadow. That light is us.

"Go see it. You'll be glad you did."

ABOARD THE *LAZARENE*, THE LAZARENES CHOOSE THEIR DOORS and walk through them. The great family of minds is separated for the first time since leaving the Calder Mill. Most go to the Second World. Others decamp for more distant shores, deciding to explore, to see what else might be found. The Round of Doors itself is cut out from the *Lazarene* and brought into the Second World so the ship's people can find their way back if they should ever want to.

How is this possible? That a thing that holds a world within it is moved into that world intact?

Ask the Lazarenes.

Some few want to stay. They go through the Echo Door and exit the Echolands in other parts of the world, for now there are many hilltops above the Haunted Forest, and doors open to everywhere.

When everyone is gone and everything that will be needed is taken, Automen aboard the *Lazarene* move the great vessel to a spot in the western Pacific Ocean above the Mariana Trench. Precisely placed explosives crack the ship like an egg, rattling off in sequence like a string of firecrackers.

The *Lazarene* splits down the middle, along its length, the two halves pushing outward and away before beginning to sink. As they fall, more explosives detonate, and the ship disintegrates into sections and shards and scraps. What hits the bottom of the trench is little more than dust, and even that will vanish in not much time, due to the science of its creators.

But the ship still sails. On the surface floats a three-masted cutter with a hull of all but indestructible live oak, with copper paneling below the waterline to prevent barnacles and other sea creatures from finding a home. It holds mighty batteries powered by lightning and the tides, and engines that can propel its bulk at impressive speed if the doldrums hit. One of its decks is a garden that can produce enough food to feed hundreds, with sunshine brought in by cleverly angled mirrors. Aboard this ship are laboratories and libraries and chambers for study and experimentation and education.

A wondrous, endless vessel.

III. TWENTY

THE PACIFIC OCEAN.

14°40′47.7″N, 137°32′50.4″E

LILY STOOD ON THE FOREDECK OF THE *LAZARENE*, AT THE RAIL. The sky was clear and the ship's sails were full. It ran ahead of the wind at a brisk pace. Lily could have asked one of the Automen for their speed, or even checked the instruments at the pilot's station, but it didn't really matter. They'd get there when they got there.

That, right there, she thought. *That's why people like to sail.*

The ship was headed northwest through the Pacific and would maintain that course for many days yet before cutting west through the Luzon Strait between Taiwan to the north and the Philippines to the south. From there it would make slight adjustments until it arrived at a small island on the southern coast of China.

The *Lazarene* would sail into Hong Kong harbor, let down one of its launches, and Automen aboard that small boat would row Lily Barnes ashore. They would then return to the ship and it would sail away. What happened to it next would be up to the ingenious machines that were now its only crew.

"You sure you want to go back to Hong Kong?" Peter Match said.

He was standing to her left and looked fine. Looked healthy, in shorts and a T-shirt and bare feet, his long hair blowing in the wind.

"Yeah," Lily said. "Even China wouldn't throw the woman behind the Repair Manifesto in jail. I won't stay long. Just a few things to do, then I'll head back to England to see my mother."

She turned to look at him.

"What about you?"

Peter shrugged.

"I really don't know," he said. "I'm the worst person who's ever lived—and I'm also not. I think I'll let the world decide what to do with me. I'd like to spend time in the forest, if they'll let me. I think I could do some good there. Help set things right, at least a little."

Lily nodded. They watched the sea for a while.

"Do you think we'll actually make it work?" Lily asked. "As a people, I mean. We have the answer right in our hands. What do you think we'll do with it?"

"I think humans are selfish," Peter said. "And I think nothing feels better than love. Giving it and getting it. It's those two impulses, fighting each other, that make us go. For a while, too much got piled on the selfish side of the scale. Now love's getting a chance. We'll see."

He turned and walked away across the deck.

"What are you going to do?" Lily asked.

"There's a piano down in one of the staterooms," Peter Match said, without looking back. "Thought I might write a song."

III. TWENTY-ONE

THE ECHOLANDS.

JANE MORELLO WALKED THROUGH THE FOREST OF SOULS, HER arms outstretched, her fingertips brushing against the branches and leaves, seeing and feeling lives as she did.

This is wild, she thought.

She'd come through the Los Angeles door—anyone could, there were no restrictions—though she had worn a hat and sunglasses to hide her face.

The Pyre had worked the way she planned, but then this . . . this place . . . who could have expected something like this?

It went against everything she thought, she believed in, she taught.

Or maybe it didn't. Aunt Jane was still thinking it through. Mostly, the arrival of the forest had complicated things. She felt like her goals, once basically achieved, had been set back by some as-yet-unknown amount.

Other people were visible here and there, from all over the world. They were mostly engaged with touching trees themselves. Their own, people they knew, people they didn't. The Echolands had quickly captured humanity's imagination, and Jane had to laugh.

A day after she used the Pyre to destroy mankind's memory of itself, it went ahead and found itself a new one.

Good times.

Jane stopped. She'd had enough of sightseeing. After all, she'd come to the forest for a reason. She closed her eyes. She used the technique she'd read about in the news stories, laid out by that woman in her Repair Manifesto (the existence of which Jane found very amusing; turnabout was fair play, after all). Aunt Jane focused her mind, and when she re-opened her eyes, a tree stood before her, like nothing she'd yet seen on her walk through the forest.

It was no taller than most, but it was *broad*, like a huge oak, spreading its branches over a vast area. It stood alone, the center of a gigantic network of connections to other trees around it. Interlaced twigs and branches and limbs, but always outward, as if the tree had reached out to snag the others. None reached back. None were connected. They were ensnared, not embraced.

The tree in the center of all this *blazed*, like the sun itself, like a blacksmith's forge. So bright it was almost hard to look at. Around it, trees were only flame, ashen or black. No blue, anywhere.

Jane stepped forward and put her hand to the trunk of her tree.

Embrace joy, she thought.

She closed her eyes.

She saw.

She opened them.

Her tree was now black, as if it had burned and died a thousand years before.

Jane burned, and fell, and died.

III. TWENTY-TWO

HONG KONG.

22°17'34.9"N, 114°10'23.4"E

Lily sat on a bench in Tsim Sha Tsui, watching the little boats skim and skip between the large ships crossing Victoria Harbor, an entire little ecosystem atop the waves.

Across the harbor, the city's skyline gleamed in the sun, all the beautiful buildings of the Central and Admiralty and Wan Chai districts. Over there was a Door, and inside it was a forest. Within that forest was a tree. For a time, the tree was grey. Now it was a bright, vivid blue.

In Lily's hand was a puzzle, a small, flat wooden square inset with smaller wooden tiles in a grid, each with a bit of a larger image on them, mixed and scrambled. One square of the grid was empty, and the tiles could be moved in and out of that empty space, shifted until the image was reassembled.

Lily set the puzzle down. It was unsolved.

Someone approached her bench.

Lily Barnes looked to see, blinking against the light.

"Hello, David," she said.

EPILOGUE.

THE ECHOLANDS.

1835.

Luis Pedrona carried Molly Calder through a door. It was not yet called the Echo Door; this name would come later.

The old woman weighed almost nothing in his arms, and he set her down gently atop the hilltop, resting his hand against her back so she could sit upright.

Molly looked around her in wonder—at the deep blue sea of forest, the looming mountain and the fortress beyond, and the great white shining moon-sun casting light across it all.

"What . . . what is this, Luis?" she said.

"It is all of you," he replied.

He put his hand on the side of her face.

"Do not breathe too deeply, Molly," he said. "We do not have much time here. You must do something for me."

"Tell me," she said.

"Close your eyes. Think of Apollo. As clear and strong as you can."

Molly asked no questions, only did as she was bid.

Apollo Calder was far away, but she brought him near. After

so long, he was emotions more than memories—she recalled the steadiness, the joy, the optimism, the foolishness, the hope. But, yes, some memories too. Apollo telling her a bawdy joke and laughing, laughing, laughing. Apollo reaching out to take her hand. Apollo falling that day in Essex and the fear in his eyes. Apollo singing to himself as he reviewed the contracts of sale that would bring them the Mill.

"Open your eyes, Molly," said Luis Pedrona.

She did, and was surprised to see that one of the trees had drawn close.

"Reach out," said Luis.

And Molly Calder did.

ACKNOWLEDGMENTS

AH, YES, THE FAMOUS LITTLE NOTE AT THE BACK OF THE BOOK where I get to acknowledge (that's why they call it the "Acknowledgments"!) all the people who have helped me to bring this story into the world. We've got a bunch this time around, so brace yourself.

The Endless Vessel is a big book. It's my longest novel (there's a version that's over 20K words longer too), by far the longest in-production creative product of my fiction-writing career and the most ambitious in terms of format, content, and scope. It took a lot to bring it into the world. I hope you enjoyed it—and if you didn't, well, I set out to take a big swing with this one, and maybe we can agree there's value in that.

I wrote this book's first draft (there were six by the end, which isn't uncommon for my novels) over the first and second pandemic years. I would guess that isn't too surprising, considering the story's themes. I think we writer types tell stories about things we deeply believe, want/need, or fear. *The Endless Vessel* has all three in it, which makes sense. That's all I've been thinking about over the past few years. Perhaps you're the same.

First and foremost, I would like to offer my gratitude to my family—my wife, Amy, and my daughter, Rosemary. It is not always a simple or easy thing to have a writer in the house. We demand special care and feeding, especially when deep in the grip of The Muse. They are wonderfully patient and supportive, and if this book is good, they are a huge part of the reason.

Another massive thank-you must be given to my editor at Harper Perennial, Sara Nelson. This is our third book together, and she's been unflagging in her belief in my writing. This novel was particularly tricky for me. It took longer to deliver than either of us expected or wanted. She approached that situation with extraordinary patience, support, and grace, and I will never forget it.

My agent, Seth Fishman, who has been helping me navigate my career as a novelist for many years now and has been absolutely instrumental in helping me ensure I can have this wonderful, bizarre gig for some time to come. Similarly, my manager Angela Cheng Caplan and attorney Eric Feig, who have been there literally since the very first project. Their expertise is matchless, and I'm lucky to know them all.

That's true of many people at Harper, in fact—I've been very fortunate to work with many of the same behind-the-scenes and production folks since *The Oracle Year*—Doug Jones, Heather Drucker, Megan Looney, Amy Baker, Lisa Erickson, and more. They're all amazing and chose to believe in this strange book when they didn't have to. May we create many more together.

Laura Anastasio for her astonishing cover design, and Jama Jurabaev for his work on the special edition cover. Marco Bernardini for designing the incredible Lazarene Map as a supplemental piece for the book (as well as *Chronicles of the Lazarene*, the companion novella to *The Endless Vessel*). They're all straight-up magicians.

My assistant, Tommy Stella, who has read this book many times in many incarnations and did a good deal of the early research for me—a series of weird, unrelated subjects that I'm sure made little sense at the time.

Other early readers: Shawn DePasquale and Mandy Romanuk, who offered many helpful suggestions over multiple drafts.

I did a ton of research for this book, and a lot of that involved talking to subject matter experts who were very gracious with their time. My brother Sam Soule helped me with modern and archaic naval matters and terminology. Cavan Scott gave the manuscript a once-over to make sure I was getting the Britishisms right and offered a thought about the most recognizable landmark when flying above Bristol. My former AP English teacher at Hong Kong International School, Kent Ewing, and my onetime fellow student there Shoumitro Goswami, who gave me valuable insight into the current state of Hong Kong. (I intended to return for a visit myself during the writing, but the pandemic had other plans.) Charles Seavey and Natasha Taylor at the Essex Shipbuilding Museum for offering up their valuable time and priceless insight into the shipwright's trade. Aaron Mahnke for pointing me in the right direction when I was researching the rise of the Spiritualist movement in the nineteenth century. The kind folks at the JSTOR online academic research library, who assisted me with locating obscure documents about eighteenth-century Massachusetts, and the staff at the Lowell National Historical Park and various historical destinations in Boston. The authors of the many books I read for research—particularly illuminating were *Materials* by Christopher Hall, *A New Order of Things: How the Textile Industry Transformed New England* by Paul E. Rivard, and *The Maritime History of Massachusetts, 1783–1860* by Samuel Eliot Morison.

My many friends and colleagues who offered everything from encouragement to story thoughts as this beast of a book came together over nearly four years: Andy Deemer, Nate Chinen, Ryan Browne, Scott Snyder, Peng Shepherd, Chuck Wendig, Michael Siglain, Daniel Jose Older, Justina Ireland, Amy Vincent, Rob Barocci, Shawn Hynes, Chip Zdarsky, Mark Paniccia, and of course, you—the person who is reading this thinking "Wait, there's no possible way this jerk could have forgotten *me* . . . I was *instrumental*!" Unfortunately, I have. Not purposefully, not with malice aforethought. . . but it happens. But I acknowledge you here, and you're not wrong—you were instrumental.

Finally, obviously, and truly: to my readers, especially those of you who have been here since the start. You make it all happen, just as much (if not more so) than anyone on this list. Because of you, the voyage continues.

Thank you.

Stay the course, embrace joy, reach out. See you on the next ship.

Charles Soule
Beacon, New York
March, 2023

ABOUT THE AUTHOR

CHARLES SOULE is a #1 *New York Times*–bestselling novelist, comics author, screenwriter, musician, and lapsed attorney. He has written some of the most prominent stories of the last decade for Marvel, DC, and Lucasfilm in addition to his own work, such as his comics *Eight Billion Genies*, *Letter 44*, and *Undiscovered Country*, and his original novels *The Oracle Year* and *Anyone*. He lives in New York.